"A unique and riveting story",
"Entrancing flow of events",
"Captivating!"

SPIES LIKE US

L. Russell Records

outskirts
press

CHAPTER 1

"**C**'mon, Morgan! We're going to the beach." I was already set to go with my new bathing suit, swim mask and fins our uncle had got me at Willoughby's Department Store on Main Street. The mask and fins were that sea green like those Navy SEAL guys. My new bathing suit was blue with a bright white stripe down both sides. I was walking around in my new fins, slapping them down on the old, weathered wooden boards of the steps down from the porch. The boards were a nest of wooden splinters, and also, they were blazing hot. I heard back from Morgan upstairs, "Just a minute, Eth." Eth was short for Ethan, my name, Ethan Calloway.

I was just two months from turning eighteen and was going to be a senior in high school. Morgan was my little brother, a year younger than me, very smart, imaginative, but lacking any fear. Like the time we went for ice cream and we found him outside in the dairy barn, helping to milk the goats. He didn't seem to care that we found it a bit odd, he just grinned broadly.

People used to get us confused when we were little kids. We both had dark hair and dark eyebrows. Now, we are quite different, with me being a bit taller but losing ground rapidly to Morgan. Morgan favors our Mom with his dirty-blond hair, blue eyes, and muscular build. He likes to wear his hair a bit long. If we were in California, he would be taken for a surfer dude.

I look more like my Dad, kind of what people call "lanky" with my Dad's black hair with streaks of red. I like it military-style, like my Dad always does. There's some Irish somewhere in our past, so

I have green-blue eyes, like my Dad.

Morgan is a natural athlete, while I am more of a thinker. I can play sports, but I have more fun trying to figure things out. We both spend most of our time out in the Texas sun so we look a bit like Indians. We like it that way, a boy's appearance is important to him as he moves into manhood.

A boy had to have his own brand of dignity. Morgan was into everything without regard to how it made him look or what people said. I felt that it was better to "set your feet before you go off half-charged", as my Dad always told us. Morgan ran right square into luck, good or bad, but something interesting usually turned up. Morgan usually came out on top, though. I don't know how. Was it the fact that the universe moved in his favor because he pushed on it in a certain way, or was it just plain luck?

We had grown up as Texans, out on the plains just south of Dallas. Our Dad was a Naval Intelligence Officer, and had worked at the Naval Air Station there. It seems like a strange place for a Navy base, but they do have a lake and a runway that sticks out in it. Navy planes flew in and out every couple of days. Three years ago, Dad left the Navy to go work for a big security software company. This meant he had to do a lot of travel, much of it out of the US.

We had just moved up from Dallas to my Dad's shore house in Pocasset, Massachusetts, and it was a beautiful early-summer day. The water was clear and there was a light breeze blowing from the West, causing a light chop along the beach. Our new little sloop was bouncing up and down on our dock down the beach like an eager puppy. We didn't know enough about sailing yet to take her out, so today was just going to be beach time.

Our move from Texas to Pocasset was something of a mystery to us. Our Mom had moved out two years ago; she had been more involved in Dallas high society than in being a mom, and with our Dad working in Europe most of the time, Morg and me are pretty much on our own here. Dad said that Pocasset was closer to his work, and he had grown up near here, in a town called Duxbury.

When you live in Dallas, Texas, you wish for blue water oceans and long, sandy beaches. We have lakes down in Texas, but we've had little rain for the past three years, and many of them are going dry. The water here is clear and cold, and Cape Cod and the endless Atlantic Ocean are a huge change from Texas. Getting out in our new sailboat seemed to me to be the first step in our transition to going from Texas to Cape Cod. Quite a change for a couple of young Texas cowboys.

CHAPTER 2

We loved living in Texas with its wide open plains. To the West of Dallas there were mountains in the Big Bend region. A few years back, we went there to a "Cowboy Experience Ranch" for four weeks while my Dad was gone on one of his very frequent trips.

We lived in a bunkhouse with eight other kids. Bert was our adult leader, called the "Trail Master". Since I was the oldest at fourteen years old, Bert appointed me as the "Wrangler" for the rest of the kids, meaning I was supposed to make them obey the rules of the ranch. "Get up at 0700, go to bed at 2200, no unsupervised fires, no smut, no running around after dark, and be safe at the firing range." Pretty simple, and I had no trouble with the kids as Morgan was my "enforcer" who coaxed the others into obeying. Over the next three weeks, we learned to ride, take care of horses, repair a saddle, handle and shoot both pistols and rifles, herd a few cattle, and live, just briefly, in the wilderness.

The first challenge was to learn to ride a horse, which neither one of us had ever done. We first had to learn the "ropes" so to speak. We learned to bridle and saddle my horse who was named "Cherokee". As I approached the horse he looked back at me, judging whether I was fit to ride him. But he actually helped me get the bit in his mouth, the bridle over his ears, and let me throw the saddle over him and cinch him up. He stomped as I reached under him to get the cinch, and I jerked back and fell on my butt. Everyone got a good laugh over that. I did get the cinch into the saddle rings, and he stomped again as I tightened up the cinch the second time.

I learned that horses bulge out their stomachs when they feel the cinch, then relax so you can tighten the cinch so the saddle doesn't rotate around and dump you on the ground. I could imagine me in a pile on the ground with the saddle on top of me and Cherokee laughing at me, and I didn't want to end up like that. It's not a good start if your horse thinks you're funny.

I found out that horses can judge your mood from your facial expressions, so I assumed the expression of sincere cooperation and trust. Horses also remember you from those expressions, so it's good to look friendly all the time.

Morgan followed my lead as he saddled his horse, "Fast Billy" with a little bit of help. He climbed up and the saddle wrangler adjusted his stirrups down to the proper length. We did a little practice in the corral, turning left and right, and giddy-upping and whoa'ing. Then we headed out to see what "cowboying" was all about.

That first ride was great as we went up a mountain trail in a long line. The trail snaked up along a ridge then down to a stream where we stopped for a rest and to water the horses. We took a different path back, down the stream bed through a grove of trees smelling of spruce. From then on, I was hooked on both horses and riding, and so was Morg. He and I got permission after the first week to go out by ourselves after morning classes anywhere on the 5,000 acre ranch as long as we stayed together and got back by supper time. We explored the ranch from East to West, and along the ridge of the Chiso mountains that bordered the ranch to the south. Bert had told us that over those mountains was Chihuahua, Mexico.

We rode all over the ranch on Fast Billy and Cherokee, and we got to ride them through the canyons, across streams, and to gallop wildly across the plains. After a while, we learned their moods. Dumb horses don't seem to have moods, but smart horses can be sleepy, nervous, lazy, excited, and cantankerous, all in the same day. You learn how to read them, how to encourage them when they are unsure, and how correct bad behaviors. You learn to turn them hard to chase cows, and how to make them backup out of danger, like if you see a rattlesnake on the trail, coiled up and ready to strike, as well as to help hold calves down during branding. You understand when they need to rest, when they are thirsty, and when you just let them pick the best way down a rocky ravine. You learn to be a horseman, and you and your horse become a team. And Morgan and I had learned those lessons.

CHAPTER 3

During the last of our four weeks, under the leadership of our Trail Master, Bert Connors, our entire camp packed up bedrolls, saddled up, and rode out to the farthest edge of the ranch, up on a tall ridge overlooking a wide valley. Our food and other gear was carried in a small covered wagon which was also the cook's larder, and was drawn by two ancient mules. We made camp in a little clearing in the spruce trees up on a small plateau. There was a beautiful view over the rest of the ranch, all the way to the river, almost ten miles away. We set up tents, a central fire pit, and a latrine behind a large bush. Teen boys are more bashful than most people think.

We camped out for four days, taking day trips on horseback or on foot to see Indian cave paintings. The paintings were made with dye extracts from local plants and had a common theme: "I was here, look what I did, this is my world", and tried to convey ordinary elements of their lives hundreds of years ago.

We found a little stream nearby, and dug clay from the stream bed to make primitive clay bowls, leaving them in the sun to dry and then baking them in coals from the fire to harden them. Most of the bowls got broken before we left camp, but we had fun and learned something in doing it.

Some guys went over the ridge to a small stream to test out their camp-made fishing gear that they had carved or fashioned from wire, and then, when they came back, they ate beef stew like the rest of us. We enjoyed hearing about their attempts at catching the tiny, elusive mountain trout. We ate our meals sitting around the campfire on logs or rocks, expertly cooked by Cookie, the ranch chef, beans and beef and cornbread, flapjacks and bacon, and apple pie, skills developed around many similar campfires. We really enjoyed Cookie's food, but we also were also hungry for seeing more of the huge ranch.

On one of our explorations, Morg spotted a cow down in a ravine with a small fast-flowing stream. Morg said, in his newly-acquired Western slang, "Eth, that there cow needs a-rescuing!" I looked down there and said, "That there cow looks fine to me. What wuz ya' thinking?", getting into the cowboy role. He pulled the rope off the tie on his saddle, and started uncoiling it. I said, "You gonna actually try and rope that critter?" Morg nodded, then said, "Eth, Here we go." He uncoiled a loop in the rope and kicked Fast Billy, turning down to the ravine. The cow looked up, unconcerned.

Morg moved in for the "kill shot" and spun part of the rope over his head and threw it towards the cow. Somehow the loop ended up over the cows' head. We looked at each other, astonished. The cow seemed to act like two "cowboys" riding up on it and roping it was no big deal. It just stood there in the stream bed, chewing it's cud. Morgan tightened the rope and the cow looked back at him, but just shifted its feet. I asked Morgan, "Now what?" He said, "Well, I guess we'll have to release the prisoner." Morgan got off his horse with his rope and walked over to the cow. I thought he was going to go up to the cow and apologize.

As he started loosening the rope, pulling the loop up over the cow's head, the cow suddenly lunged forward and took off running down the stream. Morgan still had the rope loop in his gloved hand and the loop suddenly tightened and trapped his left hand against the cow's neck. He was pulled off his feet and now he was being dragged by the sprinting cow down the stream. The rope trailed behind them and I kicked Cherokee to go after him. I jumped down and grabbed the flailing rope out of the stream. If it had snagged on a rock, both Morgan and the cow would have been in serious trouble. Morgan had started running with the cow instead of just being dragged. That kid was amazingly fast and he was able to keep up since the rough stream bed slowed the cow to a fast trot.

Then unbelievably, Morgan swung his leg over the cow's back and climbed aboard and hung on by holding the cow around the neck. They bounded down the stream, water splashing everywhere. I thought about tightening the line to slow the cow down, but my brother's hand was trapped by the loop and I was afraid I would hurt him. The cow, who was still befuddled by all this, decided to climb out of the stream and slow to a stop. Fast Billy just trotted up to us and stopped. Frankly, he looked a bit puzzled.

Morgan slid off the bony top of the confused animal and freed his hand from the loop. He was soaking wet, and covered with mud and sand from Stetson to boot toe. He held up his left hand and I could see that his hand was bleeding from the rope loop cutting through his glove. He looked back at me with a broad grin, and said, "Well, I guess I got that one tamed!" Once again, Morgan had leaped right into a situation that could have gone badly in any number of ways, and rode out a hero. I wrapped my bandanna tightly around his hand and we rode back to camp, leaving the still confused cow in the "rear view mirror".

Back at the ranch house, Cookie, the ranch nurse, also the cook and spiritual advisor bandaged up Morgan's hand, then he asked suspiciously, "How'dya gets that rope burn? Ya out messing with my cows?" Morgan looked at his hand then up at Cookie. "There was a cow stuck in the stream, and we needed to get him out." Cookie asked, "Hmm...Was he just drinkin', or was he stuck balls-deep in the mud?" Morgan turned red in his cheeks, and slowly replied, "Maybe not balls deep, but the water was definitely up to his knees." Cookie asked, "His knees, or her knees?" Morgan laughed and said, "Guess I didn't check." Cookie advised, "You better check first. If you mess with one of our bulls, like as not I'd be sending you out on Air-Flight rather than putting a Band-aid on yer hand."

CHAPTER 4

One morning, there was a visitor to our camp. He was a tall, rugged looking man, carrying two rifles and a pistol, slung low on his hip. He had a gray brushy mustache, green eyes, and deeply tanned and wrinkled skin. He was introduced as Ranger Thad Wilson, our firearms instructor. He was a no-nonsense man, deeply concerned about two things, safety and accuracy. He was also an ex-Delta Force soldier and was now a Texas Ranger.

He called us together, and set forth his rules, which boiled down 1) follow all instructions or get kicked off the firing line, and 2) take care of your weapons and they will take care of you.

From Ranger Wilson, we learned to shoot both pistols and rifles. Our pistols were the modern Ruger .22 caliber version of the old Colt .45 Peacemaker, called the Wrangler. We learned how to load it with six rounds of "long-rifle" bullets and fire accurately single-action and double-action at targets about ten meters out, stuck on a set of old posts at varying distances. With the Rugers, we learned rapidly that if you didn't just squeeze the trigger slowly instead of pulling it, your shots would end up low and to the left of the bulls-eye, even at short range. He would watch every target and he could see after every shot whether we were squeezing the trigger. He would correct us after every shot. That took practice to learn.

Then we learned to shoot the Winchester Model 94 rifle at 20 meters that fired the 30-30 bullet. It looked like the cowboy rifle in all the old westerns. We felt a bit like old West cowboys. My accuracy got better each time we fired, especially with the Winchester. Our Trail Master Bert had a beautiful Henry "Golden Boy" rifle that he let us pass around. It was a beautiful golden rifle that only he fired.

Thad Wilson, who we learned was a mid-East war veteran, also had a modern rifle, an AR-15, an "Armalite Rifle (AR). It was a semi-automatic rifle that fired a much smaller bullet, a .223, but at higher speeds. It had a 15-round magazine. Just a few of us got to fire it, the two shooters with at least 80 percent hits. I liked it because it was much lighter and had less kick than the Winchester. I was shooting 90 percent with it. It also looked cool.

We spent the rest of the day cleaning all the weapons, and learning to reload the shells. As we packed up the pistols and rifles, Ranger Wilson called us all together for the last time. He said, in a serious adult voice, "Boys, guns are primarily for the defense of your country, your community, and your family, and for hunting. Keep your skills up, you may need them desperately someday. If you ever pick up a gun for your own defense, I want you to remember something very important, a word that can save your life. That word is "RANGERS". When you say that word to yourself, you must change the state of your mind from being a victim, to being a Warrior. You must forget about anything except your mission to maintain the upper hand, and to kill if you must. Remember this word: "RANGERS."

On the last night of the camp, the camp leaders handed out awards for various skills. I beat Morg in shooting accuracy and got the medal called "Expert Marksman". Morg got an award for the camper first able to start a fire. It was called the "Fire Wizard". It wasn't all that hard with the flint and steel kits we got, but he got his going in about a second, while some of the kids never could get a fire going inside the one-minute time limit. I gave Morg my own special secret "merit badge" for cow roping, since I was the only witness to his heroic but stupid act which we never reported. It was a tiny clay cow with a piece of string around its neck. He smiled and slugged me in the arm when I handed it to him, so I know he liked it.

We really enjoyed and learned from our ranch experiences.

When we got back home, Dad asked us what we had learned. We told him about Morgan's "up close" bovine experience and he laughed and hugged us both. We related our training with pistols and rifles, and the awards we got. I remember this as one of the only times that our Dad had shown such interest in us. My Mom listened to our stories, and frowned. "You both could have been killed! Wild horses and dangerous cattle, and GUNS! I was worried to DEATH that you would come back with broken bones, bullet wounds, or a skull fracture!" We stared at her in shock. We had just had the biggest adventure of our lives and she was worried about having to take care of us and ruining her social life. She left the room, shaking her head. But those feelings, good and bad, only lasted for a few days, then we were back into our so-called normal routine.

But we were different now, we had lived the cowboy life for almost a whole month. We had learned to deal with danger, handle both horses and weapons, and be more self-sufficient. Mother had once again withdrawn from her duties of helping us become men. But we could do it on our own, after all, We are Texans, now and forever.

CHAPTER 5

The next couple of years went fairly well; I was a freshman in high school and had my friends on the track and the football team. I played linebacker but I wasn't all that good. I did really like finding my way through the line and tackling the opposing quarterbacks. My grades were good because I worked hard at it, and I enjoyed learning. When I got into high school, I became interested in mechanical things. We had a good industrial arts department and our instructor, Mr. Prejean, knew everything about engines and transmissions. My best friend, Jimmy and I took an old Pontiac engine apart, rebuilt it, and got it running again. Some other guys put the engine and transmission in a hot rod body, put wheels on it, and seats in it, and we all jumped in and drove it triumphantly around the parking lot, yelling at the top of our lungs.

I also started reading about airplanes and the Air Force because they had the best airplanes. Flying one of the fast jets had to be a great thrill. My Dad went to the Naval Academy and became an officer, but he wasn't a pilot. I read about the Air Force Academy up in Colorado. But going to college, any college, was so far off on my horizon that I put it aside and forgot about it.

Morgan followed in my footsteps pretty much, but seemed more interested in girls than I was. When we went by to pick him up after school, I would see him at the pick-up area with a different girl almost every day, just the pretty ones. I guess that they all felt the element of danger with him, which I've heard is the supreme attraction. I guess I gave off the element of "not-too-interesting". I had no interest in girls in general so I really didn't get to know any.

The one woman I knew well wasn't likely to inspire me to learn much more.

In the next couple of years we could tell that things were collapsing in our parents' marriage. We didn't want to believe it, and kept wondering whether it was somehow our fault. With my Dad's constant travel, and our Mom's careless attitude about being a wife and mother, we wondered fearfully how long it would last.

Dad called us every couple of weeks or at the end of the month from where ever he was. That could be places like London, Paris, Berlin, Zurich, or Baghdad. Mother continued her active "social" life, attending any charity event where she could dress up and go out. We would hear her answering the telephone, "Oh, Hi! Yes, this is Cindy." She would listen attentively, nodding her head. "Yes, I'd LOVE to come out to your event. Yes, you can COUNT ON ME." Then she was out there "Saving the Whales", "Fighting Cancer", and "Helping the War Orphans". War or not, Morgan and I felt almost like orphans every single day.

Our parents were there for us just at the minimum level prior to abandonment. Our Mom Cindy seemed like she loved us but she could never seem to focus on being a family mom. She was an East Texas beauty, with a perfect face and long blond hair, and had won several regional beauty contests. She didn't seem to be able to re- member to keep food in the refrigerator and on weekends she forgot to cook us breakfast...or lunch. Dinner was usually left over from what she brought home from her lunch out "with the girls". My Dad was gone so much as we were growing up that he didn't seem to notice. His job was super high-stress and he never seemed to have a thought or much time for us while he was gone. But Morg and I really didn't expect or need much, and we had learned to take care of ourselves and each other.

CHAPTER 6

Our Dad was Kirby Calloway. He sold computer equipment and software for security stuff, mostly to foreign customers like governments. He was really smart and he used to be in the Navy, as I said, he was in Naval Intelligence. I guess that means he kept track of the bad guys and what they were up to.

He wasn't a Navy diver or a Marine, just a regular kind of officer. He had left the Navy after six years, and started working for this big software company. When he was home, he would spend hours upstairs locked in his study talking on the phone. Sometimes, we could hear him speaking in a foreign language, which was normal I guess, given his job.

When he was home and not working, he was a pretty good guy. He would throw the football with us and was teaching Morgan how to throw a lot of different passes. He told us stories about the Naval Academy and the dedication it took him to stay there and not "wash out". He told us stories about the places he had visited, all across Europe and down into India and over to China. He had walked on the Great Wall and seen the Taj Mahal. He had seen Big Ben and the Eiffel Tower. He told us, "Guys, I really want both of you to come with me on one of my trips sometime. But for now, I'm moving around too much for us to have a decent visit. But I'm planning to finish up what I'm doing, then we'll have a chance. I really hope so."

CHAPTER 7

Then one day, we knew something was really wrong when we got home from school. My Dad was home from a trip and we could hear them quarreling in their bedroom. Then, when things got quiet again, their door flew open and Mom came storming out with her suitcase, her long blond hair flowing down her shoulders and her make-up flowing down her face, flush with rage, and mixed with tears.

She kissed Morgan goodbye and grabbed me by the shoulders and said, "Ethan Russell, I expect you to take care of Morgan. You are his brother and you are responsible for him". I savagely thought "That's YOUR Job", but held it in. Morg was staring straight at the ground, and I kind of teared up, and looked over at my Dad, standing up against the wall with a grim look on his face. "Ok", I said, and that was the last thing she said to me. She walked down to the end of the driveway rolling her big black suitcase, and a car pulled up, she got in, and that was it. We got birthday cards the first year and then nothing.

But when she left us, we were really hurt, especially Morgan. She had treated him really special when he was little, always hugging and kissing him, until he got embarrassed and his cheeks turned red. He would start squirming to get out of her arms, laughing. But I know he loved her and liked being treated like he was special to her.

My Dad stayed around the house for a few weeks to make sure we were ok. We weren't, of course, especially Morg. He slept in my bed every night, and I could hear him talking, blaming himself, and sniffling. I comforted him the best I could. He was my brother and I swore hard at my Mother for causing him so much pain.

One morning sometime after, just after school was out for the summer, Dad told us that we were going to leave Dallas and move to the little town of Pocasset in Massachusetts. We didn't want to leave our school and our friends, but Dad said it was important. He never said why, exactly. It was something to do with his business, he said.

He told us to pack up our stuff and be ready to "deploy", which was the word he used. He brought in two big new suitcases with the roller feet and told us to only pack our newest clothes and toothbrushes and stuff like that. We didn't have enough stuff to fill even one of the big suitcases, so we filled the other one with our toys and games.

Morgan had a teddy bear that he had held on to all these years. He picked it and looked hard at it, then tossed on the pile of stuff we weren't taking. He looked at me and said, "I don't think I want Teddy to go with us. He will have to do without me." Teddy lay in the discard pile, face up. I felt momentarily like laying on the pile with Teddy. But Morg grabbed the handle of his suitcase, the toy one, and pulled it out of our room and down the hall. I grabbed mine as well and as we rolled along, I remembered the sight and the rumble of our Mother rolling her suitcase down the driveway and out of our lives, and I swallowed hard.

My Dad took us out to dinner that night before we left for Pocasset and told us how much we would like it there in the summer. He described a quiet little town on Buzzard's Bay. He had bought a shore house three years ago but we'd never been there before. He said he used it as an overnight place between overseas airline flights. He talked about the Cape, places like Hyannis and Provincetown. He told us about the Pilgrims that had landed nearby in Plymouth, near where he grew up, and he made it sound like a great place for a couple of boys to finish growing up. He'd bought us a little sailboat and said he would teach us to sail on some weekend when he was home.

CHAPTER 8

We loaded up our meager stuff into a cab van. As we pulled away, we looked back at the house we grew up in, feeling a mixture of sorrow and disgust. We had many great memories of a few family events, but mostly the things we did at school and with our friends. I'm sure Morgan was leaving a few broken young female hearts behind.

The flight to the East was uneventful. Morgan slept most of the way and I just listened to music on my headset. Dad was reading reports and emails from the folders in his briefcase. We didn't talk much. I wondered why we had to move, leaving our high school friends behind. We were torn between remorse from leaving Dallas and expectations of a possible new life in an interesting new place.

We landed in Boston and got a Boston Coach that pulled out of Logan Airport and headed south through downtown. I looked at the scenery and thought it might be nice to see the Revolutionary War sites in Boston. We crossed over the river and I could get a glimpse of the white dome of one of the famous colleges in Cambridge, Harvard and MIT. Again, too far off on my horizon to think about.

We passed through an expanse of blue-collar homes in Quincy and then down into the wooded areas around Marshfield. Soon we were crossing the Cape Cod Canal in Bourne. We took the turn off Rte 28A and pulled into our new home town of Pocasset. We turned onto Shore Road and passed a number of smaller cottage-like homes and then there was the beach and a few bigger homes. The Coach turned into the driveway of one of them.

It was a substantial two-story house with a large front yard. It had a large covered front porch. The upstairs windows had little balconies on them, painted white. Way in the back of the house there was some kind of little building. The smell of the salt air blowing off the beach was a pleasant change from dusty Dallas.

We dragged our roller bags up the wooden stairs to the porch and through the glassed-in double front doors into the large living room with a wooden parquet floor. There was a set of large couches facing a large coffee table with a few picture books laying there. In the corner, there was a large bar with a marble top and three tall bar chairs.. There was a spiral metal staircase leading up to the second floor, and I wondered how we would get our big luggage bags up that swirling metal structure, but Dad led us through a central hallway to the back of the house where there was large circular staircase going up

We dragged our bags up the stairs and when we got to the second floor, Dad said, "Your rooms are down to the right, my room and my office is off to the left. The bathroom is in the middle. The other two rooms in the middle are empty. Go get settled." I took the room on the left in the front of the house, so Morgan got the room on the back overlooking the marsh.

I put my bag up on my bed and went over to the window, raised the blinds and looked out over the road to the beach. There was a small balcony outside, I opened the door and stepped out. A few cars whizzed by and there were a few people out on the little beach across the road throwing a football around. Morg came into my room and out to my balcony, saw the football game and grinned. He said, "At least they play football here." Morg had been the quarterback on the tenth -grade football team and he was really good. In Texas, that's saying something. Football is a religion in Texas. I wondered if the local high school even had a football team. He'd be a junior and could try out for the varsity QB position.

We went downstairs via the spiral staircase where Dad was paying the cab driver. He looked up, and asked, "What do you think?"

Morg and I looked at each other and I said, "It's pretty nice.

There's a good view of the beach from my room." Morgan chimed in, "Not from mine, all I can see is a dumb swamp."

Dad laughed and said, "Well, I hope you don't have to spend too much time inside. There's lots of stuff to do out in the town and out on the Cape. And it's never so blazing hot like Dallas. And I bought you a little sailboat so you can learn to sail and go exploring. It's out on the little dock over on the beach."

"You remember your Uncle Mark, right? He lives here and he'll check on you when I'm gone."

We looked at each other. Great, another adult we can't rely on.

There was a smell of fresh bread wafting through the air to mix with the ever-present smell of salt air.

Morgan asked, "Is there anything to eat? I'm really hungry."

Dad laughed again and said, "Yeah, there's a big kitchen and I've hired a cook to come in and cook meals for you. Or you can learn to cook for yourselves."

I smothered a laugh. Not anytime soon.

We went over to the dining room table off the kitchen. There was a pretty young girl bouncing around between the stove and the table. She looked up, smiled and said, "Hi. I'm Marie. Why don't you sit down. Dinner will be ready in a minute or so."

We had a great meal with biscuits, mashed potatoes, and meat loaf. Marie was our cook, but she wasn't the old grandmother type. Instead, she was a young woman and a culinary student at a nearby college. Also, she was pretty and friendly, so it would be cool to have her cooking for us when we needed her.

We had a couple of nice days with Dad. He had gotten a rental car and we drove around the city, looking at the sites, except there weren't any. There were just the kind of buildings you'd see anywhere in America. Apparently, Pocasset wasn't famous for anything except as a get-away from Boston traffic. After the third day, he got a phone call and left again. Business must be good.

CHAPTER 9

As Dad had warned us, we had an Uncle Mark who was the Postmaster in a neighboring town. He looked in on us, usually by surprise like he wanted to see if he could catch us doing something wrong. He rarely did. Me and Morg were "squared away" as my Dad said. We had to be, it just had to be that way. But now, it was time to get wet. I looked out at the waves in the small cove bouncing our new and untried sailboat around, and the small island beyond and wondered what adventures we would have.

"C'mon Morgan. The guys will be waiting for us at the pier." There weren't really any guys at the pier, we didn't know anybody yet. That phrase was left over from Dallas where we always had a crowd of buddies, ready to go have fun somewhere.

I started walking down the board walk across from the house but I sat down on the end of the walk to take off my fins. I'd be catching sand with them, flipping it everywhere, and probably fall on my face. The warm sand felt good on my bare feet.

I finally got tired of waiting for Morgan and went back in the house. I called for him, and heard a muffled noise from upstairs. I went up the spiral metal staircase to the upper floor and found Morgan in my Dad's bedroom, way back in their huge walk-in closet, sitting on the floor in front of an old chest. He had somehow unlocked it and the lock was lying on the floor in front of him. I got momentarily excited thinking it might be money or something we could sell for cash. We needed money to eat that day.

It wasn't that we were poor. We were rich, but "we" were poor, Morg and I. My Dad made lots of money but he never seemed to leave us enough if he was gone more than a week, and he had been gone longer than that this time. We needed cash.

"Ethan, come see this." Morgan had pulled out an old Manila envelope and dumped out a stash of letters, documents, two envelopes, and a bunch of old pictures, some from our babyhood. We both grabbed for them. They were mostly of Morgan as a toddler: there was only one picture of me, standing in the driveway of our Dallas house with my arm over Morgan's shoulders. I was standing up straight like a soldier while Morgan was leaning forward against his backpack straps like a paratrooper ready to jump out the door and yell "Geronimo"! I could tell he was yelling at me to let go of him. The other pictures were just baby pictures; I couldn't tell whether they were Morg or me.

There were four sealed envelopes in the folder, stuffed with something. We opened one of them excitedly and it spilled out a bunch of $100 dollar bills. There were fifty bills in that envelope and in the other ones...We whooped! We were set for spending money. That would cover our eating money and then some. We wondered where the money came from. We giggled about our Dad being a drug lord or some sort of Federal agent. But he's just a salesman, or so he said. He must be a really good one.

There was another sealed envelope in the big envelope. I shook it to see if I could tell what was in it, but nothing was loose, so I opened it. Considering the status of our "open family", I didn't think we had any secrets left.

In the envelope was a picture of a beautiful woman with long black hair, with a figure I had already learned to appreciate, standing on a city street, it looked like Paris. She was wearing a nice black dress and a pearl necklace and was making a pose for the photographer that made me excited for some reason. Morgan remarked, "That's a pretty woman. I wonder who she is? Do you know, Eth?" I didn't have an answer for Morgan. "Probably someone our Dad knows for work." I could guess at lots of other possibilities, but didn't really want to know, since my Dad had never mentioned her.

If he wanted us to know, he would have told us. Our experience with "Mom's" wasn't one we wanted to repeat anytime soon.

We put everything back in the chest except for some of the money and locked it with its key. As we started out of the closet, I noticed a large black hang-up bag on my Dad's side of the closet. I thought, might as well complete the burglary and I zipped it open.

Inside there was a black woman's nightgown. It felt smooth to the touch and I guessed it must be silk. On the hangar were some other items of woman's clothes, a fancy bra and some long white wool socks, all brand new. I looked at Morgan, who was mesmerized by our discovery. "Is that Mom's?" I said, "Mom has never been to this house, so I don't think so." I zipped the bag up again and shoved it all of the way to the back of the closet, almost out of sight. It looked like some woman had been here before us, and was apparently coming back.

CHAPTER 10

As I started to leave the closet, I noticed a large door hidden on the back wall. I moved some clothes out of the way, and examined it more closely. There was a key lock on the right side down by the floor.

"Morgan, where did you get the keys to open the chest?" He said, "In the bottom left drawer of Dad's desk."

"Are there any other keys there?" Morg said, "Yeah, there's a key ring with a bunch of keys. The key to the chest was a different kind, and it wasn't with the others", he replied.

Morgan was still sitting on the floor of the closet. I pushed past him, left the closet, and went down the hall to my Dad's office. It was a converted bedroom. I hadn't been in this room before, but it had a great view of the beach, just like mine in the opposite wing of the house.

I went over to his large wooden desk and pulled open the bottom left drawer. In the drawer there was the key ring with three keys and a stack of mail wrapped by a big blue rubber band.

I took the keys back in the closet, pushed past Morgan again, and sat down in front of the closet.

Morgan asked, "What exactly are you looking for now?"

I replied, "I really don't know, but there's likely a key on the ring that fits this lock."

Morg crawled down and looked over my shoulder as I inserted the first key in the lock. It was a good guess and it went in and turned.

The solid metal door swung open easily and I peered inside,

seeing nothing because of the dark of the closet.

"Morgan, go get us a flashlight." He scuttled back out of the closet and quickly returned with a big flashlight. He came to the back of the closet with the light on and shined it in.

At first we couldn't make out anything because the closet was at least three feet deep. But then the torch caught the glimmer of metal and we saw clearly what the locker contained.

There were two black AR-15 style rifles, a shotgun, two large pistols, one silver and one black, one smaller black pistol, and a wall rack loaded with all different types of ammunition.

"Whoa!" Morgan remarked. "What is all this stuff?"

I reached in and pulled one of the rifles off the rack and cradled it in my arms, like we had been taught at camp. I looked at the markings on the left side. They read, "M16A2". This wasn't an ordinary rifle, this was a combat sub-machine gun.

It had a large square telescopic sight on the top rail, and a folding forward hand support and a flashlight attached to another rail on the bottom. This was a true "Assault Rifle".

I put it back and pulled out the silver pistol. It was heavier than I thought it would be, compared to the Colt .45 revolvers we had been trained with at the ranch. But, then we were only shooting .22 caliber guns.

It was a Remington 1911 .45 caliber semi-automatic gun. It would be a handy gun to have in a fight. I checked to see if it was unloaded and passed it to Morg. "Wow, this is a serious pistol", he exclaimed.

There was another .45 in the rack as well as a smaller pistol. We put the .45 back on the rack and pulled out the smaller black pistol. It was a Beretta 9mm semi-automatic. It looked brand-new. I recognized it from any number of cop shows. I looked closer to the rack and saw that one of the spaces reserved for a Beretta was empty. I guessed that Dad had it with him.

We were stunned by our findings and put everything back where we got it and carefully closed and locked the steel door. Morgan looked really worried. This was so far out of what we thought about our Dad that it was hard to deal with. Why did a computer salesman need a gun? Or a secret vault full of them?

CHAPTER 11

We came out the closet, shut the door, and walked into our Dad's office to return the keys. Looking at his desk, his chair, and the things on his desk suddenly took on a whole new and sinister feeling. Having an armory a few steps away put even common things in a different light.

Morg remarked, "Well, that's a whole lot of new stuff to think about." He wasn't ready to form any conclusions either. I said, "You're right. It sure is." I had to ask myself, who was our Dad really? It's really disturbing when you don't know but all the evidence points to trouble. That closet wasn't filled with...Oh, I don't know. Old "Life" or "Sporting News" magazines? Anything but guns. Money and guns together tell a dangerous story.

We climbed down the spiral staircase to the main living room. We collapsed in the opposing couches to consider what we had just seen. We could speculate, but we couldn't come up with a concrete answer. We would need to have Dad explain it to us. But not over the phone, in person. He needed to come clean with us.

We left these thoughts behind as we turned back to the immediate task of learning to live in Pocasset on our own.

Map of Pocasset Harbor Massachusetts

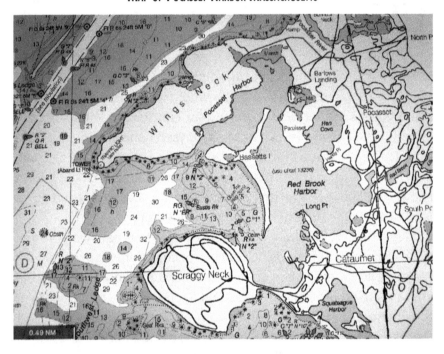

CHAPTER 12

Pocasset was a typical Cape beach town. The main road ran through the middle of town where it became "Main Street" rather than Rte. 28A. Hwy. 28A was a spur off Rte. 28 that ran south along the "elbow" of the Cape. The main Rte. 28 ran down from Boston all the way to the end of the Cape, ending in Provincetown. Main Street was a collection of small tourist shops, City Hall, the police station, a gas station with outrageously expensive gasoline, a coffee shop, a department store, and a church. The people living there were labeled as "townies". There was a small airport just east of town, and we heard a Cape Air flight come and go once in the morning and once in the afternoon, as well as the occasional small private plane. Once, we had seen what looked like some kind of Warbird, a World War II fighter plane roaring overhead.

Shore Road, where we lived, was the road that runs along the shoreline, with houses like my Dad's just across the road from the little beach and the water. Between Main and Shore Road was Bishop Lane, where the homes from the last century or two were built. The people who lived on Bishop were sometimes called the "Royals", the families that had lived there since the days when whalers and swordfish and lobster barons lived with their families spanning multiple generations. Some had taken the side of the British in the Revolutionary War, so there's the source of the name. Some of them were hanged after the war, but there were still enough "patriots" left to re-settle on Bishop Lane.

There was a strict protocol between people living on one street or the other. But one thing was clear, the elite lived on Bishop Lane and they were the ruling class. Kids like us who just showed up on Shore Road were tourist kind of people, whether they had lived there for years or not. We were expected to leave at any time to go back where we came from and do whatever we did there.

One Sunday afternoon, Morgan insisted we go skateboarding down Bishop Lane. I was sure that this was one of his ideas that would lead to trouble. I tried to talk him out of it, but he said, "We've been sitting in this house for a whole month and we haven't made any friends or enemies yet." As usual, this idea led to trouble, but also to opportunity.

The sidewalks were cracked and uneven, great for challenging skateboarding, but as noisy as a concrete grinding mill. I bet Morg that the people of Bishop Lane between 250-278 had never heard such a racket. Adults of that particular gentry were too cultured to come out with a rolled up newspaper in hand, waving it, and yelling at us. Instead, they walked quietly out to the top of their driveways and stood there with arms crossed and their reading glasses on the tip of their noses. After we had seen four or five of them come out and stand like the "Children of the Corn", we got the idea, kicked up our boards, and started walking.

We had gotten to about 100, where Bishop connects back up to Main, when we saw three or four boys on bicycles laughing and yelling at the porch of one of the houses. We strolled over to see what was going on. There was a pretty girl with red hair, knitted into a ponytail standing on the porch and staring at the disagreeable flock of boys.

As we sidled up, we heard them taunting her, saying "Wanna go on a date tonight? Then all of them laughing. One of the littler ones, yelled, "I'll show you a real good time! Ooo-la-la!" pointing to his crotch. That was followed by more raucous laughter.

Now, Morgan and I are from Texas, and even though we didn't have a good example from home to follow, we knew that in Texas, men didn't act that way. I didn't know how we could successfully intervene with the four-to-two odds, but we stepped in anyway.

The group of boys was momentarily startled when I walked into the group and grabbed the leaders handlebar, and said something stirring like "Away with you, varlets!" I don't actually remember what I said, because just at that moment there was a blast of noise from a motorcycle exhaust followed by the screech of brakes. The guy whose handlebars I was holding fell over, taking another bike with him. We all looked up to see the Avenger, a tall, powerfully built young man wearing a green flight jacket riding a heavily-chromed red Harley-Davidson softail. He looked around the group, and said, in a clear Texas accent, "Ya'll boys get out of here!"

The boys scrambled to untangle their bikes and leave, standing on their bike pedals to accelerate out of reach. Morg and I just stood back until they were all headed down the highway and then we looked at the newcomer. He looked us over and said, "Guess ya'll weren't any part of that, right?" We shook our heads, and Morg said, "They were harassing that girl and we thought we'd break it up." I thought, sure we did Morg. I had hoped to try to point out their bad behavior and get them to stop, but I had no idea what the quarrel was about, so I guessed that loud motorcycle noise and an intimidation from a stranger worked even better.

CHAPTER 13

The rider said, "Are ya'll from Texas?" Morg and I looked at each other and grinned. "How could you tell?" The rider laughed, and said, "You sound like cattle rustlers!" I looked at Morgan and laughed. His attempt at cattle rustling in the past hadn't been the biggest success story of his life. He stuck out his hand, and said, "My name is Falk." We shook hands and then took a better look at him. He was about eighteen, older than us, and had a confident air about him, like he was a person who had many stories to tell.

Falk looked around. The boys who had been harassing the girl with the ponytail were long gone. The girl on the porch had disappeared too. He asked me, "What was that all about?" I replied, "I don't know, but it seemed like they were mad about not getting a date with her, or something."

Falk put his kickstand down, leaned back on his bike and then he laughed, "I think it was more than that. Her family moved here last year, right into this house on Bishop. The old guy who lived here since forever, he died, and they bought the house. Her dad is some bigwig in the Coast Guard and works in the big station over in Hyannis. Those kids were from over in town. I've seen them before in school."

"So why don't they like her? I asked. "It seemed like they were making fun of her." That's all I could figure from what I saw in the few seconds she was on the porch.

Falk speculated, "Her name is Wendy. She has two problems. She and her family moved into the sacred ground of Bishop Lane, into old man O'Brien's house. That's not allowed here. O'Brien should have willed it to one of his kids to keep it in the family. As one of the elite, he should have married wisely to a rich local girl from another rich family, and he should have had tons of kids and filled that creepy old house with tons of grandkids, anything to promote the royalty. But he didn't."

"The old man O'Brien was a sour old guy who was married a long time ago, and his wife just disappeared. She either got fed up with him and left, or her body is in a cooler down in the basement. Nobody ever investigated, either way it would have looked bad. So when her family bought the house, they broke the Rule of The Royalty of Bishop Lane. The realtor was from Boston and didn't know the Rule, but when the Royals found out, they told her to take the commission money and get out of town, fast."

I volunteered, "But that doesn't explain why they were bothering her. It must be something else."

Falk said, "That brings me to the second point. The older one, the one whose handlebars you grabbed and you told him...what?...I only heard the word "barley". What was that?" I mumbled something stupid.

"Okay, here's what I think. He's from the town, and figured since she wasn't really part of the royalty, he could ask her out. The guy, Pauly, works for his dad as a house painter. Nothing wrong with that, but I guess she wasn't interested. I'm sure her dad had a vote, too. She's only sixteen. So, he got pissed off because if she had gone out with him, he could tell his buddies that he was moving up the class scale, up to the Royalty. So, she was in a double jeopardy deal. If she went out with him, the Royals would hate her and her family even more than they do now. If she didn't, the townies would say she wasn't a Royal, but trying to act like one. Either way, she couldn't win."

That seemed clear to me now. Wendy was a princess trapped in a tower besieged by dangerous varlets. Yeah, that's exactly the thought that went through my teenage boy mind. The sound of Falk's motorcycle starting up brought me back to my reality, strange as it seemed right now. Falk yelled at us over the sound of the red Harley with big dual pipes, "You guys should come out to the airfield sometime! I work out there and I got some stuff to show ya!" He roared off down Bishop Lane, causing at least one of the "Corn Children" to come out and disapprove.

Morgan and I went back to our low-rent hovel on Shore Road after our encounter with the the local gentry. Actually, the encounter was with some horny townies on bicycles, a stranger in a flight jacket on a motorcycle, and a string of disapproving looks from the Royals. Not bad for a Sunday afternoon, I'd say.

CHAPTER 14

We decided to take some of our burglary money and go downtown to have a nice lunch. Morg could eat any quantity of any food group. He said, "Let's go get a couple of burgers at Quincy's." Quincy's was the premier burger place on Main Street, and one of the few places that didn't specialize in seafood. The local seafood was Quahog clams and lobster and it was great. Shrimp and some other fish were flown in from Florida, Louisiana, or China. It was hard to tell where it was coming from, but it was great if you fried it. We had great local fish too, cod, flounder, swordfish, and even shark. But today it was to be burgers at Quincy's.

We walked up past Bishop Lane over to Main Street. Sunday was always busy with people from Boston and Rhode Island coming out to the Cape to fish, go out to one of the islands that were offshore from Pocasset, or just lying out in the late summer sun. It was a typically beautiful day for this time of year before the short Fall and what could be a brutal winter. The Cape doesn't have the tall, deep forests of maple, hickory, and other trees that color the landscape up north. It seems to go quickly from Indian summer to the first gale and snowfall, or so we were told.

We walked into Quincy's and looked for a booth near the windows. The tourist traffic going from souvenir store to store usually included girls in bikini tops and short-short jeans. Today, there was quite a show. Morgan and I watched and graded the beauty pageant outside the window. We ordered two bacon cheeseburgers each with their fabulous onion rings while we watched the show.

While we were waiting for our burgers, we noticed two guys come in, look around and take a booth not far from us. Morg said, "Those are two of the guys from this morning, not sure what they want besides burgers." I looked over at them and they were busy studying the menu, one that they already knew by heart.

The guy whose handlebars I had grabbed finally looked over at me, feigned expressed surprise at seeing us, and said, "What are you doing here? Where is your motorcycle buddy? Is he going to rescue you again?"

I ignored him for as long as I could, then turned to him and said, "Hey, if you got a problem with Falk, take it up with him."

He sneered back and said, "What were you doing there at the bitch's house? You after some?"

I replied, in the calmest voice I could muster, "My brother and I noticed that there were a bunch of assholes screaming in the street and we thought we'd check it out. Men that we know don't act that way. What were you doing it for?"

My poke at him could have had two outcomes, he could have taken it to the next level, or he could back it off. Morg was prepared for option one. I could see him tense up but with a broad grin on his face. Sometimes that grin scared me. If anyone in that booth stood up, it was on.

Pauly looked down at the table, and responded, "That girl is a whore and a bitch. She doesn't belong living on Bishop Lane and she's a snob who hates boys. She's probably a Lesbo."

I looked at Morg and I could see him relax a bit. I also noted that a police officer had just come through the doors and walked behind our two booths. I know they saw him too.

I saw that this was over now, and I just said, "Well, if that's true, why don't you just leave her alone. Morgan popped up and said, "I've never met a girl that was both a whore and a Lesbo. If I was you, I'd steer clear."

Just then, our food arrived and we dug in. As expected, it was great food and we ate everything down to the last onion ring. The other guys ate their food in silence, but kept looking over at us.. As they left, the guy Falk had called "Pauly" told us, "I don't want to see you newbies over there on Bishop again." Morgan and I looked at them and broke into hearty laughter. These Townies ranked just above the guys roaming our town landfill.

CHAPTER 15

The little beach out in front of our house was never very crowded and today was no exception. We got our suits on, leaving our masks and fins behind and went down to the waters' edge. As summer heat was coming to its peak, more of the beach houses were opening up, and more and more tourists were making the drive down here for lobster or clams, or to continue on to Hyannis and way out to Provincetown..

The few kids our age that lived on our street were the sons and daughters of people who had lived here for many years yet they never acquired any status like the people on Bishop Lane. I guess the comparison was years here, versus centuries here.

The water was finally warm enough for us to swim in. We had been used to the 90 degree waters of the Texas lakes which was more like a warm bath than a natural lake. And there were both hot springs and cold springs in Texas. You could take your pick.

We waded in to our waists to get the important lower parts of our bodies used to the cold, then we pushed off the sand bottom and swam out to the line of bouys marking the swim area. We held onto the rope line, treading water, and we looked back at our house.

It was an imposing two-story house with a big front porch. There were four white double columns rising from large stone footing up to the roof. There were little balconies off the two upstairs bedrooms with white railings. The porch had smooth gray paint which matched with the white walls and green shutters of the house. It looked indestructible from out there on the bouy line.

Morg was floating on his back and I could see his toes sticking out the water. He turned to me and asked, "Ethan. How long do you think we're going to be here? When do we go back to Dallas?"

I thought for a minute, and dunked my head back, washing my hair back out of my eyes. "Dad never said we were going to leave here but he didn't say we were going to stay either. I think we're kinda parked here for now."

I immediately thought how really unfair that was to us. We were growing up fast and had already passed many of the hurdles of manhood. We were living like adults now. It wasn't fair, we deserved some kind of childhood. Maybe we were living our childhood in parallel with our manhood, if that's even possible.

I looked over at Morgan, who had his eyes closed and was just floating along in the slow swell of the waves. He was a good looking kid. Blond hair and blue eyes will set a young man apart up here with all the black-haired European immigrants. It sure worked in Dallas. He'd probably already passed one of the hurdles of manhood back in Dallas. I envied him.

I looked back at the house, now part in shadow from the sun setting behind it. We could go back, sit on the porch, and watch the happenings on the beach or the sidewalks bordering Shore Road. We could have crossed our arms, lowered our reading glasses and disapproved of all that passed our view, but we weren't old enough or regal enough for that.

CHAPTER 16

A few days later, I told Morgan, "Let's ride out to the airport and look up Falk." He replied, "I think that guy has his shit together. That should be fun. Let's go."

The ride out to the airport was about six miles by bike. We rode down Shore up to Main, then headed east out of town, past Quincy's and the Willoughby Department Store. Once we were out of town, the sea breeze picked up and we felt the sand being blown across the road off the big dunes. We felt it in our teeth as the grit went everywhere. After six miles, we saw the turnoff to the airport, and we could just see a few buildings and hangars in the distance. As we got closer we could see one big hangar with its wide doors open, so we headed for that one. We could see Falk's red Harley parked over in a corner of the hanger.

Just inside the hangar, we saw a skinny dude with a greasy rag hanging out of his back pocket, wearing dark sunglasses and a turned-around baseball cap on his head. He was peering deeply into what seemed to be an airplane engine on a stand. It clearly wasn't Falk.

Morg looked around the hangar and not seeing anybody else, he called out. "Sir, we are looking for Falk. Is he here somewhere?"

The dude slowly pulled his head out of the engine and turned toward us. He looked each of us over carefully, seeing two young men who looked remarkably alike, except for a slight difference in height and age. The taller one had the stubble of his first beard hugging his face.

He took off his sunglasses, rubbed his eyes, and jerked his

thumb towards the sky. "Falk is up flying right now. His plane just came out of its 100-hour check and he's got it up to see if it's fixed right."

I thought that might not be the best way to see "If it's fixed right" but hey, if it's gonna happen, it's gonna happen up there. I can't recall where I heard that before but it seemed to have an element of truth. The stress on the engine is hardest when it's being used for real. I learned that back in auto shop in Dallas.

I said, "Thanks, we'll wait a bit and see if he comes back." The head with the backwards baseball cap went back into the engine block. We walked through the hangar and out to the ramp. We looked up in the sky from horizon to horizon and didn't see anything, but then we heard the sound of an engine running very rough. As it got closer, the sound got louder then quit completely.

Then there, just over the trees at the far west end of the runway, we saw a small, high wing plane turning to line up with the runway. It didn't look like it was in trouble, there was no fire or smoke, but it looked to be very low. But the propellor wasn't turning, it was kind of stopped at a 45 degree angle.

As it got near the end of the runway, we saw the flaps come down, the plane nose up, then apparently rapidly settle to the ground, bounce up once, then slow and stop. It had to be not more than 100 feet from the touchdown end of the runway.

We started running toward the plane to see if we could help the pilot if he was injured. Then, to our surprise, the airplane engine started back up and it started moving toward us. We stopped running and walked back to where we had begun, looking back at the now-moving plane.

The plane had picked up speed, made a gradual left turn and then came to a stop in one of the airplane parking spots marked on the concrete.

Somehow we suspected that the pilot would turn out to be Falk, and we weren't disappointed.

The little planes' engine quit and the propellor slowed to a stop.

We waited while the pilot was cutting switches and fooling with other controls, but then the left-side door opened. It was indeed Falk, in his white T-shirt and well-worn jeans, deck shoes, and his dark aviator sunglasses. He flashed a big smile, walked over and said enthusiastically, "Hey, guys, I'm really glad to see you. I thought I might not see you 'til school starts."

I returned, "We're glad to see you, too. Wasn't sure for a while there," I said, gesturing at the trees at the far end of the runway.

That reminded me. We only had two weeks until the start of school. Morgan and I were both going to be in a new and foreign high school in Pocasset unless our Dad showed up and took us away to some other strange place. Actually, we were liking living in Pocasset so far and weren't looking forward to moving again. Not even back to Dallas as that house had few happy memories for us, except for our school and our friends. I'm sure Morgan missed his collection of girlfriends. We had developed both friends and enemies here and we liked it. I still wondered how ponytail Wendy might fit into our little drama.

We smiled back and stepped over to look at his plane. Morgan put his hand up on the smooth curved front of the wing, and asked, "Is this yours?"

Falk, laughed and said, "No, it's not mine...yet. It belongs to the Company. You want to take a look at it?"

He said, "Crawl up on the front seats." There were two seats in the front and two smaller seats in the back, and I got into the left pilot seat while Morgan went around to the other front seat. The panel had a confusing array of all kinds of round gauges, switches, knobs, and the control wheel sticking out of the panel.

"How do you fly this thing with all of these gauges and all the information coming at you?"

He laughed again and explained, "It's not hard once you understand how planes fly and what information you need to look at. You don't need all of it all at once and all at the same time. I'll teach you if you want."

Morgan asked, "Why did you crash when you were just landing?"

Falk looked sheepish and explained, "I was trying an engine-out landing and I got a little short and low and I couldn't get the engine started in time to make a normal landing." He took a deep breath. "So I pulled up, dumped the flaps to get more sudden lift, then plopped her on the ground, which killed all my energy, so we just stopped on the runway. Please never try this just because it worked for me this time. I don't know why it worked, it could have turned out very badly."

I didn't know what to say. The fact that a pilot could have that kind of knowledge and control over a machine like an airplane was amazing to me. But I had to know more.

"Falk, could you take us up and give us a flying lesson? I'd be happy to pay for the plane or the gas."

He shook his head, and said, "I only have my solo license. Because of our Company insurance, my Dad said that I can't get my Private until I am eighteen. So I can't take up passengers...officially."

I took his drift. I asked, "What if you had a charter for a couple of wealthy unofficial passengers? Don't pilots do that all the time?"

He looked up at me and smirked. "Yeah, I guess I could do something along those lines." He thought for a minute and said, "Meet me tomorrow at noon if the weather is ok. I'll give you a shot at flying my plane." Not you Morgan, you are really too young. You can ride with us though."

Morgan looked down and shoved his hands in his pockets. He was dramatic that way sometimes. He'd get his chance someday.

CHAPTER 17

We woke up to a bright blue sky once again and headed out to the airport on our bikes. It was over six miles, and it occurred to me that two "Men of Means" like us shouldn't have to travel by pedaling everywhere. After all, we had four envelopes with more than $20,000 stuffed in them. Just behind Willoughby's was a used motorcycle repair and sales shop. I don't think it even had a name.

We parked our bikes on the side of the store and went inside. It smelled of old carburetors and burn-out engines. Behind the counter covered with motorcycle magazines, there was a guy with purple spiked hair and green sunglasses, kicked back in his chair.

When he saw us, he leaned forward in his chair with a bang, and said, "What's up, guys? What can I interest you in? Drugs, bikes, or hair doo?" I wasn't sure how to answer him, but Morgan stepped up to the counter and demanded, "We need a couple of good rides! What have you got?"

"I have three or four you can choose from. You got cash?"

I replied, "Let's see the bikes."

He took us back into a smelly, filthy, and dark garage behind the storefront. "They're here somewheres. Yeah, there in the back." We moved around a pile of broken frames, motors, fuel tanks and pipes to the back of the dark garage and saw a row of dirt bikes lined up there. There were two that looked to be pretty new and in pretty good shape. Since they weren't completely street legal, we wouldn't need driver's licenses for them. Getting my license was at the top of my list, but again, I needed an adult to sign for me.

"How much?" I asked. "The Yamaha is $650 and the Coolster is $700," he responded without hesitation. They were both 250cc bikes with extended forks for rough off road conditions.

I thought for a second, then suggested, "How about $1200 for both?"

He said without hesitation, "Cash?" I pulled the money out of my jeans, counted it, and gave it to him. He counted it, then shoved it in his jeans then he turned around and waved us back into the office. "We got some paperwork to finish then you can get them out of the garage and go." I went over to the counter and signed the titles while Morg went around to get the motor bikes. He pulled them up to the sidewalk, while our other bikes were forgotten for now.

They were both half-full of gas and mixture so we cranked them up. They were very loud, so we were careful to not goose them and attract the attention of our single active police officer.

We rode them slowly down the road until we got out of town. Then we cranked them up until we got the front wheels off the ground, and raced all the way to the airport. We flew through the wide turns between the dunes. We chased flocks of seagulls off the road, squawking and struggling to get their long wings out of our way. It was as much fun as you could have on two wheels, unless your two-wheeler was an airplane.

CHAPTER 18

When we pulled up, we could see Falk's little airplane in its normal parking spot. But next to it, there was this beautiful warbird, a P-51 Mustang which apparently lived in one of the other hangars.

We parked our skinny little dirt bikes next to Falk's gleaming red Harley and headed over to admire the World War II fighter.

Falk was standing next to it and talking to a tall, skinny, gray-haired guy in a flight suit. In addition to a black leather patch with silver Air Force wings, there was a brightly colored patch on his breast. It read "Thunderbirds", the fabulous Air Force precision flying team

We walked up to listen to their conversation. Falk and the Mustang pilot were talking about approach speeds for landing the Mustang. I could tell that he was impressed by the questions that Falk asked him.

Falk saw us, and turned to introduce us. "Colonel, these are two of my aviator friends, Ethan and Morgan Calloway. We're going flying in a little while." He squinted a bit because he knew Falk only had a solo license, but quickly realized that Falk was competent in the air and we'd be safe.

We shook hands and Falk introduced him as retired Colonel Fred Whittier, a former Thunderbird Pilot. He told us, "Nice to meet you guys, and I'm glad to see you interested in flying. We need more pilots in the Air Force right now with all our new planes." He looked at me and asked, "You look almost old enough, have you thought about going to the Academy with Falk?"

I had looked at one of the Academy brochures that my guidance counselor had back in Dallas, but that was a long time ago. "Sir, yes I have, but I've just started thinking about it." Was Falk going to the Air Force Academy? That was news.

Colonel Whittier replied, "Well, it's not for everybody, but give it some thought. Now, I've got to get this bird down to DC for an air show. Good luck." We all backed off to see the start-up of the beautiful aircraft.

He turned and climbed up on the wing and threw his leg over the cockpit ledge, and settled into his seat. His crew chief helped him get his parachute straps fastened, and the cockpit switches set, then he crawled into the tiny back seat. Col. Whittier then slid the clear plexiglass canopy shut and locked it. Then he waved at us, called, "CLEAR!", and cranked the huge four-bladed prop over a few times until it caught with a huge burst of smoke and noise.

We backed up even more to watch the Mustang warm-up then taxi-out. It hesitated at the end of the 3,000 ft strip of concrete for a while as he prepared for take-off, then with that unmistakable roar, rushed down the runway, gaining speed until it took off, folded up its landing gear, and turned south before disappearing into the haze.

CHAPTER 19

We all walked back over to Falk's plane in silence, all savoring the experience we had just shared.

Then I asked, "Falk, are you going to the Academy?" He looked at me and laughed, "Not for another year. I have to make it through high school first and I have another year." He added, "I have an automatic appointment if I want to take it, so it feels like I'm pre-ordained to go there."

I tried not to act surprised. "Why is that?" He turned away towards his plane, and then replied, "Because my Dad won the Medal of Honor."

I stood there, stunned. He didn't volunteer any other explanation, so I didn't pester him for a response. I looked at Morgan, and he opened his eyes wide and let out a low whistle.

Falk then said, "OK, let's go. Morgan, you climb into the right rear seat so you can watch me from back there. Ethan, get over in the right seat in the front. You can be my first "wealthy, unofficial" student.

He went over the checklist and pointed out the various instruments and gauges and what they meant. He showed us how the control wheel and the rudder pedals wiggled the little flaps on the wings and tail, and how the flaps went down.

He started the engine and we taxied out and lined up on the runway. After checking the engine by running it up, he turned to us, visually checked our seatbelts, and announced, "Ladies and Gentlemen, welcome to Wealthy Unofficial Airlines. Anything that happens beyond this point is not legally my fault, since I am not allowed by law to take passengers, even Wealthy and Unofficial passengers. Please hold on tight!"

He slowly pushed in the red throttle knob and we heard the engine rev up to a mild roar, not the throaty snarl of the Mustang, but enough to get us moving down the runway. After using up about a third of the runway, we slowly lifted off, then tilted left to climb up to a few thousand feet. We were flying along the southern coast of the Cape and we could see the beaches, the quaint little towns, and the offshore islands of this special part of New England.

After we were stable at altitude, Falk told me to take the wheel, which I had been excitedly waiting for. I made a few shallow turns, a bit of a climb, and then a bit of a dive back to our initial altitude. I watched the instruments change as we turned and climbed. I could see the altimeter increase as we climbed and decrease as we dived, with the turn indicator swinging back and forth as I turned. The information on the round dials was beginning to make sense to me. I was in heaven, both mentally and physically.

I turned back to Morg and yelled above the noise, "It's no harder than riding a horse! You should try it!" He was looking out the window, and without looking at me replied, "Screw you." Oooh. An angry sixteen year-old is not a pretty sight.

It actually reminded me of horseback riding; the beast was responsive to my gentle moves and moved in the direction I wanted to go. I wondered what I would have to learn to have the control over it that Falk had shown, even in his almost disastrous landing. He seemed to know intuitively what to do to control the plane, and what it would do in response.

I looked back again at Morgan. He was watching attentively at every move I made, and he had an imaginary control wheel between his hands and was following me through the maneuvers.

As I got more comfortable with flying, I started looking at the ground and looking for landmarks on the ground. I could see the town of Falmouth and the many ponds leading to the ocean. I turned and flew down along the island chain on the southwest coast. Falk said, "Let me have her." I released my grip on the control wheel and Falk took over. My hands were cramped, and I realized how tightly I had been holding the wheel. Falk saw me looking at my still-clenched fingers and laughed. "All it takes is a light touch."

He took the controls and dove down to just over the tree-tops and circled over a couple of the larger islands. He pointed out one particular island near Pocasset Harbor. "That one was used by the booze smugglers during Prohibition to hide their cargos that came in by boat," he said as he made a wide circle completely around it. Then he said, "There are some caves in it that they used to hide the booze and their piles of money. There was also some gold coins they found. Really, really, old. Some people think that they were Viking coins like the ones somebody found up in Nova Scotia."

"There is an old story of a "Golden Throne" somewhere on one of the islands. That's all I know. People have stopped talking about it. Maybe somebody already found it. Don't know."

I asked excitedly, "Like a real throne, like a King sits on? Why would there be a "Golden Throne" off a little island down there somewhere?"

Falk shook his head, "No, not like a Kings' Throne. It's supposed to be a little throne that the Virgin Mary sat on. A little one. The rumor that I've heard, and I'm only reporting what I've heard, was that it was a little worship statue of Mary and Jesus that the Spanish had on a treasure ship that was attacked by pirates, Blackbeard, I think. It got traded up the coast and was headed for a museum in Boston when the ship was lost in a fierce storm off New York. Somehow it ended up around here somewhere. That's the rumor."

I found that story intriguing, that there might be Viking relics down on one of those islands, and maybe even some pirate loot. I was skeptical about a "Golden Throne", but now I had a strong interest in learning to sail our little boat and going out there to take a look.

I looked back at Morgan and I could see the cogs in his mind spinning as well. We exchanged looks and a smile. He was on board with the plan.

After an hour or so of flying up and down the Cape and circling some more of the offshore islands, Falk turned the plane back toward our little airfield. He circled it once, reduced the power and turned to line up with the runway. He laughed and assured us, "This won't be like my last landing. This one will be smooth as a baby's bottom." And it was.

We secured Falk's plane with tie-down ropes then he locked the doors. The wind off the Atlantic can change direction and speed rapidly and planes have been lost in a sudden gale.

I knew now that flying was going to be in my future, maybe not right away, though I was going to fly with Falk whenever I could. The physics of flight were a mystery to me, and I needed to re-focus on learning all I could in school.

CHAPTER 20

High school for us was due to start in two days. Morgan and I shared our concerns, which were many. First of all, we needed new clothes, but we had plenty of burglary money for that. All we had was the few sets of clothes we'd crammed into that one suitcase back in Dallas. We didn't have any clothes for cold weather.

Secondly, we didn't know very many people and most of the ones we did know, hated us. We didn't want to get into a school-yard fight on the first day of school. I knew Falk would be there, but I didn't want to rely on him. Morgan and I knew how to fight. After all, we are brothers and we've gotten into many scuffles, brother versus brother over the years. Morgan had also been to ka-rate classes for two years back in Dallas and won his tournament to get his junior black belt. After that, I decided to not start any more fights with him.

Privately, I wondered whether we'd see Wendy, the girl with the red ponytail from Bishop Lane. And then, most of all, we needed our parents or some parent to register us. We couldn't just walk in there like two out-of-town orphans.

I called Uncle Mark and he said, "I can't. I'm not your legal guardian. Sorry, you need to call your Dad."

We hadn't heard from him in over a month. I tried to call him on his cellphone, but I got an answering machine in a language I didn't understand. I left a message. "Dad, this is Ethan. We need you here to register us in school. We need you to come home."

A few hours later he called. I answered. He said, "I got your message and I understand. I will take care of it." I asked, "Are you coming home?" He answered after a brief pause, where he was talking to someone else. He replied slowly, "Maybe, but either way I'll take care of it. I will be moving out of Paris soon. Can't tell you where yet. Sorry, I have to go. Bye for now."

I hung up with a deep concern over what might happen next.

The next afternoon, a cab pulled up outside our house. It stopped, then turned into our driveway. Morgan and I hesitantly went out on the porch. Someone got out of the cab and turned to pay the driver. It seemed to be a woman in a long grey coat and a big, fur-trimmed hat. She had flowing, long blond hair. Then she turned around to look at the house through her dark sunglasses that glinted in the afternoon sun. She saw us on the porch and she waved.

It was our Mother.

CHAPTER 21

She yelled at us, "Come kiss me!" We trudged down the stairs and across the yard into the driveway. She rushed up to Morgan and grabbed his face with two hands and planted a big wet kiss on him. "OH MY GOD, Look how big you are now!" He smiled back at her with a look of happiness that surprised, even frightened me.

She turned her attention to me now. She pulled me in and gave me a surprisingly strong hug. "And look at YOU! You are practically a MAN, Ethan Russell!" My teeth grated at hearing my whole name like that. "Russell" was her brother who had never expressed any interest in us, and whom we had never even met.

"OK, grab my bags and let's go take a look at this little "love nest." I was surprised at her characterization of our house as a "love nest". It certainly hadn't been for Morg and me, though after school starts, you never know. It could be a real party house with no adults around. We both grabbed two of her bags and headed up to the stairs to the porch. The bags were heavy and awkward, and I thought to myself, Is she planning on staying forever?

I immediately thought of the ramifications of that. What if she is moving in to be our Mom again? What if she is laying some kind of trap for Dad when he comes back here and the quarrel resumes?

CHAPTER 22

I had nothing but fear and trepidation as I lugged her junk up the stairs, through the double doors, and into the living room. I looked back and Morgan was dragging the famous black roller suitcase that she had left Dallas with into the room. He looked very happy to see her. That added to my dark mood.

I didn't want her back, and I didn't want her living here. This was our house, Morg and me, and I didn't want to see it turned into some kind of weekend resort for my Mother and her socialite friends.

"So, boys, where are you going to put me?" she said as she looked around and surveyed possible places for her nesting.

Morg volunteered, "You can stay upstairs in Dad's room! He's never here."

She looked at Morg strangely and said slowly, "Well, if there's no other room, then I guess it will be ok. Now how do I get there? I'm not going up that silly staircase. That thing looks AWFUL. A person could DIE falling off that thing."

She was referring to the steel spiral staircase that was a prominent feature in the living room, leading to the upstairs. Morg and I used it all the time without any thought about using the rear staircase.

Morg again volunteered, "Of course not. Come through here. There are real stairs back here". He led her through the central hallway to the rear stairs. The rear of the house had at one time been the front, with the grand staircase facing out to what had been the reception area on the old driveway. Morgan was dragging that

AWFUL black roller bag. It's funny how a person can fixate his hate on something like that black suitcase.

We all went up the back stairs and turned left to go past the bathroom and two spare bedrooms into what we had been calling the "North Wing" of the house, where my Dad's bedroom and office were located. It struck me that I had never seen him sleep in that bed, but I suddenly imagined him and the lady in the picture, her wearing the nightgown in the closet, as well as the long white socks warming her slender legs.

Whoa! I stopped my mind thinking down that dark alley and returned to the present. I had pushed the nightgown way into the back of my Dad's closet, behind some of his suits, so I was sure Mom wouldn't find it.

She took off her sunglasses and looked around. We waited for her judgement. "It's so quaint, isn't it. Just a lovely little get-away for a romantic weekend."

I could draw two conclusions from this, neither one very positive. One, she was planning to bring some new boyfriend or two down here for a "lovely" Cape vacation. Or Two, she was planning to ambush Dad when he showed up with Paris Girl, a name I just invented for her. We needed to call her something because it was obvious that she was going to play a part in our little drama, possibly an inflammatory one. I couldn't help but flashback to Morg, the "Fire Wizard." Maybe a better name for her would be the "Fire Witch", but that was too harsh for a woman we'd never met.

Mom turned to us and clapped her hands and said, "You guys SCOOT while I get settled. I'll be down after I get cleaned up."

I couldn't imagine her ever needing to "get cleaned up". She never had a single blond hair out of place, but we headed down the spiral staircase.

When we got to the bottom, I told Morgan, "Come out to the porch where we can talk."

He followed me outside and we collapsed into a couple of the big wooden chairs.

He just sat there until I said, "I wish she hadn't come. I hope she gets us registered then leaves and goes back to New York."

He shook his head slowly, then looked out toward the beach and said, "I'm glad she's here. I hope she stays. Maybe she's ready to be a real Mom."

I turned toward him savagely, "You can't possibly believe that! I don't know why she's here, but it's not simply to walk us to school and sign papers then leave us. Didn't you see how much luggage she had? She's planning to live here, at least for a while."

He looked shocked at my outburst, but then he said, "I want her to stay. I want my Mom back." I could see tears in his eyes. But those were the same little boy tears he cried when she left. I still hated her for that.

So we sat there, me in my anger, and Morg in his expectation of a happier life than the solitary lives we had been leading without parents. I didn't think of it as solitary, I saw it as freedom from adults who didn't have our best interests in mind.

CHAPTER 23

I called Marie to see if she could come over and fix a meal for us. Marie showed up just in time to get a dinner together for our "welcome" for Mom. She had two bags of groceries to replenish our empty refrigerator and to create an interesting meal for Mom and us. The word was out somehow that our Mom had showed up here from New York and was some kind of high society woman.

Marie took me aside and asked, "Do you want me to make chicken or steak?" I considered it, but then said, "Can you make both? We are real hungry and haven't had anything to eat today

She looked at me disapprovingly, "I told you that I could come over any time you needed me. You haven't been using me. And I'm already paid for!" Her response touched off something in me. Was I becoming attracted to this slightly older woman? She was pretty, funny, and could cook like the best French chef. Of, course I didn't know any French chefs but I'd seen them on the cable network.

"I'm sorry. We could really use more help from you." She smiled, and said, "OK, chicken and steak. Now get out of my kitchen!" She made a movement with her hand as if to spank me, and I scooted out of her reach.

We heard Mom coming down the back stairs. Morgan's face lit up, but the best I could do was a fake smile. She had a blank look on her face, and I guessed she had been drinking. When we brought her luggage up to my Dad's room, one of the bags had a clinking sound, like it was full of bottles. I thought, "Well, that's one bottle down, at least."

She sat down at the end of the table, the head of the table as it would be called if our Dad was around. She looked at us and then seemed to come back to life.

Then she said, in her excited little voice, "Now tell me everything and don't leave a single thing out!" I looked at Morg and he looked eager to be first, so I just folded my arms and sat there.

Morgan started, "We have school starting in two days and you need to come take us down there and get us enrolled, or we will get arrested for truancy." I thought, way to go, Morg. That might get her attention.

She laughed and said, "Of course we will, honey. We'll go down to that school and get you both properly enrolled." The way she said it enraged me, it was like she was demeaning him just because he liked school and wanted to get started. She dragged out the word "enrolled", like it was a dirty word to her. I thought that it was typical of her not to value being committed to something, something important, especially to Morgan.

He smiled broadly, and said, "We already have our school clothes and we can take our bikes to get there."

She said, "Well, that's just fine, but how far away is the school?"

Morg replied, "It's only a couple of miles from here, not far."

She sighed, and said, "Well, that's good, but tomorrow I will need to take you. Where's your Dad's car?"

That caught me by surprise. I didn't know Dad had a car here. Morgan looked at me quizzically. He certainly didn't mention it when he left. I thought quickly, "Well, there is that old garage back behind the house. We haven't had time to go explore it."

She said, "Well, tomorrow you need to go down there and see if he left a car in there. It seems to me that he has cars everywhere. I have no idea what he is up to, but he seems to like his cars."

CHAPTER 24

I thought to myself, "No way we're going to wait for tomorrow. We'll go down there after she goes to bed and see what, if anything, is in there."

We met in the hall at about mid-night and slipped down the back stairs to the porch and then out to the rickety, old garage. It hadn't been painted since it was put up in the 1930's, and most of it was old weathered wood. There were a few boards missing on one side, so we turned on our flashlights and peered through the gaps, but we really couldn't make out anything inside, so we tried the front door. I should have thought of the fact that it would, of course, be locked.

I told Morg, "Why don't you sneak upstairs and get that key ring out of Dad's desk?" He replied, "No way. Mom will wake up." "No, she won't, she's out like a light in the bedroom across the hall from his study." Morg considered the risks versus rewards for a minute, then said, "I'll be right back...unless she wakes up."

I waited in the dark by the door of the old garage. I couldn't imagine that there was anything of value stored in that broken-down shack. It would have been stolen long ago. You could probably knock the whole thing over if you leaned on it.

We unlocked the big Master Lock with one of the keys, and slid the door open. It took a lot of effort as it was jammed in tree roots that had buckled the frame. When the door was fully opened, we shined our flashlights in to see a large shape under a brown canvas tarp. We found the ties around the bottom and slid the tarp back off the car into a large pile on the floor.

Underneath the tarp in the light of our eager flashlights was a charcoal gray Maserati. As we walked down the side of the car, avoiding tools stacked along the side of the garage, we got a better look. On the side of the hood was a metal name sign that read Levante AWD with the Maserati trident.I guessed that AWD meant All-Wheel Drive. It had four black leather seats, two leather bucket seats in the front, and two smaller seats in the back. The perfect family car for a family with one small kid and a dog. Or two teenage boys. With two dogs.

We slowly pulled the cover back down over the beautiful car and re-tied the straps. The car was locked or we would have gladly gotten behind the wheel. What we could see through the dusty windshield looked like a spaceship, and we decided that our next task would be to find the keys.

The other minor issue was that neither one of us had a drivers license. I was old enough to get a learners' permit, but I doubt I could take the car to Driver's Ed, but I thought, wouldn't that be a thrill for the teacher if I drove up in that rocket ship. Taking it to school with Mom might be an issue. One of us, Morg would have to cram in the tiny back seat...with all of our books.

As we stumbled our way out of the garage, I noticed that the floor was solid concrete with a steel plate near the far end, instead of the gravel in the driveway. No big deal, but I noticed steel I-beams set into the concrete at the four corners of the garage, and other steel beams supporting the old wooden roof. I guess it wouldn't be so easy to push over as I thought. At least our car was well protected, but I wondered about the outward appearance of the garage. If someone was spending money on reinforcing the garage, why not replace all the broken boards on the walls? Was it just meant to be a deception?

I didn't point out the steel beams to Morgan. I thought that I would keep it secret for now until I figured out what it was for. It just added to the changing mystery about our Dad, Kirby Calloway.

We slipped back into the house and creeped back upstairs and into bed without waking Mom up. We had to get to school tomorrow to register and Dad's dream car wasn't going to get us there.

CHAPTER 25

We woke up early and got our "first day at school" stuff together in our backpacks. Then we went downstairs and had breakfast from warming up the left-overs from the night before. I had learned from Marie to fry eggs, so I served up steak and eggs. Not bad for my first-ever cooked meal. We waited for Mom to come downstairs and go out to the garage. Pretty soon, she came swirling down the stairs, her high heels clicking, and, without hesitation said, "Out to the garage." We jumped up and followed her down off the porch and out to the garage.

Morgan pulled out the key ring and we went through the process of the night before of getting the door open, rocking it over tree roots. We then went in and pulled the tarp off the car, pretending like we were seeing it for the first time. Once again, Morg and I were awed with the beauty of that amazing car.

Mom stuck her head in the garage and surveyed the sight of the beautiful car sitting surrounded by shovels, rakes and miscellaneous junk.

"OH, MY GOD," that's what he left us to drive? That's so much like him, only thinking about himself! This is so typical. That man never considers what other people, especially his family, might need or prefer!"

I doubted that Dad had any thought of us piling into that car to go to school, or anywhere else for that matter.

"Well, Ethan, get in there and start it up and get it out of that old garage before it collapses on it." Morg had become an expert on burglarizing Dad's desk, and had come up with a set of keys on a

Maserati electronic key fob that obviously belonged to the car.

I took the keys and squeezed into the space between the car door and the rakes and shovels that we had tripped over the night before. I unlocked the door with the electronic key, and opened it and slipped into the tight little bucket seat.

It was dark in the cockpit and I couldn't see any way to turn on the inside lights. I fumbled around and found a switch that clicked on two lights in the roof, shining down in the dash. I had never driven a car before, but I figured if I could fly a plane, I could drive a car, even one that probably cost more than our house and could go over 200 miles per hour. Just that thought sent a little electric thrill through my body.

Like any teenage boy, I looked forward to the day when I would be able to drive, so I watched my Dad drive so I knew the basics. But, I admit to being a bit scared. This was unlike anything I'd ever seen.

I saw that a red push button was lit up; I guess it knew I was ready to go. I hoped that it didn't know how little experience I had at this driving thing.

I hit the red button and the engine roared to life on the first crank. There was none of that cranking noise; it just exploded into life. The giant computer screen in the middle came on to show three rows of apps, like a cell phone. I didn't dare touch any one of the buttons, I was afraid the car would rise off the ground, tuck up its wheels, and fly out of the garage.

I let it warm up until the RPM subsided, then felt for the gear-shift. Lucky for me, it had an automatic transmission, not a clutch and a set of gears. I pulled it into "D" and it edged forward out of the garage onto the gravel driveway. I tried the brakes and it stopped on a dime, tossing gravel. I pulled it completely out of the garage so we could finally see the whole car in the sunlight, crunching and spitting out gravel again.

Mom looked at the little car admiringly. I could see the wheels turning in her head, imagining herself blasting along some highway, with her golden hair streaming in the breeze, and setting off the sophisticated gray of the magnificent automobile.

"THIS WON'T DO, will it? I don't want look to like some European diplomat pulling into the school parking lot."

"OK, put it back in the garage and give me the keys." I backed it carefully into the garage, noting that the rearward visibility was terrible. Then, reluctantly gave her the keys.

"OK, get your stuff together. I'll call us a cab."

CHAPTER 26

We went upstairs and got our backpacks and made sure we had our birth certificates. I had to search around to find my grade report from Texas but it turned up under some comic magazines and an old English essay. I guess I hadn't emptied my backpack since we left Dallas.

We met downstairs in our new school clothes. Mom was dressed like she was going to a cocktail party. Morgan was all smiles, while I was feeling very uncomfortable, both from the stress of going to a new school and from worrying about what Mom will say to the school people that could ruin our reputations before we even got started.

The cab was already outside and we climbed in. I sat in the front and Morg sat in the back with Mom. It was the same cab driver that brought Mom to us, and I thought, maybe we only have one here. That wouldn't be a huge surprise. I leaned forward to see his name badge. It was Frank. I said, "Good morning, Mr. Frank", and Frank smiled and grunted his response.

The high school was located a block off the main road. It had that 1980's look, two stories, brown brick, big windows, and a rounded facade over the main entrance with a scroll showing the year of its construction . Yep, 1989.

The cab pulled into the line of cars dropping kids off. We were in the only yellow car in the line, and I unconsciously slumped down until we got to the drop off point.

As we got out, there was a teacher or an administrator with a sign that said, "NEW STUDENTS", and she was waving the sign and yelling, politely, "If you are a new student to Pocasset High, please follow me." There was a small group of students with their moms, looking around nervously, so we became part of that group, and followed her inside to several rows of chairs set up in the gym. We all filled out a couple of pages of forms, then we waited to be called in for an interview.

Mom muttered, "I CANNOT BELIEVE we have to wait. I'm SURE people here have somewhere else to be." I tried to recall our previous registrations back in Texas, but since we had been in the same system the whole time, we didn't have any that I could recall.

Pretty soon we were called into a small office for the interview. We walked across the smooth, wooden gym floor with Mom clacking her high heels on the polished finish. Mom and Morg sat down in the two chairs that were there, and I stood behind Mom.

The interviewer looked up from her stack of student files and said, "Oh My Goodness, let me get another chair. Honey, could you get a chair from the classroom and bring it in here?" I assumed that I was "Honey" and got the missing chair and pushed it into the room, causing a loud scraping screech as we adjusted all the chairs to make room.

Mom gave her our forms and she took them and adjusted her reading glasses, which were connected on a long pearl chain around her neck.

She was a rather plump older woman with a round and pleasant face. She smelled like a bouquet of old flowers. She read through our forms, our health records, and then asked for the rest of our documentation. She considered all of that while we sat in silence. Except for Mom, who was fidgeting like a First Grader.

She looked at Mom and smiled. She held out her hand; Mom was totally unprepared for that and dropped her reading glasses on the floor. I went looking for them under her chair and put them on the desk in front of her.

"Welcome, Mrs. Calloway." I could see Mom wince. "I'm Mrs. Devers, the school guidance counselor. Your boys' records look like

L. Russell Records

everything is here, and I've looked at their grades reports and, my, you have two smart young men here, don't you."

Mom looked up and smiled, looking down at Morgan, and putting her arm around Morgan's back and touched me on the shoulder. I could feel her fingers drumming nervously on my arm.

"Well, thank you," Mom said. "My husband and I have always thought that our boy's education was the most the important thing to us."

I thought quickly that any reaction I would have to her statement, any reaction at all, would have dire consequences for both Morg and me. Morg stayed as still as a desert mouse hiding from a rattlesnake.

"Here are a couple of forms for you to sign." She pointed down to the bottom of the two forms, and handed her a beat-up ballpoint. She waved away her hand and reached into her purse for a $300 Lamy fountain pen, and scribbled her name at the bottom and handed the forms back to her.

Mrs. Devers took the forms, and asked, "Will Mr. Calloway be around during the year? We are looking for a 7th-grade softball coach."

Mom replied, "Mr. Calloway's business keeps him on the road most of the time. I doubt he will have time."

I suddenly knew what was coming next, "Well, what about you, Mrs. Calloway?" She took a quick look at the Mom's signature, and quickly said, "Oh, I'm sorry... Mrs. Cynthia Walker. I assumed you would be...have the same last name as the boys."

Mom said, wearily, "No, we have been separated for several years, and I now go by my maiden name."

"Well, that's fine, then. Would you have some time to help out with some of our school activities...PTA, bake sale, cafeteria help, welcome committee, football usher, car wash?" The quality of the job offerings dropped as Mrs. Devers noticed my mother's inattention. Mom was looking down at her phone as if she was hoping a phone call would rescue her.

"I'm sorry. My work schedule will keep me very busy over the next few months. Maybe in the Spring."

Mrs. Devers looked at me, then Morgan, then back at Mom. "Well, of course, that's understandable." Her expression had changed from warm and friendly to aloof, and even a bit icy.

"And will your boys be ok when you are not at home?" she questioned.

"Why, yes, they will. Their uncle lives in Falmouth and will be watching over them, plus they have a full-time nanny and cook. They will be fine. And I won't be gone that much." Obviously, she hadn't yet learned to spare the truth from abuse. Mrs. Devers gave me a motherly look, and I felt her warmth compared to Mom. It was like standing next to a fire barrel while building a snowman.

For the first time, I was beginning to get some idea of what level of involvement Mom was planning in Pocasset, and I was neither happy nor unhappy about it. If she was gone for a week or two, it would give Morg and I plenty of freedom, while we could still maintain the illusion of having parental authority and loving concern. I was still mostly concerned about her bringing any boyfriend home to ruin our still-gracious image of our Mom, and having to deal with some random New York adult trying to act like our weekend dad.

Mrs. Devers stood up and turned to look into a filing cabinet for our class schedules. She pulled out two file folders, one for each of us, gold for me, red for Morgan, and extracted a sheet from each of them. "These are your class schedules. There is a map in most of the hallways showing the classroom locations. Locate your classes on the map and don't be late for classes. Today is just for campus tours, just find a group led by a teacher and follow along. Classes start on Monday. And boys, welcome to Pocasset High. I expect to see good things from you two." She looked at both of us over her glasses and smiled warmly.

That made me feel good, and I looked at Morgan and I could see he was feeling it too. We were going to have a great time here with Falk and possibly Wendy, if I could get the courage to talk to her. We had a nice little sailboat, a great beach, a bunch of offshore islands to explore, our dirt bikes, and a pot of money to spend. I wondered whose money we were so freely spending, and when, not if, they would want it back.

We walked outside the school entrance where Mr. Frank and his cab were still waiting for Mom. She waved us away and climbed into the car. "Have fun, guys. I'll see you at home later."

CHAPTER 27

We turned around and looked for a tour group to join. We found one and moved into the main hallway. There was no sign of Falk or Wendy, but then I realized that the tour was only for new students, and there were about twenty of us of all ages. I guess Pocasset was the place to be these days.

We fell in with the group and walked down the main hallway looking into empty classrooms with the usual stuff on the walls; American flag, map of the US, big white boards, still showing last semesters math work. There was a chemistry lab with the usual equipment; beakers, Bunsen burners (Who was Bunsen anyway?), and a periodic chart of the elements (I wonder if all of them have been discovered?). The next room looked like geography with a huge lighted world globe (I wonder which country our Dad is in now?).

We went to the gym and stood around to watch some of the basketball team trying to make shots. From what I could tell, we were going to have a disastrous season. I saw a guy in our new students group who was about my age looking at me, and when I returned his gaze, he smiled. He was short and partially bald with very short hair. He looked like a wrestler. He was wearing a plaid shirt with a handkerchief and brown shorts.

He wasn't one of Pauly's gang so I walked over and introduced myself, "Hi, I'm Ethan. You're a new kid too? Where are you from?"

He said, "Yeah, How ya' going? I'm from Australia and my Dad just moved us here from Perth. He works in Falmouth, he's a marine biologist. I'm Colin McCready."

He spoke with that strange lilt that Australians seem to end every sentence with, like every statement is a question?

"That's really cool! So, what do you think of America so far?" I asked. I had never met anyone at all from another country and was really curious to see what he thought.

"Yeah, I haven't seen that much of it yet, but it's huge like Australia. We landed in San Francisco, which is bonzer, and spent a couple of days there, then flew into Boston, so I've seen a little of both coasts. I guess there's more in the middle to see."

I pulled Morgan over to join us, I laughed and responded, "We're from the middle, Dallas, Texas. And yeah, there is a lot in the middle."

Colin looked apologetic, and said, "The middle of Australia is mostly just the "Outback" and there's not much there, just some huge stations and a bunch of kangaroos out in Whoop Whoop. Hullo, did you say Texas?"

Morg replied in his sometimes used, but always available Texas twang, "You got that right, Partner."

Colin brightened, and said, "Texas! We hear a lot about Texas in Oz...I mean Australia. You have your cowboys and we have stockmen and ringers. People say that Texas is the US state most like Oz. You've got mountains and deserts, and coasts too, yeah?"

Morgan replied, "Colin, we have all of that and wide prairies and even swamps. Something for everyone."

Then I said, "I would really like to visit Australia. It seems a little like America a long time ago, like during the frontier days. Are Australian people like Americans, I mean in the things you like to do, and stuff like that?"

Colin thought for a minute, and then said,"Yeah, nah. Not sure yet. You two mates are the first ones I've really met, my age and all. I'll let you know when I find out!" We all laughed at that, and then Colin said, "My town, Perth, is a great sailing town. We hosted the America's Cuppie a couple of years ago. That's one thing I thought I'd like about 'round here. Do you guys sail?"

I thought about it for a second. I had my heart set on getting Wendy on my boat...to teach us to sail, of course.

"We have a boat, but we're still learning how to sail it. Once we get it figured out, we'll get you to come out with us. There are a lot of places we could go. Buzzards Bay is huge and there are a lot of places to go explore."

Colin replied, "Yeah, let me know when. I'm a fair sailor myself and I could probably teach you a few nuggets."

I said, "We'd really like that. There are a few places we want to go explore. Buried treasure, you know."

His eyes lit up. "You really think there is treasure out there somewhere?"

"We've heard a few rumors and we plan to check them out. This place has been visited by the Vikings, English, and even a few pirates. I'll definitely grab you when we go looking."

"Too right! Make sure you do." Then all both ran to catch up to the school tour.

CHAPTER 28

It had been almost a whole week of school and I had only seen glimpses of the famous red pony tail disappearing into a classroom or going the opposite way down a hall.

We were all going through the process of getting class sizes and teachers sorted out with kids and their parents stopping by to complain about their kids' schedules or registering them for school activities.

Morgan seemed to have things on his schedule pretty much figured out, and he was taking most of the basic classes I had taken back in Texas last year. Three classes in the morning, then two in the afternoon plus gym. We'd have plenty of time after school to ride our dirt bikes and maybe go flying with Falk. Falk was in all of my classes except he was taking honors math and physics. I guess he had tested up to take harder classes.

My class schedule had a lot more choices in it, and it looked a lot more interesting. I was taking calculus, French, American history, chemistry, english again, and of course gym. The school had a reasonable athletic department, with a new basketball arena, a separate gym with a weight room, and a football stadium, which was ok, but not up to Texas standards. We'd seen it all on the tour we got on the first day. I was also taking drivers education. Wait 'til the instructor sees my ride! No, not going to happen. That car needs to be kept a secret, which I guessed is what my Dad wanted.

When classes start, I usually claim a desk over by the windows and about half-way back. I like to look out at the clouds and daydream. Not just stupid mental dreaming to get out of thinking, but taking time to really try to figure important things out, things that were usually in the last chapter or from another book. I figured if I was either in the front row or the back row, I'd get called upon a lot, so maybe I could be invisible in the middle. I didn't mind getting called on when I was ready, but I had a habit of reading far ahead of the lesson, and if I got called on for today's lesson, I had to stumble back to that page. I guess then I looked stupid or disorganized, which I hated.

I really wanted to do well here in school. Wherever my future was headed, I needed to be a lot more educated and smarter than I was as a seventeen year-old boy.

I also wanted to learn more about girls, a species that I had previously ignored. Maybe my body was giving me suggestions that it's time to wake up and start being a man.

I was also thinking about how to approach the "little red-haired girl" when all of a sudden, I turned around and there she was, right in my face.

Her face was red and very agitated. She was not as pretty as I thought with her face all screwed up. "You are one of those awful boys that were yelling in front of my house! If I ever see you again, I will immediately call the police and report you for assault. Do that again, buddy boy, and you'll be the one who gets assaulted!"

With that, she turned and marched away, looking for her next victim from the boys hanging out with Pauly.

I stood there, stunned. I had never been accosted by anyone like that before, let alone a woman-girl that I thought should be there thanking me for coming to her aid. I literally had nothing in my brain but shock and unfounded guilt.

She had stopped down the hallway, looking at one of the bulletin boards showing where the classrooms were located. She looked back at me and glared.

I gathered my strength and walked up to her. I had no idea what I was going to say to her. Was I going to apologize for being in that awful gang, was I going to try to convince her that I was actually a good guy? I just couldn't put those words together.

She heard me walk up behind her because I think she expected me to and was waiting.

She turned with that same ferocious face, "Now what!"

I looked at her pretty face and her wide, angry green eyes. "Do you know how to sail?" I can't believe I blurted that out.

She looked startled, "What?"

I was glad that I hadn't said something completely deranged.

"I asked if you know how to sail. My brother and I have a new boat but don't know enough to try to sail her."

That caught her completely by surprise. She said, guardedly, "Yeah, I know how to sail. But why would I teach a creep like you?"

I said, "Yeah, I wanted to ask you about that. What were those boys yelling at you about? We are from Texas and we thought those guys were being very ungentlemanly. We walked over to tell them so."

She stood there, studying me. "So, you weren't one of those boys?"

I started to relax a bit. When I first turned around and saw her inches from my face, I thought she might hit me. I saw her clenched little fists.

"No, M'am", I said, laying down a little Texas gentleman. "We came over and tried to calm things down. Falk was the guy on the motorcycle who was the one who chased them away, actually it was all three of us, me and my brother Morgan. And Falk."

She thought about that. She still didn't look convinced.

"I'm Ethan Calloway, my brother is Morgan Calloway. We just moved here from Dallas...Texas." I wasn't sure she knew where Dallas was.

Now she smiled. "Yeah, I know where Dallas is. I'm Wendy Stillman, and we moved here last fall, just before the winter. My dad is in the US Coast Guard and we used to live in Fort Lauderdale... Florida."

Now it was my turn to smile. "What does your Dad do in the

Coast Guard?" I had never met anyone in the Coast Guard.

"He is a helicopter pilot, and he runs the Coast Guard Station in Hyannis", she informed me. "If you are out on your sailboat and get in trouble, he'll come rescue you," she smiled.

I was getting to like her smile. I said, "Well, if we leave the dock without knowing how to sail, it's a sure bet he would need to rescue us."

She laughed, and when she did, her green eyes dancing with humor.

"So, don't they have lakes in Texas? I thought everything was better out west."

I replied, "We have lakes in Texas, but now we need a gully-warsher to fill them back up."

"A "gully-warsher?" What's that?

I realized then that my Texas accent and lingo was "gettin' out of the corral", so I answered in plain English.

"It's just a really strong rain, better if it rains hard for a couple of days to fill up the bayous and lakes."

"Bayous?"

"Yes, small rivers. We have a lot of small rivers, especially down south."

She smiled, and I turned a bit red when I realized she was teasing me. I'm sure they had bayous in Florida.

She turned and looked down the hallway. "Hey, Ethan, I've got to get to class. Do you have English now?"

I looked at my watch, and realized that I did. "Yeah, let's go."

We headed down the hallway for class, and she turned to me and said, "I wouldn't mind going out on your boat. I could show you the ropes," she said smiling.

The little joke went over my head until I had time to think about it. Of course, sailboats have ropes, probably lots of them and I vaguely remember that they all had different names. Oh, boy.

But I was thrilled. In two minutes, I had gone from almost getting pummeled to having something like a date on my new boat. I could see that that might be an opening line for a lot of future dates.

I said to her, "Yeah, I'd really like that, and so would my brother Morgan. We do pretty much everything together. He's my backup."

Then, she turned her head and said, "But I need a quid pro quo."

I vaguely thought that meant some kind of a deal, something for something. "What did you have in mind?" I had no idea where she was heading with this.

"You're from Texas, right. I want you to teach me how to ride a horse like they do in Texas. We had stables down in Florida, but I didn't get to ride much."

I thought to myself, what a deal for me. I hadn't seen a single horse since we'd gotten to Pocasset.

She added, "There are stables down in Falmouth, we can rent some horses there and they have all these beach trails down by the bay."

Well, that was even better. For "Quo", I could show off my ridin' and ropin' skills to her as well as teach her the ways of the horse beast. And for "Quid", she could teach me to sail.

As I settled into my desk by the window, she took a desk in the middle of the classroom, just to my right, so we could talk in class if the teacher didn't catch us. Then she said, "What about tomorrow after school? It's still light until about eight."

I turned to Wendy, "That would be great. What do we need to bring?"

She replied, "Have you ever gone down to your boat and seen what condition it's in, and what equipment it has on it?"

"Not really, I've just walked down there and looked at it. It looks brand new and the sails are bundled up on the poles. There is a little cabin up in the front and there may be other stuff in there. It's about 25 feet long, so there's plenty of room for three or four people."

She replied, "Well, the first thing we'll do is sort it all out. Then, if we have some wind, and if everything is in order, we'll take her out."

I nodded my head, then realized I hadn't thought about Morgan and what he was doing. And no telling about Mom and what she would say.

Having negotiated a peace with her, I took a longer look at her out of the corner of my eye. She was very pretty in kind of a English countryside way. She had fair skin and, of course, her red hair that now I could tell was streaked with blond. She was average height and looked quite fit. And her womanly features were pronounced and nicely shaped. Again, I felt those new feelings pushing through my body. Until the teacher came in, and that ended that.

CHAPTER 29

The next day dawned fair and cooler. We had a few rumbles of thunder and a splash of rain overnight, but I pretty much slept through it. When I opened my window, I felt the cool breeze blowing in my window and rattling the windows. If we were going sailing, I guessed that having a windy day would be a plus.

We never mentioned going sailing to Mom. She seemed wrapped up in her own world, and she, like our Dad back in Dallas, was spending a lot of time on the phone. Except that from what we could hear, it sounded like she was either talking to a little child, or a lover. Lots of baby talk and throaty laughter. It wasn't pleasant for Morg and me to hear, so we avoided her. I dreaded the announcement that she was going to have guests coming down from New York. In my mind, there weren't two more different cultures than Texas and New York. We made jokes about them, and they made jokes about us. Morg and I still had our cowboy hats and if some arrogant New Yorkers showed up, we would wear them in defiance.

We rolled our dirt bikes out of the garage and down the street towards the marina before we cranked them up so she wouldn't know about them. We'd probably have to deal with her when we got back from our sailing lesson after school today.

The school day dragged by as we trudged through it, waiting for the bell to ring and our sailing to begin. Morg and I usually had lunch together, but today he was late. I stirred my peas around while I waited impatiently. When he showed up, he looked excited.

"Eth, the football coach asked me to try out for the team. He said that they were looking for another quarterback. I'm going to do it. Sorry about the sailing lesson. I bet you can handle that on your own." He gave me a sly look and smile.

I started to respond when a pretty auburn-haired girl came over to our end of the table, clasping her books in front of her. She looked at Morgan, then at me, then back at Morgan. "You said you would have lunch with me. I'm sitting over there," she said, pointing to a table at the far end of the cafeteria.

He looked up at her and said, "Yeah, I'll be over there in a minute." She stepped back, but didn't leave. Morg looked at me, then back at her. "In a minute. I'm talking to my brother." He introduced me to her, I learned that her name was Carmen. She walked away, then stopped and looked back. I smirked at Morg, if they walk away, but stop and look back, you've got them.

"Yeah, I guess I can handle that boat and Wendy on my own," I said, with an air of confidence. "Good luck with that one," I said, gesturing to Carmen.

He picked up his books, got up and made of quick show of running, then slowed to his normal walk. I thought, "He's been here less than a week, and he's already landed one." He had some sort of flair about him that, in addition to his good looks and athleticism made him a "chick magnet". But then I thought about Wendy. I wasn't doing too badly myself.

CHAPTER 30

I looked around after school, but Morgan was nowhere in sight. His bike was still locked up to the rack, so I guessed he and Carmen were out walking hand in hand, exchanging loving glances. Then I remembered that he had the football tryout that afternoon. I silently wished him the best.

He had been a great QB in Texas and I bet he would be as good or better than anyone he would face today. But, there are high school politics to consider. If the mayor's son was trying out too, and could throw the football at least 20 yards, that might be a problem for Morg. I was sure that he would do his best. That was the essence of his nature. Look for challenges, throw yourself right in the middle of it, and come out victorious. Sometimes that really worried me. It might not work in all situations. What's to do about it if your little brother is a natural-born hero? And you're not. I chuckled at myself. He was family, and it's good to have a hero as your brother.

I needed to find Wendy and head down to the boat. We had agreed that I would pick her up at her house on Bishop Lane. Then we would go down to the pier and I would learn to sail from my lovely teacher, Wendy.

I started up my bike but was suddenly startled by Pauly coming around from behind me and grabbing my handlebars. "Hey there Texas! Remember us?" I looked around and there were several of his accomplices standing around me. I also saw that an audience was forming. I guess I hadn't gotten the notice of my beating, which was apparently scheduled for right now.

"Yeah, I remember you. You guys been out baying at the moon

or yelling your filth at another defenseless girl at her home?" Pauly shouted, "Well, I told you not to let me catch you hanging around that bitch on Bishop. It's time to pay up!"

I was waiting on his next move. I could sense his buddies moving closer behind me. And here it came, a right cross aimed at my jaw.

I was helped by the fact that the handlebars were between him and me, so it took only a small backwards duck to see his fist whiz by my head. On the other hand, then I leaned forward, swung my left fist and connected with the underside of his head, knocking him off my bike. I wasted no time in gunning my bike as I felt an arm trying to reach around my neck. I think I might have run over Pauly's leg just a little bit as I made my escape from what had been staged as a mass beating.

I'm not much of a fighter, but my Dad had taught me that if you hit with the first punch, you would have several options, one of which was to escape, which I took in this instance. I knew it wasn't over with that punk, but I had yet to figure out how to get rid of him.

I rode around the block a couple of times to calm down and burn off the excess adrenaline that had pumped into my body during the brief encounter. Then I pointed my bike towards Bishop Lane.

CHAPTER 31

Wendy had agreed to teach Morgan and I to sail in exchange for me teaching her how to ride horses. I definitely thought I was getting the best of the deal. After that brief skirmish with Pauly's little gang, I headed over to Bishop Lane and Wendy's house.

I drove my bike up in her driveway. I didn't see any other cars so I guessed her Dad wasn't home. I don't know why I thought that mattered at the time, but I checked it off as one less hoop to jump through on our first "date".

Her home was a stately Victorian house with marble roof supports. I went up the wide stairs to her porch and walked up to her front door and started to knock. The door opened suddenly, and there stood her father. He seemed surprised to see me. He was a tall man, slightly graying, and he looked like a Navy Admiral in his starched whites and chest full of medals. He almost ran over me in his hurry to leave.

"Oh, sorry son! I didn't see you out there." He looked at me as if sizing me up as a recruit into the Coast Guard. "I'm Captain Stillman...And you are?"

"Hello, Sir, I am Ethan Calloway, a friend of Wendy's from school. We're going sailing." It all came out in a rush. He stood back and took a fresh look at me, reassessing me as someone who might not be trusted to take his precious daughter sailing.

He tilted his head and said, "So, you're the Texas boy who has never been on a sailboat and wants my Wendy to teach him. And you are going to teach her to ride. Have I got it right?"

"Yessir", I managed to reply.

"Well, do you at least know how to swim?"

"Yessir. I played water polo at school in Texas. My Dad went to the Naval Academy and he taught us to swim when we were, like two years old."

He laughed, then said, "I went to Annapolis as well. What class did he graduate in?"

I thought that Annapolis was only for naval officers, but told him my Dad's graduation class. Every navy brat whose Dad went to the Academy knows that.

He looked surprised, and then said, "His class was one year ahead of me. I don't think I knew him, but it's a pretty big place."

I thought that they all knew each other. It's one of the smallest colleges, you'd have to know everybody else. But I guess it didn't work that way.

"You've got life jackets and all the other safety equipment aboard, yes?"

I admitted that I hadn't checked all of the stuff that was on the boat. I had never even set foot on my own boat, if that's how you say it.

"Sir, I'm sure Wendy knows what we need, and we'll go through it to make sure. We'll get anything missing from Willoughby's."

He nodded his head, then slipped on his white hat with gold braid and said, "You and Wendy have a great time. But be careful. I don't want to come looking for you."

Just then, I saw that Wendy was standing just behind the door, waiting for her Dad, the "Captain", to clear me for sea duty with her. She had changed from her school clothes into jeans and a red halter top that emphasized her figure.

He strode off the porch and around to the garage. A few seconds later, an ancient but apparently well-maintained Volvo wagon appeared from out of the garage, rolled out the driveway, then disappeared down the street.

I thought to myself, good luck, Pauly, getting through that

sea-worthiness check.

Wendy touched my arm, and said, "Well, you might as well meet my Mom since Dad passed you."

We walked into the living room where her Mom was coming out of the kitchen. She was a short woman, with red hair, an apron, and she wore her readers down across her nose. She smiled warmly and beckoned me to sit on the couch. Wendy sat in a big plush chair across the room.

"You're Ethan, is that right? Wendy says you're from Texas and are going to teach her how to "Cowboy", right?" She continued to smile and I began to feel that I was getting set up for something. My native caution was sending me messages that Wendy was not all she seemed to be at first.

"Yes, M'am. I'm from Dallas, Texas. My brother and I learned "Texas cowboying" a few years ago, and I think I'm a good teacher."

"That's reassuring, Ethan. I wouldn't want Wendy to be doing anything that might be too risky." She smiled that somewhat mysterious smile again.

"No, M'am, and I'm looking forward to learning to sail with Wendy. I think she will be a good teacher, and I have got a lot to learn." Boy, I wasn't kidding. Horses are pretty simple once you get your horses' attention. I didn't think you could say that about sailboats. And I knew that wasn't true for women.

"Well, Ethan, you and Wendy take things nice and slow. You're only sixteen. You've got your whole life ahead of you. Don't rush things."

I got her "drift" in that warning, if I might use a nautical term. I probably knew less about sixteen year-old girls then I did about sailing, and we already know how that stands. But it did, once again, tingle something inside me, and I didn't know what to do about it.

I looked at Wendy sitting across the room and saw her smiling at me, and I smiled back. I wondered if she had a bit of tingle too.

Her Mom furrowed her brow, and said, "We moved here last year in the middle of the school year, and she's had a bit of a time making friends. The "Captain" has high standards for anyone he will permit to do things with Wendy, like you know, go on a date. But since you met him at the door and he didn't throw you off the porch, I guess you'll do...for now."

I didn't know what to say without getting into trouble. She had laid a number of trapdoors for me to fall through. I decided to just ride it out. At least I wasn't lying in the yard with a broken arm.

"M'am, you have a lovely home," I remarked. Actually it reminded me of the lobby of the one funeral home I had visited. It had maroon walls, heavy, dark furniture, and a carpet that looked like it had come from Persia 1,000 years ago. A variety of tapestries were hanging from the walls, and I kind of expected "Lurch" to come out from one of the gloomy doors and offer us drinks.

She looked around, then turned to me and said, "Most of the furnishings here came with the house. The previous owner died here after a long illness and left all of this behind. We haven't had time to redo anything but the kitchen and Wendy's bedroom. And we haven't even been down in the basement to see what's down there."

The immediate thought through my teenage boy mind was, "Don't open the freezer." Falk had warned me about the disappearance of the old man's wife.

"Would you like some lemonade?" Wendy's Mom got up and headed towards what I assumed was the kitchen without asking for a response.

I turned to Wendy and said, "Your mom is really nice."

Wendy smiled, and responded, "Yeah, she is. Don't take her too seriously about me not having enough friends. I'm pretty picky, especially with my girlfriends. They can really be snarky. I do have a couple of good girlfriends."

She added, "It's the boy's here up to now that I have problems with. I really don't know why. All I have done is to refuse to go out with Pauly to the Christmas Dance last year. He jumped me at school two days before the dance and asked me to the dance. I might have gone with him if he wasn't so persistent. I needed permission from my Dad. When I didn't give him an answer right away, he started getting nasty to me. He and his little band of creeps."

I said, "Well, that makes two of us. After Morg and I walked into Pauly's little party in front of your house, I've been on his list. He and his goons tried to jump me after school. It didn't amount to much, but it isn't over either. I've got to watch him."

She changed the topic to something more positive. "You have a younger brother, right? Morgan? You guys seem pretty close."

Just then her Mother came back from the kitchen with a pitcher of lemonade and some tall, etched glasses. She poured the cold lemonade and looked up at me, "It's good to have a brother or sister. I wish Wendy would have had a sister. It just wasn't in the cards."

I couldn't imagine my mother making and serving lemonade to me and my friends. It was nice to be visiting a home that seemed normal to me. I also started to relax, but then realized I was actually in a job interview. It was too soon to let off. Her Mother seemed to like me, although it was too soon to really tell. It would certainly be based on how she judged the way I treated her only child. That was the big trapdoor.

Her Mom said, "Ethan, please call me Miss Hilda, it's what I'm used to. The Coast Guard has its own protocols and the Captain's lady needs a fancy title."

I chuckled and said, "Of course, Miss Hilda. That name seems to fit you."

Her eyes grew wider, and she asked, "Do you really think so? I like it but I'm not sure about the other ladies at the base. It sounds so Southern. We moved up here from Florida, you know, and it felt more appropriate down there. Wendy was born there, in Ft. Lauderdale. She's a Florida girl."

I had no idea what a Florida girl was, but I pictured palm trees, white sandy beaches, and Wendy in a bikini. Ok, I got it now. It was time to go learn to sail.

"Yes, M'am, we'll be careful sailing and going riding." She walked us to the door, saw my two wheels out in the driveway and looked it skeptically, but closed the door without making a typical parent comment. I think she was putting her trust in Wendy, not me.

CHAPTER 32

Wendy hopped on the skinny little seat on my dirt bike and we rode the few blocks down to the pier where my little boat waited impatiently for its "Master and Commander" and to spread its wings out in the bay. Well, that's what went through my teenage boy mind.

Morgan met us at the pier. His bike was parked against the little shed. We walked over to him, and I introduced him to Wendy. Normally, Morgan wasn't too impressed by his little girl friends, but Wendy was a woman by his standards and a very pretty one at that. He looked her over quickly, then said, "Hi, glad to see you." I think he meant "glad to meet you", but on the other hand, maybe he didn't.

We walked down the wooden pier, which obviously needed a few boards replaced, past several other boats and got to our boat. It had been covered with a custom-fitting tarp since we got it and it had never been opened up. I didn't know what to expect when we opened it for the first time.

Wendy surveyed the boat from the pier, then found the zipper to open the cover and get onboard. She zipped it back and stepped gingerly from the pier to a small step just inside the boat. Then she began folding back the cover until the whole boat was opened up. There was a great salty-musty smell wafting out of the boat but it quickly blew away.

Wendy was clearly impressed. It looked like everything on the boat was brand-new, from the sail covers to the bright finish on all the teak wood. The inside of the boat was painted white, which contrasted with the deep wood trim. There was a small seat near the back and a seat across the middle of the boat. There was a small cabin in the front from which the mast protruded. I clambered over the middle seat and sat in the rear seat, which I assumed is where the captain would sit and issue orders to the scurvy crew.

There was a little cabin up in the front that had a small locked door. I looked at Morgan, the key master, who was still standing on the pier, looking unconvinced about this deal.

"I thought it would be bigger", Morg offered skeptically. "Are we really going out in that thing?"

Wendy told Morgan, "Get in the boat, open that little door, and hand me everything in there." Morgan sat on the pier and scooted his legs into the boat, then stood up uneasily. Then he pulled out a different set of keys and unlocked the little hatch and started pulling everything out, handed the objects and devices to Wendy, and she laid it out like a display on the dock.

"Ethan, get out of the boat and come back on the pier. We are going to start at the beginning."

It was harder than I thought to get in and out of the boat. Every time I moved the boat tilted over, throwing me in that direction, and banging my legs on the side of the boat. I guessed that my new collection of scrapes and bruises was what they mean by "sea legs".

She pointed out each of the strange looking objects and devices on the dock and started naming them and telling us what they were used for in sailing the boat.

Wendy then ordered me to get back in the boat. She handed me the rudder and tiller and told me how to attach it to the back of the boat...er, the stern. I man-handled the rudder and tiller over the stern and after a struggle that cost me the skin on two of my knuckles had the "pintles" locked into the "gudgeons". To me, these words sounded like 17th century English like in an old "Capt. Blood" movie.

She passed me an oar for paddling, if we had to. Then she handed me a set of ropes with pulleys on them, and then a bag which she said was the jib.

Wendy climbed into the boat and said, "Stay where you are and just watch me. This will all make sense later. Then she started attaching the lines and pulleys at various points on the "boom". I said, "Why is this pole called the boom?" She replied with a smirk, "You'll find out soon enough."

We reached up, took off the cover from the boom and saw the mainsail, still tied to the boom. She reached to the base of the mast and took off a rope and attached one end to the top of the sail. The jib stayed in its bag for now. The main sheet cover was stored, I meant "stowed" away in the little cabin with the jib bag.

The little cabin had just enough room for two people to get out of the rain, if it wasn't full of equipment, of which there appeared to be a whole lot left in there.

She reached into the cabin for some bulky orange things, then she handed them to us and said, "Here are your life jackets. Put them on. I don't care if you are an Olympic swimmer, this water is deadly cold, even in the summer. If for some reason, you get dumped in, you won't be able to stay afloat long without it." I thought it was time to ask a stupid question, "Why, will it sink?"

"No, but in about ten minutes you won't be able to move your arms or legs to swim because of the cold. In thirty minutes, you'll be dead. I guess I should have said "stay alive" rather than "stay afloat". Someone will probably find your body when it washes up somewhere."

After she said that, I thought, I hope the Coast Guard has a rescue helicopter handy. But I hoped it wasn't her Dad flying it. Sinking on my first time out is not a good way to make an impression.

We put the old life jackets on and tied them with their little cloth ties. They smelled like they had been put away wet and I was suddenly reminded of the smell of a horse blanket after a long ride, except for the fishy smell.

Wendy now started naming off the various nautical terms, pointing to the various parts of the little boat. "Bow, stern, mast, boom, halyard, sheets, rudder...use these names from now on." I didn't think I'd have to learn a whole new dictionary just to go sailing with a pretty girl on a nice summer afternoon.

I was still a bit confused so I asked, "What are those ropes?" pointing to the ropes banging against the mast.

She looked at me sternly, and said, "Rope is something you buy in a store. Once it gets on board a boat or ship, it becomes a "line". There is only one rope on a boat."

I thought about that for a second, then asked,"What is it?" I kept wracking my brain. Fish rope? Tieing-onto-dock rope? Anchor rope? I couldn't make a guess.

She replied, "You don't have one, so it doesn't matter."

She had a way of throwing out a challenge like that, so I had to figure it out. A man was supposed to be able to do that, figure out tough problems, especially when a woman asks them.

Morgan was still digging in the front cabin and sorting out the remaining objects and devices in there. Then he pulled something shiny out, it was a bright brass bell with a little support that hooked on the outside of the cabin. There was a little ringer with a knotted piece of string hanging from it. Morgan installed it and rang the bell repeatedly until Wendy told him to stop. She folded her arms and grinned slyly, "Now do you know what the only rope on a boat is?"

Morgan volunteered, "This thing?" he said holding on to the little string on the clapper.

Wendy laughed and said loudly, "YES, You guessed it!" "It's called the bell rope and it's the only rope, everything else is a line."

I shrugged and said, "OK, can we go sailing now?" It was starting to get dark and there weren't any lights on the boat.

Wendy said, "Yes, but it will have to be short. I will sit in the stern and steer, Ethan, sit on the side of the boat next to me, and for now, Morgan you sit on the middle seat, but on the right side. I'll have you switch with Ethan so you can try your hand at steering later.

I slumped down on the side of the boat with my back

uncomfortably against the "coaming". I could tell the wind was blowing from the northwest, from our right side, and this seemed important to know.

She had already untied the lines to the pier and she had Morgan pull on the halyard and raise the sail. It fluttered in the wind until she put the rudder over, and we started a slow turn, the sail filled with wind, and off we went.

Over the next thirty minutes, she showed me and Morg how the boat reacted to the wind at various angles, and how to use the "main sheet", a little rope hanging down from the pulley on the boom, to change the angle to best catch the wind. And I found out why they call it the "boom" when we tacked once and I wasn't paying attention. I was watching the water flow around the boat as we turned, thinking, "I wonder how the water knows how to move out of the way of the boat." I suddenly found out why it's important to move out of the way of the boom as it switched from one side to the other and cracked me in the back of my head.

Morgan couldn't stop laughing, saying, "I've been waiting for that to happen! It's missed you by inches three times, and it finally connected!"

I turned to him and accused him, "Why didn't you warn me?"

He laughed and said, "She said "tacking" and you're supposed to duck. I saw you duck three times before. I thought you had figured it out. Maybe you learned something new, big brother!"

We both took turns steering the little boat, and I could feel the change in energy and speed when the sails were set to catch the wind at the right angle. After a few minutes on the helm and trimming the sails, I felt that Morgan and I were ready to take her out on our own, or better yet, if Wendy went with us. Our next trip should be out to one of the near-by islands, especially the one that Falk had pointed out from the air. Perhaps the fabled "Golden Throne" was still out there somewhere. We needed to look for it before the winter had set in.

By now it was almost dark, and as we headed back to the dock,

Wendy pointed out the red and green lights that marked the deep water channel out of our little cove that had come on when it started to get dark. There were two red lights in a line on the left side of the channel, and two green lights in a line on the right side. In the daytime, there were red triangles and green square signs. I guessed that was significant, and Wendy noticed me looking at them and said, "All you have to know is "Red Right Returning". Anywhere in the world, if you are coming into a port, and want to stay in the channel, keep the red lights on your right and the green lights on your left side. Otherwise, it's "Red Right To Texas".

Finally, something that made sense to me. If you want to get back to Texas, just keep the red lights and red triangles on the right all the way home on the Intracoastal Canal.

CHAPTER 33

School continued. I judged that the classes were easier here than in Texas. I thought it was because the classes were smaller, and the teacher took things slower. I have to admit that I was learning more in depth than I had before.

I ran into Colin coming out of my last class, and he grabbed me by the arm and said, "How ya' going, Mate. When are we going sailing?" I saw Wendy down the hall, and she waved, but I did not want to get them together yet. I was sure Colin would be so much more exotic and attractive to Wendy than me, so I needed to keep them apart, for now. The last thing I wanted was for them to have a romantic encounter on MY boat.

So I threw my arm around Colin and corralled him out the side door off the main hall and said, "Have you looked outside? It's going to be a great afternoon for sailing. Let's go."

As we headed for the boat on my bike, I told Colin over my shoulder, "Ever since we moved here, I've always wanted to go out to the islands and explore them." We arrived at the pier and I leaned my bike up against the shed.

I continued, "There have been rumors of old Viking coins found in a cave, and we've heard something about a "Golden Throne". There used to be pirates and booze smugglers around here and maybe they left some behind."

Colin replied vigorously, "Sweet as! Let's go find it!"

We went down to the boat and I noted that some of the other boats that had been on our pier were now gone to winter storage. The season can't be over so soon. We took the covers off and got her ship-shape and ready to go. I hoped that Wendy wasn't out taking a walk down on Shore Road. I didn't want her to see me going out on a sail with some guy she didn't know.

Colin stepped in the boat carefully and sat on the cabin top so he could cast us off. He also started taking off the sail covers and removing the sail ties. He looked in the little cabin and saw the jib bag and turned to me and asked, "Do you want to put up the jib, Cap?" We haven't used it yet but I felt confident enough to try something new, besides Colin seemed completely at ease on the boat like he sailed her many times before. He was going to be good crew. "Yeah, let's put her up. The halyard is attached to the mast cleat, there." Colin pulled the little sail from its bag, attached the halyard, and fed the port and starboard sheets back to the cockpit. It hit me that I was beginning to pick up some of the sailing lingo.

I sat on the stern seat and fitted the rudder into place. I took a quick look around and we were the only boat in the water so it was safe to leave the pier. The wind in the cove was fitful, coming out of the North, trending to the West, a bit off the bow. Colin cast off, removing and throwing the bow lines up into the cabin. He turned to me and asked, "OK, to raise the jib?" I nodded, and he pulled the little sail up the mast. It immediately caught the wind, and pushed our bow slightly away from the dock. Colin quickly raised the main sail and we headed out into Buzzards Bay. He paused from trimming the sails, and asked over his shoulder, "Where di'ya wanna go?"

There was a long, thin island called Basset's Island blocking our little cove from the worst of the Atlantic swells that rolled around Cape Cod and into Buzzards Bay. I yelled at Colin over the wind, "We're going around the island to the South, then we'll turn to the North and sail up to that large hill!" The island was mostly sand, with a marsh and various small piles of glacial rocks dotting the marsh. There were a couple of summer homes located near the north side. The rest of the island was sand dunes or low marsh except for a large hill on the north side of the island, where it was the widest. I headed south out of the cove to the southern end, then we turned the corner and headed north, circumnavigating the small crooked island. It took about an hour to sail over to the north side of the island, tacking back-and-forth against the north-west wind. With Colin's expertise, my tacks got crisper each time, getting caught "in irons" only once, meaning I didn't turn the boat fast enough to get all the way over to the other tack. Getting stopped and stuck with the sails flailing noisily with the rudder not working caused me a minute of mild panic. Colin grabbed the port jib sheet, and pulled it back into the wind which pushed us around on the port tack so we could regain our speed. Colin remarked, "Again, that's why it's called being "in irons."

We sailed close by the large hill which formed a small cliff on its western border, looking for evidence of a cave among the rocky ledges and crags. We were completely around the north side and kept looking.

I asked Colin, "Do you see anything? He rescanned the hill, but shook his head, then remarked, "We're gonna hafta go exploring on foot. Can't see anything from here. And it's getting dark. We'll hafta come back during daylight and look it ova."

I agreed, and turned the boat to run crosswind to the west wind to pass along the west side of the island. If there was a cave, the only way we were going to find it was by walking and poking around.

We passed by what looked like a run-down summer home. Its door was open and off its hinges and banging in the gusty wind. There is no way to get to the island except by boat. I suspect that the shack was abandoned. I thought it might be nice to have a little house on an island someday but not a beat-up shack on an island that you could throw a rock across.

It got very cloudy and there was a sudden chill in the wind. It was time to go in and put the boat away. We might get one or two more weekends before the first snowfall when it'll be time to put our new toy away for good. A thought just crossed my teenage boy mind. Actually, our boat wasn't just a toy, it was a way of potentially going anywhere we wanted to go by water. It was a bit small for the open ocean, but there are plenty of ports along the shore of Buzzards Bay worth visiting.

We continued north and sailed into Pocasset Harbor, then turned back South-East at the Red No. 8 bouy. There were several lobster boats coming in to offload at the docks. The crew handling the cages gave us a strange look. Little toy sailboats weren't supposed to be out here at this time of year.

We put the boat away and zipped up the cover until the next exploration of the island and the big rock hill. Colin jumped on the back of my bike and I took him home in the near-dark.

CHAPTER 34

rode my bike past the football field to see if the team was still practicing. The stadium lights were on and there was plenty of activity on the field. It looked like they were running some sort of scrimmage, so I parked my bike and climbed up in the stadium seats near the 50 yard line. There were plenty of dad's there cheering on their kids. I know our Dad would've been here if he could and I suddenly felt very sad and alone. But that passed quickly as I focused on the game and my little brother.

It was hard to make out individual players on the field but then I was able to find my brother. After all these years together, I knew how he walked, how he stood, and how he ran. I was pleased to see him as one of the opposing quarterbacks.

His side was on offense now and I saw him calling his team into the huddle, and then breaking with the hand clap. Morg came up to the line, looked left and right, then faded back a few yards. The right tight end went into motion, and then when the ball was hiked, Morgan danced patiently in the pocket, dodging one tackler, and then found his wide receiver cutting across the field at top speed. Morgan sailed a pass which carried him into the end zone and the score. A few dads cheered while other dads groaned. A few of them called out to their sons with congrats or criticism. That play was Morgan's favorite play back in Texas when his good friend Chase was a wide receiver. Chase would scream to the end zone at top speed and Morgan would nail him with a 25 yard pass in just a tiny corner of the end zone. No one could defend it.

I waited outside until Morgan got cleaned up and dressed.

When he was leaving the stadium exit, some girl with auburn hair and wearing a cheerleader uniform was waiting to meet him. She rushed up to him and kissed him. The fact that he seemed to be expecting that sort of treatment from that particular girl indicated to me that my little brother had been busy after school when he said he couldn't go sailing with me.

I waited by the fence until they got their little welcome ceremony done, then they saw me and waved at me, leaning on the fence. Now I recognized her.

They walked up to me and I straightened up and turned to meet them. I gave her my best smile and even extended my hand. She offered her hand and I bowed slightly, then I kissed it. Morgan made a show of pushing me back, "Take it easy there, brother!"

"Eth, remember, this is Carmen." She was indeed a beauty, with wide set green eyes and long brown hair. I thought they looked like the perfect high school couple. I was sure I would see more of her.

I pulled Morgan aside with my apologies to Carmen. "Make sure you don't mention anything about our "sailing" to Carmen, she doesn't need to know ANYTHING about it. We're going to look for "It" this weekend; make sure you're free on Sunday."

Morgan replied, "Sure, but Carmen doesn't care about anything but football." I added, "And a certain quarterback, yeah?" He smiled, a little bit embarrassed. "I won't say anything, but I'm not sure about Sunday. Coach may call a practice, the O-line is never gonna protect me in a real game without more work."

"So how's your chance of making first string?" I asked. He answered slowly, "I'm not sure, there's another guy who's pretty good, and he's a local." "Well, I know you're working hard. You better get back to Carmen before she wanders off with the other QB. I'll see you at home."

CHAPTER 35

The one remaining loose end was to introduce Colin to Wendy, which was really worrying me. I was totally on new ground here, trying to win over my first girl. I wanted to do it in a way that made it look like Wendy was already mine, not available to anyone else, especially Colin. I decided to walk Wendy home from school, and have Colin meet us about halfway at the ice cream shop on Main Street. That way, Colin would see that we were on a date and not move in, at least for now.

I waited outside Wendy's social studies class until the bell rang. I had already asked Colin to meet us at the ice cream shop later. She came out and gave me a nice smile. I asked her, "How'dya like to get some ice cream on the way home?" She answered "Sure. But first there's someone I want you to meet. He's just gotten here from Australia, and he tells me he's a good sailor, too. We should ask him to go sailing with us!"

My heart fell into my shoes. My lack of experience with girls was making me paranoid about losing Wendy before I even had won her.

All I could think to say was, "Sure, that's fine, but I need to tell you. Colin and I are already friends and we've been sailing a couple of times.

Now it was Wendy's turn to be surprised, but not in a good way. "You've been going sailing without me? I thought we had a deal! Why didn't you say something, I was sitting at home waiting, thinking about you and the boat."

"Wendy, I'm really sorry, I ran into Colin in the New Students tour and he started talking about sailing, so we went out...a couple of times."

"What! How could you do that? You don't know enough yet to go out and be safe!"

"No, Wendy. You were a great teacher and with a few "nuggets" from him, we were good to go."

She turned way from me in anger and disgust, and started marching down the hall with her little fists clenched. She got about ten feet, and ran right into Colin.

She grabbed him by the arm and turned around and headed back to me, with her face still flushed and angry. By now, a few other students were beginning to notice. She shoved Colin toward me so hard that we just about collided. "Ok, now here we all are! What's going on with you two?!"

Colin was totally "in irons". I guess he hadn't had to deal with an enraged "Shelia" back home. I put my hands up and offered, "Wendy, we'll tell you the whole story, but not here. We need to go somewhere private. Colin offered, "Let's go over to my house. It's not far, and me Dad's at work. Mom is off shopping in Falmouth. It will be fine."

We went around to where we left our bikes. Next to my dirty little dirt bike was a newish Triumph Bonneville, a famed British classic from the early days of motorcycle speed trials. Wendy looked at my bike, then at Colin's and said, to both of us, "I'm riding with Colin." I immediately thought, time to open the bank again, meaning the stacks of bills we had found up in Dad's closet, and to upgrade my ride. With Mother home, maybe I could get the coin from her. But an unregistered, loud, dirty little speedster with no lights wasn't up to the British challenge from Down Under.

Wendy climbed on the back of Colin's beautiful bike and we started for Colin's home, me making an awful racket and his Triumph purring along.

Colin's home was a nice place in the "salt box" style, classical New England. We parked the bikes in his drive, and of course, mine fell over on the gravel. We went inside and stopped in the entry way. His house looked like a cross between a library and a nautical museum. There were stacks of files everywhere, and shells, shark jaws, mermaid statues, and even a couple of old whale spears crossed and hanging on the wall. I looked at it, looked at Colin. "Isn't your dad trying to save the whales?" He just shrugged.

CHAPTER 36

Colin said, "Let's go in the study." The study looked like the public library with hundreds of books along the walls, and an old chart of Perth and the waters around it. There were charts of the waters north of Cape Cod spread around the table. Colin stopped in the kitchen and grabbed three beers out of the refrigerator.

We all sat down, Colin and I on a leather couch and Wendy in the chair next to his Dad's big desk. Colin put the beers on the table in front of us, then cracked one open and started drinking it. When we didn't reach for a cold one, Colin said sternly, "Ya can't plan a treasure hunt without a pint. Take one! I'm not drinkin' with the flies!"

I had never had a desire for a beer before, but now seemed like the perfect time to try one. I grabbed one and popped off the top. I took a little sip. It had a bitter taste I couldn't describe and it made my nose tickle with the foam. I put it down. My drinking career would have to wait. Colin looked at Wendy. She crossed her arms and said, "My Dad would kill me. He spends half his time picking drunks out of the water with his helicopter."

So now it was time to get down to business. I had learned that Aussies are impatient people and they like to get right to the point, fast.

Colin started. "Ethan and I took the boat over to the island off the harbor entrance, and we found the smugglers cave! We think there is treasure in it, and we're going to find it!"

Whoa, boy, I thought. Wendy doesn't know the whole story,

and she doesn't want to go digging underwater into a water-filled cave. But she did look interested, sitting straight up now.

Colin continued, "We've been over there and we found the cave entrance. We can get through it by sliding in under a ledge, and then we can dive in to find the rest of the cave and the treasure."

Wendy, much to my surprise said, "When do we go? This sounds like a great adventure!"

"Wait", I said, throwing my hands up, "We don't know how dangerous it might be inside, and we really don't know about any treasure. It could be nothing." I was still worried about Wendy and Colin together, but then realized that we would make a great team, especially with Morgan, and eventually, Falk. I let it go.

Colin had to say it. "Well, what about the "Golden Throne? You've been talking about it since I met you. That's why we went over there!"

Wendy was further intrigued, "What about the Golden Throne? What is it?"

Reluctantly, I told her all the stories I had heard about Viking coins, Pirate gold, and of course the religious relic, the "Golden Throne."

She thought for a second, "Even if there isn't a pot of gold, or some pirate's stolen golden throne, it sounds like great fun! When do we go out there?"

Wendy's enthusiasm was contagious, but I still had concerns. But I said, "OK, then it's settled. We'll go out treasure-hunting in my little boat to our little neighborhood cave, and we'll grab the treasure and split the profit evenly. Morgan and I will split a share. How does that sound?" We all grabbed a bottle of beer, Wendy's never been opened, and raised them into a toast. "To Adventure, to the Search for the Golden Throne." Then we all laughed at ourselves.

CHAPTER 37

Colin and I had found the cave entrance on our first trip ashore. It was hidden by a grove of trees, and we only found it by wedging ourselves between the trees and the rock cliff. The trees had grown tall since the 1930's and we had difficulty getting around them. There was a small opening underneath an overhanging ledge, and we had to get on hands and knees to see it. It looked like there had once been a larger entrance but new rock had been piled on to hide it. We laid on our stomachs and slid in.

When we crawled through the entrance, we discovered that the small cave hid the fact that the real cave extended down into the water. We would have to make a dive into the cold water to get inside the cave to look for any treasure that the Vikings, the English, the Pirates, or the rum-runners had left behind. With all that traffic over the centuries, surely they had forgotten something down there. So now we were returning with the right gear to make a dive into the dark cave waters.

Colin sat up on the bow of my boat with his shoes off and his pants rolled up, his feet dangling over the side, with the anchor sitting in his lap. He raised his hand, and called out, "Three more feet!"

Wendy was on the helm, steering us straight for the beach, avoiding sharp rocks on either side. I was on the sail trim, pulling the sheet in and out to edge us slowly towards the beach. Morgan was assisting Colin with the anchor line.

Suddenly, Colin called, "Ok. Stop! We're on the beach. We felt the thump as the bow slid up the beach. Then Colin slipped off the bow and took the anchor up to the edge of the beach and dug it in. Morgan went forward and tied off the anchor rope...er, line. I had the thought that the damned thing maybe SHOULD be called the anchor rope, but quickly dismissed it. Wendy would never go for it.

We all slid into the water and waded ashore, taking our swim gear with us. The cave entrance was hidden by a small grove of trees. It was under a rocky ledge which made it very hard to see unless you were really looking for it. Wendy spotted it first.

Colin led us in, getting down on his belly and sliding under the rock and into a small, sandy rock ledge. We all followed him one by one and got in without any injuries except our scraped bellies. I had a rogue thought about Wendy and her body having a harder time than we boys. I didn't dare look at her during her slide in.

We put our masks and snorkels on, then sat down on the ledge with our legs in the water to get our fins on. There was only the light of my new flashlight, and the cave was pungent with the smell of rotten fish and seaweed. I had bought an underwater light at Willoughby's to shine our way to the treasures of the cave, and maybe point out any lurking dangers.

Wait, did anyone consider that the cave might be haunted by the ghosts of pirates? I know they usually killed the crew that buried the treasure, and their ghosts were likely still haunting the cave. Too late to worry about that, so I didn't mention it. But just then, there was a low, ghastly moan. We all stopped to listen to it. It sounded like the low moan of dead pirates trapped forever in the cave. We looked at each other for courage, then we laughed nervously.

I slid off the ledge into the water, turned my light on max lumens, and ducked down into the water-filled cave. The water was only neck deep, and I could see that the cave looked like large bowl, partly natural, but also shaped a bit by man where some sharp rocks had been broken off. I shined the light around the cave from top to bottom and there was no reflection of gold or silver coins, and no Golden Throne. No pirate skeletons either.

By now, everyone was in the water. Colin cried out, "Crikey, we didn't need this gear, we could just walk in." But he took a step further and slid off the ledge to the deeper water. The middle of the cave was about twelve feet deep, but there was always air to breathe above. The cave was about twenty feet long.

Everyone went underwater and held onto the rock ledge. I shined the light around again. Everyone swept their eyes all around the cave. Still no gold treasure, so I nodded to Colin, then I swam down into the bowl. I started looking for a tunnel or something that would possibly lead to another room. Colin and Morgan quickly joined in and searched the bottom and the wall for anything that might lead further.

Morgan suddenly tugged on my arm and pointed. At the bottom edge of the bowl on the far side was the entrance to a rugged tunnel, about two feet wide. It was partly covered in rocks that had been pushed aside by the tides. They had fallen down a bit so I could see the entrance. Morgan reached for the light and indicated he was going in. He was the best athlete, so it made sense for him to go first. If this cave had been made as a hideout, then the tunnel would have been safe to use. "I suspect that not many gangsters were great divers, so they must have made it big enough to go through, and there must be something interesting on the other side."

Morgan took the light from me, swam over to the entrance and started pulling down the rocks. I looked back for Wendy, and she was just floating back there, watching us with her red hair in a swirl around her head, her lovely body silhouetted from the light coming into the cave above.

Morgan came up for a quick breath and then headed for the tunnel entrance. He swam up to it, shined the light into it, exploring its width and to the extent he could, discover how long it was. After satisfying himself it was reasonably safe, he swam in and all we could see was his fins, flopping around, then disappearing. We waited about a minute, getting more and more concerned. The tide was starting to turn, and there were strong currents drawing Morgan into the cave.

I looked at Colin and he signaled OK, which means surface, so we all went up for a breath. Colin spoke first, "Get a couple of breaths. We'll wait for one minute then you go in after him. That tunnel is too small for more than one person so no one else goes in until you or Morgan gets back. Got it?" We all nodded in grim acceptance. I couldn't imagine my little brother meeting his death in a dark, underwater cave.

Just then Morgan popped up, startling us all. We had been planning a rescue but now here was the "survivor". That was "so Morgan", and I was relieved beyond measure.

He sputtered out, "There's a big room above water on the other side. It looks like some kind of storage room, there are open and broken wooden boxes everywhere...And guys,...I found it! I found the Golden Throne!"

We stared at him in disbelief. Could the legend really be true? Colin interjected an Australian phrase we hadn't heard yet.

"Fair Dinkum?, you really found it?" Colin questioned, barely containing his excitement, and resorting to one of his arcane Aussie expressions.

Morgan was grinning ear to ear. "Yeah, it's right there among the boxes. It's unbelievable!"

We all dove and raced to the entrance with Morg leading the way. The excitement was electric. We clawed away the rest of the rocks at the entrance and looked inside. The tunnel was solid rock and looked like it had been mined out to almost a perfect oval about four feet wide and three feet high, perfect for moving boxes of booze or pirate gold through.

We surfaced again. I said, "Morgan first, then me, then Colin, then you Wendy." She glared back at me. "OK. Morgan then Wendy, then me." Her glare faded and she nodded vigorously. Then I ordered, "Let's go!"

After swimming about ten feet, I could see a faint light above

Wendy's fins, fluttering in my face. The sight of Wendy's legs kicking just in front of me was tantalizing. I surfaced with Wendy and Colin just behind. Morgan, who still had the light, crawled out onto a rocky ledge and then onto a sand beach. Everyone else followed and within a few seconds we were all out of the water. There was a small beam of light coming through a tiny crack in the ceiling that barely illuminated the dark chamber.

Morg shined the light up to the roof and around the walls of this larger cave. We were in a large room with rock walls and a sand beach on a large rocky ledge. It smelled like the tide line and dead fish (or pirates), and the air was almost too stale to breathe. There were wooden boxes everywhere, broken open by pirate bands, "tomb robbers " or others, maybe Federal agents. We could again hear and feel the low moan of the wind blowing across the small hole in the roof where the light filtered in.

Then Morgan shined the light on our item of supreme interest.

It was a household toilet, sitting on the ground, and spray-painted gold. I walked over to it and stared. Once we had gotten over the shock of the discovery and recognized the beauty of the joke, we howled with laughter. Colin pounded me on the back and yelled, "Bonzer, Bonzer!" Morgan and I hugged while staring at the "treasure". Wendy and Colin danced around, and then Colin pulled her in and kissed her. She looked like it was no big deal, but gave me a quick glance. Rage rose up inside me but I quickly shoved it down. What was I thinking bringing them both along?

Wendy escaped Colin and came over to me, grabbed me and gave me a salty wet kiss. My rage turned instantly into ecstasy. We looked at each other for an instant, then she turned away to consider the "business" at hand.

I didn't dare to open the closed top of the toilet. No telling what was inside there. Morgan walked over to raise the top, but I sat on it. I guessed the smugglers had brought it in here for their "sanitary" needs. Much later, someone had painted it gold and hence, the "Legend of the Golden Throne" was born.

All that the scoundrels who started the legend had to do was mention the rumor of a golden throne at the hardware store, the coffee shop, or maybe Willoughby's, and some fool would go looking for it. Apparently it had been discovered many times due to the many initials all over it. We hadn't included a magic marker in our dive kit so we couldn't sign our work as intrepid visitors to the "Cave of the Golden Throne" had done. Previous visitors who had left their names behind on the toilet like "Jimmy + Janis" had been able to keep the myth going by not revealing its dark secret.

We returned back through the dark tunnel, its mysteries revealed and our fears gone. We climbed back out of the tunnel entrance into the late-afternoon sunshine, and laid out on the beach to warm up. I felt, for the first time, that we were coming together as an improbable team. I looked at each of them in turn, valuing each of their abilities; Colin, the indomitable Aussie, Wendy, the beautiful sailor, Morgan, the unstoppable athlete, and me. I was still working on my exact contribution to my new team, but I settled on this. I was the leader of the team. I came up with ideas for fun or trouble, and I was the chief worrier, that's worrier, not warrior.

CHAPTER 38

When I woke up, I jumped to the window looked out to see a the black Ford SUV parked down Shore Road. It had been there on and off since Mom had come back, most of the day and into the night. I couldn't connect the appearance of the strange vehicle there with Mom's arrival, or anything else. What were they expecting to see? Two teen boys riding their bikes? No, our dirt bikes couldn't be any reason for them spying on us, unless they were concerned that they weren't street legal, and we were riding them to school.

Or was it something about Mom that had them out there haunting us? With her living as a socialite in New York, I'm sure there were people in her life that had questionable backgrounds. We were likely to have some of them visiting us. I hoped I could sort out the good ones from the bad ones.

I had considered going down there and confronting the guys in the Ford but now I thought better of it. Maybe they were highway department guys just counting cars down Shore Road. Ha, good joke.

Today was Saturday, and it was my birthday and Morgan's birthday. Morgan's birthday and mine were a month apart, and since we never had a big crowd for either one, we decided to celebrate on the same day. I had thought about whether I should remind Mom, but decided against it. Maybe she had it in her big social calendar notebook she always carried.

I got up and opened my bedroom window then pushed the door open and walked out on the little balcony. The sun was just coming up and I could see a line of dark clouds approaching from the south-west. I guess summer was about over here up in the northeast, and we would start seeing storms rolling in until the first cold front and snowfall. I really needed to find a way to haul the boat out for winter storage, and a place to put it. We had our fun with learning to sail and our underwater cave exploration to find the mystical "Golden Throne" but now that the storms were rolling in, the boat would have to wait for the warmth of spring.

I went over to Morgan's bedroom. He was still asleep and I sat on his bed and woke him up. "Happy Birthday, Little Brother," I announced. He sat up and opened his eyes, still mostly asleep. "Happy Birthday, Big Brother", he replied with a grin, remembering our ongoing joke of a birthday.

"I asked Marie yesterday to make us a birthday cake, you know our favorite?"

"You mean the chocolate brownie with salted-caramel icing?"

"Yeah, is that ok?"

"Sure. Did you tell Mom?" he asked darkly.

"I haven't yet, but I'm going to. It's about time she was reminded of it."

We got dressed and went downstairs. Mom was still sleeping and I heard the doorbell chime. It was Marie coming to make breakfast and our cake.

"Hi Marie", we said. She had a couple of large bags of groceries with her, which Morg and I took to the kitchen. She nodded toward the car and said, "There are two more in my car. Would you please go get them?", she asked sweetly.

We retrieved the other two bags, and while walking up the stairs, I asked, "This seems like a lot of food for just a couple of meals, doesn't it?"

Marie responded, "Your mom asked me to make something special for dinner tonight, and you shall have your brownie cake."

Morg and I looked at each other in surprise. Did she remember our birthday?

Just then, Mom came sweeping into the dining room. She was wearing the black nightgown under her pink robe that Dad had bought for "Paris Girl." I thought that I had hidden it well in the back of Dad's closet. I was stunned into silence. When she saw me looking at her wearing it, she pulled her robe closed all the way, giving me a sweet look.

"Boys, I have a surprise for you tonight." We looked at each other in anticipation of the news, whatever it was. It was going to be a surprise, either good or terrible. Was the nightgown some kind of indicator?

Her eyes sparkled with excitement. "I have a friend coming down to stay with us for the weekend, and you won't guess who it is!" We waited breathlessly, we dared not guess. "You know that new FBI detective show on cable, the one set in Boston? Our guest is Tory Stevens, the star of the show! He will be staying in town for a few days while they shoot some scenes out on the beach on one of the little islands out there. He's invited you boys to come out and watch the shooting!"

Morgan and I looked at each other again. Morgan shrugged his shoulders and headed back upstairs to his football video game.

I was surprised at the news, and I asked myself if this was the new boyfriend, or just someone from her work in New York. I then recalled sharply that was the same question I had asked myself when we pulled the picture of "Paris Girl" out of the envelope. I guess it was unfair to hope that two attractive people like our parents would not find love interests where they worked or traveled.

I thought about the show; it was about a Texas FBI agent who had been transferred to Boston to work cases but also investigate some reports of corruption in the office. I hoped that they had gotten a real Texan for the role.

With these developments, I guessed our birthday party was out the window. But now it was time to bring this up. "Mom, do you know what day this is?"

She looked up from her breakfast and I could see her searching her memory for anything significant. "Why, yes, honey. Isn't this your birthday? You didn't think I'd forgotten it, did you?"

I felt a twinge of guilt for thinking she wouldn't remember it, but then knew for a fact that if I hadn't challenged her, she would have never recalled our birthday.

"Come let me hug you! You are so grown up!" She pulled me in and gave me a nice motherly hug. Ok, she had me.

"We're going to have a great big dinner tonight and Marie told me she is making your favorite cake for you and Morgan."

Hah. So Marie tipped her off. I guess I'm ok with that. At least we would get our brownie cake.

Later, I went into Morgan's room where he was sitting on his bed and playing the Madden Football video game. He looked up as I walked in, but didn't say anything. I plopped down in the chair next to his desk, and just watched him play. He was a lot better than me with his faster reflexes. The longer I sat there not saying anything, the more nervous he got. After a few minutes, he threw down the game controller, looked at me, and said, "What do you want?"

"Mom remembered our birthday. You should go down and get your birthday hug," I said sardonically. He looked up, surprised. "Really?" "Yeah, really."

"And we are having a big dinner tonight complete with our cake and whoever else shows up."

"You mean the movie stars? That might be fun!" he replied.

I got right to it. "I don't like Mom bringing some stranger down here to stay in our house over the weekend. I don't care if he is a famous actor. I saw that show a couple of times, but I thought it was dumb."

Morgan had returned to his game, but answered anyway. "Mom says he's staying in town, not in the house. I liked the show and it'd be fun to meet him. We've never met any movie stars before."

I tried to think of the positive side of this development. Morgan was right. We had never met any movie stars before, and I thought they would have no interest in meeting a couple of teenagers, and thought we'd probably spend the time in our rooms playing video games. Our Mom would want them to herself, especially her hero, Tory. I thought of the movie stars I liked, and then the guys I didn't like and just hoped for the best.

I immediately thought of the TV show we had been to in Dallas when we were little kids. Mom had got us tickets from a friend of hers for the taping of "Benny the Dinosaur" or something like that. The show's manic theme song suddenly flooded into my mind and I had to force it out.

Since it was Saturday and our birthday, we decided to take the bikes out to the seashore and ride them on a track someone had set up on the dunes. We rode about ten miles East, past the airport, and found the place. It was located on some big dunes and had those goofy flags surrounding it, which they probably stole from a used car lot.

There were a large number of riders and bikes there, so we signed the release and paid $20 a piece to get a number for our bikes and to join a group. Each group rode in kind of an informal race for ten minutes, then another group rode for their ten minutes. We weren't that experienced, so we kind of stayed on the side while the more experienced riders whizzed past us, throwing up great plumes of dust and sand into our eyes and teeth. Both of us dumped our bikes at least once in the deep sand at the far end of the track.

During one of our break periods, we saw several of the kids from our classes and made a few more friends. One of the best riders, Billy Towers, came over and gave us a few tips on how not to get run-over on the track. We found out that his nickname was "Fast Billy" so we had a private laugh over that. I wasn't sure who best deserved the name, but "Fast Billy" the horse was eons ago, so I guessed the bloke on the bike got to keep it.

After we had burned most our gas and eaten enough sand, we decided to head home by way of the airport. Falk was there, but he was teaching an introductory class for new pilots out in the hanger.

He saw us and waved us to seats in the back of the group, so we sat down to listen. Falk had drawn big circles on the board which represented the airplane's instruments during various maneuvers. He would rub off the dry marker and redraw the arrows on the circles to show climbs and turns. He had blue marker dust all over his left hand and his white T-shirt.

That part about the maneuvers was pretty interesting, but when he started talking about FAA Rules and Regulations, we got up and slid out with a wave back to Falk. We had enough school Monday through Friday.

We headed home, then saw a big Mercedes sedan parked in our driveway. Mom had pulled the Maserati out of the garage and there were a couple of people standing around with her, talking about the car. One of them opened up the car and slid into the seat.

This made me mad, as strange people were at our house and sitting in our car, me and Morgan's car. We pulled up behind them, and I gunned my bike to make as much noise as I could. Everyone turned around, startled at the racket. I could see my Mom was displeased, but then her expression turned to pure charm.

"Come over here, boys. I want you to meet our visitors." The first guy was a short bald guy with strangely big glasses. Mom introduced him as the director, and a second guy who looked like the first guy but with hair and without glasses stepped forward. Was this the famous star? I asked myself. No, he was introduced as the producer, and I guessed he was the boss.

Just then a remarkably handsome, tanned, tall man with an engaging smile crawled out of the Maserati. He got out, looked back at the car, then looked at me in a very friendly way and said, "I hope you don't mind me sitting in your car. It's quite a beauty, isn't it?"

His acknowledgement of the fact that the car was mine, and of course, Morgan's, put me in a different frame of mind.

"No sir, you're welcome to take a look at it. What do you think of her?"

He looked back at it in admiration and said, "Well, she's one of the most beautiful cars I've seen. How would you like for us to take a drive in it, maybe later this weekend?"

I, of course, thought he meant me and Morgan, but then I thought maybe he meant just Mom. But he was looking at me.

"Yes sir. I really would. I'm getting my learner's permit in school and I'll be driving soon."

"Whoa there, cowboy! Let's take it a step at a time," he said, glancing at Mom. She looked back and smiled at him. He could have said almost anything to her and she'd probably agree and smile at him.

Mom then clapped her hands and announced, "Let's go inside for dinner. Marie has created quite a spread for us."

We all headed into the house up the back stairs to the porch and then into the rear dining room off the kitchen. The smells coming from the kitchen were heavenly. I was amazed by how elegant the table settings looked, with crisp white tablecloths, two vases of roses and other flowers set in the middle of the table. We had never used this room before, and it looked like it was out of a movie set. I guessed that was exactly the effect Mom wanted. She directed where each of us was supposed to sit, she at the head of the table with the director and producer to her left and right, and Tory at the other head of the table, with me and Morgan on each side.

We all took our places, and Marie and a helper she had brought started serving us. It felt like one of those state dinners we had seen on TV. We got our salads first, then roast beef and potatoes and green beans. Everyone started eating with Mom having small talk with her little band, while me and Morg just ate in silence, watching the party. Tory looked at us and smiled at both of us while he was eating and listening to his producer talk about his plans for new episodes. The show was very popular despite my critical review, and there was already planning another season. Mom listened attentively with frequent gazes down at Tory, who just smiled back at her.

After the main course was over and the plates were cleared off,

Marie dimmed the lights in the room, and entered with our salted caramel brownie cake and eighteen candles lit and arranged in four rows of four, plus two big candles in the middle, making eighteen. I was delighted and so was Morg. This party was far beyond what we expected at the start of this day. I only worried how we were going to blow out all the candles on that huge cake.

Marie placed the cake in the middle of the table and Morgan and I blew out the candles from opposite sides of the table. Thankfully, no one thought to sing "Happy Birthday". Everyone cheered and congratulated us and I looked at Mom and saw a look of love and admiration from her. My heart warmed for her, and I thought that maybe Morgan was right about her staying here and being our Mom.

Afterwards, we got the chance to talk as Marie brought in coffee and what I thought was brandy or something. Tory said to us, "Did your Mom tell you that we are shooting a few scenes around here in Pocasset? I'd like you to come watch, and maybe even be extras in a scene. We need a few local people in one of them. Are you guys interested?"

Morg and I looked at each other, and said together "Hell, yes!" Tory laughed and said, "Well, great. I'll tell you where and when, when I get more details.

After dinner, we all went into the living room and got comfortable in the big couches and plush chairs. Marie and her helper made a last pass for coffee and brandy, then gathered up their gear and headed out the back door.

After we all got settled, Mom said, "Tory, tell us a little about your show and what you are going to do here in little Pocasset. We're all DIEING to know more." Tory looked around the room, then looked at me, then Morgan. Then he said, "Well, the basic plot is that I play a Texas FBI agent that's has been sent to Boston to clean out corruption, but it's all undercover, so don't tell anybody." We all laughed at that. "I do have a real FBI Agent assigned as an expert to help on the script and coach me on FBI moves." He then did a little karate move, with a little "ki-yi" at the end which startled Mom, which made all of us laugh again.

"We are shooting a scene out on Bassett's island where I investigate a crime scene and find a body. It's supposed to be somebody with evidence against the police chief and a Congressman who ended up shot and their body dumped on the island. It was then found by a local fisherman. Then Tory stopped, looked at me and Morgan and offered, "Hey, I think I can get you boys on the fishing boat as background crew. We can get you some fisherman clothes whatever those are."

I thought about Dad after hearing that little story, and I hoped that nothing that he was doing would put him in danger. Just thinking about that sent a chill through my body. We hadn't heard from him since Mom arrived, and I urgently wanted to call him. Then I wondered again about the car that was parked down the street. I wondered whether we could get that FBI Agent to come over here and talk to the people in the car.

As they were getting ready to leave, I asked Tory, "Where were you born? I'm trying to place your accent."

Tory smiled and replied, "I was born on a farm...in New Jersey. But when I was six, my dad bought some land outside of Abilene, and I grew up there. I went to Texas Tech in Lubbock for a year before I got hooked up into acting. That enough Texas "cred" for you?"

I nodded my acceptance. Abilene was steeped deep in Texas, and I hoped he was too. Texas Tech was a great school and was as Texas as you could get. Guns Up! I was beginning to like him.

Tory and the crew left for the night and went back to his hotel in downtown. I had noticed my mother looking at him several times that night, and I wondered if she had met him up in New York on one of her trips up there in our car, Morgan and mine. I had to admit that he had been nice to Morgan and me, much to my surprise. I had expected us to be locked in the pantry while Mom's guests were here.

Morgan walked over to my room and said, "How'dya like that?"

I said, "You mean Tory?" "Yeah, I like him, and it would be great to be in one of his scenes on TV." I yawned, and said, "Yeah, it would be. Now get off to bed."

I thought it would be hilarious if Tory's scene was shot on the same beach as the Throne Cave, and someone on the crew found it. As it turned out it wasn't, so the secret of the Cave was safe with us.

CHAPTER 39

The filming was supposed to take two days, with one set of shots down by the docks in Pocasset Harbor, one by the police station, and the final one, the one we were going to be in, on the final day out on the west side of Bassett's Island where the "murder scene" was to be. We went down after school on Thursday and Friday to see the first two scenes, but they were done when we got there so there wasn't anything to see except the crews coiling up long power cables and loading up boxes of camera equipment.

On Saturday, it began snowing but we got a call to show up at Dock 4 in Pocasset Harbor. When we got there, there was one of the local lobster fishing boats parked at the dock. We were summoned aboard by some flunky junior assistant director and given tunics and hats that somebody in wardrobe thought the local fisherman wore. What they really wore was jean jackets and baseball caps, and, in contrast, we looked like Portuguese fishermen from the 17th century. One actor, a big, swarthy guy, was playing the "Captain" of the boat, while the real captain and owner of the rented lobsterman steered the boat from inside the pilot house, hidden out of sight.

We were supposed to make a pass along the shallows on the west side of Bassett's Island, allegedly looking for a lobster trap that had gone missing. The film crew was set up back in the marsh behind the little beach recording our passage down the beach, with me and Morgan looking through cheap binoculars at the beach, trying to locate our missing trap in the snow.

The "Captain" then sees something on the beach and grabs my

binoculars to get a closer look. I had made the mistake of putting the binoculars strap around my neck, so when he grabbed them, he knocked my stupid hat off onto the water. I guessed that wasn't enough of a hiccup to stop rolling so we continued. The "Captain" turned the boat toward the beach and stopped just before we ran ashore. Then he jumps into the water, runs up the beach and sees the body of a man, laying half in the sand and the marsh grass. We run to the rail and looked horrified at what we saw. Then the Director called cut, and our part was done, so we jumped off the boat to watch the rest of the shoot.

The "Cops" came and marked off the area with crime scene tape, then Tory showed up with his female partner and investigated the scene. At the end on the final cut, the "body" jumped up and started cursing, with ant stings all over his body. They took him to the hospital to treat him for shock. Great actor, though.

Morgan and I had enjoyed our role as "extras" in the filming as part of the fisherman's crew that found the body. We didn't have any lines, we just stood in the background and acted horrified at seeing the body. Actually, Morg and I were acting too horrified, and the director yelled at us, "Stop making faces back there!" So then we just tried to look just like dumb fishermen not horrified at seeing a dead body. I had never seen one, so I'm not sure what my reaction would be.

While the film crew was disassembling all the lights and sound equipment and cameras, Tory walked over and greeted us. "How d'ya like being on TV? Looks like you guys did great. Maybe a bit of over-acting, but that's typical for first-time actors." We all giggled at that. Morgan replied, "Yes, thanks for getting us in. We really had fun."

We took the lobster boat back to the dock and handed in what was left of our wardrobe and said our goodbyes to the crew. The "Captain" thanked us, but kidded us about getting yelled at. We all had a big laugh at that. Making movies is a lot of fun, Morgan and I both agreed.

CHAPTER 40

It was getting late on a Friday afternoon. Morgan was still at football practice for the game tonight. His challenger for the position of starting quarterback for the team had been pulled by the coach for some reason, leaving Morgan as the starter. I was ecstatic for him. Football had been his life back in Texas and it meant everything to him to lead the team here as well.

The tide was out and I could smell the odor from the high tide line on the beach, the pleasant smell of the sea weed mixed with the strong pungent smell of dead fish and crabs washed in from the bay. The seabirds were diving onto the shoreline, crying and squawking as they carried off their share of the feast.

I was sitting on the porch watching the sun begin to set, and wondered if the guys in the black Ford parked a few blocks down the road smelled it too. I had never seen that car with the windows rolled down, and I'd never seen the engine running for the air conditioning or heat. It probably smelled worse in there than it did out here in the semi-fresh air.

A car came down the street from the opposite direction, and it looked like a late-model red Corvette. I was surprised to see it pull into our driveway and stop. The driver's door opened and Tory Stevens crawled out and waved. "Howdy, Ethan!" Tory walked over to where I was on the porch, and I got up and we shook hands. We had become friends, adult-teenager, since the movie scene shooting out on Bassett's Island, and I wondered why he was back.

"What's up, Ethan?" he asked, taking off his dark sunglasses.

"Just waiting to go to Morg's game tonight," I replied. "What brings you back down this way? I thought you were done with shooting in Pocasset."

"Nah, the film editors didn't like the lighting on the shots over by the wharf and downtown at the police station. We're all scrambling to get them redone over the weekend. Your Mom asked me if I wanted to go to dinner with her, and since I was here for the weekend, I said, why not?" He looked at me for a minute and then said, "You ok with that?"

I replied, "Yeah, I guess so."

I was desperate to get a call into my Dad in Paris, and when someone answered the phone, they said he wasn't there anymore. They gave me a new international number, but there was no answer at that number. It seemed to me that things were getting out of hand. I felt queasy with Tory being here, even if he was an interesting guy and he was good to me and Morgan. It just didn't seem right. I needed my Dad.

"Did you say that Morgan's game is tonight?" he asked. He seemed a bit distracted.

Everyone who grew up in Texas knows that Friday night is for football, so I could see that he wasn't really asking.

"Is your Mom home?" He looked at his watch, and then with a shake of his head said, "Well, I am a little early," looking at the door again.

"She just got home a few minutes ago," I said. "Are ya'll going out somewhere special tonite?"

"Yeah, she wants to take me down to the shore in Falmouth. There's this great little place she's been talking about."

"She should be ready in an hour or so," I said. He looked at me suddenly, then laughed. "I guess you probably know how long it takes her. Can I set down out here with you for a bit?"

"Sure. No worries." I was beginning to pick up a bit of "Colin-speak", but Tory didn't seem to notice. He'd probably been around Aussies before. He was looking down the street at the black car.

"How long has that black car been down there? I thought I saw it down there last time I was here." He stood up to get a better view. Even with both of us staring at them, there was still no reaction from the occupants. Tory turned to me and asked, "Any idea what that's all about?"

"No, I've thought about going over there and asking them, but the one time I had the courage to walk down there, they started up and left."

"Hmm...I've got an idea. Follow me." He then walked leisurely off the porch and down to the shiny red Corvette. "Get in." I jumped into the right seat, waiting breathlessly for what Tory had planned. The Corvette was almost as cool as the Maserati, just a bit cheesier. He started the car with a satisfying rumble, backed out and turned onto the street, but in the opposite direction from the black car. We drove down a few blocks, out of sight of the black car, then suddenly turned right down to Main Street, then right again. I felt like I was living in one of Tory's TV episodes.

We rumbled through town, passing Quincy's and the ice cream place. I wished that Pauly and his bunch would see me and Tory go by in the red Corvette. After we got to the intersection with Shore Road, Tory turned right and drove a few blocks and up right behind the black car. No response from them. Tory turned to me and put his hand in my shoulder and said quietly, "Stay here. Take down their license plate number", nodding to a pen laying on the console. I couldn't find anything to write on, so I wrote on my hand, "N1065743", obviously a US Government car.

CHAPTER 41

Tory walked up to the driver's side and tapped on the window. I could see some scrambling going on inside the car, but after a half a minute, the driver's side window rolled down. Tory was talking to them, but I couldn't hear him. I couldn't roll my window down because Tory had the keys. I could see the driver's hand making small movements like he was in an animated conversation. There was a brief conversation, then the driver's door opened and a big, bald guy in a dark suit got out. I was frantic in fear for Tory as the bald guy towered over him. Then the other guy got out and walked around the car to face Tory as well. I tried to think of anything I could do. I remembered the pistols in the wall safe, but that was no solution at this point.

I looked at Tory and could see him tense up as the bald giant approached him with the other guy. Then I could see him relax, smile his Hollywood smile, and shake hands with them. They talked like old friends for a bit, then Tory cut it off, said goodbye, and came back to the Corvette.

Tory got into the car and waited, watching the other car. The other guys got back in their car, and after a brief delay, they drove off.

I blurted out, "What the hell was that? Who were they?"

Tory chuckled a bit. "They are FBI agents from Washington." They have orders to over-watch your house. They said it was for your own safety."

"Safety from what? What's going on that they need to watch my house!" I was alarmed. What had we gotten ourselves into, and how? I racked my brain looking for an answer. The only thing I could come up with was...Dad. What kind of trouble would he be bringing home with him, if he made it?

"Why were you having such a friendly visit with those guys who have been haunting us for weeks? It looked like you knew them. What was going on?"

Tory started up the Corvette and laid rubber for about twenty feet. I was slammed back into my seat with the g-Force. It was thrilling. He slowed the car to the speed limit and then asked, "Do you mind driving around a bit? I just got this for a weekend rental and it seems a waste not to have fun with it." "No, it's great fun", I replied, "besides we can talk."

Tory looked at me, then nodded, "Yeah, there are a couple of things I need to ask you too. Do you mind?"

I thought, good, let's get it all out on the table. I was uncomfortable with what seemed to be his increasing attention to my Mom. I was unsure if Dad and Mom were still married or not, as unbelievable as that sounds. Also, I wanted to know about his conversation with the FBI guys. What did he say to get them to leave? Were they coming back? Did he know them, and was he now part of some plan?

He started, "First, your Mom and I are enjoying each other's company, and I would like to continue seeing her. So what's the deal with your Dad? Is he ever coming back here? Why does he spend so much time away?" He paused, but I had no answer that I wanted to share with him. Then he said, "I don't need your permission to see your Mom, but are you ok with it?"

I thought hard about me and Morg and what we were doing alone in Pocasset. At that moment I felt the same feeling that I had the first time our Dad left us here in this strange, new house, alone and vulnerable, despite my efforts to compensate for it and pretend I didn't feel that way. I had promised Mom that I would take care of Morgan, and I had made that commitment and would honor it until Morgan no longer needed me.

When Tory asked me if he could see my Mom, I felt that both she and Dad were abandoning us all over again, despite that Tory was an adult that I thought I could trust, somewhat.

I decided to challenge him. "First, tell me why you were so buddy-buddy with those FBI guys who have been staking us out day and night. Do you know them?"

Tory chuckled again and replied, "It's actually funny. They are fans of the show and when I knocked on the car window, they recognized me but mistook me for a real FBI Agent for a second. When they realized who I was, they jumped out of the car to shake my hand and tell me, they really, really like the show!" He seemed very pleased with himself.

"But what were they doing at my house all this time? I really need to know. I'm worried about my Dad! Did you even ask them?"

Tory pulled the car over to the curb, and stopped. He looked at me directly and told me, "I did ask them, without telling them that you were in the car with me. I told them that I was just in town for the filming, and to visit your Mom. They never said anything conclusive, but I got the impression that your Dad may be in some sort of trouble. I'm not sure about that. But they just wanted to talk to him about some case they were working on. They seemed to think he might be coming back here soon. Do you know anything about that?"

"No, we haven't talked to him in weeks. He was in Paris the last time we talked, and now...I don't know where he is. Are they coming back?"

Tory cocked his head and replied slowly, "I don't think so. I gave them the impression that I was kind of looking after...you and your brother, and that you didn't expect him home anytime soon. I hope that was ok. You can't lie to the Feds, but you can exaggerate or forget if you are good at it. I think they will leave you alone for the next little while until something else comes up."

"Did you get their names so we can verify who they are?" I asked urgently.

Tory said, "Yes, Agents Adams and Lockhart. With the license number you copied, I can track them down. With the help of our staff agent, Agent Brown, of course. I think he will be helpful."

It occurred to me that if I was going to talk to Dad, it might be better to do it on some other phone, not our home phone. It might be bugged. There were suddenly way too many people getting involved in my life.

I mulled over what I was going to say about Tory's question about my Mom. Finally I said, "Tory, just treat her with respect and don't do anything in my house that disrespects her or this house. I know she likes you, and that's fine. If my Dad comes back, remember that this is his house, not Mom's, and they need to resolve a lot of things between themselves before other people get too involved." I included Paris Girl in that thought as well. He nodded yes and replied, "Ok, that's fine", and started up the Corvette and headed for my house. I still needed to get to Morgan's game.

CHAPTER 42

I got to the game in the fourth quarter and found a seat in the top row. There was a pretty good crowd here. The Pocasset Pirates were down by a field goal, three points. Morgan was playing QB and he looked as smooth as ever. His opposition, the Hyannis Hurricanes, had a much larger team than little Pocasset, and his O-line was having trouble keeping one particular linebacker from rushing through and sacking Morgan before he could even complete a handoff. I could see his favorite receiver, Bennet, #83, getting bottled up on the line, and not getting a chance to get free and get into position for a pass.

The teams went back and forth on the field with neither team getting a score. Then, as the Pirates punted the ball, the Hurricanes receiver fumbled the ball, and the Pirates got the ball on the 25 yard line. The Hurricane defenders seemed to be disorganized after the fumble, and in the last play of the game, Morgan called "his play", rolled out right, and hit Bennet crossing to the left, in a diving catch in the last six inches of the end zone, winning the game. The PAT was good, and the game was over.

I waited in my usual spot by the fence at the exit to the field and started looking for Morgan coming out. It was dark and I had a hard time picking him out.

Suddenly, I got a quick glimpse of Pauly's angry face, and a fist coming at my face, then hitting me just over my nose. My nose spurted blood and I saw stars. I had thought that "seeing stars" was just an expression, but it is true, you see bright stars swirling around instead of your regular vision. I was completely disoriented and held on to the fence to avoid falling. Pauly struck out again and hit me in the right ear, knocking me down to my knees this time. I was helpless to the attacks from the rest of Pauly's gang who began kicking me in the back and in my legs. I tried to get up, and when Pauly's face got close, I swung my right fist into his jaw, knocking him backwards. But, I was still getting pummeled in the back by the gang.

Suddenly, the impacts stopped and I looked up to see Morgan and Bennet taking on the gang, and putting them on the ground, one by one. I could hear their cries and the sound of solid hits. Morgan was using his karate skills to great effect and in a few seconds, the gang was flattened to the ground, including Pauly. I crawled over to him and sat on him. I looked at him and saw his terrified face. I hit him hard in the face with my right and then my left fist. I screamed at him, "Pauly, now it's over! It's over! Got it?"

He nodded his bloody head and I got off of him. I got up and Morgan came over and helped me stand. I looked around, and five defeated wanna-be thugs got up and slinked away. I turned to Morgan and hugged him. "Thanks, brother. They had me down."

Morgan replied, "Yeah, we caught them by surprise, and none of them really knows how to fight. I think we're done with that little shit."

I turned to Morgan's friend and wide receiver, Bennet, and said, with blood dripping down into my mouth, "That was a beautiful catch," I said, spitting blood at him. He backed up, then he smiled and said, "Thanks, I'm glad we were able to catch you as well."

The next day, the red Corvette pulled up in the driveway, and Tory and one other guy got out, a black guy in a suit, waved, and came up to the porch. Tory was wearing his usual, $100 jeans and a rodeo shirt. I walked down to meet them. Tory put his arm around my shoulders and said, "Let's go up into the house. We shouldn't be talking out here. Hey, what happened to your face?" I told him the usual lie, "You should see the other guy." I know that I did some serious damage to Pauly in my rage at getting jumped. I probably looked just as rough, and my right ear was still ringing like a bell.

We walked back into the study at the rear of the house. Tory explained, "Ethan, this is Agent Brown, Bill Brown. He is the FBI Agent who is lucky enough to be assigned as the FBI liaison to my show." We settled into the chairs in the small windowless room.

Mom came in and the two men rose in respect, "Do you men need me in here? I could stay in here for a while and listen if you want me to." I looked at Tory, and he did a small look-down shake of his head. I offered, "Mom, were just gonna talk about some other places Tory could shoot in next years' episodes. You don't need to stay for this, if you have something else you want to do.

She looked around the room for confirmation that she wasn't wanted, then said, "Well, ok. But let's get together for drinks on the porch when you guys get finished up. Marie and I are going to put together a few horse-derves." She snickered at her little food joke and swam out of the room.

Tory turned to Bill, the FBI guy, and said, "Bill, you got the floor."

Bill turned to me and said, "There is something going on with your Dad. When I ran the license and names, I found out that those guys weren't local, they were out of the DC office, not Boston. That's a bit unusual, I can't find out why they sent these guys up here, rather than just having the local guys drop by. If they were from Quantico, that means there is some international content in this deal. That makes it a little different.

Then he asked, "When was the last time you heard from your Dad? Is he missing or what? There was a bulletin going around showing him as someone they wanted to question, without saying why. It seems like they think he has information of interest to a number of interested parties, not just the US, and not all friendly. He paused to let that sink in, then asked, "Do you know how to get hold of him? I think you really should. You need to tell him to get back to the states before things go South on him."

I felt a cold chill come all over my body. I know he was in Naval Intelligence before, and he did a fair amount of US travel then. He told us several times that when he left the Navy eight years ago, he went to work for a big security software company. I took that to mean that he sold and installed special security hardware and software that let computers on different networks and even in different countries talk to each other securely and exchange data like orders, shipments, invoices and the like. It wasn't that different than ordering something from a US company that might come from say, China or Columbia, without giving out sensitive information to someone who wasn't supposed to see it. I replied to the agent, "I have an International number for him that no one ever picks up. I got it from a guy he worked with in Paris after he left to go wherever...I'll try to call him again in the morning and try to find out what's going on with him. You're beginning to worry me now."

"Well, don't be overly concerned. We don't have any bad news. It just seems that there is something brewing, I don't have any idea what, and some people think your Dad's the key to finding out what it is. I'll do some simple background work on it, just to listen, not to investigate, and I'll let you know through Tory if you give us permission to, what else I'm hearing. That is, when I'm keeping Tory here from acting more like a Texas Ranger than an FBI Agent."

"Agent Brown, actually I'd like to hear directly from you. Tory is a friend but I don't want to burden him with something that may be nothing. He's got to stay focused on his play job of rooting corruption out of Boston, and Pocasset if it's spread down here."

He agreed, and then he and Tory joined Mom on the porch for a brief visit before they sped off in the red Corvette.

Mom stayed out on the porch with her cocktail talking on the phone to New York. I wondered if she'd stay here in Pocasset once Tory wasn't spending weekends down here anymore.

I had a quick thought. It was time to open up our little armory and put the guns out where they might be needed. Morg had kept the key to the wall safe in Dad's bedroom, so I got it out of his drawer and went down the hall to their room. I could still hear Mom talking on the phone, and I could hear a few words, Tory...lovely weather.. They're fine....love to see you, too.

I ducked into the closet, crawled on the floor, and slid her clothes around until I could open the safe. I found a little light switch inside that I hadn't felt before and flipped it on. Everything was still in place, and I grabbed one of the M16A2's and the Remington .45 and the 9mm Beretta off the wall. I took them down to my room, threw them on my bed, and headed back for the ammo. I crawled inside the gun locker and grabbed as many boxes of the .556 rifle, the .45 ACP, and Luger 9mm shells as I could, then I locked up the safe and rearranged Mom's clothes in front of the safe again. I threw the shells on my bed, covered them with my plaid blanket, and closed the door. I loaded the Beretta and went over to Morg's room and put the Beretta under his mattress.

Mom was calling up to have me come down and have a drink and some "horse-derves" with her. I looked back at my bed and thought, we got rid of the threat from Pauly, but now there were bigger storm clouds on the horizon. It was time to grow our little army by enlisting Falk, and by getting some weapons training for Colin, because Australians weren't allowed to have guns. Those idiots turned all their guns in back in 2017 so they could all be destroyed. He'd probably fall in love with our little full automatic rifle.

CHAPTER 43

School continued as before. We got to know our teachers and while they had a few ideas different from our teachers back in Texas, they seem interested in each student. I was just sailing along, doing the minimum studying for my classes and still maxing all my tests. I really enjoyed learning, and it was easy for me. I was swimming on the water polo team, which was really more of a club, since we didn't play real games against other schools. We had a couple of really good players, but as a team, weren't ready for prime time.

Pauly stayed mostly out of sight, but when I did see him, he almost acted friendly. I guess you have to stand up and sometimes beat the shit out of someone to get their respect. I wouldn't respect anyone that wouldn't stand up for themselves, but Pauly had pushed his bad attitude too far. We had a saying in Texas, "Big Hat, No Cattle." That's the attitude that got Pauly his lesson in respect.

Morgan continued to lead the football team to a winning season, their best in the last ten years. The kid was in his element and was frequently in the arms of lovely Carmen. We had several little gatherings at our house with Carmen and Wendy. For some reason, they didn't get along. Carmen was a girl from over on Wing's Neck, where the "New Rich" lived. I couldn't put my finger on the reason, but I think it went back to her family's unwanted intrusion into what little high society that Pocasset had, based of course on Bishop Lane. I couldn't believe that Carmen had bought into that old fraud.

I spent a number of enjoyable hours on the couch with Wendy

in her living room when her mother was gone. I was feeling a physical attraction for her which was getting stronger every time I saw her. She was open to some spirited kissing on the couch, but that's as far as she would go. Girls don't appreciate what that build-up does to us if there's no...release of the tension.

Her mother was very gracious and I did get to have a sit-down, as he called it, with her father. I had a lot of questions about the Coast Guard and the things that they did around the Cape. He told me a few stories about their role in rescuing sailor from their sinking boats in a storm, about stopping drug boats coming into Little Harbor, and most interesting to me, about their discovery of a child sex trafficking operation operating out of Rhode Island. I couldn't imagine any worse crime after he told me of the condition of these young girls they found in the hidden compartments of inbound ships and fishing boats.

I asked him about how he became a Coast Guard Captain after graduating from the Naval Academy. He said, "Simple. All Academy graduates have the option of choosing another branch to serve in, up to a quota. A few of us chose to be Marines, and I chose the Coast Guard. There are a lot of Naval Academy graduates just sitting off the coast of North Korea, waiting for the ball to drop. I wanted to serve closer to home. We lived in Galveston, Ft. Lauderdale, and now here in Hyannis, rather Pocasset, and I could usually go home to my family at night. The Stillman family has lived around here for a century or more, so I'm more or less at home. We did have a six-month deployment to the Gulf a few years ago, though."

His questions for me were mostly about my family and my plans for the future after high school. I didn't get into the details of my Dad's long absences from home.

My talks with him reignited my interest in possibly going to the Air Force Academy. Since Falk would likely go, at least I would have a buddy there. My grades were good enough, but I was lacking in sports and in some kind of community service. I was playing water polo at school, but we didn't have a competitive team. It was just for fun, a chance of getting into the water when the bay froze over.

We had a succession of snow storms, one after another, and the temperature had hovered around freezing the whole time, making for a slushy mess on the roads. I was almost done with Drivers' Ed, and would get my license, but I already had my Restricted Learners, which meant I could drive without an adult in the car with only one passenger, and not at night. I still hadn't built up the courage to ask Mom to drive the Maserati which was so tantalizingly parked in our shack of a garage. Maybe Morg and I should take it out on a training drive one night soon.

CHAPTER 44

Early one cold morning, I put on a sweater and came out of my bedroom to go across the hallway and wake up Morgan for school. It was pitch black outside, and there were a few snowflakes coming down in the glare from our porch lights, which I had been leaving on lately.

I was only wearing my sweater and my skivvies and as I crossed the hallway. I was startled by a shape crossing the hallway, and turned to look. There I saw Marie coming out of the spare bedroom and into the upstairs bathroom. To say I was shocked would not cover it. It was the last thing in the world I expected. She was wearing an old bathrobe, and she had a guilty smile on her face as she looked at me, then ducked into the bathroom.

I went back to Morgan's bedroom and jumped on his bed, hard. He bounced in the air and woke up just before he touched down. "What the bloody HELL?!"

"I just saw Marie in the hallway. She wasn't wearing nothing." This meant she wasn't dressed for work, but I liked the way it came out of my teenage boy mind.

"What? You saw Marie here, in our house?" Morgan said, still trying to wake up.

"Yeah, I guess we'll get the explanation from Mom. But she's in the bathroom now, taking a shower, so don't walk in to take a pee or something until she leaves. I guess breakfast may be late."

We both waited until we heard the bathroom door open to get a glimpse of her with a towel on her head and wearing that old bathrobe ducking back into the bedroom. The bedroom door slammed shut and the show was over. I looked at Morgan and he just wagged his head, and said, "This might be interesting."

We got ready for school and went downstairs to make our own breakfast. We looked in the refrigerator, then in the pantry, but nothing seemed worth the effort. Pretty soon, Marie appeared, not wearing the white chef coat, but in regular clothes. "Do you guys want breakfast?"

Morgan jumped in first. "Sure we do. But we'd also like to welcome you to Calloway Court, since you now appear to be staying here." Well done, Morg, I thought. That was a polite way of getting to the truth. But Calloway Court? He might as well said Calloway Castle.

Marie replied, "Thank you, Morgan. Your mother asked me if I would like to live here. The furnace in the house where I was staying was broken down and I was always cold, and my roommate moved out. I didn't want to stay there by myself. I told your Mother that, and she invited me to live here, for as long as I needed to. I hope that doesn't cause any issues between us. I will have meals on time from now on, since I won't have to travel through the snow three times a day. This doesn't change anything regarding my cooking duties. If you don't mind, I'll just wear regular clothes instead of my chef coat, it's much more comfortable."

And prettier, I thought. She was wearing a tight sweater that showed off her figure underneath. I found it very interesting to watch, and it did look more comfortable. She was also wearing different makeup, it made her look younger and more appealing. Now I thought that I could get used to her living here with us.

She made us hot breakfast and we were off to school. It was treacherous going for our bikes, and it was fun to drive them on the new-fallen snow. We had been stopped once by our police officer, Sgt. Collins, for not having the bikes registered with the town, but we got off with a warning. I had worked on both bikes to make them as close to being street-legal as I could. They still weren't, and would never be, but the cops let us off.

CHAPTER 45

I tried several more times to get through to my Dad at the international number that I had gotten from his Paris office, but no one answered until late last night. It rang and rang, then finally someone picked it up.

"Yes, who is it?" said the voice on the line, in an unrecognizable accent.

I replied, "This is Ethan Calloway. I'm trying to talk to my father, Kirby Calloway."

The voice in the phone asked, "Who? We don't have any Ethan's here. Please don't call again."

"Wait! I'm calling for Kirby...Calloway. I'm Ethan!"

There was a long pause on the phone with some background conversation, and then the voice said, "He will call you." Then the phone went dead.

I sat by the phone for about an hour, and just at midnight, the phone rang and it was our Dad.

"Hello, Ethan! How are you? Is Morgan around, I'd like to talk to him as well."

I said, "Wait a sec and I'll go get him." I ran up the staircase and rousted Morgan out of bed. "It's Dad on the phone!" Morgan jumped and we both raced downstairs, making a pounding metal racket on the spiral stairs.

"Dad, we're here. I'm holding the phone so we can both hear you. How are you, and where are you? We haven't heard from you since Mom got here over two months ago."

He replied, "I've just transferred to our new office in Lagos,

Nigeria, in Africa, and the phone service is lousy. I've tried to call you several times and it went dead before it connected. I'm going to move soon to another office near the capital just outside the Federal District in Abuja, the capital city, and it has good working international connections. This is a private line but definitely not secure, so let's not get into details. I'm fine, I can't tell you exactly what I'm doing, but the work is going well, and I expect that I'll be free to come home a few weeks from now."

We were overjoyed to hear that and both said, "That's great Dad! We can't wait to see you."

Then he asked the big question about the elephant, "Is your Mom still there? How are you getting along with her?"

I said, "We seem to be working things out. She remembered our birthday." I wasn't planning to say anything about Tory, and I had my hand on Morgan's shoulder if he started down that path.

Morgan chimed in, "I made the starting QB on the football team, and we're 5 and 2. I've got a WR, Bennet, like Chase was, and we run some of the same plays. I'm having a great time here. Let's not move anytime soon!"

Dad laughed, and we could hear the pride in his voice, "That's super, Morg. I really wish I could be there to see you play. I am really trying to finish up, but my sale to the government is taking longer than I expected. I'll let you guys know when I start home from here. But please don't tell anyone about me coming home. Just say you don't have any information if anyone asks."

CHAPTER 46

Then I had to ask some of the lingering questions, as delicately and obtuse as I could. "Dad, we're driving the car in the garage. Is that ok? And we found the money you left for us and are spending it as carefully as we can. We could use some funds from you, when you get the chance."

He replied, "I guessed that you would find the car and it's ok for you to drive it, as long as you are legal. But, be careful which buttons you push, there are some features in the car that are not for everyday use. Stick to the normal things and you should be fine."

"Alright, we will. I don't want to eject Morgan through the roof."

Dad laughed and said, "There's nothing like that, but just be careful in it."

Then he added with a tone of suspicion, "How did you find that money? I've been putting money in your bank account and I saw that you haven't been using it. Don't you remember the account I told you about before I left? It's now got a large balance. The account number is in the junk drawer in the kitchen in an envelope with your name on it. That's the account you should be using, not money you might have found just laying around. What else did you find in that location? Everything in there needs to stay locked away. And replace the money in the envelopes in the same denominations. That's important, got it? That's our bailout money."

I drew a complete blank on hearing about the money he was sending us, I didn't remember any conversation we had about any bank account. I admit that my mind was pretty scrambled up at the time, and it must have just flown over my head.

"Ok, Dad. We'll start using that bank account and everything else is already locked away. We'll put the money back, just like we found it. With Mom using that closet, we've moved the location to a safer place."

He panicked, "Mom's using that closet? Oh, shit! There are other things in there that I didn't want her to find."

I tried to calm him, "We have the key to the special location and she'll never see that one. As far as the women's clothing in there, she's already wearing it. She acts like it was a present from you to her, not Paris Girl." I dropped in that last part to see what reaction I would get. Dad was already spooked, and maybe I was feeling a bit vengeful today

"Paris Girl? Sounds like you dug into my stuff and found that picture of Claire in Paris." Now he was sounding a bit irritated.

I said, "Maybe if you were home more, you wouldn't have to have all these secrets laying around for "spies like us" to discover.

He was quiet for a minute, then said, "Claire is a lady I met in Paris. That was Paris, and now I'm in a completely different country and a new job. That's over now," he said, sounding regretful.

"Well, Dad, she looks really pretty and if you liked her, I'm sure she was a nice person. That's not a problem for us," I said, looking at Morgan, who looked dubious. It was now completely obvious that our parents were mentally separated and trying to live their own, new lives. As we were.

CHAPTER 47

Kirby Calloway turned in his chair to look out the window. It was a miserable night in a city not known for hospitable weather. It was the rainy season in Nigeria in late Fall and clear days were rare. The rain poured down all the time, flooding the streets, washing away smaller bridges, and generally making life miserable for those outside the glass buildings that had big A/C systems. Abuja, Nigeria despite its beauty and native charm was nothing like Paris.

Calloway was a senior sales executive for a large American security software company. He had spent his last three years in Paris, following an at-large posting from Dallas, Texas, to the European Union. This assignment had kept him hopping between European capitals as well as the Mid-East, or the "ME", as it was known in the trade.

He was viewed as an international expert in computer security, and was employed by a well-known computer software company to help their clients across the ME and EU plan and execute computer security protocols between systems located all over his area. This sometimes gave him access to highly confidential, and occasionally SECRET information in these systems.

Calloway was a middle-aged man, rather handsome, with green-blue eyes, tall and lanky, and under his white shirt and bland blue tie was a body as fit as he could make it, given his schedule. His hair was black with little red tints, trending to be curly on the sides which his crew-cut rarely showed. He had a reddish-black beard that he kept well-trimmed.

To be able to sell multi-million dollar security software systems successfully, he needed to develop trusted relationships, and even friendships with top technology people and business executives in all these countries. This he was especially good at, since his pleasant nature, intelligence, and good looks were traits that were good at developing these relationships, particularly now, as more and more top IT roles were taken by women. He was welcomed with open arms, and sometimes open legs in several European capitals.

He generally had his selection among the senior technology women in the companies that he sold to, but he had no romantic connections with any of them. Even though many of them were beautiful and very talented, it was that combination that made many men afraid to approach them. That made Calloway different, he found them infinitely preferable to the office girls that made obvious plays for him. Not that he discouraged them.They admired Calloway's genuine friendliness and his openness, as well as his good looks. He was frequently invited to their social events; cocktail parties, boat trips on the Seine, and even in their internal retreats. But there wasn't any one particular woman for him. He found himself looking for a softer side to their personalities, rather than talking about gigabytes and picohertz.

But recently, there was one woman in particular who had caught his eye. She wasn't some kind of technologist, and she wasn't even a customer. She was a Human Relations Manager for one of his largest clients in Paris. Her name was Claire Montand. She was an American born in San Francisco, who had moved with her family to France when she was a child and had lived in Paris her whole life.

It was five months ago when they had met at an embassy cocktail party in Paris where she had come as someone else's date. He had waited to the last minute to get a date to this very prestigious party, so he ended up coming alone, which he didn't mind every once in a while. He noticed her standing by the windows in a designer white dress. Her long black hair was upswept into a chignon with tendrils of hair framing her face. Her image reflected brightly off the window, so it looked like there were two images of her. She was beautiful and charming, as Kirby could see from her interactions with people at the party, many of which seemed to know her.

Her date, some minor embassy official, seemed more interested in chatting up the men at the party, which gave Kirby the opportunity to introduce himself.

"Hello, my name is Kirby Calloway. Are you enjoying the party?" It seemed like a harmless enough opening shot.

She turned to face him directly with her light brown eyes flashing a golden center, and her face turned from an expression of boredom to an expression of annoyance. She and her date were not working out.

"It's none of your business if I am enjoying the party. And I certainly don't care if you are, either."

She spoke with a luxurious French accent that he found entrancing, especially with her annoyance. French people, he had found, get easily annoyed with Americans. Kirby could tell she wasn't having a good time, especially since she had been abandoned by her date for a younger man.

She hadn't turned away, so he tried a somewhat apologetic response. "Ok. I guess you and I both are tired of these big events. All the real business gets done when people leave to go find a room to talk and deal, leaving the rest of us to eat the shrimp and drink the martinis. I might as well go home. It's been fun."

She looked around the room, assessing whether there was something more interesting to do than entertain this dull, but faintly attractive American.

She looked at him, and then turned away. "Then go then. I'm not going with you, I have a date." She looked around again and he was still nowhere to be found. Most of the men there to make a deal had already gone off to private dinners or to a room in the hotel to talk business or politics. A few abandoned women were talking in groups, looking over their shoulders for some handsome bachelor to come rescue them. Several were eyeing Kirby.

She weighed her options, then suddenly looked back at him, smiled and shook her head, and started slowly swaying. Kirby was instantly intrigued.

"Actually, I'm having the time of my life. Can't you tell? I'm just waiting for the band to start playing."

"I don't hear any music, are you sure there's going to be entertainment?"

She laughed and taunted him, "I can imagine a place where there is plenty of entertainment and maybe even some music playing." She looked at him, wondering what he would do with that line.

"Now that you mention it, leaving this party to go somewhere with music sounds like a fine idea."

She softened a bit, then said, "My name is Claire. What did you say your name was again?" Calloway bowed slightly and gave her his business card. She looked at it briefly before handing it back to him. "Mr. Kirby Calloway. Don't you have some big deal to close tonight?"

He didn't know which one of them was steering the conversation into the bedroom, but he liked the way it was going.

Ok, don't get too cute here. "Not really. I'm waiting for my meeting with the "Institute du Technologie" tomorrow after which I will know whether there a big deal here for me or not."

That didn't seem to impress her, but she said "Ok, then. You just proved that you are harmless and slightly interesting. Let's go and you buy me a drink."

They stopped by the hotel bar and he noticed a few of his acquaintances there, waiting for drinks, looking at them together with interest. He thought, it certainly wasn't because of me; I keep a very low profile. Was it her, and was it because she wasn't with her date? Kirby hoped not, he didn't need to make enemies in Paris.

She ordered a lemon martini and Kirby ordered a Jack Daniels, rocks. They retreated to a private corner of the room and sipped their drinks.

Kirby looked around to make sure they weren't being noticed.

Everyone in the main ballroom was into their own conversations, and Kirby and Claire were easily ignored. No one else especially wanted to be noticed, either.

He started the conversation, "Are you French? You seem to have an occasional American lilt in your voice."

She replied, "I was born in California, but we moved to Nice when I was four. My Dad became a diplomat, so we moved to Paris when I was seven, and I've lived here ever since. I love it here, and will never leave!" she concluded with a cute little laugh.

Then Kirby asked, "What do you do? I think I've noticed you over at one of my client companies. I am in the software security business."

She looked at him carefully, "Yes, I remember you going into a meeting at my place. I'm your friendly neighborhood Human Resources Vice-President. I decide who we hire and who we need to get rid of. I'm a good judge of people, so I'm interviewing you now."

He was suddenly suspicious of her sudden interest. "For what position?" he asked.

She looked down at her drink, took a sip, and replied, "I have several openings right now. What are you good at doing?"

Kirby hadn't had an HR job interview since he left Navy Intelligence, so he had to think about it, assessing what he could and couldn't say about himself. His head was spinning with her flirtations.

He leaned in towards her. "I'm good at explaining how complicated things work to my clients," he explained. "I'm good at explaining the benefits, risks, and rewards, and I'm good at closing the sale. And I'm really good at keeping secrets."

She looked up at him, stepped forward, but just out of kissing distance and said seductively, "Good, I've got one for you to keep."

CHAPTER 48

Her hotel room had the same scent of perfume that he had smelled when he first met her. It was highly intoxicating.

She locked the door and came to him, inviting his kiss. He put his arms around her and pulled her in, crushing her breasts against his chest. He bent down to kiss her welcoming lips and she responded with an open mouth kiss.

He reached around her neck and found the zipper to her dress, one motion and the expensive silk hit the floor.

She reached down for his belt buckle and released it, then pulled his belt all the way through with a whipping sound. She bent down to unfasten his pants while he reached over her shoulders and undid her bra. It fell to the floor along with his pants. She stood up and kissed him again, this time more savagely, rubbing her nipples in the hair of his chest. He reached behind her again, cupping her ass, then raised his hands to her waist and slid her panties down to her ankles. She leaned back and circled him with her long, silky legs. They fell to the unmade bed, and he pulled her up around him and slipped deep inside her.

Their lovemaking was explosive for both of them, and Kirby had never been with a woman who anticipated his every move and moved her body to flow with him. It was an amazing romantic experience.

The next morning, Kirby woke before dawn, got up out of bed slowly and quietly got dressed. She lay asleep on her side. Her long black hair was draped around her shoulders and partially covered her naked breast. He took his business card out of his wallet, and threw it on the bed. Then he realized he didn't even have her whole name. She was just Claire. He took a rose from the flower arrangement and laid it on his pillow next to her. He left the room and went back to his hotel. He would find her, and had to see her again.

After that night, they saw each other nearly every day while Kirby was in Paris. He loved the city of Paris and she was a very knowledgeable guide to all the most interesting places.

Their favorite places were along the Seine River, and the many shops and cafés along its banks. There is one little spot that was their favorite. It is called the "Square du Vert Galant". It is a little green space located just on the tip of the Île de la Cité, a little island in the Seine. It was built in tribute to the mistresses of Henry IV, and they enjoyed sitting together by the water and watching the "bateaux's" go by. There, they talked about their pasts; Claire talked about growing up in Paris with her father after her mother died when she was fifteen.

Kirby told her about his two boys; their exploits in Texas, his concern for them living with a difficult woman, their mother, and his plans for getting them all together again when he could escape the crushing pressure of his job.

Little by little after their first explosive encounter, they were able to get to know each other better without resorting to steamy midnight encounters. They lay on a blanket by the River, with a view of Norte Dame. He held her, looking down at her beautiful face and half-closed brown eyes, and he wondered what she was thinking. He saw her as a passionate romantic, with a taste for adventure and a love for Parisian life and culture. He wondered if she would be happy anywhere else.

She lay in his arms, and saw him as a deeply honorable man, quite intelligent, awkwardly passionate, and torn between his job and raising his boys to be men. He had defaulted that job to his flighty wife. She was concerned about him and his relationship with his two boys, who were at the age at which they needed a father there to get them from childhood into being successful adults. She planned to find a way to help him, especially if she was ever his wife. But she was afraid she would lose him if his work took him away from Paris.

She looked up at the pale sun through the trees, breathed in the scent of the flowers and the earthy scent of the Seine. Then she turned and brought his head down, for a long, slow kiss. Ah, Paris.

CHAPTER 49

It was a typical early spring day in Paris. The weather had been perfect for weeks, and he and Claire we able to go for long walks in the late afternoon sun in the beautiful parks in Paris. He loved their time together. But he also loved the work that he did. He loved meeting with new customers, figuring out their needs, and then helping them to get all the value they can from the products that his company sold.

The offices for Security Software Inc. were housed in the business park at La Defense, Paris. Kirby was ensconced in his cubicle, reading the latest global news and the procurement notices that every modern nation puts out. He noticed an interesting convergence down in Nigeria.

They had just had an election in which a reformer candidate, Muhari Clarion had just won, despite the opposition of a powerful opponent, Kwandanbo. Even the Christian clerics like Mbaka had been against him which was surprising since that, even though he was Muslim, he had a record of opposing radical Islamic groups like Boko Haram and their war against Christians.

They were requesting bids on a wide range of services, from new construction of roads and highways, port facilities, low-cost housing, hospitals, and most interesting to Kirby, a new technology program including security software.

Kirby put together a lead report on what seemed to be a big opportunity for his security software company and took it to his boss, Helen White. He knocked on the glass door of her office, seeing her at her desk looking through some routine sales reports. He held up the folder containing his research and bid proposal. She waved him in, and pointed to one of the chairs in front of her desk.

She took a quick look at the exec summary, then touched the intercom button, and said, "Sally, can you come in here, please.?"

While they waited for Sally to make it down the hall, Helen read the exec summary again, and asked, "This looks like a great opportunity. We'll put it through the evaluation process, but I think it'll be a go. Are you prepared to go down there and ramrod this sale?"

Kirby was taken aback. "Do you mean for me to leave Paris and move to Nigeria for the duration? I'm not sure I would want to do that right now." Claire was his anchor.

Helen put on her most persuasive smile. "Kirby, this may be the biggest thing that we have ever seen. A security system for the whole government of Nigeria? Think what that would mean for your future in this company."

Sally came to the door, and Helen said, "Sally. Kirby here has put together a case for a new effort in Nigeria. Here is the information." She gave Kirby's folder to Sally. She opened it, and her eyes grew wide.

"I want a proposal team put on this immediately, and within two weeks, I want a detailed scope and cost proposal to submit. Got it?"

Sally responded, "Yes M'am! We'll get on it now." She scurried out the office and down the hallway, stopping at several doors to alert her team to the opportunity and to schedule their first meeting.

"Kirby, I know this is probably a big disruption to you personally, but the sales commission on this deal is in the high six-figure range. We'll take care of you down there, get you a house and a staff. I'll alert the installation boys and girls to get involved in the proposal to start planning what they will need down there, IF we win."

"Kirby, what do you see as our chances to win this?"

Kirby said, "Ma'm, I honestly don't know. Let me do some background research and look for some hooks and levers we have or can develop. But I really believe it's worth the investment."

Helen considered his response and her understanding of his personal situation. She had met Claire, and realized that she was at the top of Kirby's mind.

She then offered, "I know your situation with Claire. I will try to find a way of having her follow you down there if you will accept the transfer. I know that there is a lot of bad press about Nigeria, but I have heard that it is a beautiful country with a very promising future. We could really help them straighten out some of their corruption problems with our product. This opportunity is too big to pass up, both for you and the company. What do you say?"

Kirby thought very hard. He weighed the pros and cons, and the possibility of losing Claire. The possibility of six-figure commission checks and Helen's promise to help him convince Claire to come to Africa and join him finally made the decision easier.

"Ok, I'll agree to move down there and push this thing along. It's too important for us and for me, and I can see where it might be an aid to the new President, if he is truly going to be a reformer, and if he can stay in office. But I really want Claire to join me, if I can convince her."

"Well good. If you can convince her, I'll work to get her safely down there."

"Ok, I give it a try."

CHAPTER 50

Kirby left a cab waiting downstairs at the curb in front of her apartment as he arrived to pick her up.

"Where are we going? It better be some place nice, considering the work I put into looking this good for you."

She was wearing a tight-fitting silver and blue cocktail dress. Her hair was upswept again with little blue flowers.

"You'll see. It's worth the trip." Their cab wound around Paris and ascended the Butte Montremarte until they arrived at the small gate in front of the Hotel Particulier Montremarte. Claire got out and took a long look around. "It's beautiful up here. I love visiting Montremarte with you. But where are we going?"

"Look up there, go through that wrought-iron gate into the garden", Kirby informed her.

"But that's somebody's house." she pointed out to him, quizzically.. She was looking at a white, three-story building with a beautiful garden on its front lawn.

"Well, it used to belong to the Hermes family, but now it's the Hotel Particulier Montremarte and that's where we are going."

"To a hotel? Kirby, my dear. I do appreciate your thinking, but I'm not prepared to stay overnight. Look at me; I'm an evening-out kind of girl right now," and she twirled slowly around to show the silver and blue sparkle highlights in her dress. He laughed at her, and took her hand.

They walked through the front doors of the hotel, and there it was. The Maitre d' opened the door, and graciously welcomed her as if she was a frequent visitor to this very exclusive restaurant.

"My darling, this is one of the best restaurants in Paris, the "Mandragora". We're just here for dinner, and I have something to tell you."

She felt a thrill running through her body, she had been expecting his marriage proposal for weeks. Things had been so perfect for them since they met that it had to end with them together.

The interior of the tiny restaurant was decorated with large velvet drapes, which made each little alcove a very private place.

Their dinner was amazing, poached lobster and seared scallops on an asparagus risotto, with dark chocolate mousse for dessert. Claire knew the moment was approaching for Kirby to present the ring and propose, and she waited breathlessly.

He took her hand, squeezed it slightly and said, "Claire, I have some news, news that will affect us."

"Wha..what?"

"I've been offered a new job in Nigeria starting soon. It's a great opportunity for me, and for us. I want you to come with me."

She sat there for a moment, frozen with disappointment and anger. She stared at her plate with tight lips, where her Mousse is melting rapidly.

She looked at him, her eyes full of tears. "This is not what this night was for!" Kirby was mystified. What was she expecting?

Claire responded through her tears, "I love you, but I'm not moving out into the jungle with you, and live in your treehouse or whatever. You know I love Paris, and don't want to ever leave here."

"I've lived here my whole life. All of my friends are here. I'm sorry, I love you, Kirby, but I cannot agree to go live in Nigeria."

With that she said, "Please take me home. If you decide that Nigeria is where you want to be, go live there by yourself. I'm sure there will be plenty of island girls there for you to play with," she said bitterly.

Kirby intelligently thought better of informing Claire of the fact that Nigeria was not a jungle island somewhere. He had lost this round and it was better for now just to shut up. She would have time to process his invitation and hopefully accept it when she got over her apparent disappointment with their evening. What was she expecting, a marriage proposal?

They drove home in silence. When Claire got out of the cab, she was crying. "All I can say is...", then she stopped, turned away and said..."Goodbye, Kirby."

CHAPTER 51

Kirby was wrapping up his job for SSI in preparation for his move to Nigeria. He was getting his accounts transferred and new people were taking over functions that Kirby had owned. He had been individually briefing these people all day, so it came as a bit of a surprise when James "Jake" Weldon came into his office in the La Defense offices, and sat down in front of him.

Kirby looked at him and asked, "Did you have an appointment?"

Weldon laughed in his little sarcastic way. "I've heard you are going to Nigeria to pursue some big projects down there with the new President. I can say now that your work at the Institute here is done, and by the way, good job on that. Your input on the Chinese was very useful. But the Nigerian angle is really interesting to us as well. Nigeria is always such a mess; they have a Constitution much like ours, but every few years some military bozo rounds up a bunch of his buddies and overthrows the elected leader. Then they assassinate him and rule for a couple years until one party or the other gets tired of the military dictatorship and throws them out, and of course, they get assassinated. It's a great playground for us, and with all that oil money in the bank, there's lots of ways to pay for influence."

Kirby sees where this is going, and asks, "So what do you want from me?" With all the transition activities at SSI, he had momentarily forgotten about his other job. As a strictly patriotic act, Calloway had agreed to provide intelligence about Russian, Chinese, and Iranian activities that he might come across in the course of his SSI sales activity. These players were constantly struggling against each other as well as the USA for influence in Europe and the Mid-East. It had seemed like a good idea, at the time, he thought rue-fully. But, the Agency had been a good source for understanding who all the players were in a given situation.

Weldon lit a cigarette which was against all policy and good manners, then asked, "Do you mind?" He took a couple of long drags from the glowing cigarette, then put it out in the palm of his hand. The smoke cloud over his head lingered, and people sitting in the surrounding cubicles waved their hands or file folders to chase the smoke and the smell away. He tossed the butt and brushed off his hand in Kirby's wastebasket.

"We've already got a good team down there. I've assigned one of our best agents to help you out. His name is Katanga, and I think you will get along fine,"

"Katanga? Isn't that the name of the bad guy in a Bond movie? Oh wait, that's the name of a mining town in Nairobi. Are you sure that's his name?"

"Yeah, that's his name. You'll like him."

Weldon got up to leave. The smoke cloud he had created still lingered around his head.

"One more thing. We have a couple of other teams working down there. We're worried about the Chinese pushing their OROB initiatives in that region, and they've been pretty successful with it. Once you read about it, you'll see what a dastardly plan it really is. But don't worry about what the other teams might be doing. Just stick to your own guns."

"Ok, Jake. Sounds like there's plenty to do already."

"Yes, there is. We are really counting on you getting that secu-rity hook into Nigeria. That will give us visibility to everything going on in the area. Good luck with that!"

CHAPTER 52

He looked around his apartment, suitcases packed, all of his work papers and research packed in a trunk, and another opened, large steamer trunk full of software brochures and past slide-show presentations. The last thing he packed was a photo of himself and his two sons, Ethan and Morgan at one of Morgan's elementary school football games. Morgan was wearing "15" and was happiest with a football in his hand playing quarterback. His passes were a little shaky at that age, but he enjoyed playing and he worked hard at it.

Ethan was different. He was the "A" student who loved mechanical things. He had assembled his own toolbox, and had built Morgan a waving wooden passing target powered by an electric motor, and a small radio controlled Corvette convertible that he would race up and down the street until the mailman turned the corner and ran over it.

He put the picture carefully in the open steamer trunk.

He really missed Claire and the times they had spent together. He had tried to call her several times, but she had never answered. He assumed now that if they were to ever be together, he would have to move back to Paris.

When he and Claire broke up, there was no reason to hang around, besides he was looking forward to a whole new opportunity on a continent and in a country he'd never visited before. He was a little concerned at the potential living conditions in Nigeria, but SSI. had arranged a long-term stay in a nice hotel on Lagos Island, the Barcelona International.

The long flight from Paris to Lagos was a morning flight leaving at 8:00 on Turkish Airlines, landing at Murtala Muhammad International.

His first stop was going to be in Lagos because there were a number of large companies operating huge ports and logistics facilities, as well as many of the National Banks. These would be important computer systems that would need to be integrated into a national transaction security system, which was the software that he had proposed to the Nigerian Government. All the bidders were now conducting their "due diligence" prior to confirming their bids.

His other employer was also eager for him to start collecting intelligence as well.

The port city was amazingly busy at all levels. People carried fresh produce on push carts as well as on the backs of donkeys and the occasional camel. There were trucks moving through the crowds, from small pickups to multi-trailer container trucks. All were moving to and from the markets and the container ship crane docks. Most of the containers were snatched off the giant ships by the huge cranes and "flown" over to a line of trucks that were loaded up and quickly drove off to other markets and big and small businesses. The containers held an astonishing variety of goods; food, furniture, cars, electronics, and sometimes more dubious cargo, drugs, weapons, and even human slaves kept in abominable conditions.

He looked out at the Lagos harbor lights reflecting on the oily, brown water leading from the shipyards and docks in Ajegunle out to the lagoon, and eventually out to the ocean. He had decided to start his investigation by studying the movement of different kinds of cargo in and out of the ports. He was talking to the operators looking for information on cargoes of weapons, strategic materials like trillium, drugs, and human trafficking. His cover was as a sales engineer working on a proposal for the national security system. It was important to learn about the processes and system the port operators used to move and track cargo. This was a major opportunity for theft and trafficking.

There were large container ships and super-tankers moving back and forth into the Apapa Quays. His temporary office in the Leventis area overlooked the harbor, and he could see ships traveling the Lagos Lagoon channel. But his work here in Lagos was over. He now had a good feel for the major activities of the port which was a major contributor to the national economy. They were also a vital strategic resource, one that needed national oversight, which appeared to be generally lacking. He would get a better feel for the whole picture when he moved from the coastal city of Lagos up to the central city and the capital of Nigeria, Abuja.

Kirby packed up all his notes, a few videos and pictures he had taken, and caught a morning Turkish Air flight to Nnamdi Azikiwe airport a few miles from the capital and checked into the Transcorp Hilton Hotel, his home until he found a permanent residence, if SSI won the security software contract. If not, he wasn't sure. He thought he would then request a leave of absence and go home.

Abuja was a bustling modern city, with a generally reliable infrastructure for traffic and communications. The Presidential Villa was located at the historic spot at the foot of Aso Rock, a giant monolith of granite. Its geologic significance was not lost to the ancient tribes of Nigeria. Abuja had been a religious and governing hub for thousands of years. Aso rock was named by the Asokoro tribe and it means "Victory".

And it would be Kirby Calloway's new home as soon as he could establish one.

National Map of Nigeria - Capital Abuja

CHAPTER 53

The lights glaring out from the Presidential Villa below the monolith Aso Rock were not just for showing off the beauty of the rolling grounds of the provincial capital, but they also had a sinister purpose, they were to spotlight anything moving within a mile radius of the Villa. Things were a bit unsettled here at the present time. There were frequent police patrols around the wall surrounding the Villa, and anyone trying to enter was thoroughly searched. Anyone who failed the search was detained, sometime indefinitely.

Kirby Calloway had moved his operations from the port city of Lagos up to the national capital in Abuja, a city of three-million, and the art and music capital center as well. He had almost no time to get settled into his hotel suite at the Abuja Transcorp Hilton Things were rapidly evolving. His company had submitted its bid for the security software contract. Calloway had reviewed it and put his signature on it.

A new President, Muhari Clarion had just been elected, one who promised to stamp out corruption and remove illicit foreign influence in his country. That had been the pledge of all of the past Presidents, and Calloway wondered if this guy would be any different. The President and his Minister of Commerce was meeting with the commercial attaches from each interested country to give them his message and assess who were going to be his favorites going forward. Calloway already had an appointment to meet with President Muhari as soon as he got the call in his hotel room.

Calloway wasn't the US commercial attache, there wasn't one.

The last one, William Sitze, had been constantly intimidated by local thugs hired by one of the foreign companies, probably the Chinese, and resigned before the election. The US ambassador to Nigeria, Marlo Franklin, had asked Kirby Calloway to temporarily take on that role. He said that he had gotten the suggestion from President Muhari. That was a bit of a mystery for now.

His phone, which was sitting on his hotel desk in front of him, jingled with its non-specific ring. It wasn't the call he was expecting.

He picked it up and answered slowly, "Calloway."

"Hello, my friend", he heard and recognized the voice of an acquaintance from an agency company. It was Borowitz, a Swiss businessman that now worked as an agent for a number of companies in Nigeria. "We have quite a mess here, don't you agree?" Calloway hesitated. This could be just a fishing expedition. He said, "Hello Felix. Well, there are a lot of moving pieces."

Kirby decided to continue, "With the ascendancy of President Muhari, we have to find out who his favorites are. When he was an MP, he had good relations with the Igbo Christians Nationalists who were the driving force in getting him elected, though I don't think he was ever a member. He commanded the Naval division of the Armed Services that was considered the best one they had. He seemed to try to play nice with everyone except the Boko Haram. I think he wants them exterminated. And he has an uneasy relationship with General Kwandanbo."

Borowitz thought a minute and said, "I've heard about him courting the Russians and the Chinese for aid. I think he's suspicious about you Americans, he thinks he sees the CIA behind every palm tree."

Kirby asked, "Well what about the Iranians? I'm sure they would like to make inroads while there is disorder here."

"Yeah probably, that's right. I haven't seen them making a play yet, but I'm sure they would like in. Ever since Muhari exposed all the corruption of the Goodluck Jonathan regime and the Nuyongas, and the billions of oil revenue that they squirreled away in the

Caymans and God knows where else, everyone wants to get a chunk of that when the money starts flowing again."

Borowitz continued. Kirby just let him talk. Some of this might be good.

"I have a man on the inside. He was a Lieutenant in the Navy in Muhari's division, and he's a guy that Muhari trusts. He tells me who is coming and going over in the Villa." Borowitz paused to see if Calloway would volunteer anything.

Calloway offered nothing, so he asked ,"Is it true that you are going in to see the President tomorrow?" Kirby guessed his inside guy was doing his job.

"Yes, as the very-recently designated commercial attache, I've been summoned to present my America's congratulations for his "election" as well as to be a conduit for the time being for American companies who want to have a presence here. He doesn't want to be bombarded with solicitations from hundreds of companies that are eager for a piece of the pie, if there is one.

Borowitz seemed impressed. "Doesn't that make you the guy who controls which Americans see the President?"

Calloway answered, "Not really. All these companies are doing their best through low ranking officials to get them to write them into their spending plans. I have little real control over that. The best I can do tomorrow is to get clearer direction as to what President Muhari wants from me. I also have to present my own company's interests in that meeting too. That's who pays my salary, not the US government. I'm doing them a favor which I hope provides a good return on the time I'll have to spend on it."

Calloway reflected a minute on what he had learned from Borowitz.

"Borowitz, there is something you can do for me. You have been in contact with the Russians, and I need to meet their attaché. I want to play them against the Chinese who I see as barging in here, trying to push everyone else out. They seem to see Nigeria as their anchor for future expansion. And they are my biggest commercial threat"

"Yes, my friend. I would be happy to introduce you. I think you will find him to be a very interesting man. He shares many of your interests. I'm sure he would be open to meeting after your meeting with the President. And you need to meet his lovely assistant."

CHAPTER 54

Kirby took a rental car from his hotel to the front gate of the Villa and stopped at the Presidential Guard Brigade post. Actually it was its own building with its own scanning equipment, security force, and a lock-up.

Kirby was swarmed by a group of guards, so he showed his invitation to the meeting, his company photo ID, and was even asked for his Texas drivers' license. Each time he showed one of these documents, an animated discussion ensued, that Kirby couldn't read as positive or negative. Knowing the fate of those rogue visitors who fail the screening, Kirby just waited patiently, sweating it out.

Finally, the chief guard elbowed his way into the crowd of guards, looked at the ID, then looked at Calloway, and then waved him on through the crowd of gate guards and past the Villa gate.

The palace was huge with multiple white stone buildings connected by corridors lined with marble columns, and it was topped by a huge green dome.

Kirby was then directed to park in a line of cars near the main entrance to the Villa. There was a gentleman waiting at the designated parking spot, escorted by two Villa guards with AK-47 rifles.

"Doctor Calloway? I am your escort, Muhammad Bin El-Rashad. Please call me Mo." Calloway is surprised by his promotion to Doctor, but decided to let it slide for now.

"Yes, I am Calloway." Mr. Mo smiled a very formal smile, and then said, "Welcome to the Palace of Peace, the "Qasr Alsalam". Please follow me."

Calloway followed Mr. Mo into the Villa, flanked by the two armed guards. They went down a long, white stone corridor, then turned into another long, white stone corridor. Each of the hallways were festooned with native art, including carved masks, paintings of local scenes, and collections of animal heads and elephant tusks. They came to a large ornate door, decorated with golden trim and hundreds of jewels.

Mr. Mo knocked twice on the door, and it was quickly opened, showing a large room, covered in beautiful rugs and wall hangings. Calloway expected to see a Golden Throne, but instead, there was a set of large plush sofas, sitting on a huge native rug, facing a large plush chair and a 72-inch big screen TV. Just behind the largest sofa was a large Chinese secretary's desk, inlaid with intricate "Mother of Pearl" white shells in ornate patterns. The secretary, a young black woman, had her meeting schedule and iPad ready for action.

Mr. Mo escorted me to face the gentleman seated in the large chair, and presented Kirby to President Muhari. "Great President of Nigeria, Muhari Clarion, I present to you, Doctor Kirby Calloway, Commerce Delegate from the United States of America, Texas."

The President waved Calloway over to the end of the couch closest to his chair, and waved Mr. Mo to the other end, still within earshot of the conversation.

He was surprised by his addition of Texas to the end of his title, but he could see that it was greeted with respect. Texans have been producing oil in African countries since the 1930's and except for diamonds, oil revenues have made some African countries rich, while making other countries dictatorial and poor. It seemed to Kirby that was worth something here.

The President was wearing a suit fashioned after military style like an Eisenhower jacket, but made with $1000 worth of silk. He was wearing a gold Rolex and a set of large diamond rings, which set off a very ugly ring, a gold ring with a square top, with a beaver chomping on some tree limbs, the class ring of the Massachusetts Institute of Technology, MIT. Calloway looked at his own ring finger and adjusted his MIT ring to make sure the beaver was on top. He thought, well, being an MIT grad from Texas might just play well here.

"Sit down, Doctor Calloway." Then he waved to a servant who brought a pot of tea and poured three cups. Mr. Mo took his cup, so Kirby took his. Mr. Mo sipped his tea, so Kirby sipped his. The President picked up his cup, and then set it back down. Calloway guessed that he had probably repeated this little welcome ceremony several times before this meeting, and was "tea-ed out".

The President started. He looked directly at Calloway. "I've been looking forward to this meeting, Dr. Calloway. There are a number of things that I have been wanting to discuss with you. First, I understand that you are also the representative of the United States with regard to commercial dealings. I know many American companies, but in my new capacity, I do not wish to have to deal with them all. My new Minister of Commerce will now give you a list of specific needs that we have along with a rough budget in each category". He paused and waved in a short, bearded man who walked from behind the couch carrying a closed folder that seemed to have a significant bulge. He gave Calloway the large folder, and he tucked it in next to him on the couch.

"I expect that you will meet later with Minister Umanda to discuss this item of business. I trust that you will be judicious and fair in your recommendations. I need not tell you, because I assume that you are a man of honor, that some companies will seek to influence you, but I can trust that you will not be unduly swayed by such. You must also be careful with this information, as there are certain groups who would like to see it misused." He looked down at his ring, then at mine. His meaning was quite clear on that point. Two MIT graduates do not break trust with one another. He also indicated that bribes were acceptable as long as Kirby didn't violate that trust. Kirby decided right then. No bribes.

He continued, "I am also aware that you are the business representative for Security Software, Inc. Unfortunately, in your new capacity of the American attaché, I cannot consider including your company in any bidding for work for my government. I have included a letter to that effect in the documents that you have been given."

Calloway's heart sank. His commission check would have been many tens of thousands of dollars. And he would lose access to the main computer systems of the new regime, which was actually his other main goal.

Calloway responded, "Yes, your Excellency, but I think my company and our software can help protect your new government from further misdirection of funds."

The President held up his hand and said, "Yes, yes, Doctor. But this has already been taken care of. You need not be concerned any further. Now, I do expect you to attend my installation ceremony and the celebration afterwards. Thank you for visiting with me."

Mr. Mo stood up suddenly, and Kirby followed suit. Then he nodded his thanks to the President, but he was already consulting his secretary for the name of the next supplicant.

Kirby followed Mr. Mo out through the gilded doors, through the white stone hallways, and out to the parking lot.

Damn, damn, thought Kirby. Not only do I have to filter through all these company files and deal with their attempted bribes, but I have been excluded from getting the inside access that I need to complete my work here. To say nothing of my lost commissions.

Mr. Mo walked him to his government Mercedes and his driver was waiting. "Goodbye for now, Doctor Calloway. I shall be in touch to set up your appointment with Minister Umanda. In the meantime, please study the information provided to be ready for further discussions."

Calloway responded, "You know I'm not a doctor, why do you continue to address me with that term?"

Mr. Mo smiled, "Because it pleases the President. He cannot be seen dealing with people that...do not have the proper pedigrees. Since you are both graduates of that school, MIT, he has decided to honor you with the degree. Please use it from now on, if you please."

Calloway got into the back seat with the large folder, and his driver closed the door and got in. Calloway thought, well at least this morning hasn't been a total loss. He now has a new title, Doctor Calloway, even if he was not.

CHAPTER 55

He waited until he got back to his hotel room to consider the contents of the folder. He threw the folder on top of his little hotel desk, laying it on top of his closed laptop. He took off his coat and draped it across a chair, along with his tie.

He got a cold Heineken out of the refrigerator and sat down in the uncomfortable chair in front of the desk. He looked at the folder with concern and disgust. He had been frozen out of what was sure to be a very large security software contract. In addition to his commission, it would've given him the opportunity to connect with computers all over Europe and the Middle East and accomplish his true purpose. He picked up the folder as if it were a basket of dead fish and opened it.

There were two loose documents, and a sealed envelope inside the folder. He set the envelope aside, and considered the first document. It was on stiff parchment paper with gilded edges, and as he turned it over, he read; University of Nigeria, Doctor of Philosophy in World Affairs, awarded to Kirby Ethan Calloway, signed by the head of the university and Muhari Clarion, President of Nigeria.

He set it down and stared at it. Then he thought, well I guess this makes it official. I am now Doctor Kirby Ethan Calloway.

Just then the phone rang over by the bed, startling him out of his focus on his new title. He wondered who could be calling? Almost nobody knows I'm here. He got up and went over to the phone, sat on the bed, and answered it.

"Hello, Kirby? This is Helen White." Helen White was his boss at Security Software who he'd only met once three years ago, when he got the assignment to Paris. He could hear many other voices talking behind Helen White, shouting congratulations and whoops.

"We all wanted to call and congratulate you on the big win! It's the largest contract we've ever seen. Do you have a copy of the contract? We only have a fax here. Do you believe it? The order came in a few minutes ago, BY FAX!

Kirby took the phone over to his desk pulling the phone cord to its full extension. He picked up the second document, and started to read it. It was a contract for a full array of security software, servers, workstations, and consulting work for his company to the government of Nigeria. No wonder they were prohibited from bidding on the work. It had been officially awarded literally minutes before his meeting with President Muhari, before he had even entered the white stone corridors. And at the bottom of the page there were two signature blocks, a blank one for him, Doctor Calloway, and the other one, already signed by Umanda Killowon.

"Thank you very much. This is really great. Thanks. I'm looking forward to setting up shop over in the Villa to do the install, and I'll need a team, sooner rather than later."

Helen came back on the phone alone. Kirby guessed the party had moved down to Kelly's Bar on the corner down from their offices.

She said, "We will be getting your commission check in the mail as soon as the contract is signed. The first one will be for one-hundred thousand dollars, and there will be two more like that as the work progresses. The next one will be cut when we are up and running, then the final one after a year of successful operations. How does that sound to you, Kirby?"

Kirby laughed and replied. "Pretty good, but now it's Doctor Kirby, I've received a Ph.D from the University of Nigeria as well as this award. Not a bad day's work. And, oh by the way, I'm signing the contract just now. It's already been signed by their minister of commerce." Kirby did not mention the other contents of the folder. That was not company business, at least not THIS companies' business.

Helen laughed, and said, "Fabulous, just great news. Send us the signed documents. I'll get you in touch with our contracts people now to settle the details. They can take it from here. And Kirby, we will need you to stay on there for a while to set up and run the operation, for at least a year. We'll get you a house instead of that dingy old hotel room."

Kirby said, "That'll be fine, this place is getting a bit cramped. But I will need to take some time off before we get started to go home and spend a little time with my kids. It's been far too long for them to live with just the influence of their mother." He also thought about his other job the President gave him, to help select companies to bid on the portfolio of work. That was going to be a lot of work, but a great opportunity to gather competitive intelligence. He guessed giving him access to other companies confidential information wasn't a big deal in the twisted politics of Nigeria.

Helen said, "So they have been living with their mother? How interesting that must be."

"Yes, it's going to be a challenge for them. But my boys are pretty mature, I think they will figure things out. She is an interesting person, and she might be worth a surprise or two for them."

"That's an interesting possibility from what you have told me about her. I will approve your trip home for a brief visit after the win, but only if the installation schedule permits it. If your install team arrives on schedule, you'll have to get to work right away."

"Yes, Helen. I got it."

The trip home was not to be. A large shipment arrived at the government warehouse in Abuja a few days after the conversation with Helen. Kirby had been house-hunting for a new place to use as his residence and his office. The company had sent a real estate buyer to Abuja to help him locate a suitable home for the next year, at least. After viewing several estate homes, all of which were much grander than he was expecting, they settled on a two-story stone house, surrounded by an eight-foot wall, and with a small garden and a swimming pool in the back. There was a driveway that came off the main road and through a stone gateway arch to a two-car garage in the back. There were servant's quarters along the back wall for the security team, the housekeepers, the cook, and his driver. And there was a rooftop open-air garden area.

He had just walked into the house when the phone rang. He looked for a chair to sit in to talk on the phone, but the room was bare. It was from the warehouse manager and the company logistics manager telling him that a large shipment of computer equipment had arrived and needed to be signed for.

The phone rang again, and it was Helen White. "Kirby, you should be getting a call from our shipping line about the equipment we sent to the warehouse. The installation team will be arriving tomorrow. They will be staying at the Abuja Sheraton, and the team lead is Al Risdorphen. You may know him."

Kirby smiled and said, "Yeah, I know Al. We worked together at SwissBank. I think I still have his number. I'm staying at the Abuja Hilton. Who else is coming?"

"Al has put together a good team; three hardware guys to get the hardware and networks installed, and a couple of software types to get the rest of the work done. They should be ready to start work by the weekend and expect that it will take a couple of weeks to a month to get all the bank and logistics links working on top of the existing SAP ERP system. This will give Nigeria a completely integrated and secure system to do business all over the world. Your job is to keep the customer happy; keep him informed but don't scare him if glitches show up that we can fix quickly. You and Al should stay in close contact in case there are any issues that might get out that we don't want advertised while we are fixing them."

"Ok, Helen, I'll keep the President apprised, and I will keep up with Al's progress. Helen, this President is a smart cookie. I noticed a MIT ring on his finger in addition to all the usual gaudies. Somehow I feel like I have met him before but I can't place him. Oh, one other thing, this place doesn't have any furniture in it. Right now, I'm talking to you from the phone outlet in this gigantic open room. Is there a plan to get some chairs in here?"

"There will be a big truck showing up there tomorrow. It should have everything you need, office, bedroom, conference room, everything to transform that little stone cottage into a working office. And that includes your staff. They will come by there to introduce themselves."

Kirby said, "Wow, I'm really impressed. I just need to make sure I'm not living higher than the Prez. He wouldn't like it, I'd guess."

Helen replied, "It's really nothing fancy, just the basic stuff you need to get rolling."

"Thanks, Helen. I'll report back after the tornado of people and furniture blows through. I have a meeting with the Minister of Commerce this afternoon to discuss our plans to get the system in and teach them to use it."

CHAPTER 56

Kirby called on Minister Umanda Killowon in the Presidential Complex to update him on the status of the project and also the research he was doing for the President. He had a large but not particularly distinctive office, with only one picture hanging on the wall; President Muhari Clarion. Killowon was a no-nonsense guy, and they went immediately to work discussing the logistics and support they would need to configure a new computer room inn the Villa that would act as a front end to all other systems.

Following that conversation, Umanda said, "Doctor Calloway, the President would like to invite you to a state dinner with himself and the First Wife, and then a private meeting to discuss some private matters. I hope you will accept."

"Of course, I accept. When would you like me to arrive at the Villa?"

"It won't be at the Villa, it will instead be at his former residence on the hillside. I will send a car for you at 1630 tomorrow, if that is convenient."

Kirby replied eagerly, "That sounds excellent. I will await the car in the lobby." The timing was great, Kirby could be out of the way when the furniture arrived and was being moved in. When he came back, the place would look entirely different.

Calloway left the Villa and got back in his car and directed his driver to the new address on Grace Court. He hoped that the furniture and everything had arrived and been put in place.

As he drove up to his new home in the residential area of Grace Court, his Naval Academy training kicked in, and he saw the imposing structure as a base to be defended. He viewed the stone wall around it as a privacy wall, certainly not a wall that would be a significant barrier to an attack, should that come to pass. The roof and second floor might provide some defensive positions, but it was a nice home, but not a fort.

The cab drove through the archway and dropped him off at the front door. He walked in through the front door that was ajar and climbed the stairs to a large room that Kirby wanted to turn into an office space with his office, a secretary area with guest seating, and a large conference room. He walked through a large arched door and looked around. The room was clean, but bare.

Just then, there was a voice at the door. "Doctor Calloway, Sir?"

Kirby turned to see a tall, heavily built black man, attired in a tailored white belted uniform standing in the doorway. He had the build of an NFL Fullback, but the face of a sports announcer, confident and friendly.

"Sir, I am Katanga. I will be your Man."

Kirby was in a gratuitous mood and walked over to the doorway and returned humorously, "I've never had a "Man" before. What does that mean?"

Katanga looked around the bare room, and said, "Sir, it means that I will responsible for your comfort and safety, and for the direct management of the rest of your staff. I will supervise the preparation of your meals, your transportation needs, the cleanliness of your home, and its security, should the need arise.

Kirby replied gratefully, "Well, Katanga, you can see we're pretty much starting at ground zero. This place needs a lot of work."

Katanga then replied, "Yes Sir, but don't worry. I will make sure that your home is in readiness for you when you return from your meeting with His Excellency tomorrow evening."

Kirby was surprised by that response. "How did you know about that?"

"Sir, I will make it my business to be aware of anything that will affect you, your schedule, your wants, or your security. That is what it means when I tell you that I am your Man." Katanga bowed slight-ly, then asked, "Will there be anything else, Sir?"

Kirby said, with a fake seriousness, "Just find me a damn chair! I can't just walk around here forever."

Katanga replied, "Right away, Sir!" And within seconds, a wheeled chair came rolling through the doorway.

Kirby watched it roll to the center of the room and just stop. "Where did that come from?", he asked incredulously.

Katanga replied, "Sir, we will always try to anticipate your needs, and the need for a chair was obvious. When all of your furniture ar-rives tomorrow, we will return it to the person we got it from."

Kirby sighed, sinking into the mysterious chair, "Don't tell me the rest of the story, I don't want to know." Kirby then recalled that "Katanga" was the "Man" that Weldon had assigned to help him, and that made him suspicious. What was his real role here? To keep a close watch on him, or to really be his aide? Kirby decided not to bring him into his confidence until he had proven himself.

That evening, his desk, an actual chair, a coffee table, two couches, and three brand-new metal filing cabinets arrived and were moved into the big room upstairs to what was to become his office, conference room, and TV lounge/visitor area all in one.

Kirby decided to start sorting through the pile of company infor-mation, unsolicited bids, letters of introduction, personal pleas, and arrogant demands that Umanda had given him. He decided to sort them into much the same categories that Umanda had suggested, but with more emphasis on logistics and transportation, which had been his area of focus in his Naval Academy studies. He also divided the company information into new companies and companies that were currently doing projects for the country.

The other categories included construction, airport expansion, banking, hospitals, agriculture, and highways. After his initial sort, it was obvious that many vendors thought there was going to be a lot of money spent in all these categories. The previous regime, led by Goodluck Johnathan's Nuyongas PDP, had neglected to use the oil revenues generated by new oilfields to benefit the people and had actually stolen it and stashed it away in banks in the Caymans, Switzerland, Hong Kong, and most recently, Singapore.

This had been a real racket and it led to Kirby thinking, what other skullduggery had some of these vendors been involved in to enable the acquisition and theft on a national scale? Dictators need facilitators to make bad things happen and then cover them up. With that level of corruption, many other bad things can happen, too. Something to look at much closer.

Kirby gathered up his papers and walked downstairs to have his driver take him back to the hotel. When he got there, Katanga was there to meet him. "Sir, with your permission, I have arranged a different car and especially a different driver. His name is Nam. Your previous driver was known to be a part of the Nuyongas tribe and was very likely feeding back intelligence on your movements to the leadership, which, as you know is hostile to the current regime."

Kirby was surprised once again at the apparent completeness of what Katanga saw as his duties.

"Thank you, Katanga. I appreciate your thoroughness." While on one level Kirby appreciated it, but on another level, he still felt a slight undertone of suspicion.

Kirby pulled up at his hotel, and the new driver ran around the car to open the door for him, then saluted him. Kirby was embarrassed: he always tried to keep a low-key status, and arriving like Prince Harry was not helping his image. He got out and instructed the driver, Nam, not to go through such formalities in the future. Nam hop-stepped, saluted and "Yes, Sir."

Kirby just shook his head, and walked up the steps to the hotel doors. The doorman, having taken note of Nam's respectful performance, quickly opened the door, greeted him with deference, "Welcome, Doctor Calloway!", and offered to take Kirby's small satchel. Kirby refused gracefully, but then he suddenly realized that the information inside was more valuable than gold and he needed a new level of security for himself and the information, not a ratty old leather satchel.

"Hello, Doctor Calloway?" Kirby stopped and turned to face a man standing next to the elevators. The man was a large hulk, but had an engaging expression, slicked-back black hair, and a big smile, set off with two large gold teeth. He was wearing a $1,000 velvet suit.

"Hello, I am Sergei Rubenov, head of the Russian commercial office in Lagos. You are Doctor Calloway, no?"

Kirby saw him as a Russian Cossack, riding the steppes on a Mongol pony and waving a large sword. He had the thought that it probably reflected his competitive practices as well, and Kirby was instantly on his guard.

"Yes, I am Doctor Kirby Calloway. I thought we might get to meet, but it was gracious of you to wait for me here in the lobby."

"No problem, no problem. Things are moving so fast here now that I assumed you would want to discuss the recent developments sooner, rather than later. My secretary has reserved us a table in the private dining room. Let's continue our discussion in a bit less of a public place. Let's go up a level." Rubenov pointed up to the door of a small dining room up on the second floor off the main lobby. They walked up the stairs and around the balcony to the little room. The door was cut glass, and as they entered, Kirby saw that the room was illuminated by an array of candles in large brass lanterns and etched glass panes.

His secretary rose from her chair at the table that they were headed for, "Doctor Kirby, this is my private secretary, Alaina Kamoroff." Alaina looked up from her logbook, and Kirby saw a woman with the most brilliant blue eyes he had ever seen set into a beautiful tanned face, outlined by white-blond hair. She was wearing a tight, low cut white dress and her figure was amazing. She was stunning. Borowitz was right; Rubenov certainly had good taste in administrative assistants. He took her hand, but couldn't help looking a bit lower as she bowed slightly in greeting.

Kirby hesitated a second to consider what Rubenov meant by

"recent developments". "Are you referring to the Presidents' appointment of his old foe, Kwandanbo, to be his Chief of Operations?"

"No, not that. The big development was the Chinese bid to buy all of the port facilities at Lagos, Benin, and Port Harcourt and operate them for the Nigerian government. If you consider what the Chinese bid was compared to what they are spending now, it only makes sense for them to take the offer. And we know they would do a better job, more efficient, 'eta ne pravda'?" Rubenov meant "isn't that true" by his last statement. I had to agree with that. But there were also American companies that had offered turn-key operations to the Nigerians as well. He felt suddenly guilty that he hadn't yet reviewed any of the American offers, but that was what he was carrying around in his little leather bag.

Kirby offered, "Well, the question is: How does the Nigerian government view that offer? It's not like President Muhari is now short on cash. But I don't think that he's going to turn all his marine facilities over to some foreign power, even if they are the low bidder."

Rubenov slapped his leg, and said, "That's exactly what I hoped you would say. You have the best insight into his thinking. That's why the people of America and the people of Russia should band together to make sure that does not happen. We have seen what happened when they took over in Hong Kong. It was subtle at first, but soon we saw them playing favorites. If the cargo traffic increases as we expect, soon all the dock space, container unloading, and ship repair will be in short supply, and the Chinese would favor Chinese and allied ships into the marine facilities. Neither Russia or America could allow that to happen."

Kirby agreed. "That could be a problem for sure. But I'm working on my overall assessment of the opportunity set for American businesses. I'm not ready to set my priorities yet, but I will pass this along to the Ambassador. Thanks for the information, Mr. Rubenov."

Rubenov grabbed Kirby's arm as he looked to be leaving. "But wait, my friend! Please call me Sergei, may I call you Kirby? Aren't you going to tell me about your meeting with Muhari? I know you just met with him?" He framed it more like a question, like he wasn't sure that we did meet.

He thought about not saying anything about the meeting, but felt that Rubenov might feel slighted and not be helpful in the future if Kirby blew him off.

"It was a short, cordial meeting where President Muhari stressed his efforts to make the country more modern and to pick designated vendors for key projects, rather than having his subordinates make strategic decisions by just writing their favorite vendors into their budgets. He has delegated the responsibilities to Umanda, the Minister of Commerce. My job is just to weed out American vendors who have a record of corruption or failure in performance, and recommend those vendors who can get the work done without blowing the budget, as well as providing some unique value."

"We did not talk about other countries besides the United States, however I would be happy to weed out Russian companies as well, Sergei, if you would like."

Sergei considered what Kirby had said, then grinned broadly, and retorted, "We shall weed our own garden, Kirby. I suspect that you may find a few Russian roses among your American thorns."

Kirby took the elevator up to his room in the Hilton, glancing around for anyone who might get too close. He shut his door and locked it, fastened the little chain, then sat down at his little hotel desk and pulled out the thick sheaf of papers that he had already sorted by categories. Some of them were obvious winners for further consideration; large international companies with years of experience in construction, manufacturing, and logistics. But he didn't want to just go with the obvious winners; he was also looking for smaller companies that had done work for Nigeria before and that had good track records, especially local companies. But after a few hours work, he had a list of the companies by category that he would recommend to President Muhari.

Just then, he heard a knock on his door. Kirby thought quickly about who it might be, and ruled out any friendly visitors. He got the Beretta pistol out of his desk drawer and held it by his side as he walked to the door.

"Who is it?", Kirby asked slowly.

"Weldon" was the answer.

Kirby slowly cracked the door to see the visitor at his door, took off the chain, and then relaxed and opened the door. Kirby smiled and welcomed in his old friend and current CIA liaison, Jake Weldon.

Weldon saw the pistol as Kirby returned it to the drawer. "I see that you have not forgotten the protocols. You need to give that even more attention from now on."

Kirby inquired, "What have you heard in that regard? Is this related to the contract award or something else?"

"It's not the contract award. Congratulations on that by the way. That should put you in the catbird seat, and the Director is very happy about that. It does make you hugely popular in some quarters and deeply unpopular in others."

"But that's not the main problem. We know that Muhari gave you a portfolio of American companies that want to participate in the "new economy" that he has been promising to the country. He must really have faith in you. Do you know why that is?"

Kirby thought for a moment, "I know that I have met him before somewhere but I can't place him. I did find out that we both have Masters Degrees from MIT, but in different years, and I think that was a big part of it. He made a statement about "honor" involved and I think he really means it."

Weldon nodded, but warned, "We have some reports that the information in that set of documents could be very damaging to certain companies, as well as certain government officials here, and in some other countries including the good ole USA. Have you started looking through the information yet? We could send over an analyst to help you if you see the need."

Kirby considered it, but said, "Not yet, I can't have the Company obviously involved in any aspect of this right now. The President is obviously aware that you are involved somehow, but seems willing to let it ride unless it surfaces."

Weldon looked at his watch, then started to get up. "Just remember two things: people you don't know, want to know what you know, and they will kill you for it, especially if you expose serious corruption, and worse yet, if it involves foreign governments. And two, Katanga is "our man" and is your personal bodyguard. He is one our best trained agents, but you should continue to treat him as your house master. Don't go anywhere without him anymore. And three, get in there and use your new Nigerian computer access to research those companies, their transactions, and their performance histories. Flag anything that looks unusual. Handoff anything that needs deeper research, and four, don't get yourself killed."

Kirby laughed. "I thought you said there were only two things."

Weldon joined in, "Well, I thought of number four, but that reminded me of number three, which is really how you earn your REAL salary. Go earn it. I will see you in a couple of weeks."

Kirby stopped him. "Jake, is any of this going to get home to my boys? They're on their own, pretty much, back home. Their Mom is there but she is clueless about any of this, and wouldn't have any idea what to do if something went bad. I need to know they are safe too."

Weldon stopped to think. "I shouldn't think so at this point. But I know a few Washington FBI guys and I'll let them know about your kids. Maybe I can get them to take a ride by every now and then to see how they are doing. OK?"

Kirby replied, with deep gratitude, "That would be great. If they get anything, I want to hear it!"

Weldon got up to leave, and then he stopped and turned to Calloway, "There is one more thing. We're not sure that Muhari is our best choice for President. We are seeing him poke his nose into things that we don't want to see reformed. Go about your business, but I wouldn't get too close to him if I were you, "Brass Rats" or not. We'll let you know if you are getting too close to our little op."

CHAPTER 57

The four of us, me, Morgan, Wendy, and Colin swore ourselves to secrecy when we got to school on Monday. We agreed to not discuss our finding of the cave entrance, or the experience inside the underwater cave, and especially not the Golden Throne. We also agreed that if one of us was in a conversation where the Golden Throne came up, we would just say, "it's just a rumor", but not say it's not true or try to discourage anybody else from going on the hunt. We would let the determined try to retrace our path, but don't lay it out for them. This is what we all agreed to. No talking.

But I had to tell Falk. He was the one who put the idea in my head, and I wanted to know if he had gone on the quest himself or only heard the "rumors".

Falk was coming out of his last period class and I was free because I had already passed Drivers Ed and now had my real Drivers License. He saw me standing in the hallway, and came over.

"Hi, Eth. What's going on? It's been a couple weeks since I saw you, so...whatcha been up to?"

The tone in his voice sounded to me like he already knew about our exploit, and I knew exactly how he found out. Wendy.

"Oh, nothing really. We've taken my sailboat out a few times, but it's gotten too cold to go out, so she's in storage over at Green's boat storage until next season. I think they'll take good care of her."

"Hmm...did you ever go out on the islands looking for that old treasure rumor, you know, the alleged Golden Throne? We talked about it when we were flying and I pointed out where I thought the cave might be."

It now sounded like Wendy had spilled the whole story to him. I bet she was dating him and not telling me. I always thought she might really like him more than me. Maybe she wasn't who I thought she was. She didn't go anywhere with me, what was she doing with Falk?

"Yeah, we did a little poking around out on Bassett's Island, and there were a couple of interesting spots."

"Did you ever explore out around that big rock pile that I pointed out from the air? I thought that might be worth checking out."

"Yeah. That was one of the places that we poked around at. Not sure what we found though. It might have been a cave entrance."

"Wow! So you found a cave entrance? Did you go inside? What did you see?"

At this point, I had to reverse the argument and put him on the spot.

"Wow. It sounds like you've been there already. What did you see?"

Falk offered, "The entrance led to a big underwater cave. Very interesting experience. But you would need diving gear to go any farther,"

That was enough for me. I challenged him directly.

"Wendy told you the whole story, didn't she?!"

Falk was taken aback by my challenge. "I haven't talked to Wendy outside of class for a couple of weeks. Why do you care what she tells me? She doesn't know anything about the cave or the Golden Throne! So what story was she supposed to have told me?"

Now Falk is smiling. "That you and her went into the cave and found the relic?" Now he looked happy to be stringing me along.

I was totally confused at this point, and Falk was having the time of his life.

He looked at me, then gave me the "Oh, what the hell" look.

"Ok, Ethan. Here is the story, but you must keep it a life-long secret. Do you swear?"

"Yes, I swear on my mother's grave." That came out wrong. "I swear that I swear!" I had to know what Falk knew.

Falk said, "Let's take a little walk," and we walked out to the edge of the quadrangle where there were no prying eyes or ears.

Then he looked around. There was one kid walking home across the quad. Falk waited until the kid was at the far end. Then he put his arm around me, grabbed me by my collar and pulled me in close. I was almost afraid to hear what Falk was going to say.

He looked around again, then whispered these chilling words.

"I put the toilet in the cave and spray-painted it gold when I was thirteen. I was the one who started the rumor of the Golden Throne." I looked at him in disbelief, but then it all made sense. He had been dropping the rumor of the treasure for years, and gullible but determined people like me and my little gang had followed the rumor all the way to the Cave of the Golden Throne, found the secret, and kept it a secret all these years. It was beautiful.

After that moment, Falk and I became fast friends, sealed together by the secret of the Golden Throne which I would take to my grave, after possibly dropping a few rumors along the way.

I had totally misjudged Wendy. Lucky for me I hadn't jumped on her for revealing the secret. I kept having these jealous fantasies where she was in love with somebody else, Falk, or Colin, or who knows who.

But was I prohibited by my oath from telling her or Colin the real truth behind the Golden Throne? I thought about it, and finally decided that keeping my oath was the best thing, and it allowed Wendy and Colin to continue to enjoy the beautiful joke behind the "Legend of the Golden Throne" without knowing its humble origin.

CHAPTER 58

One Saturday, Wendy called me, and asked, "Have you forgotten your promise?"

For a minute I tried to remember any promise I had made to her, then I remembered, "You want to go "cowboying"? I had almost forgotten the "quid" versus the "quo."

"I called the Highlander Farms stables in Hatchville and reserved a couple of horses for tomorrow afternoon. They have a training corral, a big meadow to run around in, a long path ride through the woods, and they also have a jumper course."

"A jumper course? Can't we get a couple of Texas quarter horses and go chase some cows, not get on some English countryside jumping horse?" I just then recalled that when I first met Wendy, I thought she had an "English countryside look." Oh, boy. What was I getting myself into? I then also recalled the look Wendy's mother gave me when I bragged that I was going to teach Wendy how to ride a horse. It looks like I've been sandbagged!

That Sunday, Wendy got her Dads' old Volvo wagon, and drove over to my house. She was carrying a big athletic bag, and I looked at the huge bag with interest, and asked her, "Do I need to bring anything?"

She looked at me with concern. "Do you have any proper riding clothes?" she asked looking at me doubtfully.

"You mean like jeans and a toboggan shirt?"

"No, but never mind, just wear your jeans and...what'd you call it? A toboggan shirt? What's a toboggan shirt?"

"It's just a heavy T-shirt. I will wear my Mackinaw jacket over it.."

"What's a Mackinaw jacket?...Oh, never mind. Just get in the car."

"Wait, I have to get dressed!" I went back to my room and Wendy followed me. "So this is where you live, is it?"

She looked around and saw a very empty room, a bed that was made, an open closet door, with a few shirts and jeans, clothes and some Fritos laying on the floor, and my desk with open school-books. No Bon Jovi or Tom Brady posters, no football trophies, a set of James Cameron novels, a few Joseph Campbell books, really nothing that would indicate anything about me. Except for my cluttered workbench with tools, some mechanical stuff, but nothing was working.

I took off my "Dockers" shoes and put on my Tecovas "Cartwright" cowboy boots and grabbed my Stetson 4X Beaver hat out of the closet, then shut the closet door. Wendy looked me, nodding her conditional approval.

As we were walking out, Marie came out of the kitchen, wiping her hands on her apron. "Well, hello." she said to Wendy. "You must be Wendy. Ethan talks about you all the time. It's so good to finally meet you."

For some reason, there was a bit of an icy edge to the last part of her statement. Wendy seemed to catch it too. It surprised and worried me. There was absolutely nothing between Marie and me. Though, I admit to enjoying watching her move around the kitchen. She seemed to be wearing more casual clothes each day, clothes that showed more and more of her womanly assets.

We headed down to the stables located just south of Pocasset. The stables were located on a small ridge surrounded by tall chestnut trees. There was an office located in an elegant old house. We went in through the open doorways into a room with dark wood plank floors, paneled walls with old-looking wallpaper, and a gigantic cut-glass chandelier. There was also a huge bar with glass bottles of every description on the wall behind it. Several riders with red or black coats were enjoying their civilized drinks and talking about how many fox scalps they had taken that day. Teenage boy mind again.

We checked in at the desk there, and Wendy told me. "Wait here while I get changed." She ducked into the ladies lounge while I stood around nervously while people who were dressed like they were out of the "Great Gatsby" walked by me, thinking I was some hick from Texas. I guess my Stetson 4X Beaver gave me away. Well, I was a hick from Texas, but I knew how to ride a working horse, not one of these show ponies.

Wendy came out the dressing room. She wasn't dressed like the people I had been watching go by me, thank goodness, but she was wearing riding pants and tall black boots. She was wearing a knitted wool sweater, rather than the black suit coat that the locals were wearing.

I thought she looked great, out of a movie, but not "Great Gatsby". Her long red hair was tied by a white bow, and blew about in the wind.

"Let's go. We have a couple of experienced jumpers down in the second set of stables."

She noticed the look of fear, no, apprehension, no, actually it was fear as we walked across the stable yard toward the entrance to the stables.

"Your horse is "Big Un", and he has run in a couple of Kentucky Derbies, but that was years ago, and now they use him for jumper training. He has been down in Mississippi for the past couple of years doing fox hunting. You should be fine."

I was going to ask her why he was called "Big Un", but then I saw him. I've never seen a horse that big. Quarter horses are smaller and very muscular, while this monster horse was tall and slim. When he saw me, he immediately started prancing around in his stall, and he looked out at me like he was welcoming his next victim to the party.

I had learned of a primitive ritual where, in order to prove his manhood a boy has to face off in combat with his spirit animal and win the battle. The spirit animal gracefully loses, letting the Man-boy claim his victory. After his victory, he is allowed to choose his favorite bride from the most beautiful girls from the village. There in the stall was my spirit animal, a gigantic horse monster.

Wendy warned me. "He hasn't been ridden for a few weeks, so he will probably be a little tense for a while, but he should settle down after an hour or so."

Tense? He was tense? I will tell you which one of us was tense. I walked over to his stall and he came over to the gate to look me over. I immediately went into my "sincere cooperation and trust" facial expression to show him what a good rider I would be. He smelled my hand, and he snorted and stomped away. I guess he interpreted my sweaty palm as fear, and he was right.

One of the stablemen, Walter, by his sewn name tag, came over and went into his stall to put a halter on him, then he turned to me with the rope, and asked, "Do you want to lead him out, sir?" in a very British accent.

I was thinking and whispering under my breath, rangers, rangers. "Sure, Walter, hand me his lead."

I took the rope and Walter opened the gate to his stall and Big Un came charging out, and almost ripped my hand off. He stopped, then turned around to take another look at me.

All of my experience with horses has told me that a good horse is very smart. This is certainly true of quarter horses, and I could now vouch for whatever this enormous critter was. Oh, a Hunter-Jumper, a lethal combination if there ever was one.

Walter brought over a saddle out of the tack room and threw it over my horses' back. Big Un got even more excited. Walter cinched him up, then put on his bridle, and turned to me and asked, "Ever ridden a rein lead? This horse you have to pull on the reins to turn him. He doesn't respond to neck lead."

Great. One more thing to unlearn.

Wendy was already sitting on her horse, "Willow", waiting impatiently for me to get going. She looked over at me, and taunted,

"How is your "quo" working out for you now?"

I now deeply regret ever making that deal with her. It wasn't worth losing my life over, and I had a brief mental image in my teenage boy mind of me sitting in a wheelchair like Superman. You don't make a deal with a woman you barely know in the middle of an angry encounter.

Walter grabbed Big Un by his halter and led him out of the barn, with me walking alongside like an idiot, just holding his rope...or was it line?

When it was time to board Big Un, I looked at the stirrup and it was waist-high. I looked around for a stepladder but there was only a wooden stool. I dragged that over, stood on it, put my foot in the left stirrup and started to swing my right leg over, but Big Un took off in a fast, very bumpy trot. I bounced along with him, hanging on to his side, but was finally able to grab part of the saddle and pull myself upright. Big Un didn't lose a step while I was fighting for my life. Lucky I didn't lose my hat.

After recovering my position and my composure, I followed Wendy into the training corral, where I learned to get Big Un to turn with the reins, and stop by pulling on both. A quarter horse would have been backing up with the same command.

Then we rode down the crushed shell-covered trails through the woods next to a nature reserve. There were leaves falling and someone had a wood fire burning. The smoke blowing across the trail and the falling leaves, with Wendy in the foreground would have made a beautiful fall video. The trail led for over a mile through the trees, across a stream, and alongside a marsh where a flock of Canada geese were resting up for the next leg of their journey south.

I was hoping Big Un was burning off excess energy as we walked through the canopy of trees shedding the last of their leaves, but as we emerged, he saw the hunter course with the jumps and his ears stood straight up and he started to tremble. Wendy, who had been leading the way, looked back and saw me and my horse. She asked,

"Well, cowboy, are you ready to chase a few outlaw foxes?"

I had learned that most hunt clubs don't hunt foxes anymore. They hunt a pair of coyotes which they never catch, because the wily coyotes immediately head for the wild, instead of circling back like the semi-trained foxes do. The foxes are then re-captured for the next hunt. Some foxes achieve celebrity status after proving that they can't be caught.

At this point, my honor and my courage as a man was on the line with a woman that I thought I loved, and who didn't want to see me fail.

I summoned my courage, rangers, rangers, and called out to her, "Let's go. Let's do this!"

The first obstacle on the hunt course wasn't the high jump; it was a series of obstacles with two or three rails, offset so you had to wind your way through, jumping over each set of rails to the end.

Wendy again took the lead, and I followed her, watching her every move and shift in the stirrups and saddle. She made the first jump like she was stepping over a fallen branch on the sidewalk. I lined up for the jump, and Big Un must have had his "rangers" moment too because he took off like a rocket and sailed over the little obstacle, clearing it by three or four feet, and landing hard, then lining up for the next jump. It felt like I was on the scariest amusement park ride of all time, with me hanging on to the saddle and the reins for dear life, while the horse ride carried me across jump after jump, with me not in control, just barely clinging to the saddle. I know it wasn't pretty.

Big Un wasn't even breathing hard, and I saw Wendy heading for the next course, much higher than the first one.

She looked back at me, assessing my performance from the first set. Then she turned around and rode up next to me. She looked stunning, a super horse woman with not a red hair out of place.

""Great job, and you too, Eth", obviously giving all the credit to the horse for my survival.

"Eth, why don't you take your horse out into the meadow, then give the first set another run? Big Un is probably out of practice and could use another run or two at the first set."

I was thinking more about taking Big Un back to the barn and going inside to the bar and talking the bartender out of a beer, but instead I replied with gusto,"Yeah, were just getting warmed up. We'll stay in the kiddie pool for today."

Wendy smiled and nodded, then turned to face the intermediate course.

Big Un's ears drooped as he saw Wendy ride off, then he looked back at me in disgust.

I felt that it was time to have a conversation with the animal.

I got off and looked at him straight on. He ignored me and turned away to see riders going by, all having more fun than he was. I honestly felt like I was trying to talk to a headstrong child who didn't want to listen to me.

"Big Un!" He recognized his name and looked at me. I jerked on the bridle to keep his attention.

"Hey boy, we are going to try to have a little fun together. Let's go out for a long run, then we'll come back and do these jumps again. Ok with you?"

He looked at me, then looked away. I don't know whether he understood me, but at least he didn't openly disagree by biting me.

I got back up on him by jumping up and grabbing the front of the saddle. There was no saddle horn to pull myself up on, so it was hard work. Once I had the stirrups, I turned him towards the big field. We leisurely walked across the stable yard and then as we crossed over into a field that was covered in short grass and bounded by tall trees, his ears picked up again and I could feel him shifting gears underneath me.

I said, "Ok. Here we go. YeeHahaa!", which is a Texas phrase which even Big Un understood. He took off like a rocket again and I could feel his stride getting longer and longer as he convinced himself that he was in the Derby and headed for the finish, winning it this time. I could feel in him a passion for victory, putting behind him years of frustration in his horse life experience. Anyway, that was going through my teenage boy mind, and I felt like me and Big Un had achieved a mind-meld of sorts.

After two circuits of the field, we returned to the jumps, and Big Un and I sailed over the rails like pros, even with me wearing my Mackinaw jacket.

Wendy was back from jumping her horse over the moon. She was sweaty too, and she pulled up next to me and my horse. She noted that we were both tired and sweaty, and she was satisfied that I had undergone the rigors of humiliation over the deal we had struck months before. I had undergone the ritual, and now I could claim my bride.

She looked at me approvingly, then she leaned over to me, and she kissed me with that same salty, wet kiss. I've never been kissed on saddleback before, and this one I will remember.

We walked our horses back to the stable yard slowly to cool them down. Then we took Big Un and Willow back to the barn and turned them back in to Walter. I gave Big Un a pat on the neck and let him smell my hand. He looked at me and saw my tired and satisfied expression, that I hoped he might remember in case we came back. My spirit animal and I had become one.

Walter looked approvingly at Big Un and the look of tired relaxation in Big Un and in my eyes. He nodded, then remarked; "Looks like you and El Satif got on satisfactorily. I'm glad of that. The Prince of Egypt needed a good workout.

"Prince of Egypt? This horse you gave me was a Prince?"

Walter, patted Big Un affectionately and told me, "Big Un is his nickname. His real name is El Satif and he is part Egyptian Arabian desert horse and part Thoroughbred."

Walter took the Prince away to be receive his reward and he broke the spell I was under. Later, Wendy told me that Walter was El Satif's owner, not just a stable hand.

That's the nice thing about rented horses; you don't need to spend the next two hours cooling them down, washing them off, brushing them, then cleaning up and repairing the tack.

Wendy looked me over again, from my cowboy boots to my cowboy hat, and she said, "I expected that you would be whining about that big horse. I'm proud of you. You stepped right up into it."

The sun was going down over the bay to the West. I looked at her in the fading sunlight. She was still as fresh as she had been this morning.

We walked back down the road to her Dad's Volvo, and she grabbed my hand and held it. She looked at me, and said. In a very soft voice, "Thank you, Ethan. I've wanted to go with you to keep this part of our bargain for a long time."

I wagged my forefinger at her in fake anger. "You were sandbagging me the whole time, weren't you...you and your mother. You're an expert rider, aren't you." She held my arm, flashed an adorable guilty smile, and said "Yes, well, but you still haven't taught me how to "cowboy". I picked her up and swung her around me. "How about a lesson in that?"

CHAPTER 59

Colin and I were out riding his Triumph bike one afternoon and drove out to the end of the Cape, into the small and eclectic town of Provincetown. We stopped at a biker bar out there, and Colin's strange accent and language convinced the barkeep, who was already being yelled at by twenty or more drunken Harley drivers, to sell him a couple of beers, and we had a few beers...and then my shout! a few more.

Somehow the topic got onto the subject of firearms. Colin told me that all Australians had been ordered to turn in all their guns, shotguns and rifles in 2017. I had heard from Falk that the government spent over $300 million and only collected 20% of the total guns. Stupid government and smart people, except that the $300 million actually belonged to them. This led me to believe that Colin had a rifle or a shotgun under his bed.

"Have you ever fired a gun before?"

Colin looked serious, "No, Mate. My dad is a scientist who loves his bloody whales and sees no use for guns. Perth dance clubs can get bloody rowdy, but we use fists, not guns."

"Well, we have a different culture here. It's because we had to fight you Brits for our independence back in 1776."

Colin reacted, "Whoa, Mate! We hated the Brits as much as you did. Many Aussies came over to Oz as prisoners of the Brits for stupid, petty crimes. They brought over a bunch of Irishers, too, and they are still cranky about that. Now we are all Aussies, and we don't like the Brits either!"

I considered that; I had never heard that fact before. But, I had a point I wanted to make, and being a bit drunk made sure that I did. Then I said, "Well, maybe the difference between you Australians and us Americans is our guns, which made it so we could push the Brits out. It took two tries, as I remember, but we finally did it."

Colin finished his fourth beer, tossed it in the general direction of a trash can, and admitted, "Well, maybe that's true, but it's too late for us. In Oz, if you use a gun even in self-defense now you can go to jail for five years. So we all turned in all our guns a few years ago. Most of us anyway. Probably not the criminals though, yeah? Hmm."

I slapped Colin on the back, and said in a somewhat inebriated voice, "Colin, my good man. This is your lucky day. I happen to have my own personal submachine gun!"

Colin looked through half-closed eyes, while he popped open his fifth "Nantucket" beer, then slammed his hand down on the table, and said, "Well then, you can damn well prove it! Yeah?"

I don't remember much of the ride back to Pocasset but somehow we made it through all the small towns and sand dunes and pulled up in my front yard, still feeling a bit under the weather.

Colin still remembered my drunken boast about the submachine gun, and I was sober enough to realize how big a mistake that was. I couldn't possibly ever divulge the secret of our gun vault, especially to Colin, who talked anyone's ear off and couldn't keep a secret, except maybe for the Golden Throne. Maybe.

Then I thought of something. Just after Morgan and I found the money, and then the gun vault, Morgan had gone to Walmart or Target and bought an air-soft gun that was a replica of a Thompson submachine gun. It fired full-auto streams of little white plastic bullets that could go through a paper target at 25 feet or so. It really hurt if you got shot, I know that for a fact. But it wasn't real.

I told Colin to wait downstairs while I went up to Morgan's bedroom closet to find where he had left the gun. It was wedged into one corner. I pulled it out and went in search of the round drum magazine. After going through Morgan's desk drawers, I found it and it was loaded with 500 plastic rounds. I grabbed the gun and the magazine and headed downstairs where Colin was waiting nervously for his chance to shoot a gun for the first time. Guns are in a American man's blood, and can't be denied forever. Having our guns in the vault made me feel a lot safer to face what might be coming for us. I think that's why Dad put them there.

The Thompson replica looked and worked just like the real one, and it was heavy, too. Colin held it reverently, like some religious icon. He turned it over, looking at the details. He pulled the cocking handle on the barrel back and heard a satisfying click. Then he put the stock under his arm and raised it to aim it at the TV across the room, then swung it in an arc as if he was mowing down an attacking tribe of Aborigines. Anyway, that's what I saw in my teenage boy mind.

He brought it down to a carry position like he had seen in the movies, like the old Cagney stuff. After a minute or so, he carefully handed it back to me. He kept looking at it as I attached the round drum magazine with a satisfying clunk. I was afraid he would hear the little white plastic pellets rolling around. "Do you want to fire it?", I asked him.

"Oh no, Mate. I've never fired a gun in my life, and I surely don't want to start with this one!"

"Ok. But now you must never tell anyone about this gun. I need you to swear. I shouldn't have ever told you about it, but sitting among a bunch of wild bikers drinking beer for the first time, I was stupid drunk."

Colin looked at me sheepishly. "Yeah, we both got caught in the dunny. Never again. I won't tell anyone about your gun. But someday, you'll have to teach me how to shoot."

"I will, when the right time comes. Promise."

CHAPTER 60

I hadn't seen Wendy in a couple of days, not in class, not in the hallways. She was busy, we both were busy, I could have just missed her. After all, it was our senior year and there was lots to do before graduation .

I decided to go by her house and see if she was ok. It was a very unusual and bad day for me if I didn't get a hug or kiss on the cheek from her.

I pulled up in her driveway and saw in addition to her Dad's old Volvo, there was a red Porsche Cayman "S". I thought Wow! Her dad bought her a car, and what a beauty! Shit, now I was sounding like Colin. To him, everything is a beauty.

I knocked on the door, and Wendy's mom came and opened it. "Hello, Ethan, come on in." She seemed happy today, which was pretty much how she was all the time. No drama like my Mom.

I walked into the funeral parlor and was surprised to see Wendy sitting on the couch with Falk. I was always worried about those two together.

Falk was a very interesting person. He was always working, mostly on flying stuff. He had invented the Legend of the Golden Throne. Who does that? He was good-looking, kind of like a tall Tom Cruise. He seemed to have all the money in the world, yet he never seemed like some rich guy. He was always the nicest person. And his dad won the Medal of Honor, that meant "hero" was running through his blood. That was it: he was just some kind of heroic son-of-a-bitch, looking for a place to be that hero. And that was probably his red Porsche Cayman "S" in the driveway. Maybe we should go out and race him with the Maserati. Teenage boy mind again. The Maserati was locked safely in the old garage.

It occurred to me for some reason right then that I had never seen Falk with a girlfriend. Instead, his best friend was the guy we meet at the airfield that day, his mechanic and flight instructor. If he was gay, then he would either tell me or he wouldn't; it made no difference whatsoever to me. At least, I wouldn't have to worry about him and Wendy.

With my surprise at seeing Falk, I didn't notice that Wendy's Dad was sitting in a chair with its back to me. As I walked in, Wendy walked over and took my hand, and pulled me over to sit with her. I stopped to shake hands with her Dad sitting in his big chair.

He was dressed in a tan uniform, with only the US and a chrome eagle on his collar, and gold wings with a star and wreath on them. I had never seen him out of uniform.

He just said, "Good Morning, Ethan. Take a seat." I followed Wendy over and sat next to her.

The conversation immediately switched to be between Falk and her Dad. Wendy and I were just spectators.

Her Dad spoke, "You know what you're getting into, right? It's a long hard road. The first year, you are the lowest person on the totem pole. You have no privileges and everyone dumps on you. Your classes come at you like a fire hose, plus you play competitive sports every day. It's not for everyone, actually it's only for the best of the best."

I at first thought Falk had really screwed up and was going to be sent somewhere to do hard time. But then I realized, that her Dad was talking about the Naval Academy.

"Do you still want to do it?"

"Yes, Sir. I really do. And I want to fly helicopters like you do. I'm a pretty good pilot already, and the other stuff sounds hard, but fun."

"You know that with your Dad's Medal, you have the right to automatic admission. So all you have to do is pass the entrance physical, medical, and mental qualifications and you're in. And with the pilot's license you already have, you'll get your first set of wings after your first year."

"Yes Sir. I'm not worried about the tests. I'm really sure that's what I want."

"Ok, then. It's settled. Just get your paperwork in on time and you'll get your letter of acceptance,"

"Thank you sir, for coaching me through it. I'll try to make you proud."

"You'll make us all proud. Falk...is that your real name, Falk?"

"No Sir. It's Clarence Bosworth Falcones. My parents wanted to name me after some of their old, dead relatives. As soon as I could talk, I became Falk, only Falk."

We all had to laugh at the poor decision his parents had made in naming their poor child. Falk was definitely better.

CHAPTER 61

A few weeks later, Falk called me. "Hey, you and Morg come out to the airfield, I've got something cool to show you."
I figured he had a new carburetor for his C172, or something like that. Morg was playing dolls with Carmen or something, so I went by myself. I had bought myself a very used Harley Softail which I had fixed up, meaning I had reattached the fenders and replaced the taillight. The Maserati needed to stay in the bat-cave for the time being.

I headed through town, listening to the satisfactory muted roar of the 1899 cc engine. We riders had been warned by Officer Collins about making too much noise, so when I drove through town, I kept it muted until I got out past the gas station at the edge of town. Riding through town let you experience the different smells depending on the time of day; bacon for breakfast at Sammy's, fresh coffee at Adela's, fried chicken for lunch at Quincy's, and burning garbage late in the day.

When I pulled up to Falk's hangar, I peered through the open doors on both sides of the hangar and saw a little yellow helicopter. As I walked over to look at it, I noticed that Falk's Cessna 172 was no longer parked on the ramp, instead its place was taken by this cute little toy.

Falk came out from behind the engine compartment, wiping grease from his hands. His mechanic, Ray, was kneeling behind the engine sorting out the tools they had been using. He got up, nodded to me, and took their tools back to the hanger. I had never really looked at him before; he was a thin, older man, with long gray hair, but he had what struck me as wise eyes, blue as sky.

Falk was wearing his usual; jeans, white T-shirt, Sperry Top-Siders and Ray-Bans. I can't remember him ever wearing anything different.

He saw me staring at his yellow beauty, and came over to where I was trying to peer through the plexiglas bubble to see the cockpit.

"So, what do you think of her? I've decided to upgrade to rotary wings. I can go anywhere, fly fast, fly slow, or just stop and enjoy the view. This is what I want to fly in the Navy, so I want to get ready."

"Can you even own a helicopter while you are there? Would they let you take this with you to the Academy?" That seemed like a stretch.

"Not exactly. You can't even have a car until your junior year. But I could leave it at a nearby airport and fly it when I get a weekend off. And it's not really mine, it belongs to the Company.

This was the second time I had heard about "the Company". It must be something his mysterious, MOH-winning dad owns.

"You want to go up?", Falk asked

"Wait a minute here. Are you even qualified to fly this thing? I've heard that flying helicopters is nothing like flying airplanes."

"Eth, you've never let the issue of a silly little license bother you before. Besides, once you get her up, she flies a lot like an airplane."

Then his face turned thoughtful. "It's getting into the air that's the hard part. You know, hovering, ground taxi, that sort of thing. Oh yeah, and landing."

As much as I trusted Falk, I was highly skeptical of going flying with him in this thing. But it sure looked like fun.

"Ok. Let's go."

Falk's face lit up. "OK!"

I walked around to the passenger side, but Falk grabbed my arm and pointed to the left seat. I thought, No Way! I'm not going to try to learn how to fly this thing when Falk barely knows.

Falk corrected me. "The pilot sits in the right seat, passenger in the left. It's switched from airplanes, at least in this model."

I climbed into the left seat, still not sure if this was one of Falk's pranks. He climbed into the right seat and started fiddling with some of the switches,

I looked out the front, and out the sides. We were sitting in this plexiglas bubble, hanging out in space, not like the comfortable confines of a small airplane. It was not at all reassuring.

We put on headsets to talk back and forth, then Falk turned the ignition key and the engine chugged to a start, and the blades began slowly turning. I could then hear him. He got on the radio to warn other aircraft in the neighborhood that a helicopter was taking off. I wondered if that was normal or just for this flight, like a beginner license plate that warned you of a student driver.

The blades turned faster and faster until they were just a blur overhead. The helicopter was starting to come alive, trembling like "Big Un" looking at the chase track.

Falk looked over at me, and asked, "You ready?" I answered back, "Are you?"

He just laughed and pulled up on a stick between the seats and the helicopter slowly rose from the ground, and promptly started drifting left, then forward, then back. Falk was wiggling the stick in front of him to correct us from drifting all over the ramp. I cringed back as far as I could in my seat. I looked out and realized that we were nowhere near the parking spot where we started.

Falk slowly pivoted us around to the right, away from anything we could run into as we lifted off, and then he pushed the stick forward and revved the engine and pulled up on the stick between our seats, and we started moving forwards. But as we did, the nose dropped down so that I was looking at the ground, not at the sky where I thought we were headed. I tried to cringe back farther in my seat, but then I noticed that despite the nose pointed at the ground, we were climbing out and pretty soon the nose came up to what looked like a normal attitude. We climbed to about 500 feet and flew back towards the town. Things look so different when you are flying so low. You can see into people's back yards, see them mowing the grass, and if there were pretty girls laying out on a beach in the nude, you could see them too. Sorry, teenage boy mind again.

We flew out towards the bay, crossing Hen Cove, then flying over Bassett's Island. Falk pointed down to the rock pile and said, "There is an old story of a "Golden Throne" somewhere on one of the islands. That's all I know. People have stopped talking about it. Maybe somebody already found it. Don't know."

I looked at him, smiling because of our wonderful shared joke, and said, "Eat shit."

We flew south down towards Falmouth and I could see the Highland ranch. There were a few horses running around in the corral, and I wondered whether one of them was "Big Un".

Falk turned to me and said, "Do you want to fly it?" I was tempted but I replied, "Not on my first trip. This is so different from the Cessna, it'll take some getting used to."

He turned back and admitted, "Yeah, it's different and that's why I love it. You can do many different things with a helicopter than an airplane, especially in the Navy, search and rescue, recon, even combat. And even some Marine fighters like the F-35 can now fly like helicopters, so I'm on the right track."

"Yeah, buddy, you are."

We flew back to the airport and Falk managed to put her down right on his spot. After two or three hops, up, over, and down. It was still great flying with Falk. I hoped that he and I would have the experience of flying together sometime off in our futures. We got out and secured the helicopter blades with long ropes or lines, whatever, so they wouldn't spin in the constant wind of the Cape. His mechanic came out of the hangar and looked her over. He asked Falk, "Any issues?" Falk looked back the chopper and shook his head. "Nope, she flew like a dream, Dad." I wasn't sure I heard him right, "Dad?" Falk looked at me and saw the confusion there. "Ethan, I want to introduce you to my father, Colonel Raymond Conroe Falcones." I shook hands with him, and still in a stupor replied,

"Sir, it's a pleasure to meet you." He looked me directly in the eyes, paused then said, "Falk's told me a little bit about you and your brother and your family. Sounds like you and him might end up as Brothers in Arms. Your Brothers will be lifelong friends, people you can count on in any situation. From what I've heard, you might be worthy. I'm glad to know you." With that, he threw an arm around both Falk and me as we walked back to the hangar. I felt a sense of comradeship with both of them; a past hero and possibly a future hero. And I wondered how I might earn their respect. Would it be in combat sometime in the future?

CHAPTER 62

It was late one Friday night, and Mom had gone with a friend down to New York for a couple of days. I think that she and Tory were becoming a "set" that people in social circles could invite to parties, knowing that they would be an entertaining couple. It seemed she was resuming some of her old ways, and her days staying in Calloway Court were numbered.

Marie had come back from one of her night culinary classes at the local college, and gone to bed already, so it was just Morg and me. I went over to Morgan's room where he was playing some sort of driving game. I watched him for a while as he raced through the countryside in his simulated Porsche 922. It looked like he was racing along the Italian coast, passing castles and small villages in the night time on a road twisting along next to the sea.

After a while, something occurred to me. While he was racing some fake car on a computer, we had a real race car sitting in the old garage downstairs. Mom had taken it out a few times. She had even driven it down to New York for a weekend. It came back unscathed, probably because it sat in an indoor heated garage in Manhattan the whole time.

I said, lazily, "Morgan, is that fun, racing a fake car in a fake country?" He replied, "Yeah, I like this kind of a racing game. You can get the feel of a real car inside a computer."

I said, "Now that I've got my License from driving that beat-up school Ford, I'm thinking that we should take a drive in our own car."

Morgan put down the game controller, and looked at me with

his eyes wide open, incredulous. "Are you out of your fucking mind? We could get in so much trouble. That car is a cop magnet and we'd set off every alarm on the planet."

"Yeah, I know there are risks, but here's what I'm thinking. With the warning we got when Tory talked to the FBI guys, we know we're in danger from someone, don't know who, but we might need to make a fast get-away, and our bikes won't work for that. They'd just run us down."

Morgan considered that. He had never really accepted that we could possibly be in danger. Even with the call we had with Dad, he wasn't convinced.

"That car makes a lot of noise when it starts. It could wake the dead, to say nothing of our neighbors.. Can you imagine the shit we'd get from Mom if she heard about it?"

"OK, right. We push it out of the garage, and roll it down the street until we can start it without being seen or heard. We jump in and take a quick ride around the town then out to the airport, then back here and stop it, then roll it back into the garage. Easy as cake."

Morgan thought a minute. "Here's the fatal flaw in your cunning plan. We won't be able to roll it back up the driveway, it's too steep. Getting out would be easy, but getting it back up the hill would be impossible."

"OK, we'll have to get the speed up before we cut the engine and then coast up to the garage."

"Yeah, but it'd be facing the wrong way. We have to back it into the garage."

I looked straight at him and said in my big brother voice, "Morgan, are you going with me or not?"

He thought about it for a minute. His little snake mind was looking for a way out of my ridiculous idea.

"OK, but promise me that you'll be careful. We don't need to attract any attention, OK?"

I put on my black hoodie and Morgan retrieved the keys. I said, "We need to see if Falk wants to go on our little drive. Let's stop by his house." Morgan cringed at this complication but agreed with a pained looking nod.

We went out to the garage and opened the door. After many recent openings, the door slid open easily. I got inside and put the car in neutral. Morgan asked, "Are you going to help me push?" I reconsidered our escape plan. "Get in. We're going to fire it up in here and deal with any complaining later. "

The Maserati started with its usual enthusiastic explosion and I let it warm up a bit, then we pulled out of the garage and rolled down the driveway as quietly as I could make it go. It was downhill so we just idled all the way. I turned right on Shore Road and slowly increased speed until we were out of earshot of our neighbors.

The tricky part was to go down Main Street without attracting the notice of the police. Then I saw the police car parked along the curb in front of "Harriet's Coffee Shop". I almost panicked but continued along as quietly as possible. As we went by, we could see Officer Collins sitting at a table, no doubt with coffee and dough-nuts on his plate. He didn't notice us, so I sighed my relief. I realized that I had been holding my breath the whole time.

We drove slowly to Falk's house and I parked so that the head-lights shone directly at the house. I knew Falk was still up, and sure enough, he opened the door and looked out at us, standing in his bare feet. I saw his eyes get big in the headlight beam, and he went back inside and came out with his shoes on.

He had this big incredulous grin on his face, and said, "What the hell are we doing?" I noticed that he said "we", not "you", so I knew my new brother was now an accomplice.

"Morgan, hop in the back, and let Falk sit shotgun." Morgan got out and then slid into the small rear seats without complaining.

Falk got in, and surveyed the cockpit approvingly. "Wow, this thing is a rocket ship." I said, "Wait til you see how she drives."

I figured that if we had to go through a police-intense zone, I would let Falk drive since he had his license long before I did.

I drove carefully through the rest of the town, then out to the airport, then opened it up on Rte. 28. The car responded with the slightest pressure on the accelerator, and handled in turns like the racer she was. It was an amazing experience, and I had begun to get a feel for the car and how it handled high-speed turns in the curvy ride out past the airport.

I stopped the car out near the dirt bike track and turned to Falk. "Well, do you want to drive?" He said, "Absolutely!", and we switched seats. Falk drove out farther down Rte. 28, then turned on Hwy 6, and drove it hard down through the twisty section between the dirt track and the airport. The look on his face was he'd just finished Le Mans.

At the airport, Falk turned to me and asked, "Do you want her back?" I replied, "No, drive her all the way back to your house. We need to wrap this little excursion up pretty soon."

Falk pulled out on the highway and turned toward town, this time watching the speed limit. But, as we crossed the town line, we saw the flashing lights of a police cruiser pull in behind us. Falk obediently pulled over. I was thinking, we are so screwed. Morgan made himself as small as possible in the back seat. The cop got out, walked over to the drivers's side, and inspected the car with his high-beam flashlight.

We sat silently, then the cop spoke. "This is a pretty fancy car for you to be driving, eh, Falk?" Falk looked up into the flashlight and replied, "It was the best I could do on short notice, Uncle Bill." They started laughing, the flashlight went off, and Falk said, "Eth, Morg, meet my uncle Bill. This is Officer Collins, aka, Uncle Bill.

"Evening, boys. Isn't this your Mom's car? I've seen it around town a few times, mostly headed up the road north."

"Yessir, this is my Mom and Dad's car. We borrowed it so Falk could give us a driving lesson." That seemed plausible enough.

Uncle Bill responded, "Well, OK, but you boys are out too late to make any sense. You need to take this buggy back home and park it."

We all nodded dutifully, and Uncle Bill, said, "Have a good night.

Good to meet you, Eth." I guessed he had forgotten Morgan's name.

Falk started her up, and pulled out on the road. There was no traffic out at two in the morning. We drove into town, up to Falk's house, and Falk stopped in front. He got out, and said with a big smile, "Thanks for letting me drive your car. Sorry about the little scare back there. I suspected Uncle Bill might be lurking out there around the town line where the speed limit drops to 30 from 55. It's a nice little speed trap, and he is frequently the cat waiting for the mouse."

Ethan then said, "Falk, I'd like to ask a favor. Could you and Uncle Bill sorta follow us home? We don't want to get into any other trouble and if you could check in on us later, to make sure we get home, I'd really appreciate it. Morgan chimed in, "We've maxed out the fun meter, and we just want to get home."

Falk said, "I'll call Uncle Bill and we'll drop by in a bit to see if you're safe. In the mean time, take that rocket ship back to its moon base."

Morgan got back in shotgun, and we headed into town and back home.

As we approached the turn on to Shore Road from Main St/ Rte. 28A, I noticed a black car following us. As we got closer to our house, the car got closer and closer, and I started to turn in, the car appeared to try to push us into the drive. Instead of turning in, I turned back onto Shore Road and gunned it, bouncing across the ditch next to the street. The black car, which I quickly identified as a Mercedes, not a government Ford, tried to follow us, but I stomped on the accelerator. The Maserati leapt forward and within seconds we were doing over a hundred miles per hour on the twisty little road. I was glad to have just practiced this just minutes before.

There was a hairpin turn on the coast road, and I raced toward it with the Mercedes closing on us. The tight left turn after Red Brook Pond was coming up, but it was invisible in the dark. Good. Just before we got to it, I slammed on the brakes, and cut the wheel hard to the left around the sudden turn. We just tracked around to the new direction. As we sped away, I looked back to see the Mercedes leave the road and skid into the embankment guarding the turn. The pond waters were just down that embankment, but they stopped before they hit the water's edge. Their headlights disappeared momentarily in the dust cloud they had caused, but they hadn't overturned like I had expected. By then, I knew there was an expert driver behind the wheel, and they would soon be on us again. Time for one more trick. There was a big curve coming up, and as soon as we got far enough around the curve so he couldn't see us, I cut the car hard left onto a tiny drive that I knew went through to Bishop Lane. I stepped hard on the huge brakes and came to a stop within the trees and bushes of the little drive, cutting the lights and getting off the brakes. The Mercedes roared past us, ignoring the big skid marks and the smell of burnt rubber, and as soon as they were out of sight, I backed out and raced back on Shore Drive to our house. I skidded into the driveway throwing gravel everywhere, up to the garage, and we jumped out and we both raced to the front door. I yelled at Morgan, "There's a loaded pistol under your mattress. Get it out and meet me at the top of the stairs." I hoped that our Texas gun training on the ranch was still burned into Morgan's mind. Tonight we were Texas Rangers, not scared high school kids.

CHAPTER 63

I ran to my bedroom just in time to see the black car pull into the driveway. I threw off my mattress and grabbed the M-16 and two magazines that I had hidden there. I loaded one of the magazines and bumped it to see if the 15 round mag was locked, and I loaded the first round, and switched from "SAFE" to "FIRE" to "AUTO". Locked and loaded. I noticed that my hands were shaking.

Morg came out of his bedroom with the Beretta, chambered a round, and asked, "What's the plan? What are we gonna do?" We were both breathing hard, pumped high with adrenaline from the car chase and now from what appeared to be a deadly threat, but from an unknown enemy. What could they want?

I looked square at Morgan. "We are Rangers now. Are you good?" He looked at me with a surprised expression which then slowly turned savage, and nodded, "RANGERS!"

I whispered, "Let's see what they do next. Don't shoot unless you are directly threatened. Got it?" Morgan nodded, but his eyes were wide open and I could tell he was as scared as I was.

The house was completely darkened and dead quiet The only lights were the streetlights across the street and a tiny little light on our back porch. I went back to my room which gave me a view of the driveway. From the light of the streetlights, I could see a car parked behind our car, three shapes approaching the Maserati, opening the car door, shining a flashlight inside the car, and then having a brief talk. Then one of them went around to the back of the house, while the other two came up to the front porch. I went back to the upstairs living room where I could see their shadows on the drapes over the front room windows. The streetlights dining through the windows cast an eerie light in the living room.

They hesitated on the porch, then slowly opened the front door which I hadn't had time to lock. I could see that one man was carrying a pistol, and the other man had a short-barreled shotgun. I tightened my grip on the pistol grip of the M-16, and looked through the darkness at Morgan. He had seen the guns, too. I thought about calling 9-1-1, but didn't dare leave my post to go have a conversation at 0300 in the morning with a half-asleep operator.

The one who opened the door came into the front living room, turned on a flashlight, and looked around, seeing only furniture and the reflection off glass and mirrors. The other man with the shotgun followed him in. I waved at Morgan to drop back farther into the hall. He backed slowly deeper into the darkness, saw Maries's open door and faded into the blackness of her room. The man panned his light around the downstairs living room and then saw the spiral staircase. I heard him say in a muffled, angry voice, "Shit, Goddam it." He didn't want to climb our little spiral death trap.

Then he yelled out, "Calloway! You've got something which belongs to us and we're going to get it back!" They waited for a response, shining the light around the room, and up the stairs. We remained out of sight in the hallway.

Then it hit me. They had been watching the neighborhood for the appearance of the Maserati as evidence that Kirby Calloway had returned home to Pocasset. When Morgan and I went for our little drive, and they saw the car, they assumed that our Dad was driving it. They didn't know or care about us, they just wanted our Dad to hand over something that they valued highly. And then kill him.

I whispered to Morgan, "You need to watch for the guy who went around back, he'll find it easy to come up here on the back stairs. And Morgan, we are RANGERS." Morgan swallowed hard, nodded his understanding, RANGERS, and crossed to the other side of the hall.

Just then, I remembered! Shit! Marie was asleep in the middle bedroom. I crept down the hall and quietly opened her door. Morgan moved to the wall so I could get to her bed. Her window was open and a small ray of moonlight lit her face. I kneeled down next to her, feeling the heat from her body through the sheet. I put one arm over her body and my hand across her mouth hard, and whispered, "Marie, shh, shh, you need to wake up." She tried to sit up, but my arm held her down. Her eyes were wide open, and she looked at me and finally recognized me.

I whispered, "Marie, there are some very bad men in the house. Take your blanket and go back in your closet and cover yourself up with it. Stay there until I come get you." Her eyes continued to be wild, but she nodded, and slipped off her bed and quietly went into the closet. We had not yet moved junk out of her bedroom, and the room was still full of spare furniture, clothes, and linens so it didn't look like a bedroom, I hoped.

A loud voice called out again from the dark. "Calloway! We are not messing around with you. Come down here and bring the Nigeria stuff with you, and we'll just leave. No harm, no foul. You know we're not leaving without it." I knew he was lying. They weren't leaving us here in our own house alive. That thought infuriated me.

But it seemed like our situation was getting desperate. I could hear someone trying the back door, banging it around. Then I heard the glass window in the door break. It wouldn't be long before one of them would be up here. The other two guys downstairs were moving around too, I could hear someone in the kitchen, throwing things around and breaking glass and dishes. I patted Morgan in the shoulder as he crouched against the wall, then I partly closed Maries's door and went back into the hallway.

"Mister, this is Ethan Calloway, his kid. Our Mom is not here, and our Dad hasn't gotten here yet. We are expecting him in a day or two."

"Naw, we saw him driving that fancy car of his. That was a merry chase for sure. But that game is over. He's up there somewhere, hiding behind his little kid!"

"Promise, mister. That was me in the car. I was just out taking it for a drive. I know I'm not supposed to, but I snuck out with it. He's not here right now and I don't what you mean by the Nigerian stuff. I don't have anything like that to give you. My Dad hasn't been home in a couple of months. We don't know where he is. We just know he's supposed to be here this week or next." My heart was pounding through my chest, and I was short of breath.

They hesitated. The loud guy said, "OK, you come on down here. We want to meet you and say hello."

My heart sank into my shoes. The only bright spot was that they didn't know that Morgan was up here. I knew if I went down there, it would be bad, but if I didn't go down, it would be worse, and Morgan would get dragged into it. That was unacceptable to me. I had only a second to think up a plan, and it wasn't a very good one.

"OK, OK. I'm coming down. Just let me grab my flashlight."

I crossed the hallway to where Morgan was crouched. I checked that the M-16 was set to "AUTO" and gave it to him. I said, "Give me the Beretta." I took it and stuffed it in my pants under my black hoodie. I looked at him in the dark, not really seeing his face. "Morg, I've got to go down there. I expect they'll get a little rough with me, but here's what I want you to do. Are you good?" I whispered him my plan, squeezed his shoulder and turned to go down the stairs. I had never been more scared. I'm sure that showed on my face as I walked down the staircase like Orpheus descending into the Underworld.

As I stepped off the stairs at the bottom, someone hit me hard in the back of the head, and before I could fall on my face, he grabbed both of my arms in a vice grip while I tried to recover from the blow from the butt of the shotgun to my head. Then, I was pulled by my arms into the face of the ugliest man I'd ever seen. In the spooky glare of the flashlight, his face was as ugly as a wild Texas boar; little squinty pig eyes, pig snout, big fleshy lips, and three chins.

"You? You're only a kid. Where's your Dad?"

"Sir, like I said, I don't know what you're looking for. My Dad..." Mr. Ugly slapped me with his full palm open, hitting me just as hard as he could. My ear rang like a bell and my face was on fire from the slap. But something was awakening inside me. I wasn't going to be a victim of these creeps.

"Kid, I don't have any more time to fool with you. Where's your Dad's office? Upstairs?"

I didn't answer him, so he pushed me off into the guy who had been holding my arms, and said, "Hold him here." The guy who had gone up the back stairs reappeared in the downstairs hallway, and said, pointing to the back of the house, "Boss, there's another way up, back here."

I desperately hoped Morgan had faded into the black of Marie's room and hid within the stacks of laundry and spare dishware that we hadn't moved out of her room. And I hoped that Marie didn't freak out with Morgan hiding right next to her.

Mr. Ugly put his gun away, thought about going up the back stairs but changed his mind and decided to take the spiral staircase up. In the dark, he got tangled in it halfway up, losing a shoe which hit the coffee table down below.

"Shit. Goddam it. Bring me my damn shoe." The third guy picked up the shoe off the coffee table and went around to the back stairs to go up rather than risk the spiral.

After those two were both upstairs in the study, I could hear them tearing all the drawers out and throwing papers around. The guy holding me was getting bored I guess, so he hit me again hard in the back of the head, knocking me to the ground. The pain was terrible all through my head, and even into my eyes. I felt my personal beating was getting off to an early start. One more hit and I would be unable to hit back. It was time to act with the all the fear and hate inside me.

I pulled the black Beretta out of my waistband and I shot him twice, once in the chest, and once in the neck. The shots were deafening in the large room. Blood flew everywhere, and he grabbed his throat and fell backwards on the couch. I crawled over behind the bar, out of sight from the top floor.

Hearing the two shots, the other guys, Mr. Ugly and whoever else had gone upstairs to toss my Dad's study came rushing out of the hallway into the upstairs living room. They fired blindly into the downstairs, breaking the glass in the front windows with a large shatter and bouncing a few rounds off the marble-topped bar that I was hiding behind. I waited for them to come down, trying to see them and aim in the darker room.

Just then, Morgan stepped out of the darkness behind them from Marie's room and shot them with two bursts of three rounds before they even knew he was there. The gunshot noise rang through the house. The first one fell to the ground in the upstairs hallway, but Mr. Ugly tried to turn around to face Morgan, but Morg gave him three more rounds, and he fell backwards down the spiral staircase, only making it about half-way before his dead limbs got tangled in the handrails and stopped him, hanging upside down. One of his shoes fell off again, and landed on the coffee table. Several of the spent casings rolled down the spiral stairs, making a tink-tink-tink sound as they dropped from step to step, until they rolled into Mr. Ugly's body.

Morgan came down the back stairs and joined me staring up at the dead man, dripping blood on the parquet floor. He looked at me, took a deep breath, and said, "That wasn't the plan." We both sat down, totally exhausted by our experience. I looked over at him, then hugged him, and said, "So, what do we do for fun tomorrow night?"

We were both in shock so a macabre joke seemed not to be pure sacrilege. Three bad men were dead in our house in less than 30 seconds, and we had killed them, Morg and me. Morgan looked sorrowfully at me and said. "The guy at the top of the stairs isn't dead yet. I saw him twitching." He then burst into tears, but then stifled a sob, regaining what was left of his composure. I thought, it would have been much easier if the bastard had just died. Now we would both have to face him for months to come. I was tempted to go up there and finish him off.

The house was amazingly quiet, the only sound was blood dripping and hitting the parquet wood floor. The metallic smell of the men's blood was nauseating, especially when combined with the acrid smell of the gun smoke which lingered in the room.

Morg and I just sat there on the floor, paralyzed by the release of fear and the sudden realization of what we had done.

Suddenly, the front door opened. Morgan and I both jumped, then crouched down behind the furniture, trained our guns on the doorway, and strained to see who had opened it. As a man stepped into the dark room, we realized that we had forgotten about the get-away driver. He held a pistol in one hand, turned his flashlight on with the other hand, and looked around. He trained his light first at the body on the couch, and then on the body in a grotesque pose hanging on the spiral stairs. The horror of what he was seeing hit him, and he stumbled backwards out the door. A few seconds later, we heard an engine racing and the squeal of tires as he left as quickly as he could go. Unfortunately, he only got a block before he ran into a police car driven by Uncle Billy, with Falk riding along. He swerved the car into the woods and got out, trying to flee on foot. Falk nailed him with a tackle with Uncle Billy right behind. He quickly surrendered lying on the ground in a thorn bush after having a shotgun pointed at him.

We tried to recover our composure, when we heard a loud noise from upstairs, and once again we drew our guns. The intruder flicked on all the lights and stared at the carnage in the stairs. Her eyes flew wide open as she looked around the room. I had forgotten about her. It was Marie, wearing only her nightgown, and coming out of the dark after the shooting had stopped.

"Oh my God!! Oh my God! What happened here? Are you guys all right?" she exclaimed.

Morgan replied, with concern, "Not really. Ethan here is bleeding from the back of his head, and he is ruining his shirt."

Marie rushed down the spiral stairs, jumped over Mr. Ugly's body, ran to me and turned my head so she could look at the back of it. "Oh my God! Eth! You're a mess. Does it hurt?"

I was just beginning to feel the pain in my head as the adrenaline burned off. I sat down on a cushioned chair. Morgan quickly grabbed me by the shoulder, and said, "Don't sit there. You'll get blood all over it. I was beginning to feel very woozy, so I just sat down on the floor. Marie came over with a wet dish towel and held it to my head. I was feeling really sleepy now and just wanted to lay down.

Just then Falk and Uncle Billy came into the room. Uncle Billy was holding a big first aid kit, and when he saw me he came over and opened the kit and started pulling stuff out. As he did, he was looking around the room. "You got them both, huh?" I replied, "No." Morgan interjected, "There's another one upstairs. He may not be all the way dead yet." Uncle Bill called Falk over. "You take care of Ethan. I've got to sort this mess out. Morgan, come tell me what happened."

Falk grabbed a pillow off a couch and told me to lay down on it, with a big towel to cushion my head and absorb the blood still flowing from the wounds on my head. I looked up at him, then passed out.

CHAPTER 64

The next thing I remember is waking up in the hospital. I had no idea where I was, but my head hurt so badly, I didn't want to worry about it. I just laid there looking around with my eyes, not daring to move my head.

I saw Mom on the other side of a glass wall talking to one of the doctors out in the hallway. As I got more aware, I realized I was in intensive care, and Morgan was sitting in a chair right next to the bed.

When he realized that I was awake, he stood up and looked at me with a very worried, but relieved look on his face. "How are you feeling? You were in surgery for two hours, and then out of it since last night. You had me worried, bro." he said.

I couldn't say that I felt better since I had nothing to compare it to. I just had an awful headache and a couple of tubes in my arms. "Fine", I replied. "What's been going on since...what time is it?" Morgan looked at the big clock in the wall and said, "It's a little after seven, in the morning."

He continued, "Well, after you passed out, more cops showed up and they must have called the Feds so they showed up too. They figured pretty quick that it wasn't just a home invasion, there's more to it than that. But they aren't telling anybody what happened. No press, no TV cameras. Somebody in the FBI called Dad in Nigeria and he's going to be here later tonight."

I told Morgan. "So at least we know what it takes to get him to come home!" Morgan just smiled ruefully, "Yeah, we do."

"Who were those guys that we...killed?" I was beginning to

feel regret. The anger had faded and now what I was feeling was a sorrow for taking human life. But, I also knew at the time that we weren't going to walk out of there alive. Those guys were brutal killers and they were planning to kill us. The guy I shot was intent on just beating me to death. He just didn't feel like wasting a bullet on me. Luckily, I had a couple of bullets to lend him. Yeah, RANGERS.

Morg nodded, then he reported, "The first guy I shot only got hit twice and is expected to make it. Mr. Ugly sent him out on point, so Ugly got most of the shots. All we know now is that they were some professional thugs that do work for a variety of "businessmen" to solve problems that don't get handled in court, guys who can give people a little push.

"Morg, those guys weren't after us. They were after Dad and something that he has, something that they said belongs to them."

"Yeah, that was pretty clear. From our call with Dad, he's got information that's gonna put a lot of bad people in jail. And they are watching us to grab or kill him to make sure nobody ever hears about it. That means that we are not safe either."

CHAPTER 65

Kirby Calloway landed in Boston Logan Airport at 0215 on a flight from Newark, originating from Nnamdi Azukiwe International Airport in Abuja, Nigeria, a total flight and wait time of over 24 hours. He called ahead for a Boston Coach limo to get him on the fastest route to Wareham Tobey Hospital, where Ethan was being treated.

The Coach pulled up in front of the Tobey Hospital, and Kirby jumped out before the driver could come around and open the door, leaving his go-bag on the back seat. The driver, Mitch, tried to call out and remind him, but he disappeared into the double doors. He sighed, got out and retrieved the bag and took it to the front desk. "This is for Doctor Calloway, he was in a big hurry, must have an important case to get to."

The receptionist looked at Mitch. "Yes, he does. His son has just gotten out of surgery." Mitch looked down the hallway where Kirby had disappeared. "Well, I hope he was in time," then turned to drive back to Boston.

Kirby ran into the ICU Ward, and was intercepted by a nurse who said to him, "Follow me. Your son will be fine in a couple of weeks, he had a head injury, but should recover with no lasting effects. Here is his room. If there is anything I can do for you, just let me know."

As he approached, he saw a familiar figure with long blond hair. Cindy Walker Calloway was talking to a nurse, and she heard him walk in. She turned to face him. There was only the briefest hint of a smile. Tory had been in to see the boys, and was now just standing next to Cindy. Cindy did not bother to introduce him.

"Welcome to the party, Kirby. It's good to have you here. We think he will be okay after the doctors did a little repair to the back of his skull. But I want you to know, Tory and I are not going to be caught up in whatever evil is chasing you. We're out, and we're going back to New York!" Then she reached into her purse and pulled out some papers. "Here's your divorce decree. All you have to do is sign these papers and send them to my attorney and we're done."

Then she turned on her heel, went into the room and hugged Morgan, and tried to kiss Ethan. He turned away, not wanting to look at her. Then she walked out, with only the briefest glance at Kirby, and with Tory looking apologetic but following along behind.

Kirby looked into the room and saw his son's heavily bandaged head, but Ethan was awake and talking to Morgan. His heart leapt at seeing them together and safe. He opened the door and went in. Ethan saw him first and tears appeared in his eyes. Morgan turned to see him, and suddenly tears of joy and relief ran down his face.

Kirby gathered up Morgan out of his seat and they fell onto Ethan, hugging them both fiercely. "Dad, were so glad to see you! We have been worried about you." Kirby was speechless, just rejoicing at the hugs of his two wonderful boys. Morgan quipped, "Uh... Dad you smell like Africa." They all laughed, and Kirby said, "Well, you would to if you had been traveling for almost 30 hours. I'm sure I probably smell like a water buffalo or worse." "Morgan chipped in, "I was thinking more like a hippopotamus, Dad."

Ethan opened up, with an urgent tone in his voice. "Dad, what is going on? Why was the FBI watching us, and why did those guys come looking for you, and deciding to kill us?!"

Dad loosened his grip on us, and turned to the nurse waiting outside, and made a go-away signal with his hand. She looked annoyed but she turned around, then stood at the door to prevent anyone from coming in. He told us this:

"What I am going to tell you is secret and very sensitive information. We have uncovered a human trafficking and drug ring that works on a global basis. There are some people here in the US, very highly placed people, that have a role in it. We are in the final stages of our investigation and expect criminal action to result. I guess one of these people thought I was home and had the information with me. I'm really sorry you guys got caught up in this. I still need to finish it. That's why I have to go back right away. I have made a commitment to the President that I must keep, and who I now consider to be a friend. Do you both understand?"

I nodded my head and so did Morgan. So that was behind all of this. Dad has made a commitment to a guy in Africa that could get us all killed. Somehow, I found myself admiring my Dad for that. After all is said and done, the commitments you make and keep are the only things that truly define a man. Dad stayed with us for two days. I slept most of the time while Morgan had to go to school.

Wendy and her family sent flowers, but I think her Dad told her to stay away from me until this got sorted out.

On Day Three, when I was awake and somewhat lucid, Dad told us, "There are some loose ends here that it's hard for me in Nigeria to uncover. I know this is a tough thing, but could you guys try to trace the guys that attacked you? You have their names and I'm sure the local cops will assist you if you ask. They would probably welcome your help."

Morgan volunteered. "Dad, we'll take it as far as we can. And we'll be careful."

I was feeling pretty good at this point, but I still got dizzy when I got out of bed. I tried walking around my room, and it seemed to help.

I stood up and hugged my Dad, and so did Morg as he prepared to leave. I suddenly realized that Morgan was taller than me. I also realized how much I loved my brother and my Dad. Our family has been through an unbelievably horrible experience and it wasn't over yet.

CHAPTER 66

After a whole week, I was more than ready to get out of the hospital and go home. The doctor just told me to take it easy and call him if I had any dizziness or vision problems. I didn't and wouldn't.

The whole episode left me with more questions than answers. The thugs who attacked us in our own home were looking for something that my Dad had or knew about. It was obvious now that all of this was related to the horrible facts that he was finding out about human trafficking. Dad wouldn't discuss it in detail with us, and left for Nigeria as soon as the doctor cleared me. He said he had to leave or he would endanger us all over again. He stopped to have conversations with the Washington FBI, and they didn't seem all that happy with what Dad told them. From what he told us when he called from Dulles, I couldn't tell whether they thought he was guilty of something or not. It was very confusing. It was getting very hard to figure out who to trust.

Morg came into my room and sat on my bed. "Eth, I'm afraid of all this. Those guys will be back again. Well, not those guys, exactly," Morgan chuckled. "But they know where we live and they apparently didn't get what they were after, whoever they were. Other than the little information that Dad gave us, we don't have any information that would be of any value to anyone. I'm tired of playing defense, it's time for us to pull together our offense."

All we knew was they were common bad guys, hired by some company in New Jersey that seems to not exist. The FBI is pursuing the lead but they have nothing.

From that moment on, I decided that Morg and I were going to have to look into this ourselves. But this would have to wait.

The next morning, I got up early and went out to my balcony. It was a crisp, cloudy morning with a threat of snow. The wind was gusting out of the West, and the low clouds were scudding along just over the hilltops to the North.

I came in and headed for the bathroom down the hall. I was surprised to see Marie coming out of my Dad's office with a yellow note pad. She was fully dressed like she had been up for quite a while.

"Good morning, Marie," I said. "What were you doing in my Dad's office?"

She looked down shyly and replied, "I'm working on a new recipe for tonight's dinner and I needed something to write on. It's complicated so I didn't trust myself to remember the whole thing."

"Really? What is it?"

Marie had a blank look for a second, then she replied haltingly, "Ah, it's a beef dish. I know you guys like that. It has a lot of herbs and some red wine, and it's called..ah..beef with wine and herbs."

Somehow this didn't ring true.

Then she changed the subject completely.

"You were so brave the other night. I was hiding in the closet, but I could hear everything. I could hear them beating you downstairs and I was crying. Morgan was hiding in my bedroom and I was afraid they would come in here. They were tearing up the office and throwing things everywhere. But when I heard the two shots downstairs, the guys in the office came running out, then Morgan jumped out of the door and shot them. He SHOT them, right in front of me. After things got quiet, I came out and saw the guy laying on the couch and then the guy upside down on the stairs. I was so relieved that you were ok."

She had moved closer to me, and reached out with her hand and stroked my face. "I was so worried about you, I was afraid you were hurt." She moved even closer, and looked into my eyes, and kissed me. Her lips were warm and wet, and she made it more and more passionate. I was thinking about Wendy's kisses while I was kissing her, but I buried those thoughts and responded just as passionately to her. Then she pushed me away, and told me, "Come back to my room later tonight. I need you with me. I'm afraid those guys will come back."

I went back to my room, with thoughts swirling in my mind. I wanted this same experience with Wendy, but she had cut it off with me. Marie had tempted me on several occasions with appearing in skimpy nightwear, but now it was moving into something much more serious, something that I couldn't resist doing. I decided that it was time for me to step up.

CHAPTER 67

Late that night, I knocked softly on the door. I heard her say, "Come in, Eth. And shut the door. Lock it." I couldn't see anything in the blackness of her bedroom, but after a few seconds I could see her bed, and the split between the white sheets and the coverlet, which she had thrown to one side. I could then see the outline of her figure on the bed, and she moved to light a tiny little candle. The flame rose, then began flickering in the slight breeze from the drafty windows.

She was wearing a short little pink silk top, and nothing else. She was lying on her side facing me. Her right breast was cradled in her arm and her left breast was illuminated by the candlelight. She laughed softly, and said, "Come over here, you idiot, and slide in. I'm getting cold."

I put the Beretta on the nightstand, then dropped my jeans to the floor, and kicked them under the bed. I wasn't going to need them again tonight with Mom gone overnight.

I was almost eighteen and I've never been laid. For most of my life, I didn't notice girls and didn't seek being friends with them. My only experience with girls or women was with my mother and I thought girls were petty, unintelligent, and just a drag on me having to put up with them.

Then I met Wendy and fell in love with her. She was smart, curious, and would try anything. Except she wouldn't have sex with me. After that wet, salty kiss in the romantic darkness of the throne cave, I suddenly felt my repressed sexual energy explode. We had gotten pretty close a couple of times, lying on the couch in her living room, with her blouse open down to her waist. The beauty of her body filled my mind and pushed me close to the edge. But at the last minute, she would turn away from me, and call out, "We can't, no, we can't!" I could feel the repressed energy in her body, too but, she wouldn't...well, take the final step with me. After that steamy night experience which started on her living room couch, and continued in the Maserati until she called it off, she wouldn't speak to me, and she wouldn't explain it. She just shut down completely, even in class. And now, after the invasion of our home, she had another good reason to avoid me.

When Marie moved in with us at my Mom's invitation, I was annoyed at her turning our house into a boarding house for women. That was before Wendy and I peaked, and after that, I welcomed her being here. Outside her job and school, she was very smart and we talked about books, movies and even a few poems. I was even inclined to write a poem to her as an English assignment, but it was so transparent that I tore it up. All I would need is for something like that to start floating around school and I'd be done for with Wendy, and probably Colin, too.

But now, I had an opportunity to finally cross the barrier into manhood, at least that was what was going through my teenage boy mind. And from now on, there would be no "teenage boy mind" anymore. That would slip into the past tonight.

I clumsily climbed into Marie's bed and laid down next to her. I could smell her perfume and it went right to my head. She could feel my tension growing out of what little control I had, and pulled me on top of her, at the same time pulling me into her. I was frantic now, and with a few thrusts of my hips, I felt the radiant hot blast of my orgasm, wave after wave totally ravaging my body.

I fell over to my side, pulling her with me into an embrace while I recovered my breath. All I could say was, "Oh, that was the most incredible feeling I've ever had." I felt like I was turning inside out.

She laughed a very throaty laugh, pulling herself close to me.

After snuggling in close, she whispered, "Don't head on down the trail just yet, Cowboy. The Rodeo's just getting started." She turned on her side and wrapped my arm around her, holding my hand under her breast.

After the briefest of naps, I came out of my orgasm-induced coma and woke up. She had turned me onto my back and was stroking my earlobes, then touching my face lightly. Then her hand played across my chest just tickling my nipples, until her hand rested on my stomach. I could feel her fingertips drumming lightly on my waist, then she stroked my thighs, working slowly inward until she started stroking me up and down. Then she laughed and straddled me, pulling my manhood inside her. She began moving up and down and I could tell she was working towards an orgasm of her own. I was trying to restrain my own climax by thinking of strange things like...building a concrete sidewalk in front of our house. Anything but the growing pressure in my body. She began breathing hard and calling, "Oh! Oh!" Then she then let out a shriek that scared me, thinking that I had hurt her. She gasped two or three times, then laid back, totally relaxed. She turned to me and said "Oh, Ethan, that was marvelous." Then she turned over and nestled her naked bottom close to my groin, and pulled the covers over us both, and said with a sigh, "Goodnight, lover."

I woke up sometime after midnight, and turned on my side to face her. Her beautiful face was lit by the glow of the candle, and she must have felt me roll toward her. Her eyes opened slightly, and she gave me the smile only a love partner can give. I know I was grinning back at her. She whispered, "Good Morning", then pulled me to her, rolling underneath me. She put her hand behind my head, and pulled it down for a long, slow, deep kiss. "I want you", she said in an urgent whisper.

I rolled over on top of her, holding up my body with my arms. I looked down at her, enjoying the curve of her breasts and the beauty of her blushed nipples. I pushed myself into her, spreading her legs, which she then curled up round my back. We made love until we were both exhausted, then rolled away to get some needed rest.

Later, in what seemed to be the morning to me, I got up and sat on the side of the bed. It was still dark and the sun coming from the other side of the house was barely lighting the Eastern sky at all. I had to look hard to find my jeans laying on the floor and struggled to put them on. I realized that I still had my socks on, and chuckled at that thought. I found my T-shirt and pulled it over my head as I walked out of the door to her bedroom. I passed Morgan on his way back from the bathroom shower, and he barely looked at me. But he stopped and asked, "Marie?" I nodded, and he nodded, then tried to pop me with his towel. He turned away back to his room and said loudly over his shoulder, "Finally!"

CHAPTER 68

Juan Ruiz stood on the second floor balcony and stared angrily at the unloading schedule on his clipboard. He could see that they were very late by looking down at the handcuffed lines of young girls and a few boys just now coming out of the container box and lining up on the floor of the old warehouse, under just a couple of dimly lit bulbs. Once the men got the people unloaded, they went into the back of the container and brought out eight cases of Chinese Fentanyl. It looked like the girls who were last to get off were woozy from laying next to the Fentanyl for the last two weeks.

Ruiz was used to the horror of what he was doing. It had been going on, night and day for over three years. He was a small man in stature, but he was seen to his men as a brute who would deal with any situation with force and a consideration for profit. He always carried two weapons on his belt; a twelve inch Gerber knife, and a Sig Sauer P226 9mm pistol, which he had gotten as a gift from a friend, taken from a dead US Navy SEAL in a botched raid against Maduro. It was a trophy beyond any other.

Juan Ruiz was the son of a drunken Brazilian army sergeant and a mother who offered her favors to any low-life would buy her a cachaca. His mother took out her frustrations on him as the oldest child of a brood of seven little brothers and sisters of unknown parentage. He left home at twelve and joined the gangs that roamed the "favelas" up on the hills above Rio de Janeiro, living a life of violent crime. His hatred for women was well-founded and deeply embedded in what passed for his soul. After an attempted robbery of rich tourists on Copacabana beach, he spent seven years fine-tuning his murderous skills in the over-crowded prison in Pernambuco. He had escaped during the riots in 2012 and began his drug trafficking career before being recruited for this job which he saw as an upgrade.

There was another container load due within the next hour, and they could hide only one at a time on the tiny, broken-down loading dock. Such was the price of anonymity when the whole place needed to go back to looking abandoned by first light.

The smell of the place was awful; human sweat, human waste and vomit from some who fell ill due to seasickness or disease.

Ruiz wiped the sweat and stink off his forehead and wiped it on his heavily-stained pants. His small body was uncomfortable in the never-ending heat of this Venezuelan port. His face reflected in the window on the platform, outlining several large scars from knife-fighting battles before he perfected his skills.

The captives looked up at Ruiz above them on the second story platform, him looking down on them like some sort of God who would rule on their fate. Ruiz was mesmerized by the sight of all the women under his direct control, and watched as they were washed down with large hoses and water from the dirty harbor. Some of the women had lost their clothing from the wash down, and tried to cover themselves with whatever scraps of wet cloth were still hanging on their bodies. Ruiz enjoyed watching them trying to cover up.

Ruiz surveyed the awful scene and smiled. This was a better bunch than usual; more young women, particularly Orientals which were in high demand in the UK. Some were even still wearing the party dresses that they wore when his "recruiters" picked them up. He turned on the PA system and picked up the microphone and ordered, "Separate the old and short ones."

He felt a tug at his sleeve, and saw Rodrigo waiting for a command. "Sir, it's time for the sorting for transshipment. We need you down below now." Ruiz turned with him and walked down the stairs, going through a locked door into a windowed room where he could view all the captives, now dripping with water,

His men went out to the lines of chained captives, unlocked them, and pulled away a small number of old or unattractive people. When they unlocked the chain, one young man escaped the line and ran back across the dark building, furtively looking for a way out. Some of Ruiz's men ran out of the sorting area after him. Ruiz yelled out, "Don't shoot him, he's worth a lot of money." But when the escapee resigned himself to not having any way out, he stopped and kneeled down with his hands over his head. Ruiz's man clubbed him over the head with his rifle butt, then several others dragged him back to the lines.

Ruiz's men continued to sort out this batch of human assets; pretty young ones of White, Hispanic and Asian heritage to be sex slaves, young men for labor in mines, middle-aged African and southern Asian women designated for house-keeping, and the older ones designated for shipment to China for what was probably organ-harvesting.

They were all moved into separate rooms where they were fed and clothed, and allowed to rest for a while. They were given a two piece white garment to replace whatever clothing they had left. They were given a cup to get water from a dirty trough, and they were fed from a large pot of steaming rice and beans, the first food some had had for three days or more. A few of Ruiz's men walked among the young female captives, picked out a couple each, and disappeared into the darkness with them. Other men came and joined them, singing and drinking and waving bottles of tequila.

The women didn't scream or resist, they just followed the men away. They returned a few hours later, sobbing. A few of the older women tried to console them, but they looked out into the darkness, wondering if the men would come for them next.

Ruiz thought to himself that it had been a long time since he had any recreation himself. He went down to the room where the young girls were sleeping. He walked down the aisle where they lay asleep, many for the first time in weeks.

He decided against taking any of them. They were worth a pile of money to him. Instead, he opened the door to the ones headed to the Chinese. Many of them were awake and sitting and praying in small groups. He looked at each one in turn, then went back and grabbed the one he wanted by the hair and dragged her away, hitting at him, and screaming. The other ones started a howl and scream with a sound which would chill the Devil's balls.

He dragged her into a spare storeroom and threw her to the ground. Some other men, who were resting or smoking around the area, jumped up, grabbed their rifles and bedrolls and ran away.

The woman was in her early twenties and probably could have been in the younger group except for the fact that she had one lame arm, probably caused by disease or some field injury.

Ruiz grabbed her by the shoulder and stood her up. She looked at him, whimpering, waiting for what came next.

Ruiz ripped the top of her clothes off, then punched her savagely in the face. She fell backwards with blood gushing from her nose and mouth.

He pulled off the rough white pants they had given all the women and threw them to the side. He pulled off his pants as well, keeping the belt with the knife close at hand.

He got down to his knees and pulled her legs around him. He roughy raped her, getting his enjoyment from her quivering body underneath him, and the terrified look on her smashed face from which blood was still flowing freely. She uttered no sound which irritated Ruiz. He expected some appreciation for his decision to pick her to have sex with. He pulled back from her, then he asked her, "Have you nothing to say?'

In response she drew up her legs, and shouted 'puta'! then kicked him in the face with both feet, knocking him on his back. When he arose, her face was pure anger and rage. Ruiz's rage matched her own, and he took his big knife out of its sheath, and crawled back over to her. She showed no fear as he plunged the knife deep into her abdomen over and over. Then she screamed out with the pain, and this further excited Ruiz in his blood lust. He saw the look of horror and pain in her eyes as he poised the knife over her again, then plunged it sideways into her breast and past her rib cage into her heart. Her last words were "Oh, Dios!" The light in her eyes faded quickly as he withdrew the blade, wiping it on her long hair. Her blood was everywhere, Ruiz was kneeling in it as it flowed in all directions from under her body. Ruiz stood up over her, the blood from his legs dripping on her corpse. He took one long look at her, feeling the animal satisfaction he had desired in his body and mind.

He put on his pants which were also soaked in her blood, and re-sheathed his terrible knife on his belt. He walked out of the store-room and called out, "I need someone to come here." His voice was unmistakable and within seconds, two of his guards came out of the darkness into the light of the single bulb overhead.

"I need you to cleanup that mess, gesturing into the doorway behind him. One said, "Right away, Boss" and they went through the doorway. One of them cried, "Oh, God, and the other one vomited violently. Ruiz tightened the belt on his pants and kept walking. He walked over to one of the cleanup hoses and poured clean water over his head until there was no trace of the blood from the woman he had just brutally used for his own satisfaction. The blood red water spread out over the floor with nowhere to go.

Rodrigo suddenly appeared in front of him.

"Sir, the next container has just arrived. Shall we unload it now?"

Ruiz looked at the man, who was terrified by Ruiz's looks. "Wait until I change clothes and go to the tower. I will give you the signal then."

From the first batch that night, most were asleep when the trucks drove up to take them by sea to brokers in various countries where there was a need for workers or other needs like the Chinese. The old ones commanded a great margin since their organs could be resold at a fabulous profit. The young women would bring in the next level of profit, but there were more of them, so the total income was higher.

Just then, the dockside door opened and the next container arrived for processing. Ruiz smiled, and thought about the cash accumulating quickly in his accounts in the Caymans, where he planned to take a couple of senoritas in a couple of weeks. He could already taste the margaritas and smell the coconut oil on the warm skin of two lovely girls curled up with him in his cabana. These girls had no knowledge of his depravity yet, but they sensed an animal passion in him that made being there with him sensously exciting despite the danger.

The phone in the wall rang, and Rodrigo said, "Sir, it's for you. You should take it in your office."

CHAPTER 69

Ruiz raised his thick eyebrows, then frowned, and walked slowly back into his office and closed the door. Inside his office, he could no longer hear the screams as the new assets arrived and those processed were pushed out the doors to their final destiny.

He picked up the phone and pushed the button on the line with the blinking light.

"This is Ruiz."

"Ruiz, I just wanted to alert you to some recent inquiries that we are getting from the FBI into our operations on our "mining" shipments. I don't think they really have any reason to follow up with you, but you should be careful, more careful than normal."

"So, what are you asking me to do? I am already just operating at night, and our shipments are only half what they were only three months ago. I have recruiters all over the world asking me why we aren't taking more product."

"We just need to be careful. From now on, I need you to send all the cash to a new bank account in Nigeria. I will email you all the details over our secure line. Use our trusted courier to move it."

"Ok, Sir. Is that all?" Ruiz asked, in a very irritated way.

"Look, Ruiz. I do not need any attitude from you. Just do what you are told."

"Yes, Mister Congressman."

"Damn it, Ruiz! This is a secure line but never use that expression again, or you will be replaced, or worse!. DO YOU UNDERSTAND?!"

Ruiz hesitated to calm his nerves. "Yes, I do...Sir."

"Then just get on with our business and be more careful!"

Ruiz slammed the phone down, and spit out between clenched yellow teeth, "I will kill that el Cabron if he screws this up for me. Or anybody else who interferes! And Rodriguez, tell the captain of the boat leaving tonight that he will have me as a passenger."

CHAPTER 70

Congressman George Washington Hilton warmly welcomed the delegation from the Massachusetts Chapter Against Child Slavery and Sexual Abuse (MCACSSA) into his Washington office. "Come in, welcome, I'm so glad to see you all," he said as his all-female guests wearing white gloves who now filtered into the semi-circle of chairs his staff had arranged in front of his desk. The scent of old lady perfume wafted through his office. They exchanged pleasantries about the mild winter, and, of course, speculation about the fate of the Patriots after Tom Brady. New England women are rabid sports fans at any age.

When the talk ceased, the chairperson Ms. Georgia Allen spoke. She had a look of grim determination on her face.

"Congressman Hilton, we wanted to ask what specific bills you are prepared to sponsor to end the filthy practice of stealing children from their dear mothers and selling them into a life of abuse and perversion."

Hilton was a big man, with a white balding head, a long nose, and long, bony fingers that he would use to punctuate every point. When he was angry, his eyes would bulge out, terrifying his opponents who didn't know him. He was not a man to be trifled with; he had spent twelve terms as the Congressman representing the 15th District, and he was the chairman of the House Intelligence Committee. He had a Law Degree from Harvard and had graduated Summa Cum Laud from the University of Vermont. He was a respected Congressman and was holding out for a Federal Justice appointment so he could retire. He wasn't known as a pleasant man.

But his wife, Ellen, was just the opposite. She was from an old New England family, the Reveres', and she was the picture of friendship and hospitality, especially when it came to people who donated to their fund, "Protecting Women Globally" (PWG), which she ran.

But in response to the question from Chairperson Allen, he smiled, somewhat uncharacteristically, showing two rows of perfectly inserted white teeth.

"We have several bills in conference as we speak. The issue we are dealing with right now is the consideration of opportunity and their human rights. Young women who live in small villages in impoverished countries need more opportunities than just growing up poor. Sometimes they need a boost out of poverty and a chance to make more money for their families. Yes, dear ladies, we know of horrible things going on, and we will take strong action to stop these atrocities, but we must respect human rights, especially those of women all around the world, as well as their right to immigrate to these welcoming United States. Don't you agree?"

Many of the women of MCACSSA nodded their heads solemnly, while some of the others were not satisfied with the answer. He then mentioned his and his wife's foundation.

"My wife Ellen and I have established a foundation, the PWG, for caring people like you who want to donate to the work of helping those people." He handed out brochures that described the work that the foundation was doing in third-word countries to improve the living conditions and education of women living there.

"Please consider our Foundation in your giving plans."

Ms. Allen was not to be diverted from her purpose. "Are there bills close to being passed that will specifically target organizations that are engaged in the human trade, especially their banking transactions?" Ms. Allen was unconvinced, as were several other women.

Congressman Hilton replied, "Yes, that is a great point. We are looking for banking institutions that have funds that may have origins that we can't trace. Some governments make that extremely hard, as you may know. But we are right on top of it, we have Federal agencies that specifically track these types of transactions."

"Ladies, it is so nice to listen to your concerns and I hope to take action on your behalf to eliminate this scourge from our planet. I invite you to come back soon and meet with me again soon. My aide will escort you down to a special lunch we have arranged for you with several of my most experienced aides. I trust you will have a nice time during your visit to your Capitol."

The ladies were escorted out of his office by his aides, with a few ladies turning around and waving goodbye with their white gloves.

Hilton's chief aide came into the office and shut the door. "That was a big nothing burger. Do you think they left happy?"

Hilton wiped his brow with the handkerchief he took out of his suit jacket, and shuffled the papers on his desk while he composed his answer.

"There is only that one woman who matters, that Allen woman. She is a problem because her husband is a Senator on Foreign Relations and Immigration Committees. He could launch an investigation, but it wouldn't go anywhere. They've gotten this trafficking thing so wrapped up with immigration reform that they will never unwind it. I'm not worried. I told Ruiz to slow down and start moving all the money into the new Nigerian accounts. Our bank there is owned by the second most powerful man in the country. It will be safe there. That will slow them down if they are trying to track the money. I'm not worried. But, just in case, tell Jimmy that we might need a more skilled crew ready to go. And I suspect that Calloway will uncover the operation in Venezuela and we need to be prepared to burn it out."

His chief of staff nodded his head in agreement. "I'll get on that right away. But what about Calloway?"

"I've sent a man to check him out. He's moved out of the Hilton and into a fort near the Federal zone. He has security guards all over the place. I think the President himself is protecting him. But, I think we can turn some of his guards."

"Then we'll take them down together!" the aide bragged.

"No. We'll lay low until he comes back to the States. We've scoped out the house now and know how to take it. But we'll wait until we see Calloway developing something we can't have exposed. Then when he runs back to the states with the evidence, we'll take him out either on the way home or when he gets to that place in Pocasset. And the kids too. I'm still grieving for those two idiots we sent last time."

This caused Congressman Hilton and his Aide to erupt in laughter. "Can you imagine four tough Jersey thugs gunned down by a couple of kids? How on this planet could that happen?"

Hilton turned serious. "I want them dead! Do it right next time!"

CHAPTER 71

The next morning, Kirby packed up his office supplies, toiletries, and his 9mm Beretta into a small bag. It was finally time to leave the Hilton for his new digs in the Asokora neighborhood on Grace Court. The important documents along with his evaluation and analysis papers were crammed into his old leather satchel. His clothes were already packed into three suitcases from the night before. He looked around the room twice to make sure that he had not left anything behind. As he started for the door, he heard a loud knock, a bam-bam-bam. He jumped back and pulled out his Beretta 9mm pistol. Before he could say anything or ask who was at the door, he heard, "Doctor Calloway, it is I, Katanga, and I am here to collect you."

Kirby opened the door a crack and was relieved to see Katanga standing there with a bellhop and a cart for his luggage. "I'm very glad to see you this morning, Katanga. I'm also very glad to say goodbye to this hotel suite after three months. But why did you make so much noise when you knocked? I almost shot through the door."

Katanga explained, as he ordered the bellhop to load the luggage and take it into the hallway. "Sir, I beat on your door in that fashion so that in any instance you will know it is me." Kirby nodded, "But in the future, could you tone it down just a bit?" Katanga, smiled and replied, "Maybe just a bit."

As they headed out of the room, Katanga stepped in front of Kirby, "Sir, you must permit me to go first, in case any introductions need to be made." Kirby took that to mean in case they met any opposition.

Kirby stepped back and decided to follow Katanga's instructions with regard to this new protocol.

Kirby then asked, "How is the new place coming along? I'm very excited to see it."

Katanga replied, "Oh, Sir, there are still a few things out of place, but I think you will enjoy your new surroundings. I think you will find a surprise or two."

Nam was waiting with the car, and still did his little salute when Kirby entered the open car door. Kirby asked Katanga, "Where did you pick Nam up?" Katanga looked at Nam, who smiled crookedly, and replied, "I served with him for a time in India. He's a retired Gurkha and can't put his uniform back in the closet."

Katanga sat in the front and watched keenly all around the car as they made their way back to the new office-home. The traffic was busy today, with everything from Mercedes limos, buses, taxis, pushcarts, sports cars, and even men riding donkeys.

Arriving at Kirby's new home in Asokoro, they pulled into the front gate under the arch and stopped in front of the door. The staff was assembled on the front steps, and Katanga introduced each one; the cook Ansarra, the housemaid, Sumara, the grounds keeper, Ikihi, and the head of the security guard, Bosin. A few of Bosin's guards stood in the background in their light green shirts and dark green pants uniforms.

After an introduction from Katanga, the group politely applauded Doctor Calloway and then went back to their respective duties. Katanga led the way into the house, and Kirby eagerly followed him in. The change in the appearance of the house was stunning. All the furniture had arrived and been placed expertly. Rugs with Nigerian themes covered the floors. Just inside the door, Kirby was greeted by the company-provided decorator, Janine, and she led the tour of the house. Several of her staff accompanied them. Kirby was most interested in the upper floor and his office area. As they climbed the stairs, Kirby noticed the new Nigerian wall hangings and paintings. When they entered the upper floor, Kirby was immediate impressed. What he had asked for was to convert the largest room upstairs into a joint office space and conference room. A long conference table made from dark Nigerian mahogany dominated the room, and large whiteboards covered one wall. A new wall had been added to separate his large office area from the conference room. His office area now included his large mahogany desk, an intercom box, a seating area with several large chairs and a matching sofa. There was also a desk and a visitor's seating area for Sumara near the door. Behind his desk on the wall was a photograph of the President of Nigeria, Muhari Clarion.

Kirby walked over to his new desk and sat down in his new chair. He couldn't help smiling his pleasure at the dramatic change in the whole house in such a short time-frame.

"Katanga, you and Janine have done a wonderful job here. I am very pleased."

"Thank you, Sir. Welcome to your new home."

Katanga reminded Kirby, "Sir, you do have the dinner with the President this afternoon. You will likely need to spend time preparing for the meeting, so I will ask everyone to leave now and return to their duties."

The small group of staff and visitors that had formed for the tour broke up and Katanga and Kirby were alone.

"Sir, I have one more surprise for you. I thought it would be best to save it for last and when we were done with the formalities.

Katanga spoke into the intercom, "Sumara, would you escort our special guest in, please?" Kirby rose to his feet, not knowing what to expect. The door to the conference room opened, and standing in the doorway was a very familiar figure.

It was Claire, wearing the same black cocktail dress as she did on their last night in Paris.

Kirby could not hide his love and desire for her as she rushed to him. She kissed him with the same passion as she had during their wild courtship in Paris. As he inhaled her perfume, he recalled their walks in the Butte Montremarte district, the hill that the white

Church of the Sacred Heart, the Sacre-Coer, is built upon. It was the beautiful Paris of the Belle Époque, Paris of the past. They had roamed its gardens and cafes, and it was there that they fell in love.

"I've missed you so much! I've decided that I am unable to live without you", she whispered in his ear."

"But, also, I cannot live without Paris. You must take me back often."

Kirby countered, "Oh, are you going to stay here with me? I don't remember inviting you."

"Well, you didn't, you damn fool. Katanga did. You have him to thank. He told me this place needed a woman's touch, so here I am. This place looks awful, by the way, it looks like a men's club."

She looked around his office with disapproval. "Why don't you have any flowers in here. Isn't this where you work? How dull it is. How do you get anything done." She walked around the office, playing with the items on his desk, then seeing the picture of her in that same black dress and pearl earrings.

"Oh, God. You must think I don't have any other clothes. Well, I do, and I am going to change as soon as you show me where it is that you live. Then you are going to take me out to the best place in this rough little town and show me a good time!"

"Claire, my love. Please get settled in and then I will take you to some beautiful places. But first, I must honor my promise to have dinner with the President. Do you mind terribly?"

"The President...hmm. I guess I can let you go for that. But tomorrow, I want to have some fun!"

"Sumara, would you show Ms. Claire Montand to her room and help her get settled?"

"Of course, Sir."

Claire reluctantly released Kirby's hand and followed Sumara around the hall into his bedroom. She looked back, and blew him a kiss. They say if they walk away, but look back, you've got them. The thought of that made Kirby very happy.

CHAPTER 72

The President's car arrived inside the front gate at just before 1630. It was a brand-new armored Cadillac, similar to the "Beast" driven by the US Secret Service, but smaller. Katanga escorted Kirby outside and they both got into the car, which quickly sped away. Kirby had the thought that he and Katanga were likely the first passengers in this luxurious ride. They were headed for President Muhari's private residence, not the Presidential Villa. The route took them through the National Arboretum and up into a jungle located on a small hill near the Usama Dam. As they approached, they were saluted at several checkpoints of armed soldiers, and then after a turn in the road arrived at a small complex of buildings flanking a central, larger building, which Kirby assumed was the residence. All of the buildings were constructed of white stone. There were flower beds everywhere, flanked by growths of tall bamboo and Queen palms.

The President's car stopped in front of a large stone portal along a palisade of stone columns. It had a British Colonial feel, but was clearly Nigerian inside in design and flair. Kirby was surprised to see Mr. Mo again waiting for them, and he came over to the car and opened the door.

"Good to see you again, Dr. Calloway. I hope the drive over here was pleasant enough?"

"Yes, it was interesting. I hadn't been in this area before and it's quite beautiful when you get out of town."

Mr. Mo smiled and said, "Yes, it is rather pretty up here. Would you please accompany me?"

Calloway and Katanga followed him through the portal into a garden with lilacs, bougainvillea, and tulips. A small waterfall filled the air with its bubbling sounds and the sounds of rushing water. We came to a large wooden door, just plain light teak planks, arranged in an interesting pattern, but not encrusted with the jewels like the door in the Presidential Villa.

The door opened, and we were met by Muhari's "junior" wife, Adela, who welcomed us and escorted us into a large dining room. She was about thirty years old, wearing a beautiful flowered dress and flowers in her long dark hair. She insisted that we move to our chairs that were marked with an elegant name tag. There were several other guests in attendance who Kirby recognized as Ministers and business leaders. The table was set with beautiful silver tableware with ivory handles and ivory colored plates. Carved crystal water glasses set off the lights from the crystal chandeliers. I looked at Katanga and I could tell he was suitably impressed.

We stood behind our seats until we heard the ringing of a bell, then a loud gong. The President entered through a door at the other end of the room with his First Wife. He was wearing a white naval uniform with his ribbons and medals. He was the Admiral of the Nigerian Navy before he became a politician, and Kirby thought maybe he, like many veterans, felt comfortable wearing the uniform. His wife, Ururhu Amsawa, looked about forty, but could have been much older. Her hair was swept into a bun and adorned with small yellow flowers. Her dress was a bright golden wrap that highlighted her dark skin.

He came down around the table with his wife, greeting all the guests. He greeted Kirby and Katanga. "Welcome to Anaguan House. This has been our home for many years and it is a pleasure for us to have you visit. Please be seated."

Kirby and Katanga both bowed, and then Kirby said, "Ururhu, we thank you for inviting us into your home." She smiled, then dipped slightly before moving on to the next guests.

The dinner consisted of five courses, including a roast of water buffalo, which Kirby thought tasted like a cross between bison and ribeye steak. There was little conversation during the meal, as the food was entertainment enough with its uniqueness and taste. After the meal, President Muhari stood and said, "Doctor Calloway and I will meet in the study privately for a time. Please enjoy the desserts and after-dinner drinks. Thanks for coming, Mr. Katanga, and I will deliver your charge back to you safely in an hour or so."

With that, Kirby and Muhari walked out the rear door, and walked down the hallway to President Muhari's study. It was full of books from all countries, eras, and cultures. One wall was maps of Africa from the earliest days of exploration by the legendary Dr. Stanley Livingston.

They settled into facing large, leather chairs. Muhari's chair was placed in front of a stuffed roaring lion hanging on the wall. Kirby waited to see what the President wanted to discuss.

Muhari asked Kirby, "Do you remember your days as a Navy Midshipman? Especially the summer training in riverine operations?"

Kirby replied, "Yes, of course I do. Every day as a cadet gets burned into your brain. That's why the training sticks with you."

Muhari's face showed a wry smile. "Do you remember an exchange cadet named "Clarion" from Nigeria? He would have attended that training with you, the night river training program that you commanded."

Kirby thought back through his life as a Navy Midshipman and suddenly recalled a face, "Yes, why of course! Sub-Lieutenant Clarion? That was you! Now I remember, you were that guy that insisted on commanding his own boat, and got his crew to back him up. He was a determined son of a bitch and a natural leader. Yeah, I remember you now. How about that?..Sir."

Kirby was still in a daze thinking about those challenging military training exercises along the James River at night and his command of the fleet of small river attack boats, one of which had been commanded by the new President of Nigeria.

Muhari then explained, "When I heard you were coming to Nigeria to sell me a security system, I decided to award it to you and your company based on my past impression of you. I didn't know until later that you were a "Brass Rat" as well. In this job, it is very difficult to find people that you can trust. My country's history is about one military coup after another. We only returned to democratic rule in 1999, and even then corruption and outright theft was the rule from the President on down. I decided to run for President to try to stop it. As you might have heard, I have plenty of opposition, some of it very dangerous."

"But for now, I have the upper hand. I personally control almost a trillion dollars in cash located in banks all over the world from oil revenues stolen by a succession of corrupt regimes. I plan to spend it to reform the government and finally deliver the services and infrastructure that our country desperately needs, and to root out and destroy the remnants of Boko Haram."

Kirby was mystified. "So, exactly, what is my part in all this? I have all the information Umanda gave me on American companies and I suspect there is some monstrously bad behavior in there somewhere. But why did you give this task to me? I appreciate the new house and my elevation to Doctor, but what do you expect me to find that you couldn't?"

Muhari stood and walked over to the map of Africa, and paused for a minute, tracing the route of the powerful Niger River on the map. Then he answered, "A few years ago, when I ran the Nigerian Navy, I employed a US consulting company to help me streamline logistics operations. In the process of doing so, I learned an interesting thing about consultants. They rarely come up with anything really new. Usually, the answer to whatever issue you have is already known somewhere in the organization. The consultant's job is to find that answer and elevate it and help sell it to a very resistive management as something new from outside the organization. It's the old story about the prophet is never listened to in his own town."

"That's why I've asked you to provide your recommendations on what companies I can trust to get the job done, while they are not ensnared in our corruption which is so prevalent. You are an outside voice who will likely be listened to. If I were to do this investigation, it would immediately be seen as a political attack. So I must warn you; you and your advice are expendable if you prove to be wrong. And, more importantly, I want to find out if there are activities going on that are hidden from view unless someone peers deep into things that don't seem rational. I fear the worst. You need to be very careful."

"Or you can tell me now that you want out. But if you do though, all of it goes away; the software contract, the house, the servants, everything that you haven't even had time to enjoy. Do you understand me?"

The tone of the meeting had suddenly turned deadly serious. Kirby had already experienced the first taste of danger, and he knew what he was getting into.

"Yes, Sir, I do. I'm going to start digging into this as soon as I get back to my new home."

Muhari softened. He looked at Kirby and smiled. "I understand you have a special visitor. Take some time to enjoy being with her. But be careful going out in public with her. She could be a target for kidnapping. I'm sure you would do almost anything to get her back in that awful instance."

Kirby stopped to think about the gravity of that. When she walked in, all he could think about was his joy in having her with him. If she was ever endangered, he would do anything to protect her.

"Yes, Sir, You're right about that. But I have confidence in my "man" Katanga. And I will take your warning to heart."

Based on the urgency of the situation, Kirby decided to divulge what he had learned from his quick analysis of the data Umanda had given him.

"Sir, I have found some patterns in the logistics and finances of the ports that seem very irregular to me. I can't describe it now, but I think with a little more digging I can get to an answer. This is where I will concentrate. The recommendations for most of the activities that Umanda outlined are pretty clear. It's the ones that stick out that need to be checked out. It could be nothing, but then again it's very irregular for a logistics pattern of shipments and transfers of money. I'm getting the impression that the activity here in Nigeria is only part of the story.

Muhari was suddenly very interested. "What are you finding? Can you explain what you are seeing?"

"Sir, I really need to validate the truth of what I think I am seeing in the data. I don't want my preconceptions that there must be corruption in some segments to have me finding data that conveniently plug into that prejudice. But I'm afraid that it might involve human trafficking and slavery."

The room was silent, as President Muhari considered what Calloway had told him, and the evil it represented. Then Kirby asked, "Sir, weren't you a Catholic when you were at the Academy? I seem to remember that you would attended Mass at the chapel when I did."

Muhari looked down at the ground and then looked skyward. "I am a spiritual man. I find comfort in my relationship with the Heavenly Being. It does not matter what we call Him. He knows his name."

He continued, "This country has vacillated between being a Christian or a Muslim country. We have many tribes that are always fighting for control. I converted to Islam shortly after our Independence in 1999. The Muslims are always more forceful than the Christians. Many are radical, and if I did not take control as a Muslim, I would never be President. General Kwandanbo is always edging toward the next election, which will be in four years. I have that much time to correct as many errors as I can that we have created for ourselves over the past 30 years. If I am weak, some of my students in the military will see that and attempt a coup. This country cannot stand another military takeover. We rededicated our country to democracy again in 2003, right here by the Aso Rock. This rock represents our democracy now, and I have pledged that we will not be turned away from our true destiny again."

And then, "That's why I need your help in getting the best and most trustworthy companies to work with me and Umanda to get us moving again. And, Kirby, I know you have dual loyalties. I know you are working with the CIA." He let that hang in the air for a moment.

"I'm not sure what that means to you, and to me. But I do know I can trust you, that you know how to do the right thing. I need you to remember what we have been through in the past."

Kirby was deeply moved by President Muhari's deep feelings for his country and his honesty with him. He felt the gravity of the commitment he had already made to the President. CIA or not, he was going to keep his word to this leader. If there was value to the Company, so much the better.

"Sir, I agreed to your request a month ago and I will be true to my word." Kirby meant it. He was committed to helping Muhari finish his vision. His Naval Academy service ethic was still strong in him.

Mr. Mo showed up at the door, and Kirby realized that the dinner was over. Kirby turned to the President and bowed slightly to acknowledge their conversation. Katanga met him as he came into the entranceway. Mr. Mo walked them out to the President's limo, and drove in silence back to the new Calloway home and office in Grace Court.

CHAPTER 73

Katanga and Kirby walked to the door together. As they met at the door. Kirby was moved to shake hands with him, still in the trance of his meeting with the President. Katanga reacted quickly to the unexpected hand, and grasped it firmly. "Sir, I take it that things went well in your meeting?"

Kirby smiled happily, and then told Katanga, "I need a couple of your best logistics and financial analysts here tomorrow, we've got a lot of work to do!"

Katanga replied, "Yes, Sir, I actually told Langley to put two on the plane a couple of days ago...in case you decided you needed them after your meeting with the President."

Kirby looked at Katanga with a mix of surprise and admiration. "You said your job was to anticipate my needs. Did you learn that on the Farm? Some kind of magic?"

Katanga rolled his eyes up, laughing, " No, Sir. It just comes to me. My tribe in the Congo was a tribe of witch doctors. I guess some of that rubbed off on me."

Kirby laughed too. "That must be it then. If I lose my wallet again, can you call on the magic to find it for me?" Katanga laughed but Kirby suddenly remembered something very important.

Kirby looked around, and asked, "Where is Claire? I thought she'd be here when I got back."

"Yes, Sir. She had dinner here earlier, and then she decided she needed to rest from her long flight. I think you will find her in your bedroom, Sir."

"Thank you, Katanga. I shall be retiring now."

Katanga smiled broadly, "I wish you a lovely night, Sir."

He went into the bedroom without turning on the lights. Claire was asleep and breathing heavily, lost in her dreams. Kirby slid in next to her, trying not to disturb her. She sensed him moving next to her and turned toward him, still half asleep.

"Kirby, are you back now? Come over to me."

Kirby sat on the edge of the bed and removed his clothing. She snuggled up behind his back as he undressed. He could feel her warmth and smell the French perfume that he loved when mixed with smell of her skin. He sincerely hoped that he hadn't selfishly brought her into danger, but then he remembered that it was her idea...and Katanga's.

CHAPTER 74

In the morning, Kirby dressed then went into his office. Katanga appeared as if by magic.

"Good Morning, Sir. I hope you slept well."

"Thanks, Katanga. Can you arrange to bring the analysts over this morning so I can brief them and get started on the investigation?"

"Sir, they are awaiting you in the conference room having coffee."

"All right!" Kirby exclaimed. He pushed back his chair, and bent down to unlock his safe and get the documents Umanda had given him along with his own notes.

The two fresh-faced analysts stood as Doctor Kirby Calloway entered the room,

"Thanks for coming to assist in this effort. We have a unique intelligence-gathering opportunity as well as a chance to do a great favor to the President of this country. That's how I want you to view this work. Now please sit down and let's get to work. The first thing is to get a feel for the country and the key players. Katanga has assembled a playbook for you, get started with that."

In the meantime, the Security Software team had been busy. Kirby dialed up Al, the project lead, to check on the status of the work. "Al, this is Kirby. How is the project going over there?"

Al replied, "We had some holdups at first in getting cooperation from some people. They were slow to give us passwords and all the IP addresses to the systems they had, and some of their banks were even slower. But when I showed around your letter from the President they all started falling in line. Also, we heard that Muhari was a real bad-ass when he ran the Navy. They were talking about him making somebody walk the plank into shark-infested waters for disobeying him. The people we talked to didn't know if it was true, but they acted like it was."

Calloway thought back to his days in riverine operations on the James River, and the exchange Nigerian sub-lieutenant Clarion that he had under his command, the one that demanded command of his own boat over the heads of several senior middies. Midshipman Captain Calloway had given it to him, and then had been impressed by his skill on the water and in leading a team.

Kirby had worked with Al at a major security assessment and then a software upgrade at SwissBank in Zurich. Al Risdorphen was born from Swiss immigrants, and was almost a Swiss himself. They both found the Swiss bankers to be highly professional, very accomplished outdoorsmen, and totally tight-lipped. The chief of the group was Director Horatio Sorobet. He was in his 80's, tanned, over six feet tall, and incredibly rich. Sorobet was cordial, polished and he was clearly the leader of this very social little community. Partly because of Al's heritage, and partly for business courtesy, both he and Al were treated to many parties as well as skiing trips for the winter they were there. The only skiing Kirby had done was up in Vermont while he was a midshipman, and he found the Alps very challenging. There were easier runs, but the majority he found tended to deep blue or black. But their Swiss clients were patient teachers and Kirby soon learned to almost keep up with them.

"The only remaining bank to turn over their keys is the Kwandanbo Bank. They have been real assholes. I guess Kwandanbo and Muhari don't get along? But, doesn't Kwandanbo work for the President?"

Kirby sniffed, "It's complicated."

Risdorphen continued, "Well okay, that's way over my pay grade. We just got the keys today, and we'll work them into the test flow starting now. Most of the subsystems checked out fine, and if everything works out from here, we'll go live in two weeks. And we'll be putting in the secure line over to your office today or to-morrow. That way, you'll be able to see everything and brag about us to the President."

Kirby nodded, "That's great news, Al. We'll both be making a little money when that happens. Kirby had an idea. "Hey, Al, I have a couple of guys doing some work for me here. Not company employees, but I could make it look like they were. But I'd like to send them home with you and your team, if that's ok."

Kirby could imagine Al tugging on his beard and shaking his head, "Uh...I don't know about that. They check us pretty carefully going out. Has to do with their work rules and immigration. Let's talk about it later."

"Ok, Al. Never mind. Once again, great job to you and your team. Please pass that along from me. And let me know when your team is flying out."

CHAPTER 75

The two analysts took over the conference room, and Katanga locked it and posted a 24-hour guard on its door. The analysts were two youngsters pulled from the bowels of Langley's "Criminal Investigation" section. Both were single young men, highly motivated to serve their country.

The oldest one, who was no more than twenty-five years of age, Bob Hayes, had actually been through agent training and had served briefly in the field in Poland, but had asked to go back into Analysis Branch due to family issues, or maybe family pressures. As Kirby could attest, life doubling as a businessman but also serving as an impromptu CIA field agent was a difficult situation to balance with his duties at home.

The other one, Kent Simmons, had entered service after the two years as a Mormon missionary in Ethiopia. He had first-hand experience as he had seen Christian children being dragged away by traffickers. He was very eager to get started, pulling up research from the CIA country files, as well as newspapers and other journalists' work, even before he arrived on site.

After meeting them, and welcoming them to the villa and the team, Kirby acquainted them with his view of the situation, his goals for their work, and a warning about talking to anyone about what they were doing. They were assigned two of the six bedrooms in the villa with instructions not to leave without Katanga assigning them a bodyguard. Soon, they would be at as much risk as Kirby was, and he was determined not to lose one of them to kidnapping and murder. For that reason, he and Katanga had tried to compartmentalize the information so it would be hard for either one to gain the wider view. But at some time, they would all have to know everything, and then they would all be at great risk. If these guys were as sharp as they appeared, it wouldn't be very long before that was the case, then they would have to leave suddenly and safely back to the US under armed escort. But there was much work to do over the next several months.

CHAPTER 76

One morning, Katanga came in to Kirby's office while he was looking through records, "Sir, you have a visitor this morning. It is the Chinese trade representative. Here is his card."

Kirby was not surprised, in fact this meeting was overdue. "Very well." Kirby gave the card a quick glance and then put it under his notebook. "Katanga, please have him get comfortable out there. Maybe Sumara can get him some chai. But make sure he can't overhear the young lads in the conference room."

Katanga stepped out and closed the door. Kirby checked his schedule, looked at his email, and did a little search on Google, then got up and went to the door and opened it.

"Welcome, Mr. Le Ming. I've been wondering when we would find time to speak."

Le Ming returned Kirby's firm handshake with one of his own. He had a smile on his face but Kirby had not ever learned to read the meaning. He had seen it to be both a good thing and a bad thing, but he was unable to figure out which one.

"Yes, thank you, Dr. Kirby, and also congratulations on your new home. It looks like you are open for business here now."

"Yes, we are all quite comfortable here now. Thank you for your interest."

Le Ming appeared to look around the office and said, "I thought you would have a big staff by now, with all the involvement you now have with the President." Now his face did show a high level of interest.

"I have all the staff I need here. We also have a team doing a bit of systems work in the Capital and the Presidential Villa. That seems to be going well and that team will likely head back to the US by the end of the month."

"Of course, we heard about that contract you won...no, excuse me, were awarded to do the security software work in the Capital. Congratulations on that as well."

"Why thank you, Mr. Le Ming."

"You may have heard that my government has proposed to reduce cost and eliminate the inefficiencies on the ports of Lagos, Apapa, Port Harcourt, and Benin? Could I ask if this work has been mentioned to you by the President?"

"Mr. Le Ming, you must know that all discussions between my company and the President are highly confidential."

"Ah, of course, certainly. So you will know, we have also proposed to bundle the work package with some very attractive financing and offered some very low labor rates as part of the deal. Had you heard this from anyone else, perhaps?"

"Well, let me think, Yes, I did hear something about it over in the bar at the Barcelona Hotel in Lagos. Why, is it supposed to be a secret? The word seems to be out on the street, and in some of the bars around town. I think I heard about it in the Russian Tea Room as well."

Le Ming's facial expression did not change but Kirby could see a slight red shade in his cheeks.

"We were hoping to keep it confidential until all the details had been worked out. Then you may have heard that we are teaming with Kwandanbo's bank to cover all the financing."

It was Kirby's turn to show a blush, but not for the reason that Le Ming probably thought. It was looking more and more like Kwandanbo was scheming behind the President's back with the Chinese. They didn't need Kwandanbo's money. They have plenty of yuan. But they needed his power base to get the ports contract.

Le Ming continued, "We feel that President Muhari would see the benefit of what we are offering, especially if someone he trusts makes a recommendation to him."

"Yes, I am sure that he would be inclined to listen to me on this matter," Kirby offered. But not in the direction you would like. The Chinese Communist Party had developed an international aid strategy called "One Belt, One Road" (OBOR) that provided industrialization assistance to third-world countries with extremely lucrative prices. The Chinese had developed this program as a way of bringing third-world countries into their sphere of influence. But, one of the problems with the "One Road" program had been the Chinese practice of flooding the country with hordes of unskilled Chinese workers and also delivering dangerously sub-standard work, and then tightening the screws on the financing to gain concessions in real estate and state monopolies. There were also concerns about the diseases brought in by theses workers.

Le Ming continued, "We, of course, would see this assistance as a valuable service to Chinese business interests in Nigeria." He then waited for Calloway's response, to what was a very thinly-veiled bribe. His eyes were blinking at twice the rate as when he walked in.

Kirby just looked at the papers on his desk, then looked up directly at Le Ming.

Kirby asked, "Mr. Le Ming, is there any other matter that you would like to discuss?"

Le Ming thought for a few seconds, then said, somewhat mysteriously, "I just wanted to restate my government's position, as I have said to your Ambassador, that China is not responsible in any way for the increases in Fentanyl shipments to the United States. This is not our doing, and we pledge to help the US to stop any such shipments."

"Thank you, Mr. Le Ming. I will, of course convey this promise to the Ambassador as well."

Bob knocked twice, two little mouse raps, poked his head in Ethan's office. "Sir, we have something to show you if you have time."

Kirby could hardly wait to get rid of Mr. Le Ming, so he stood, and Sumara came and escorted him out. The feeling was that a dark spirit had left the room.

Kirby bolted out of his office, put his arm around young Bob, and grinned broadly, "Please, please do show me!"

CHAPTER 77

Kirby had read every bit of information from Umanda, plus the stacks of articles, bank accounts, telexes, emails, and just letters from hundreds of entities all over the globe, and he was unable to draw any firm conclusions.

Bob took him over to a large whiteboard on the wall. Kent stood in front of it with a wire stick that might have once been a fly swatter. In the middle of the board was a large circle that had the letters "RZ" inside it. Along the left side of the board were small to large circles that connected to a few larger circles. On the right side of the board was a drawing of a very large school of fish in a pond, and to the left of the fish were a number of large circles.

At the bottom of the middle of the board was a series of drawings resembling banks.

There was also a little picture that resembled the US capital at the bottom of the board.

None of the objects on the board were connected as yet, but ex-missionary Kent had a fistful of colored markers, red, green, and blue.

Kirby looked the board over and asked, "Ok, so what? What does this all mean?"

Kent began, with the air of a Harvard business school lecturer talking to a class of First-years.

"Doctor Kirby, this is a useful model for understanding the complex flow of transactions that would occur between any legitimate business entities in a global business network. We, Bob and I, call it the 'fish model'." They both chuckled at their little joke while Kent drew a few more fish in the pond on the board. "We've tried to identify all the organizations and personages that we see interacting, and then we've been able to identify the different real organizations that fit into the various functions that make the fish model work. And we have records of money transfers between the entities. Most of them are in cash but when banks get fussy there are records of those as well." While he was speaking, he was drawing red and green lines with arrows pointing in the direction of movement. The green marker arrows were for money and the red marker arrows were for "product", the fish.

He went on to show customers purchasing "fish" from brokers, usually in the same country, then these brokers contracting with shippers to purchase the fish from "RZ". Kent clarified, "The green lines show money changing hands, and the red lines show the fish being delivered to the customers. The "fishermen" catch the "fish" and sell them directly to the shippers who deliver the goods to the end customers via "RZ".

"Are you with me so far?"

Kirby nodded, he was impressed by the simplicity of what he was seeing. If he could put company names, or even peoples names in the circles, and track the financial transactions on the board through account numbers and interbank transfers, he could pinpoint where there were possibly fraudulent activities going on. It was all so much clearer now.

Bob tapped him on the shoulder to break him out of his trance, and said, "Dr. Kirby, there is one big problem. What are the fish? There are no records of customs and health checks on the shipments. There are no records of compliance with fishing quotas. There are no export licenses, and the fishermen, whom ever they are, haven't got licenses either. It doesn't make sense. There are people obviously buying fish and receiving fish, but no fish. There are NO FISH."

"And who or what is "RZ? We have some evidence, including a bunch of fish money coming from that entity here to Nigeria into a bank owned by Minister Kwandanbo. It was simply a cash deposit, and it appears to be the first one of its kind. Kirby was very interested now. "How much was it?"

Bob cleared his throat. "Umm..it was over $80 million dollars. And as soon as it landed, there were big checks cut to several US companies. We are trying to track down where the money really ended up now. And there is almost always some kind of clearing house that looks at all the incoming orders for fish; grouper, pompano, tilapia, and the like, and matches those requests to what's in inventory or in the pipeline. But there are no available records of inventory, or any orders, just pipeline shipping manifests."

"So we haven't been able to put a finger on the brain, the clearing house. We thought at first it was "RZ", but now we don't think there is enough evidence for that. "RZ" now looks more like an inventory management and transshipment point. We need to locate the central intelligence, if we might use that term," Kent said with a smirk. He turned to the whiteboard and drew another circle, drew money arrows from "RZ" to the circle, and then labeled it "CI".

Kirby was amazed by what Kent and Bob had been able to accomplish using the information Umanda had given him, but also his access provided by Kirby's new security system to any company data system in Nigeria and many banks around the world.

"Guys, you've done a masterful job of all this. So you're telling me we have two or three remaining questions. Where did the money from "fish" sales end up in the US, and what exactly, are our "Fish? Any ideas on this?"

"Sir, our best guess is human trafficking or drugs or weapons or some combination. There's not a lot of profit in guns; the market is flooded with them. I can buy a slightly used AK-47 for fifty bucks. An M-16 costs about a hundred bucks. They just flow from conflict to conflict. Both the US and China will send a dozen pallets of guns to pretty much anyone who asks for them. So our guess is human trafficking and drugs."

Kirby thought about the consequences of all this information.

If Kwandanbo was himself involved, which obviously his bank was, then he had a big pile of money to pay for some rogue military men to unseat Muhari or to buy the next election. Either way, he could create a lot of mischief. If he was tied to human trafficking, then he would also be branded an international criminal that if proven, would likely eliminate him as a threat. Muhari could have his bank assets frozen or even seized. That meant that Kwandanbo would be a serious threat to Kirby and his operation if what they knew leaked out.

Kirby's face turned deadly serious. "I think we may be in serious risk here. I'm going to phone home and get us some military help."

Both Kent and Bob nodded solemnly, and then looked at each other like, "What have we got ourselves into here?"

CHAPTER 78

Kirby reflected on the second question: where was the money ending up in the US? If the companies that were receiving money were just shell companies, then they were laundering the money before passing it to the principal. But what was the principal offering in exchange for the money? It had to be something of real value. Kirby had a realization. It had to be a government official that had enough power to force our system of oversight to overlook the issue, only someone in Congress could stall or weaken legislation that would put an end to human trafficking. They had been trying to put an end to drug trafficking for years and had made little progress. Now it was apparent why.

"Boys, I probably don't need to tell you how explosive this information is. I don't want any of this put in official communiques. We have to assume that if it is a Congressman involved, he could have spies in the CIA. We've recently seen how that organization and the FBI can be compromised, so take extra efforts to secure this information."

Kirby had a second thought. "Sorry guys, but I'm restricting you to the house for now. Once you wrap this up, I'll get you out on a private charter or an Air Force plane. We need to keep this out of official channels, got it? And don't say anything to any of the house staff, including Katanga. Let me be the one who fills him in with the minimum that he needs to know."

Kirby needed to close one more housekeeping task. If Al's installation team got caught up in this mess, it would be innocent US citizens and his friend who could be killed. He called Al's cell phone.

Al picked it up right away, and Kirby could hear airline boarding announcements being made in the background. "Hello, boss. Glad you called; we're on the way out now. Is everything ok?"

"Yeah, Al. It is, just wanted to make sure there were no last minute problems with you and your team getting home. And Al, I'm getting great reviews from two of our users. Good work, buddy!"

"Anytime, Kirby. Just go win some more like this one. I'm already spending my second commission check."

With that out of the queue, there was a third question that Kirby kept to himself, and that was, who was the "central intelligence" in this operation? The most obvious answer was stunning. What was the Company operation that Weldon had warned him to stay away from? It had something to do with the President. What had Weldon said? It was:

["We're not sure that Muhari is our best choice for President. We are seeing him poke his nose into things that we don't want to see reformed. Go about your business, but I wouldn't get too close to him if I were you."]

What was it that Weldon and the Company didn't want to see reformed?

"Ok, guys. We need to get this wrapped up soon. I want you to concentrate on two things. First, who is "RZ" and how do we find him and the transshipment location. Secondly, I want..." Kirby was interrupted by Bob, who raised his hand like a high school student.

"Sir, I think we already know the location of the trans-shipper "RZ". The money was carried to Nigeria by a courier that we have been following for years. We track all of his movements. It came from Caracas, Venezuela. We even have an address on the Calle Atras where the money was picked up!"

Kirby was overjoyed by that bit of information, but now he was conflicted as to how to respond. In normal times, he would ask Langley to send a team into the site to investigate. But now, he felt that he couldn't trust Weldon, and he was leery of anyone else in his chain of command.

He suspected now that Weldon and other CIA agents had gotten to the truth of the human trafficking operation, and had discovered who was really in charge. But...instead of turning him in to international law enforcement, they cut themselves into the profits. That was what they didn't want discovered. But, Kirby realized that this was just speculation on his part, he had no real evidence. There was only one way to find out for sure, and it was extremely risky and dangerous.

He would have to disclose his concerns to Weldon, and tell him that he plans to focus his investigation on the CIA link. Weldon's reaction would be the tip-off. Kirby hoped that he would be supportive, but if he wasn't, that would prove the case.

Kirby returned to the business at hand. "Next, I want you to try to link all we have discovered to any Congressional members who we can find to have links to the smuggling operation. Emails, phone calls, corporate board, strip clubs, country club memberships, maybe a vacation or trip to Venezuela, anything that would establish a link to "RZ" or "Mr. Big", and I need it right away. I'm going to try to arrange extra security for us now. I have managed to piss off the Russians, the Chinese, Kwandanbo, and now maybe even our beloved CIA, or some rogue part of it. Be as covert as you can with your searching; I know there are folks out there that are aware of what we are doing and will not be happy with us if we seem to be closing in on the truth. Warn me if you see anyone making a fuss about what you are doing."

Kent looked puzzled, "Sir, making a fuss?"

Kirby chuckled, "Yeah, it's a Texas way of saying that someone is alert and planning retaliation. That's "making a fuss."

CHAPTER 79

Kirby was not expecting a call from the FBI in Washington, DC and when Sumara asked him to pick up, he feared the worst. He knew the FBI was watching his house in Pocasset, and this could only be bad news.

"Is this Mr. Kirby Calloway, the doctor? This is FBI Special Agent Brown. We've been keeping an eye on your house on Shore Road. We have some bad news, unfortunately."

Kirby's heart stopped waiting for the news.

"Sir, are you there?"

"Yes, I'm here, what news do you have? What's happened?"

"Apparently there was a home invasion at your house. Your wife was not at home, but the boys were there."

"Tell me what happened!"

"Yes, sir,

"Well, it looks like your two sons tangled with four local thugs who had entered the house. Two are dead, and..."

"Wait, you're telling me my two sons are dead?!

"No, sir, no. Your sons took 'em out, all of them. You must have raised them right, sir. They defended the house, just like you must'a taught 'em. You should be proud of them. But, your oldest son, Morgan, was injured in...

"Wait, Ethan is my oldest son, which one was it?

"Ah, yes you're right. It's Ethan that is your oldest son. Sorry, I got them mixed up."

"Well, sir, he is in the Tobey hospital in Wareham with a skull fracture. They asked me to tell you that you should come home as soon as you can. I don't have any other details. Your other son, Morgan, is just fine."

"Thank you, Agent Brown. I'll leave right away." Kirby's hair was raised on his head and his heartbeat doubled inside two seconds from hearing the news.

Kirby pressed the intercom that Katanga had just installed.

"Katanga, we need to talk. Can you come up here? I'll be in the bedroom."

"Yes sir. I'll be right up."

He then called in Sumara from the visitor sitting area. "Sumara, I need you to book travel for me back to Boston Logan on the first available flight. Bring me back in five...no four days. Use Katanga's CIA code word to get whatever priorities I can.

Claire was working at the little desk in their bedroom, and she looked when Kirby rushed in.

"What's wrong?! I can see it all over you!"

Kirby pulled out his go-bag and stuffed a few things in it.

"Some thugs broke into my house in Pocasset, probably looking for me. The boys took care of them, but Ethan was injured. I have to get home right away."

"Oh, my God! How bad is it?"

"I don't know. That's all the information that I have. But I'm leaving on the first flight out."

Katanga rushed into the room. "What is it?" He was obviously concerned.

"I'm going back to Boston ASAP. Ethan is hurt and I need to be there."

"Ok, boss, I'll keep the pressure on our guys, both the analysts and the troops."

CHAPTER 80

After his trip back to the USA, he returned by "first available-govt priority" to Abuja's Nnamdi Azukiwe airport, another 30 hour flight, but it felt tougher because he was flying East. He had picked up about ten hours crossing time zones, and his awareness was completely out of whack. He took a cab from the airport and went home and was met first by Katanga. Katanga took him on a tour of their defenses. Kirby struggled to change his focus from the boys to the situation at hand.

"Welcome home, Sir. I hope that things at home are well now. We are making good progress here now, measured by the daily additions and changes on the whiteboard upstairs. We have had some people looking over our defenses from that building across the street. I would think that would make a good observation post and possible sniper point. We will need to consider that if conditions worsen here."

Kirby looked around, noting the location of some new firing posts on the roof and second floors. He was satisfied, so he headed upstairs. Claire met him at the top of the stairs with the warmest of welcomes.

Then he went into the conference room, thanking the guard who guarded the room 24x7.

Both Bob and Kent rose from their work and greeted him, but quickly turned to the progress on the investigation. "Sir, we are on the final round of research, and we hope to have names in all the boxes soon." Kirby was glad to hear that, but it just moved up the danger level at least one notch.

He left the conference room and nodded to the security guard to lock it, which he did, then stood back at the position of a relaxed "parade rest" in front of the door. He could hear faint talking coming from inside the conference room, clearly being overheard by the guard. That would have to be taken care of.

Kirby had seen Katanga earlier out in the little courtyard drilling the guard in combat skills, and they looked sharper every day. Good, we will need them, and soon. Kirby walked back down to the main door where Katanga had his office off the main hallway. Katanga noticed him coming and stood up behind his desk. He noticed the worried look on Calloway's face.

"Sir, it looks like you are concerned about our situation. Can I help?" Kirby walked into the office and closed the door. He motioned to the chair behind Katanga's desk,

"Sit down, Katanga, I need to fill you in on how our little investigation is progressing and what may be coming our way."

"First, how well are your guards trained if we get an armed incursion here?"

Katanga was not surprised at the question. "Sir, they have basic hand to hand fighting skills but not anything good enough against a well-trained army of ninjas, for example. However, they are quite skilled with their rifles. We have been practicing repelling an armed force coming through the main gate and a few over the walls. What kind of attack are you anticipating?"

Kirby thought for a minute. There were many possibilities at the moment. He looked at Katanga and with a sober voice said, "The results of this investigation are going to be troublesome on a number of levels. Anyone with a lot to lose might try to close down our work and steal the findings or destroy them. I believe it will be Kwandanbo's forces backed by a rogue CIA group, I'm guessing that it might be anything to ten to twenty fighters with varying skills. There will be a sniper. We have a few taller buildings around, so if we had enough men, we could patrol those ahead of time."

"Next, I want you to change out the guards in front of the

conference room, and move them away from the door. I think there have been leaks back to Kwandanbo and maybe to Weldon, and we need to bottle this up now. Got it?"

"Yes Sir. I will take care of this personally and with prejudice, if necessary."

"You and I are going to make a call right now back to Langley for additional support. We need to make plans to evacuate this building as soon as we finish our work. We need to stay here for now because of the secure link we have here to the central computer, but as soon as we can drop that link, we're out of here."

"You're not going to call in James Weldon on this?"

Kirby looked down, shaking his head. Then he looked at Katanga and said, "Katanga, I think he's involved in this. He warned me about going too far, and to me that's a clear enough sign. I am going to call him, but only to see if he is really in or out. If he is involved, then my call will be the trigger that starts it all." If he is not, he will rush to our aid."

"But first, let's see what Langley says about getting some help here. Shall we start with "Hostage Rescue?"

Katanga dialed the number on his secure phone for the group at CIA headquarters that was responsible for situations where a CIA post was endangered of being overrun.

The Officer in Charge answered the phone within less than two rings. Katanga identified himself and after a brief delay, he was validated.

Katanga then described their situation, their location, and what they viewed as the threat. The Officer in Charge responded, "Sir, can you hold the line? I need to connect you with my supervisor."

Katanga repeated the situation to the unnamed supervisor, who then asked, "Let me understand this. You are saying that you under immediate threat by a rogue CIA unit? Am I reading this right? This is going to have to go all the way to the top. We'll call you back. Wait for our call."

Kirby remarked with disgust. "These guys will never come

through in time. They will have to go investigate and will hit the same roadblocks we did. We may have just alerted them."

Kirby headed back to his office. He had decided that now it was time to brief President Muhari, and he called the Presidential Villa. To Kirby's delight, Mr. Mo answered the phone.

"Hello, Doctor Kirby. Are you calling to see the President? He is quite busy now. General Kwandanbo has raised an army and has demanded that the President resign immediately and leave the country. He is at the Mambilla Army Barracks now to assemble his troops for what seems to be an armed conflict. It is a bad time!"

"Mr. Mo, I need to see him very urgently. Can you please tell him that I have important information about Kwandanbo that he can use to defeat him."

Mr. Mo replied, "Yes, Sir. I will, but it may be a while until he can get back with you. I will give him your message."

Kirby then thought, what a fucking great time to call Weldon. Everything seems to be coming together, and at the same time falling apart.

CHAPTER 81

Morgan came downstairs and said he was taking the Coolster bike out to E. Sandwich beach for the day. I think he was wanting to learn how to surf, but I think he just wanted to show off to Carmen. He didn't know how to surf, but it would take him about two rides to figure it out.

That left me alone to consider our situation.

I was sitting downstairs on the couch just wondering how we could extract ourselves from this whole bizarre situation. There were so many moving parts: things that didn't fit together, things that were so unfinished, and apparently so dangerous.

We had gotten back all the guns after we were cleared of charges, partly because our Dad has a Federal Firearms License, which was another useful bit of information, and with the provision that we would lock them up safely out of reach of children. I laughed at that, which children did they mean? There were no more children in Fort Calloway.

Morgan and I had come an awfully long way since we left what seemed like the safety of the plains and mountains of Texas. Even though I was now seventeen, and Morgan was sixteen, we were no longer kids. Our parents' way of life, and the promise our Dad made to some President in a far-away country had pulled us apart as a family, irretrievably. And now we were men, Rangers.

The thing we had wanted most as kids was to have a family with a full-time at-home Dad and a full-time female person who loved us and wanted to act like a Mom. We thought that was what most parents wanted for their kids. When Mom came back to live with us, Morgan was overjoyed and I was skeptical, and we were both right-sort of. She came and stayed for our last two years of school, and her boyfriend Tory had become an interesting friend.

They were now both back in New York where Tory was continuing his role as an FBI Agent on cable TV, and Mom was doing what she always did, socializing and meeting people. We threw her a little going-away party, which she said she liked, but it was clear to us that New York was calling her. I watched Morgan to see his reaction, but now, at this point in our lives, he didn't need her anymore.

During the time she was living with us in Pocasset, she was oblivious to most of what Morgan and I did, and we grew out of needing a Mother. She was just another interesting person that came and went from Fort Calloway, as Morgan had started calling it, just between us.

Dad was another issue. We couldn't figure out what all his loyalties were. He was making big money from his company's work in Nigeria, but there was something else going on, and it had appeared with armed men outside our house one night. When he finally told us that he as also assisting the CIA, the pieces began to fall together. He kept promising that he was going to finish up and come home, but he could never pull himself away for long. We couldn't figure out what was so important, what he had committed himself to doing, and how it was going to affect us. Our Dad has asked us to do our own investigation of the guys who had attacked us, without actually running them down. I guess he had never met "Spies Like Us" before. We weren't going to stop.

So I had decided that it was time that Morgan and I started looking into things here.

The remaining issue I needed to deal with was Wendy. I saw her in the school hallways after that last date, and though we were in English together, she had moved over to the opposite wall. She used to sit right next to me. I guess our episodes on the couch and the final incident in my car finally drove her away, to say nothing of the danger in hanging out with me. She wasn't ready to make love with me, and I hoped not with anybody else. I respected her for that, but at the same time, I had a man's body and needs. And I loved her and it seemed that was a natural progression.

But I can understand her point; maybe the first time shouldn't be in the cramped back seat of a Maserati. The first time should be in a darkened room, with candles gently lighting up the room, music playing, and a big bed with satin sheets...and pillows, lots of pillows. And if you have all of that, it has to be with someone you love, not just someone you just wanted.

I was the one that torpedoed our relationship, and I was desperate to get it back, but I didn't know how. When I went up to her, she just lowered her eyes and turned away. That broke my heart.

This went on all winter, and neither of us went to our senior prom. Big deal. Then on the last day of school in our senior year, I saw her looking at me across the classroom. I looked back at her, and she turned away, but she was smiling. After class, I tried to follow her, but she kept leading me along until we were out on the quadrangle.

Then she stopped, turned and looked me straight in the eyes. Her arms were folded over her chest. It looked like she was about to deliver a speech. I feared the worst.

She took a deep breath, looked down again, then looked up with a strict face, like a teacher who had caught you doing something wrong.

"Ethan, I really like you, in fact, I love you. But what you want from me, I'm not prepared to give you. But I love when you hold me, and when you touch me, I feel a thrill all over my body."

"But I can't have sex with you, at least not yet. I want to be in a total relationship, not just a weekend date." She paused. "Now, you talk."

I understood all she was saying, in fact, I agreed with her. I wanted that total relationship that she talked about as much as she did. But that greedy little sex monster in me was pushing me harder and harder. But I wanted her back. I wanted to love her and have her love me.

I put my arms out to her and she rushed to me. I could feel her passion as she kissed me with the lips I had learned to love.

"Wendy, I want you back, and I will keep things safe for you. Please be my girl again!"

"I am, I am your girl! Forever if you want!"

I didn't take that as a marriage proposal, though it hit me that way. I hugged her and kissed her again and again. I had no more words to answer her, so I just answered with my arms, lips, and my body.

Just then, I became aware of a teacher approaching. It was Mrs. Broward, and she didn't look happy.

"Stop what you two are doing. You, Wendy, need to act like the decent young lady I know you are. And you, Ethan, need to cool your jets. That behavior is inappropriate anywhere at school. School is over now, and you two have the whole summer to go necking if you want to. Now, please leave the school, you are now graduates."

We walked back to the school hand in hand, for the first time in months. As we walked in to pick up our books, we saw Colin standing there, smiling at us. I wondered what Australian metaphor would come out of his mouth.

"Crikey! I have to deal with you two again?"

Then he came over and hugged us both. "She's all right now!"

And now, we did have the summer ahead of us again. I'm betting on a very interesting one, but at least I'd have Wendy to share it with me.

CHAPTER 82

A few days later, one fine summer morning, Morgan, Falk and I were at the airfield talking about aircraft engines, and all the issues we were dealing with now. Falk assured me that he would help us whenever we needed him.

My interest in mechanical things had reawakened and Falk was describing why aircraft engines had two of everything, at least having at least two wings made sense.

Uncle Billy came by on patrol with a new addition to the police department. Uncle Billy introduced him as Junior Officer Ray Watson. He was a young black deputy, about twenty-two years old. To my mind, he wasn't a good fit to the department. For one reason, he was way too smart. He was up to date on all the latest social media, and was an expert in the police computer systems. Morgan and him immediately hit it off, talking about cheats to the latest computer games.

After they left, Morgan came up to me and said, "My new buddy, Officer Ray Watson has access to all of the cop investigation systems and some of the Federal ones. And he has a lot more interest in finding out what happened to us than all the rest of "Law Enforcement". Why don't I try to get him to find out more info on the guys that attacked us? There ought to be a lot of chatter about what happened and this could lead us to finding out who it was, and who they worked for."

I agreed. "We can cover a lot of ground that way, and then we can go looking for the assholes. If he's willing to let a "kid" like you sit beside him while he investigates our little incident, that might help Dad a lot."

The next day, Officer Ray Watson and "junior detective" Morgan took one of the police laptops into an unused room. Officer Billy Collins looked in on them, and said, "Get as much information as you can without stirring up a hornet's nest, and report back to me."

They started by entering the name of the surviving thug, Mr. Leroy Boudreaux. Apparently he was born in Nova Scotia, had no permanently address except for a POB in Muncie, IN. He had a rap sheet that included burglary, armed robbery, and attempted murder. There were two known associates. One of them was dead, recently, thanks to us, but there was a live one, living in Boston, MA, Mr. Joe Corecelli.

Officer Ray Watson contacted the Boston PD and arranged an interview with Mr. Corecelli. They waited a few days for that to come back, but in the meantime went through the same procedures with the dead assailants, Mr. Ugly, who turned out to be Mr. Alfred Gronsky of Pembroke, MA. Ray, seeing the name, remarked, "I've never seen a Gronsky that wasn't ugly."

The other guy was Wilfred Plotski, of Gloucester, MA. Officer Ray remarked, "I've never met a Plotski that wasn't stupid."

The Boston PD report came back on Corecelli; just another robber and bully, and not very good at either one. These guys were all a bunch of local ugly, stupid henchmen.

The next track that Morgan and Ofc. Watson investigated was to go through the dead men's driver's licenses and retrieved cell phone records. Two of the cell phones showed multiple calls from the same number in Franklin, New Jersey, from what appeared to be a liquor distributor. I knew what Morgan was going to do next, and it was going to be fun.

Morgan called the number and pretended to be Justin Boudreaux, who was the thug still in the hospital in a coma. Boudreaux had received calls from the bar the afternoon of the attack. The phone rang six times, but it was finally answered. We three clustered around the phone to listen to the action.

"Yeah? this is Tony's ABC Liquor Distribution. What can I do for you?"

"Tony, this is Justin. I'm out of the hospital and I need my money."

"What? You're out of the hospital? How come you're not in the lockup?" Tony seemed to take the whole thing as a joke.

"They're treating as a simple robbery attempt. I got a dozen of those already and beat them all. I bailed out of this one, and I need my money from the job. NOW! I'm coming over to get it." Morgan was talking in his deepest, nastiest voice, and so far the guy Tony was buying it.

"Ok. Wait. I'll get the boss." He stepped away from the phone and yelled where Ray and Morgan could hear it. "Billy, go get Tomas. It's the guy who did the bungled job in Mass and he wants money. Good joke."

There was a pause and the sound of laughter in the background, then Tomas came on the line, "Listen, asshole. That job was so fucked up I can't believe it. You let two little kids screw you, and you and Arthur are the only ones alive. No fucking way I'm giving you any money. And that's the last job you'll ever do for us, you fuck-up!"

Morgan tried again, raising his voice, "I want my fucking money and I'm coming for it!"

"Yeah, you can just go...wait a minute! You ain't Justin. Who is this!?"

Morgan hung up the phone, and he and Ray fell over laughing. They had now met the whole family, and the money man was a thug named Tomas. Billy was probably the local muscle. Arthur was the get-away driver who almost shit himself falling backwards out of the house and getting arrested by Uncle Billy. It didn't take long on the cop computer to figure out who "Tomas" was, and to get his phone records, too. It turned out that Tomas had made frequent calls to an untraceable number in Northern Virginia, and they found bank transfers in the millions of dollars to a foundation in Arlington, Va.

We were going to need more horsepower to take this farther. It was time to call Dad with the information we had found. I watched Officer Ray and Morgan go after these guys just using basic spy techniques; research, logic, and deception that had watched our Dad do. And a few movies and TV shows. This spying stuff was fun, despite the danger.

CHAPTER 83

We went home and waited until about midnight to call Dad's private number. I was surprised when a woman with a slight French accent answered the phone.

"Hello, Kirby?"

I guessed immediately it must be Claire. I thought, ok, here goes.

"No Claire, sorry, it's Ethan. I'm my Dad's oldest son."

"Ethan? I was expecting your Dad to call me on this phone. You sound like him, really. Things are really confusing around here. I think we are leaving soon. He's downstairs talking to Katanga. I'll have him call you when he gets free. Goodbye."

Her first call with his boys who were strangers to her caught her off-guard.

"No, wait! Claire. Me and my brother Morgan are looking forward to meeting you. We have a picture of you that...our Dad gave us."

"Well, Ethan, that is kind of you to say. I am looking forward also to meeting you both. Your Dad keeps promising to take me back to America, but he hasn't been able to keep his promise as yet. He brags about you both all the time. He really loves you."

"How are you feeling, Ethan? I understand you were injured recently in some sort of burglary, yes?"

"Yeah, there was a little incident at our house, but I'm fine now."

"That's wonderful to hear. Did you call to speak to your father? Of course you did. I'm being silly. I think he is in his office. I'll run fetch him."

I really liked talking to her. She had a beautiful, friendly voice, and now I could match it to her picture. Wow. Dad's doing alright for himself.

It was Dad. "Hello, Ethan, is that you?"

"Yeah, it's me, and Morgan's on the line too. Morgan, tell him what you found."

Dad cautioned, "Wait. We need to be on a secure line, and I need to be in my office for that. Give me a few minutes and I'll call you on that line."

A few minutes later, our phone rang, and Morgan answered, "Hello, Dad?"

"Yes, Morgan, go ahead with your...report." That sounded strange to me. It was suddenly like we were spies reporting in, and it was a good feeling.

Morgan laid out what he and Officer Ray Watson had been doing, including the part where they duped the crowd in the liquor store in New Jersey and were able to see phone records up to Northern Virginia, but were unable to decode the untraceable phone number. Dad wrote down the number, and said, "I've got some guys working for me that can dig this out. Thanks for going the distance for me, both of you!"

CHAPTER 84

"**M**org, there must be more we can do to help Dad. Do you still have Tory's number?

"Yeah. Here it is. What exactly are you thinking?"

"Listen. Dad is trying to get back home, but it sounds like the bad CIA guys in Nigeria are trying to track him down. He had to escape from them, and now he and Claire are still on the run. Now, we don't know where he is or how he's getting home."

"So, let's call Tory and explain it to him. He knows those two FBI guys in Washington. You remember them? Maybe he could get the FBI to look at it again, and maybe they would like to help. You know, Spy vs Spy? Give me your phone."

It rang four times until somebody answered. "Hullo, George Mason, what can I do for youse?"

"Hello, Mr. Mason. We are trying to reach Tory, he's a family friend and we have to advise him of a death in the family."

"Sure, sure. He's on the set, but I'll go get him."

"Morgan, Why did you say that? You didn't need to say that."

"I just wanted to. That should get Tory's attention."

"This is Tory, who is this?

"Tory, it's Ethan and Morgan. Sorry about the death in the family story but we needed to talk to you now."

"Ok. What is it? Must be important, right?"

"Yeah, it is. Our Dad exposed a rogue CIA group in Nigeria, and he's trying to get home, and he's at great risk. He can't just fly to La Guardia or something. They have tried three times to kill him to prevent him from getting home with his evidence, and we want you to alert the FBI that he needs help. Can you help us explain this to your FBI contact and get them to help?"

"Wow! This all true? This would make a great segment for my show. But, OK. This is really serious, I got that. Let me see what I can do. I'll call Agent Brown and fill him in. Expect to hear back from me in a day or two. OK?

"Ok, we appreciate anything you can do." We hung the phone.

"What do you think, Morg?"

"We should have called Agent Brown ourselves. Didn't you say that's what you weren't going to do. Not involve Tory?"

"Yes, but I wanted to see if he could help us. Not like a Dad, but someone we trust to deal with things that two young men shouldn't have to deal with all on their own."

An hour later, the phone rang. I picked it up and answered, "Hello, this is Ethan Calloway."

"Son, this is Director Fred Smith of the Washington Division of the FBI. I've been listening to a story I have a hard time believing." He was saying that, but I didn't get that he didn't believe us.

"Yes, sir. I know it is hard to believe, but our Dad is in trouble. He was asked by the CIA to gather intelligence for them in addition to his real job. And when he found out about the illegal and awful things they were doing, they have been trying to eliminate him and his CIA team. I think my Dad and Claire and his other friend are in very serious trouble."

"OK, understand. Let's talk about how we can help. I have no issue going up against the Agency when they cross over and start threatening or even killing American citizens at home or abroad. We'll take care of it. Give me everything you know."

We spent the better part of an hour filling in the picture for Director Smith. He hung up, saying, "I'm going to assign this to one our best agents, Special Agent Lockhart. I think he is already familiar with the case. Apparently, someone in the CIA asked his unit to watch you a few months ago. He'll take it from here."

I remembered Agent Lockhart as that bald-headed monster

who Tory and I bounced from the black Ford on our street. He was one of the two guys watching our house. I was glad of their help, and Lockhart sure knew where Fort Calloway was.

We weren't sure when Dad was going to show up or how. We were just waiting to hear from him, but I had the feeling that it was going to be soon. And I knew Wendy and her Dad were in on it, and that made me feel better.

I was sure things were going to start happening soon after my call. Within a few hours, we had two FBI agents in front of our house. One was in front of the house and one was on the back porch. I assumed that there were others out there somewhere watching. I went out to talk to them.

"We're glad to see you guys here. Thanks for coming."

"No problem, son. We've been briefed that you've pissed off the Agency and need protection. Is that about it?"

"Yes sir. We had some bad guys try to hit us about a month ago."

"Really? I hadn't heard that. How'd that turn out?"

"Well, we killed two of the bastards, and the other two were arrested."

He turned to face me with a new look of respect. "No shit? So we're not here just to babysit you boys, but to add firepower?"

I laughed. "Yeah, but we'll leave it to you this time, Ok?"

CHAPTER 85

When I went back inside, I was startled to see Marie sitting on the couch, sobbing. I sat down beside her, not knowing what to do.

"You are going to hate me, I know!"

I replied, "Why? What do you mean?"

"It wasn't your Dad who hired me to be your cook, and it was me that convinced your Mom to let me stay here."

I was throughly confused. "Marie, what are you talking about ?"

"I needed the money to go to culinary school. I couldn't afford it on my own. So when this guy came into the bakery where I worked, and sat down for coffee, and started asking about my work and everything, then he asked me if I knew the Calloway's. I said, yeah, everyone knows them. They just got here this year. So then he says, how would you like to be their live-in cook? He said I know they need help, and he showed me a help wanted ad. Then he said, "My company is willing to pay for your school and a little more if you will cook for them. After a while, you can probably make the case to move in over there. I know they have lots of room, and they have a very nice kitchen. I'm sure you would fit in well with the two boys that are living there."

"What do you say? Here's $500 cash to go towards your tuition." He laid a stack of $50 dollar bills on the table under his napkin.

I thought to myself, this is too good to be true. "What do I have to do?"

Then he said, "I work for the government. We are concerned about what their Dad is doing in Nigeria, and we just want to have someone who will keep a diary of things going on over there. Just a record of who comes and goes, and any suspicious talk that you might pick up on. Just write it down, and we'll get back with you to collect it. See, it's simple, just write down what's going on there and keep us informed. Ok? And there is a $250 bonus if you agree right now. Ok?"

"I took their money. It seemed harmless enough until all of this started happening. I even went into your Dad's office to see what I could find. Then I realized that this guy was on the side of the people who were trying to hurt you, and your Dad...and now me. I couldn't do it any longer."

The little incident in the hallway where I caught her coming out of Dad's office was now clear. She was looking for anything she could report on about us. Basically, she was spying on us.

I was torn between my concern for her and my anger at the guy who put her up to this. I couldn't be angry at her, so I just gave her a big hug.

"So what was the big intelligence score you reported to your handler?"

"I couldn't find anything; you guys are so boring." We both laughed. "I just told them what you liked to eat and then about the home invasion. The guy seemed surprised by that."

"Yeah, he probably wished he'd thought of it first."

"Well, Marie. Your days as a spy inside Fort Calloway are over, though we'd be pleased if you'd stay on as our cook, and our friend. Now, if you see the bugger again, I will be on the street corner to citizen-arrest him as a co-conspirator to the invasion. We can tell the cops that you were a double-agent giving us intelligence on him. OK?"

"Yes. Yes. Thanks Ethan, and the other night...that really was my idea. I mean it."

I gave her another big hug and a kiss. Morgan was walking down the stairs and saw me kissing her. He yelled out, "Get a room!"

CHAPTER 86

Kirby walked back to his quarters. Claire was there, getting ready for bed, in her nightgown and brushing her long black hair. Kirby looked at her and wanted to pick her up and throw her in bed, then pull the covers over both of their heads. She noticed him and smiled, "When do we start having some fun?"

Kirby reset his mind from thinking about sex with Claire, to the more serious matters at hand.

"Claire, I have to talk to you about something very serious. We'll have fun later. But right now, here's what's going on. He explained to her the investigation, his promise to Muhari, and the possibility of an attack. "Just in case, I want you to have this gun to protect yourself. I've carried it for years and it's my lucky gun. But don't shoot anybody unless your life is threatened."

He took out his black Beretta and handed it to her. "It's loaded and chambered. But the safety is on. All you have to do is push this lever up and then pull the trigger. She took the gun from him and looked at it like it was a hammer, just a tool.

She looked at him, smiled coyly, and said, "You sure know how to show a lady a good time! Now get out of here and take care of us, and your work."

Kirby kissed her, then went back to his office.

Just then, Bob and Kent burst into his office, carrying several boxes of files. "Kirby, we finally got everything!" He didn't even notice them using his first name in their exuberance. "That's great! What's everything?"

Bob spilled several files of phone records, payment notices, and thirty or so other documents on his desk, all clipped neatly together. "We can prove that the money that "RZ" moved, and by the way, "RZ" is Juan Ruiz, into Kwandanbo's bank, and much of it ended up in three companies in Idaho, New Jersey, and Iowa. But these are all real companies; little, rather unsavory businesses that would pass the money through for a fee. Then they are laundering money through their local banks up to a couple of accounts that are owned by several foundations that are owned by US Congressmen or their wives, most notably the now-less-than Honorable George Washington Hilton of Massachusetts."

"Whoa, slow down. Take a breath. I think I got most of that, but what you're telling me is that the fish money that was deposited in Kwandanbo's bank ended up feathering the nest of the Congressman from the great state of Massachusetts, George Washington Hilton?"

"Yes, but only some of it, about five million dollars. The rest of it, less expenses, went to the mastermind, Mr. Central Intelligence himself, a Swiss Banker named Horatio Sorobet. We haven't fully identified who was actually doing the brokering, but we do know one of Sorobet's foundations got all the money, less expenses of course. The brokers were just low-level managers, matching orders to supply. We'll get them later."

Kirby almost choked. Holy Shit! Horatio Sorbet was one of their sponsors on the security project at SwissBank, Al Risdorphen's rich buddy. That will be a horseshoe in the gut for dear Al.

Kirby interjected, "Let me guess, the expenses were monies kept by Kwandanbo to finance his little army of rebellion that's now threatening the President."

"Yes, Sir. And we have linked James Weldon to the operation by coming across secret communications between Weldon and a dirty CIA agent named Kwasse who is in Sorobet's operation. Weldon was spying on Sorobet, and when they saw the huge piles of cash, they threatened him, then cut themselves into a big share of Sorobet's profits. That's what they didn't want us to find. They were discussing their issues with us and the investigation, and their plan to "clean things up". We think that means taking out the warehouse in Caracas. And we think we know how they are going to do it, or rather get US to do it. There's a memo to the head of DHS, describing the need for kinetic action there to destroy the drugs and money sitting there; no mention of the risk to people."

"Great, now put it together, create an exec summary and hooks to all the evidence you can point to."

Kirby headed back to his office, and in his mind he saw the whiteboard again, but this time there were names in each of four big blue circles. Dangerous names.

CHAPTER 87

Claire was getting very bored being quarantined as it were because of Kirby's insistence that she stay inside their home. He was basically ignoring her with everything going on, as well as his growing concern for his boys. She had been out to the little garden in the rear courtyard, and had appreciated the wide variety of flowers; bougainvillea, orchids, and birds of paradise. She had considered going for a swim in the little pool, but she didn't think the guards up on the walls seeing a well-endowed woman in a black bikini swimming laps would be a secret for long, especially with iPhone cameras. But she really wanted out, over the wall.

Kirby's house keeper, Sumara, noticed how restless Claire was becoming, and with the native warmness that is so much a part of the Nigerian culture, decided to offer her friendship. Sumara was a local girl that had lived in Abuja all her life, and she knew everything about the local area, especially the nearby marketplace. She and Claire were getting to know each other in their confinement and she found that Claire was interested in all aspects of Nigerian life and culture.

One day, she brought in some samples of the fabrics from one of the local fabric marts as a gift for Claire. Giving gifts of fabric is part of the culture of arts in Nigeria. Claire was entranced by the brilliant patterns and textures of the Nigerian fabric. She exclaimed, "Sumara, I've never seen fabrics like these, the colors, the patterns, they are breathtaking. Could you take me to one of the markets so I can see for myself?"

"Missy, I don't think so. Master Kirby has told us that it is too dangerous for you to go out without a bodyguard. It would not be safe."

Claire was insistent, "What about you? You come and go as you please everyday."

"Yes, Missy, but I have to go home. I live about a kilometer from here and I feel perfectly safe walking there. The open market where the fabric stores are is just a few blocks farther over."

"Really? Are they open now?" Claire was getting excited about the prospect of getting out of this stone fortress, as she was beginning to view it. Her life in Paris was so active; parties, walks with Kirby along the Seine, and shopping, yes SHOPPING!

"Ok, we're going, Sumara. You can be my escort. We will act like you are just walking home with a guest. We won't tell anyone especially Kirby and Katanga. We won't be gone long, nobody has to know. I know what Kirby would say."

"Are you sure Missy? We would be taking a chance."

"Yes. I know but I have to get out. I feel like a trapped animal!"

"Well, Ok. But you must wear Nigerian clothes so you don't stand out. Sumara wrapped Claire in one of the bright orange and green fabric samples she had brought, being careful to let the inseam label show, as is done.

"Now you must have a drawstring purse. Here, you can carry mine. You need a shawl for your hair. Let me look, yes, here is one of mine that I carry in my purse. There, you look almost Nigerian, except for one thing." "You mean the color of my face?" Claire asked timidly.

"Yes, that, but I meant the color of your lipstick. You should not use so red a lipstick, it should be just natural, just pink." Claire took a tissue to wipe the red lipstick that she favored off her lips.

"You are tanned enough to look like a light-skinned Nigerian, so don't worry about that."

"Now all you need is a hat, a big one. Do you have one?"

"Yes, I do, let me get it."

Sumara looked at her from top to bottom. "Missy, I think you should dress this way all the time here. You are so beautiful. Now, we need to go."

Sumara then walked through the building to make sure they could avoid Kirby and Katanga. Kirby was in the locked conference room with the analysts. Katanga was out in the rear courtyard, instructing the guards on bayonet drills. He feared that their hand-to-hand fighting skills were lacking, so he was training them how to fight with a rifle and a bayonet. So the coast was clear for them to go out the front gate.

One of the guards named Tontu stopped them. "Where are you going, Miss Sumara? And should you be taking Lady Claire with you? You know Doctor Kirby has said no leaving."

"We are only going to the market, and we shan't be gone long. So we are going now. Move out of the way."

The guard was not willing to give up yet. He asked, "Lady Claire. Is this alright with you?"

"Yes, Tontu. It's alright with Dr. Kirby. We'll be right back."

Sumara and Claire held hands as they walked down an unnamed stone road towards the Shekinah Plaza, where the market was located.

They arrived at the market, and Claire marveled at the shops packed together that featured all manner of Nigerian products, from brightly colored shirts and scarves, wood carvings, and even swords with carved wooden scabbards. Someone had a boom-box playing music. Like all Nigerian music, it had a strong drum beat. When Claire asked, Sumara said, "That is Tiwadara. He is a national hero."

At the end of one row of shops, Claire saw a row of fabric dealers with hundreds of bolts of beautiful fabrics, including greens, blues, oranges, and amazing weaves of flowing patterns crossed by horizontal bars of different colors. There were tie-dyed prints of flowers of all different colors. She found the one dress, the one she had to have. It was a white dress, tie-dyed with Kono Blue, and with layers of embroidery and fine lace in various floral patterns all over the dress around the neck. She had seen dresses like this advertised in Paris shows for thousands of Euros. Claire pulled it off the rack and draped it over her arm to fully appreciate it. It weighed almost nothing. She asked the shopkeeper, a young girl not more than fifteen years old, "Did you make this dress?" The girl replied, "I made all of them", pointing to the whole rack of dresses. Claire just smiled in amazement. "How much for this one?" Claire asked about the dress she was holding. The shopkeeper never hesitated, "That one is forty Euros, or if you have US dollars, it is thirty-five Dollars. The young girl hadn't figured out whether Claire was French or American from her accent.

Claire gladly pulled thirty-five dollars from her borrowed draw-string purse and gave it to the young shopkeeper. Claire thought for a second, and asked, "It's so beautiful. Would you accept five more dollars for it?"

The girl smiled, and said, "Thank you for understanding the juju in that dress." She bowed slightly, and gracefully accepted the additional five dollars.

Then Claire noticed something else that she had to have. It was a brightly colored shopping bag, blue, orange, and black, with what looked like magical emblems all over it. There was what looked like a orange cathedral protected by flowers and tridents on a blue background. "And this too." The girl pulled it down from the rack and said, "This one is five dollars, but I give it to you for free."

Claire responded, "Thank you so much, but you don't have to do that."

Then she did something unusual. She came out of her stall and came up to Claire, motioning for her to listen to her whisper.

"There are some boys following you. They are Bakassi and they think they are magical. They roam around looking for what they think might be evil. I think they are following you because you are different. You dress like a Nigerian, yet you are European. They don't understand that. That bag I gave you also has juju. It will protect you."

Claires' face shone its appreciation. But Sumara was immediately terrified. "The Bakassi shouldn't be here, they are from Anambra." She was trembling. "They think they are carrying magic machetes, and they use them to test people to see if they are evil inside. If they are, then they kill them on the spot.

Claire grabbed Sumara by the arm, and said, "We're going now. We have magic too now. Come on."

Then she looked around, and asked Sumara, "Which way?"

Sumara pointed back through the rows of various shops, and they began walking very fast down that way. Claire looked back and saw a group of about eight or nine young men, wearing black shirts with red sashes, and stripes painted on their faces, walking along behind them, not exactly chasing them, but definitely closely following them. And they were all carrying machete swords.

Claire whispered to Sumara one word, "Faster!"

They picked up the pace, but the boys matched them and now began closing on them. "Down this way!" Sumara cried, and they turned right down a narrow street. The mob of painted boys made the turn, and started running,

Sumara cried, "Turn left here", and they suddenly turned down a wide street, and Claire saw the wall of her new home just ahead.

Claire cried out, "Stop!", and Sumara almost fell as Claire came to a halt and turned to face the advancing mob. She raised her hand, and commanded to the mob, "Stop Now!"

The mob slowed, but then their leader came forward and drew his machete from its scabbard and approached Claire with a wicked grin on his face. His face was completely painted red, with black stripes on his cheeks. His short hair was stiffly pointed out of his head, and some of his white teeth were blacked out.

Claire took off her hat and scarf, and stood her ground. She was terrified, but she struggled not to show it. "What is it that you want? You must go away and leave us alone!"

He held the machete up, shining brightly in the African sun, and walked up to Claire and laid it across her chest. She closed her eyes, shuddering as he did it, expecting the cut of the blade at any second.

Instead of cutting her with the wide blade, he held it to her for what seemed like an eternity, then suddenly raised over his head for what was surely the deadly slice.

But instead, he held it in the air, and turned to his mob which had congregated around them. An exultant cheer came up, and the mob was suddenly joyfully celebrating.

The magic machete had failed to find evil in her, and the mob of boys left to go look for evil in someone else.

Claire was trembling, and she and Sumara hugged and cried.

Just then, Katanga and four of his guards, including Tontu, came rushing out of the gate arch and surrounded them. Katanga looked down the road at the retreating mob of boys and shouted, "What the hell were you doing out there? We specifically told you not to leave the compound without an armed escort. There are much more dangerous people out there than these stupid Bakassi Boys. Now, both of you silly women, please go inside, please."

Claire was still clutching the package with her new dress in it and the magic shopping bag. As she entered the compound, Kirby rushed out to meet her. She ran to him and they hugged with tears in her eyes.

She pulled away from him, wiped away her tears, and said, "Wait until you see me in this dress! It's magical!"

CHAPTER 88

"THIS IS CBS NEWS: We interrupt this program to bring you the latest video report from our journalist, Karen Lopez, in Caracas, Venezuela. We want to warn our viewers of some possible graphic content."

Karen Lopez, an attractive but worried-looking correspondent grasped her microphone tightly, looked intently at the camera and announced, "From what we understand, US Homeland Security Reaper Drones have struck and destroyed what was supposed to be an unloading facility for terrorist weapons and drug shipments here in Caracas."

"What we are seeing is the remains of a large warehouse and what looks to be a number of casualties inside. From reports we are getting, this was also some sort of classroom for immigrants learning a trade before being allowed to immigrate into the US, the UK, Europe, and other countries where skilled workers are in short supply."

"Apparently, US Intelligence had received reports that the facility was tied to the Sinaloa drug cartel, and was also being used to store large quantities of drugs and also cash. There was no link to a school on the same grounds. We have on the line, Congressman George Hilton, chairman of the House Intelligence Committee. Congressman Hilton, what are we seeing here in this horrible footage?"

"Look. Karen, we had received credible intelligence that this facility was used by one of the major drug cartels as a place where they stored vast quantities of the drug Fentanyl as well as huge bundles of cash from their operations to smuggle the very dangerous drug from China. Their plan appears to be to smuggle large quantities of the very dangerous drug Fentanyl into America through various American seaports, most recently in Providence, Rhode Island. Federal agents just seized a boat there, linked to this facility which was loaded with Fentanyl, but unfortunately, the crew seems to have escaped. My office has led the fight against these types of crimes, as well as the awful crime of human smuggling. We will, I assure you, continue to battle these crimes with every means available to us, including the US military and the Department of Homeland Security."

"Thank you Congressmen Hilton for joining us as we watch this awful fire which seems to be destroying everything including the warehouse itself. Oh! There it goes now, falling to the ground. More news at Eleven! This is Karen Lopez, live from Caracas, Venezuela."

CHAPTER 89

Kirby's housekeeper and aide, Sumara, came to his office and switched on his TV. "Sir, I thought you'd want to see this." Kirby watched the CBS News report with great alarm, then thought, "What a truly fucking great time to call Weldon. Everything seems to be falling apart here, and everywhere else. They needed to get a team into that warehouse operation, but now the fucker has gone up in flames. He picked up the phone on the secure line, and dialed the 10-digit number with deep concern, and almost fear. This could be his death sentence.

His phone rang eight times without an answer. Kirby tried to visualize the office where Weldon worked and how far away he might be from his phone.

"Hello, this is James Weldon's desk. Can I help you?" It was a somewhat harried sounding female voice, probably his admin.

Kirby was so startled by the pickup that he almost dropped the receiver. His nerves were on a razor's edge.

"Uh...Yes...This is Kirby Calloway, and I'm trying to reach James. Is he there today?"

"I'm sorry, no. He was called back to Langley rather suddenly. I can transfer this call to his office down there if you like, or I can just take a message."

"Yes, please transfer the call. I need to speak to James urgently."

There was a brief interlude of music, which Kirby thought was very strange considering the nature of the communication.

"Hello, Kirby, I thought I might be hearing from you."

"Hello, Jake. There are some very interesting things going on right now over here. Have you been watching the events unfolding?"

"Not really. There are some other issues we're dealing with here. The Chinese, the Russians, the Iranians, you know."

Kirby could feel his heart rate increasing and his heart beat pounding in his chest. It seemed that Weldon was purposely being evasive. It could not end like this, with Weldon shutting down the conversation that Kirby desperately needed to have.

"Ok, then, here it is. You told me that Muhari was not the Agency's choice for President. Now there appears to be an insurrection sponsored by Kwandanbo aimed at overthrowing Muhari and seizing control to institute some sort of military dictatorship again. I'm asking you directly whether the Agency is supporting the overthrow of a recently elected President!"

Weldon answered, "It's not as simple as that! We have other interests there that you are not aware of, and I told you directly, no I <u>ordered</u> you directly, to avoid them in your inquiry because of the sensitivity of the operation." He hesitated, and spoke slowly, "Now, what have you done?"

Kirby could hear the sound of a pencil being tapped on a desk.

"Weldon, does your little operation have anything to do with the smuggling of little girls and young women? Does it have anything to do with that boatload of Chinese Fentanyl that just landed in Providence? Does it have anything to do with massive payoffs to at least one American Congressman?"

Tapping...

Kirby raged. "I think it does and we're going to bring back the evidence and dump it all in the lap of the Attorney General himself." Kirby could hear the sound of an office chair being pushed back violently.

Weldon screamed, "Kirby, you'll be damned to hell if you do!"

With that threat, Kirby slammed down the phone. With that, it was on.

CHAPTER 90

Kirby spoke to his two young agents. "Here's what I want you to do. Disconnect the phone and computer lines inside the conference room. Create three paper copies of the key evidence with your summary of findings, one for each of you and one for me. These are going to be the only three copies. Make three digital copies of everything and write to a digital disc. Again, one copy of everything to me, and two to you guys. Pack up all of your personal things, and dress in the darkest clothes you have. Then sit tight. If you need to call home, use the remaining line in Katanga's office."

"We may be facing some sort of attack, but if that occurs, go into into the kitchen in the middle of the house. If for some reason the attackers get into the kitchen, just kneel down and give them the information. It's not worth dying for. They will likely take you back to their camp, and trade you later for some scumbag that they want back. But all of that is very unlikely. Very."

Kirby thought to himself, if they get that far, they will kill everybody, especially these two who are carrying a bomb in their heads for some very evil people. That would be a real tragedy.

"As soon as the attack is over, we have arranged separate cars for each of you. You will go by separate routes out to a small hanger at the edge of the airport. Katanga will meet you there. Inside the hangar is a private jet that will take you home, you and your precious cargo."

"If Katanga is more than say, um...thirty minutes late, tell the pilot I said to leave without him. Go straight back to your home branch and wait until I get back and call you. Don't talk to anyone. Ok? You good to go?"

Both men nodded a grim agreement, but then Bob asked, "What about you and Claire? How will you make it out?"

Kirby grimaced. "We will have to find our own way home. It might be through Paris or Switzerland. I've heard they are both pretty this time of year."

Kent looked over at Bob, and then looked up at Kirby. "Sir, can I ask you a question? Are you really CIA?"

Kirby smiled grimly. "Actually, no. When I was in Paris, a former old friend, James Weldon, asked me to help him understand what was going on in the French Science Institute, one of my software clients, around technology exchanges with the Chinese. It seemed innocent enough at the time, but now it's turned into this. Weldon showed up in my SSI office as I was preparing to leave for Nigeria, and asked me to continue to feed him information. I agreed, thinking I was being patriotic or something, and I thought getting CIA insight into the local politics could help me win that software contract. Now here we are. I do probably need to ask for a CIA paycheck after this is over", he said with an ironic smile.

The two men nodded, then shook hands with Kirby, seeming to appreciate but not fully understand Kirby's decision. Then they went to make preparations to leave. They seemed to Kirby to be very ready to leave Nigeria, and he thought, but why?, he thought grimly, things are about to get real interesting here.

Kirby went down to the ground floor and out into the front courtyard where the stone arch circled over the driveway which led out the street. Katanga had installed steel doors under the arch that could be swung closed if needed. The walls around the house were only eight feet tall; this place was designed for privacy, not defense. In the distance, he could hear the sound of small arms and machine guns and occasionally a mortar explosion, and in the growing darkness there were constant flashes of light preceding the explosions. It looked and sounded like the battle for the Presidency was underway.

Katanga came out of his office and called out to Kirby, "Sir, the President is on the line. It's important that you talk to him now!"

Kirby ran to take the phone.

"Yes, Mister President! Are you well?"

"Yes, Doctor. It looks like we have a standoff at present although a few enthusiasts on both sides are still firing away. What is it that you wanted to say to me so urgently? I guess we will not have time to meet. Is it something about my friend, Mr. Kwandanbo?"

"Yes Sir, it is. We have discovered and we have evidence that he and his bank are deeply involved in human trafficking, an international crime, and he is subject to arrest and trial by the World Court. He is involved in a global trafficking and drug smuggling operation, and we have identified all the principals, including a respected Swiss banker, and a US Congressman. And Sir, a splinter group of our own CIA is involved with Kwandanbo and his attacks against you. I fear immediate retaliation against me from that rogue element. I am requesting asylum and protection from your government, Sir, for myself and Claire."

"Kirby, you need not be so formal with me. After I win this little war, you and your lovely Claire are welcome to stay with me as long as you need to until this thing is sorted out."

"Sir, that is very generous of you. But, are you sure you will win this war? I still hear gunfire."

"Yes, yes. I am sure of it. My Presidential forces, my Naval Marines are now encircling General Kwandanbo's ridiculous little army and will arrest him shortly. I have kept them fully funded and well-trained for just such an eventuality. The World Court can have him when I am done with him, if there is anything left of him to bring to trial."

Then the President sounded concerned, "But what about Katanga and your other staff? Do they need asylum here?"

"No Sir. I am flying them out as soon as it is safe. But, can I ask? Would you have any Naval Marines that you could lend me? Just until I get my people safely out with their hand-carried evidence."

"Why, I shall see if we can spare a company or two to add to your protection. And as soon as you can safely travel, you must bring your beautiful Lady Claire over to my home and spend a few days with my wife Ururhu and myself. To enjoy the peace."

"Thank you, Sir. It would be a great honor. For old times, and new times."

Kirby hung up the phone, and Katanga brought him a combat vest like the one Katanga himself was wearing, and he put it on.

"What's your preference for a sidearm? You going to keep that 9mm Beretta, or do you want something that a man would carry?"

Kirby laughed. "No, I gave that one to Claire."

Katanga nodded, and shook his head in worry for her.

"Ok, what do you have for me to choose from?"

"I've got two choices for your shooting pleasure tonight. An old Colt Python .357, which is the "Dirty Harry" revolver, or I have something in a new Ruger .45 Range Officer, which I prefer simply because it has an eight-round double-stack magazine."

Kirby picked up both guns, and was a bit surprised how heavy the Colt .357 was compared to his expectations. He knew it would be heavy, but this thing was a cannon.

He put the .357 down, and racked the slide back in forth on the Ruger .45. He was satisfied and told Katanga, "I'll put the Ruger on my right side, and if you aren't going to use the .357 yourself, I'll take it also."

Katanga shook his head. "We will need that gun, somebody else wants to fight."

Bob Hayes stepped out of the shadows in the big room. "Sir, I'm a qualified field agent, an Expert marksman, and with your permission, I'd like to join the fight."

Katanga handed him the weapon and a box of cartridges. Kirby reached out and shook Bob's hand, then put his arm around him. "Make sure they don't get us both, Bob, that only leaves young Kent to get the story out."

Katanga got a call on his walkie. He turned to Kirby, "There are some guys with guns walking up the street toward the front gate, and there are some other guys a few blocks over circling around behind the rear wall."

Kirby looked at Katanga. "Is it time to shut the front gate now?"

"Sir, I recommend that we leave it open. If it's less than ten guys in the front, I'd rather take them in the open."

Kirby shrugged. "Makes sense to me. Let's do it that way."

Just then, they heard a loud scream from the top floor of the building across the side street. They looked to see a figure dressed in black and camo tumbling off the building, still clutching a long-barreled rifle and hitting the ground below with a loud thud. On the top floor, a man with a light green shirt and dark green pants stepped out of the darkness to wave, then disappeared again into the dark.

"I guess that was their sniper," Katanga quipped. "Now, it's time to take cover!" Katanga took cover behind a wide column on the porch, while Kirby and Bob crouched behind the low wall guarding the entrance to the house. Two black-dressed men simultaneously tried to enter the courtyard from either side of the arch. From somewhere, the invisible guards shot both of them. They fell into the entrance, lifeless. Two more tried to sprint into the courtyard and hide behind the hedge beside the driveway, but they quickly learned that bullets go right through branches and green leaves. One tried to run back to the gate, but was hit multiple times in the back. None of the three men had taken a shot yet, the guards were doing all the work.

Suddenly, there was a wall of men rushing through the front gate, firing pistols and automatic weapons at targets they couldn't see clearly. This time, all three men took aim and fired at the rush of men. All four fell down, but two continued firing, now finding the men behind the low wall. Bullets splattered the stucco and blew chunks out of the concrete wall until the guards took them out as well.

Katanga took a small radio device out of his pocket and pushed a button. The main gate closed slowly. Two men tried to get through before the gate closed, but were shot as they tried to crawl through the vertical opening, and one man's body was caught in the door, holding it open. Katanga saw what had happened, and pushed another button, and the door closed all the way, cutting the man in half. He screamed as his lungs and stomach exploded out of his body as the gate swung shut and latched hydraulically.

Things were quiet for a few minutes, then they heard a sudden round of continuous shooting from the wall on the back of the house. The guards had anticipated the rear attack, and fired into the black shapes swarming over the eight-foot rear wall. The three men stayed in front for what they knew would be the next mass attack from the front, and soon it began. More than ten dark shapes slipped over the wall, covered by their comrades firing from behind the outer wall. Bob and Kirby, kneeling behind the low wall were not able to get a shot off due to the volume of fire. Katanga leaned out from behind the column, shot two attackers but then was hit twice, in the arm, and the right leg. He fell, but crawled back into the recess of the door, still firing. Four men rushed the wall that Bob and Kirby were using for cover, and as they got closer, Bob opened fire, shooting blindly over the wall. The sound of the .357 was unmistakable even with all the other gunfire. Kirby fired three rounds at a column of approaching figures, putting two of them in the dirt. He sensed that they would not be able to hold out much longer.

He had given Claire his Beretta with instructions to hide until she was discovered, then use the gun on her attackers or herself. She did not have the same strategic value to the attackers as did Kent and Bob, but the attackers would likely do something awful to her.

Bob was out of ammo, and Kirby had only half a magazine, five bullets for the next row of attackers. He thought about Claire, and he thought about his boys, and gripped the Ruger for what looked to be their last stand.

Suddenly there was a barrage of gunfire from outside the gate, and Kirby even thought he heard the sound of a bugle. Then there was a loudspeaker telling the attackers to surrender or die. The attackers who were left in the courtyard turned to see what was happening, and Katanga pressed the buttons to open the gate. What was left of the body caught in the hydraulic gate fell to the ground, a bloody mess. A dozen or so Naval Marines in their blue fatigues came bursting through the gate, causing the attackers inside the courtyard to drop their weapons and fall to the ground. A squad of Marines outside the gate were rounding up the stragglers who hadn't fallen after the Marines' initial attack. President Muhari had come through for them.

CHAPTER 91

The Marines cleaned up the scene, arresting or killing any of the attackers left alive. Kirby decided it was time to execute the next phase, which was to get Katanga and the two analysts on the plane and headed back to the USA. A Naval Marine medic had forced Katanga to lie down long enough to be treated. His wounds were painful, but not life-threatening. The first car, a black Toyota, pulled up with one of Katanga's hand-picked drivers. Kent came out the front entrance, took a long look at the chaos in the front courtyard, and jumped into the car with his suitcase and locked briefcase and took off. He never looked back.

A second car, a dark green Volvo station wagon pulled up. Bob went back inside to retrieve his stuff, and when he came out, he handed the .357 back to Katanga. He was shaking and seemed very glad to be leaving, but stopped to shake hands and look around, seeing the carnage that filled the courtyard. "Well...Damn." was his only comment. Then he man-hugged both Kirby and Katanga, then got his stuff and loaded up his car, and was on his way.

Katanga's ride was next, and all he had was his gun and a small duffel bag. He walked up to Kirby and both men hugged in the way that only men who have been in combat together can appreciate. Katanga walked to his car, a shiny black Mercedes, shook hands again with Kirby and got in the passengers' side. It was just then that Kirby noticed that the driver was a beautiful young woman with light brown skin. Katanga leaned over despite his wounds and kissed her, and they drove away from the scene of the fierce battle, the Battle of Castle Calloway.

Kirby surveyed the scene. Naval Marines were pulling bodies out of the courtyard and out the gate. The smell of death, blood, and acrid smoke was almost overwhelming. Kirby could not remember any of these sensations during the fight. A gentle breeze was beginning to push the gun smoke away from the house.

Kirby ran back upstairs to check on Claire. As far as he could tell, no attackers got anywhere near the house. The closest approach was the near-fatal encounter that he and Bob endured at the low wall, and Katanga's fight at the door.

He was not expecting what he encountered when he walked down the hall to his quarters. There was a fresh trail of blood down the hall toward the bedroom. Kirby started running and screamed out Claire's name, and didn't hear any response. As he entered the bedroom, he tried to find the light switch, but he fell over a body. He kneeled down with horror, and turned the body over to see the face of a black teenager, about Ethan's age. He had been shot through the chest and stomach, and was dead.

Kirby jerked up, pulling the Ruger up to firing position. He looked over to the bed and saw another body draped across it.

Frightened beyond belief, he moved to the body, and turned it over. In the dark, it looked to be wearing a black dress, and had long black hair, but when he turned it over, it was another attacker. He had been shot in the chest, one high and one low. Just then, he heard a weak, panic-stricken voice coming from the bathroom. He jumped over the bed, and pushed the door to the bathroom open. He turned on the light and there was Claire wedged between the toilet and the bathtub. She was still holding the Beretta and there were shell casings on the floor. She had blood spatters on her robe, but was apparently unhurt.

"Kirby! Kirby!" she cried out. He pulled her up and looked for any wounds. He could find none.

"Claire, look at me!" She turned to look at him and her eyes widened in recognition, dropping the Beretta pistol on the bathroom floor.

She cried, "I heard the shooting, then I heard breaking glass and went to look out in the hallway. There was a man coming down the hall with a huge knife. I shot at him and he grabbed his stomach but kept coming at me. I came back into the bedroom and he followed me. I shot him again, and he fell down in the doorway. I ran into the bathroom, and a minute or so later another one of them came at me with a knife. I heard what he said, "Don't ya be 'fraid we jus' gon have some fun's." So I shot at him twice and he fell on the bed. He tried to get up, so I shot him again. Then I went into the bathroom to hide." Kirby picked her up and carried her back into a chair in the bedroom. Then he held her until her sobbing stopped. She couldn't help looking at the body on the bed.

He looked around the bedroom, thinking how did they get up here? Kirby walked down the hallway following the blood trail, and found broken glass from a window on the side of the house, unguarded in the dark, with a tall ladder leading down to the ground.

He got her calmed down enough to start packing clothes for a quick escape and possibly a stay at the Presidents' home in Anaguan House. Once she focused on that, she was alright.

He went into his office and took the disk and the leather satchel with the evidence in it and brought it into the bedroom. There was a brightly colored Nigerian shopping bag lying in the chair, so he took it and crammed the satchel in it. He put the disk into his chest pocket, inside the combat jacket.

He dragged the two bodies over on the other side of the bed, until he could get them out in the hall. Then, Kirby was startled by someone suddenly entering the room. It was Katanga, and Kirby could tell he was terribly distraught.

"What the hell are you doing here? You're hurt and you're supposed to be on the plane out of here!"

Katanga collapsed into a chair, and wiped his hand over his eyes. "I couldn't leave. Not until you and Claire are safe. That was the commitment I made, and I am going to keep it."

"Katanga, I really appreciate you coming back for us. I really do, but we are going to be fine. We're going to stay with Muhari for a few days until things settle down."

"Sir, you aren't fine, and you won't be. I know that."

"Katanga, we've gotten the boys on the plane and they will get the story back to the people that can correct these problems. No one should care about us anymore."

"Sir, the plane that the boys were on went down just after takeoff. They are gone. Muhari knows this and that makes it too dangerous for him to have you with him. You still have powerful enemies here.

"What! The plane is down? Are you sure they didn't survive? Why weren't you on the plane with them? That was the plan."

"No, sir. I got to the hangar just after the plane took off. The plane came down in pieces, on fire. I saw it myself."

Kirby could not comprehend what this loss meant to him. Those fine young men. The chance to get the story out where it could be heard. All that was lost. Katanga stood up, slightly favoring his right leg.

He looked around, and for the first time saw the bodies of the two dead men.

"Who killed these?"

I pointed at Claire who was laying her negligée into her suitcase. She just smiled a grim smile back at him. Kirby guessed that she was getting with the program now.

"We have to find a different way out. It was Kwandanbo who attacked us, with the insistence and help from our "friends" in the Agency over here. And they are not likely to stop now."

Claire volunteered, "Why don't we just call the Embassy? You know the Ambassador. He should be able to let us come over there for asylum, or something!"

"Claire, we could do that, but in my experience they will push us off. We have a real mess here. They don't want to be caught between rival political factions in a mess the Agency created. They are professional bureaucrats, they'll have a job well after we are gone."

Kirby thought, "I have a friend who can...might be able to help. Felix Borowitz.

CHAPTER 92

"Felix, it's Kirby Calloway calling."

"Have you any idea what time it is?" He raised up, wearing only his undershirt, found his round little glasses, and looked at the clock.

"Saints Love! It's only four AM. Why would you be calling me at this time...and who is this anyway?

"Felix, it's Kirby Calloway. I need your help!"

"Well, what is it, man? Oh, Kirby. Sorry, I'm just waking up now."

"Felix, I and two colleagues, one woman, and one shot, are in desperate need of a ride out of town, actually out of Nigeria, actually today, right now."

"Gracious, Man. What kind of trouble are you and this woman in? Ex-spouse or something?"

"No, no, much more serious. Some of Kwandanbo's folks are after us. They tried tonight to kill us, and we need to fly under the radar and out of the country."

"Ok, I understand now. How awful! Well, there is a SwissAir flight leaving this morning at 7 AM for Zurich. I take it all the time. I have some free passes that you can use for diplomatic travel. I'm not supposed to have these, but can usually acquire a few. I will have them waiting at the SwissAir counter. Will that help?"

"Yes. Yes. Thank you so much. You are literally a life saver."

"So who is this woman that you need to smuggle out of the country? Is she pretty? Do I know her?"

"No, you don't, but I will introduce her and buy you a weekend in Paris to boot. Is it a deal?"

"Yes, of course, my friend. I would say, anytime, but please don't make it 4 AM the next time."

Kirby had been friends with Felix Borowitz for a long time, but tonight it paid off.

"Now all we need is a ride to the airport," Claire added.

Katanga said, "I can take care of that", and within minutes, a shiny black Mercedes pulled up in the driveway, driven by the beautiful girl with light brown skin.

"Kirby and Claire, this is my daughter Lindsay."

CHAPTER 93

We threw our travel bags in the trunk and jumped into the black Mercedes. Claire held tightly onto her shopping bag. Katanga said, "Let me introduce you to my daughter, Lindsey. Tonight she is my driver, but usually she is a First School teacher, like kindergarten in the US.

Lindsay looked back and smiled, but kept both hands on the wheel. Kirby and Claire nodded hello. "Katanga, we really need to hurry. It's 0430 now, and the plane leaves at 0700."

Katanga turned around and said, "Don't worry. I taught her what I learned in the high-speed escape course at the Farm. She will get us there."

Indeed, Lindsay drove with the confidence and skill of a NASCAR racer, weaving in and out of the light traffic between the Three Arms Zone and the airport, and by 5:15, we were at the Nnamdi Azikiwe airport. We were on the lookout for anyone that seemed to be on the lookout for us. Claire had brought a hat big enough for both of us to hide below. We all had French passports, but with the EU, we could go anywhere we wanted to without papers.

Kirby believed that Kwandanbo's men would be watching a particular airline, like those going back to New York or Miami, but all major airlines had early morning flights, so there were hundreds of people flooding the small airport. We found our passes at the Swiss Air desk. Good old Felix had given us First Class tickets to Zurich, so we headed up to the First Class Lounge, still scanning for trouble.

Katanga's leg was starting to bleed again, and nothing will get more attention in a passenger lounge in Africa than leaving a pool of blood on the floor. Everyone was hyper-sensitive since the break-out of Ebola in Africa, and blood stains were a clear indicator. Kirby sent Clair down to the concourse with her big hat to shop for a new pair of pants and a jacket for Katanga at the shops which were just opening at 6:00. In the meantime, Kirby sat next to Katanga with a newspaper under his bleeding leg and covering it with his jacket. When Claire returned, Kirby took Katanga into a men's room stall to get the blood-stained newspaper and his pants off, and then make a bandage out of newspaper and what was left of his pants.

The two of us barely fit in the stall together, it was like we were playing that game "Twister" in the stall.

We are both over six feet, and Katanga is built like a NFL tackle so it wasn't easy.

By the time we had made the change, and gotten back to Claire it was time to board First Class. Our seats were close together, so once all the other First Class passengers were seated, we spread out so it didn't look like we were sitting together. When Tourist Class boarded, we averted our eyes, and pretended to read so no one boarding could see our faces. But, some of the Tourist Class passengers looked angrily at us as they passed by. Kirby wondered whether that was just class envy, or whether some of their attackers had boarded. No one was dressed like a soldier so it was hard to tell. But their assailants could just be ordinary looking people, in other words, CIA agents.

As the flight took off, Kirby thought sadly about the tragedy with the two men who had given him the secret keys to the information he was carrying. They had served their country well, and then died at the hands of their evil countrymen. Kirby remembered their youthful exuberance and eagerness to get to the truth, and their brilliant minds. They will be missed in the Agency, at least the Agency that Kirby thought he knew.

Kirby had given Claire the package of secret documents and she was carrying it in the Nigerian shopping bag. Kirby thought she would draw more attention if she were accosted by someone intent on stealing her bag. He kept the disk to himself, tucked into his suit coat inside pocket.

As Kirby thought about arriving at their destination of Zurich, he had the unthinkable idea of going to confront Sorobet in his Zurich office. Then he realized that would probably get him thrown out of a window in a very tall building in downtown Zurich. He then decided that confronting Sorobet would take a different approach, and that his priority was to get himself, the reports, Claire, and Katanga home safely, and they were a long way from that. Sorobet could wait for justice to come if they destroyed his empire underneath him from his chalet in St. Moritz. Kirby hoped desperately that Sorobet had not gotten wind of their activities, but he realized with dread that nothing probably escaped Sorobet's view.

The final approach to Zurich was breathtaking in the morning as they flew into the airport. There was a light fog that highlighted the height of the mountains to the south surrounding this beautiful city. Lake Zürichsee stretched to the east, it's deep waters gleaming blue through the fog.

Kirby left his seat and sat next to Katanga. "Katanga, the danger might not be only on the plane, but it could be waiting for us as well in the airport. Weldon would have covered all bets."

Katanga nodded, "I'll lead the way. We'll go up into the First Class Lounge again to plan our next move, the flight to America."

"Katanga, why don't we fly into Canada instead?" They might not be as alert looking for a flight to Canada, don't you think?"

Katanga thought about it, and said, "Yes, but that gives them more chances at us in the terminal in Canada. I don't think that would fool them. They have plenty of men to cover both places. And I am sure they have told the less-informed agents to stop us at all costs. We need to find a different way in."

Kirby had to agree. Their route back to the US was blocked.

"How long would it take for us to go by train to the coast, then go by sea back to New York...or somewhere near there?"

Katanga saw where Kirby was going with that thinking.

"One day by train, a couple days to find sea transportation, then five days home from there. But you know they would still be waiting for us in New York."

"We're not getting off in New York."

Katanga jerked to look at Kirby.

Then Kirby filled Katanga in on his plan. Katanga nodded, asked a few questions, then sat back to think about it. "How exactly are we getting off a ship in the middle of the ocean and make it back to land? I'm really, really, really not a big fan of little boats, particularly those out in the middle of a big ocean."

Kirby replied, "It would take the cooperation of several men I know, and one I don't know well. But it's worth a try. Let me think it through." After a few minutes, he sat up and said, "I think it could work." Then he filled Katanga in on the plan. Katanga nodded his grim acceptance, but then he turned to Kirby. "But there is one other thing."

"What is it?"

"Could we stop using Katanga as my name? Katanga is a mining town in Nairobi. My real name is Ken, Ken Broussard. I'm from Louisiana."

Kirby was taken aback. "Why do you want to change your name now, after all this?"

Ken bent over and said, in a whisper, "This is going to be the most dangerous part of our journey. I want you to know my real name if I go down. Ok?"

Kirby bent over, and reached out his hand, "Glad to know you, Ken."

Katanga looked at the ground and whispered, "There is one other admission I need to make. He paused, then said, "I was supposed to be reporting to Weldon on you and subvert the effort if it got to close to Weldon's op. "

Kirby was disappointed but not surprised, the whole idea of a CIA agent planted in the middle of a competing op was so classically Langley.

"So when did you change allegiances? You have been a vital part of what we've been able to accomplish. We would not even be here without you."

"Kirby, once I saw the depth of the evil deception that Weldon was running, and I learned what a good man you are, I decided to pursue the course of honor. Now I'm proud to serve with you."

"Ken, thank you for telling me this. But, I never doubted you, so let's put this behind us. Ok?"

Ken Katanga looked up, and nodded ok, then took Kirby's hand and put it briefly on top of his head. "Now, I really am your man, and your friend."

Kirby looked into Katanga's eyes and acknowledged this tribute. But then he said, "We need to see if we can get some help to make this plan work. But first, I need to call my boys and tell them what's going on. They could be in danger, too."

CHAPTER 94

Kirby went into one of the private phone booth and dialed his home number. Marie answered the phone. "Hello, this is Marie."

Kirby was confused, he was unaware that Marie was living in the house.

"Is Ethan Calloway there? This is Kirby Calloway, his father."

"Oh, yes! Mr. Calloway, he's upstairs, I'll get him for you." There was a brief pause, then Ethan came on the line, with Morgan right beside him.

"Hi, Dad! How are you? Where are you? Morgan added.

"I'm safe, but I can't tell you where I am, but we've had to evacuate from Nigeria due to a little war between the President and someone who wants his job. We kind of got caught in the middle of it."

"Dad, you said 'we', is Claire with you?"

"Yes, she is, and also a good friend from Nigeria, Katang...I mean Ken, who is in the small "Club" of CIA agents we can trust.. We're looking for a safe way home now. We have made some bad people mad, and we need to steer clear of them, meaning we can't take a flight home. We're looking for another way now."

"How else can you get home? You mean on a boat?"

Kirby smiled, "Yeah, good guess. But you know I'm a Navy guy, I like boats. Listen, didn't you tell me your girlfriend Wendy, that her Dad was a Navy guy too, but he's Coast Guard now?"

"Yeah, he is. His name is Captain Rick Stillman. He runs the Hyannis station, and he's a helicopter pilot."

"That's great. I need his phone number. I need you to go talk to him and back me up; this whole story might be a bit hard to believe. So I might need a little help from the "Coasties". Wendy is still your girlfriend, yes?"

"Yes, Dad. She is my girl. I want you to meet her. Here's the number." Ethan read him the number, and then asked, "So, when are you coming home?"

"Probably in a week or so, promise."

"So you're done for good with that project you've been working on for over a year, right? Really done this time?"

"Let's say "done" for now. I still have a friendship with the President there and there is some clean-up I need to do. But when I get home, I'm home for good this time, I'm sure of that. I'll still be selling software but not having my side-line business. I've killed that one off, really killed it." he added wryly.

"When I get back, I'll have to go spend some time in Washington to report on things I've learned...at great cost, I need to say."

"Ok, Dad. We're looking forward to having you home. We've contacted some guys we trust in the FBI to watch out for you when you get here."

"Thanks, that's a great idea. One more thing, what's your Mom doing? Is she still living there?"

"Nope, she and her male companion, Tory, who we really like, are living back in New York. We're all on good terms now."

"Ok. That's good to hear. I need to go now, but I'll be in touch. And I will call Capt. Stillman and you need to go talk to him. Now, Ok? Goodbye!"

CHAPTER 95

We hung up the phone with Dad. Morgan seemed distracted. "What's on your mind, Morg?"

"What does Capt. Stillman have to do with Dad getting home? I don't get it."

I hadn't connected those dots yet, but it was clear that Dad was hatching some kind of plan to get home and avoid the "bad guys". I needed to call Wendy and talk to her Dad to give them a heads up. But what I was trying to understand was why Dad had to sneak home? Wasn't he still a volunteer member of his vaunted CIA? Why was he hiding from them now?

I called Wendy, and asked if I could speak to her Dad. She told me that he would call me, but I said that I needed to talk to him in person. She said, "Be here at six o'clock and you can have dinner with us, too."

I arrived at Wendy's house at the same moment as her Dad, and I waited in the street until he had pulled his old Volvo wagon in.

We both got out, and Capt. Stillman walked over to me. "What's so important that we needed to talk right away? Wendy called me and asked if I could come home right away. What is it, Ethan?"

"Sir, could we go in and talk in private? It really is important; it could be a matter of life or death."

"Ok, son. Follow me."

We walked up the walkway to the porch, and on through the funeral home living room and down a hallway into his study. Wendy and her Mom just watched us in silence as we walked through the house, though I could tell Wendy was really disturbed.

His study was what I expected from a Naval officer. There were hundreds of books covering the wall, and a huge map of Cape Cod. It reminded me of Colin's Dad's study, except in place of whaling spears, there was a Naval Academy Midshipman saber.

He turned on a desk light, and he gestured me into a big leather chair. He sat down in a similar chair, while I prepared my thoughts.

"Ok, Ethan, what's on your mind?"

"Sir, my Dad has been assisting the CIA over the past three or four years by just feeding them commercial information about his clients in Europe and now, in Nigeria. He and the President Muhari Clarion, have become good friends, something about the Naval Academy again."

Stillman's ears perked up at that.

"But in helping out the President and assisting the CIA, he uncovered a human trafficking operation run by some rogue agents and linked to a US Congressman. The attack that Morgan and I faced was a result of that investigation; they were looking for my Dad."

"Now he is stuck somewhere on the coast of Europe, running from that rogue unit with his friend Claire and a good friend named Katanga and he is trying to get home without being killed. They have been attacked twice in the last week already."

Stillman listened attentively, having a hard time believing the story but deeply impressed by the urgency which Ethan showed.

"My Dad has a plan in mind, but I don't know exactly what it is. He is going to call you to discuss it, but I know it involves boats."

"Boats? From Europe to here?" Now Stillman was intrigued. "What kind of boats, and why does he need my help?

"Sir, I don't know, but he needs your help, and the information he is carrying will blow this whole nasty thing apart, if he can get it back into the right hands. All I ask is for you to listen to him and see if there is a way you could help bring this very dangerous business to an end."

Capt. Stillman nodded. "I will expect his call, then, and if there is a way I can help, I will try."

"But Sir, you realize that this has to remain a complete secret?"

"Of course, I'll treat it with the highest confidentiality."

Then we walked back into the dining room and had a great home-cooked meal, Capt. Stillman, her Mom, me and Wendy. It was a first for me and it felt good. So this is what a family feels like.

CHAPTER 96

Ken suggested, "Let's start with the Zurich field office. They might not have heard of the mess down in Nigeria yet, and besides, I know the deputy station chief. When I played football at LSU, she was a cheerleader."

Kirby was surprised. "When we first met, I thought you might make a good NFL recruit but I never imagined you as a US college athlete. You were a Ragin' Cajun? I can see it now, Broussard!"

"Ok. But don't get too carried away by that name. I can always go back to Katanga, you know. And by the way, I was a LSU Tiger, not a Ragin' Cajun."

Kirby smiled, and replied fondly, "You'll always be Katanga to me...Ken."

Ken went to the phone booth and called the Zurich office. It was not a number listed in the phone book, and it didn't have an address, but it was one of the largest offices in Europe. Keeping a close eye on banking transactions was a key part of the work they did there.

The person on the receiving end just said, in a cold, monotone voice, "Hello, this is Department 143, can I help you?" Katanga identified himself, and after a brief pause, another, much friendlier voice came on the line, and asked, "Ken, is that really you?" Katanga recognized the voice. "Hello, Sarah! It's me. It's been a long time, hasn't it?"

"Yes, something like five years, yeah? What can I do for you? I assume you've gotten yourself into trouble somehow, and now you need my help to get out of it. Right?"

"Nailed it. We would first like a ride over to the office where we can regroup. We're in the First Class Lounge at the Zurich airport in ZRH Level 3, near Gates B/D. Can you send someone?"

"Sure, let's see...ok, look for a charcoal Mercedes with a female driver, it'll pick you up in one hour precisely. Are you by yourself?"

"No, I have two companions, Claire, and Kirby Calloway."

"Oh, is that the Calloway from Nigeria? He's been in the wind here a lot this morning."

"Sarah, I can tell you the story when we get there, but I can tell you, I will vouch for Calloway one-hundred percent. We need to book some unusual travel arrangements back to the States. Calloway has made too many enemies to count, and we need to go deep. We have part of a plan, but we need your help to pull it off."

"Ok, be safe getting here."

CHAPTER 97

"Ok, it's time to go." Kirby was faking the reading of an old "Travel Weekly" magazine because it was huge and covered his face, and Claire was passed out under that huge hat she'd bought. She stirred, and then sat up quickly, looking around not quite knowing where she was.

Kirby looked around the room, but saw nothing unusual or dangerous. There were a few couples relaxing or sleeping in the big chairs. There was a hefty, disheveled man at the bar sucking out the last of a Bloody Mary, and there was a blond guy leaning against the wall by the door reading a newspaper. They got up to go, then Kirby realized that the man's newspaper was upside down. He bumped Katanga's elbow, and nodded at the guy. Katanga nodded that he had seen him, and picked up one of those heavy glass cigarette ashtrays as they walked by a chair and hid it behind his back. They had no other weapons, but with luck, they would soon have one.

When the man suddenly dropped the paper and reached for his gun, Katanga sailed the massive glass ashtray like a frisbee, catching the man right in his forehead. The glass ashtray bounced back under a big recliner. He dropped straight down, and Katanga reached inside his waistband and removed his gun, a Glock19, a favorite pistol of CIA agents. Katanga kept the gun out, hidden along his leg.

No one in the Lounge showed the slightest interest in the man sitting on the floor with a bloody newspaper, right side up, covering his head. This was a sophisticated group of travelers. They didn't really want to know more about what they just saw.

They continued to walk out and down the stairs looking out into the check-in area for anyone who was paying any particular attention to them, or appeared to be crossing the check-in lines which moved slowly to the right.

At the bottom of the stairs, there were two policemen, standing, talking, and generally surveying the crowd. They didn't seem to notice the man and woman who were slowly crossing from line to line, getting closer with each move.

When the three got to the bottom of the stairs, they stopped behind the two cops and appeared to be looking for their tickets. Kirby judged the distance to the doorway to be about twenty meters, about ten seconds away for him. But Katanga's leg was injured, and it would take far longer. Outside, he could see the charcoal Mercedes pulling up to the curb, right on time.

The couple grew closer, and now the cops noticed them, saw them as a threat, but were slow to draw their weapons. The man and woman both fired multiple shots, hitting both cops and wounding Kirby in the shoulder. Katanga fired at almost the same time as their assailants, two shots each, left-right, right-left and they both fell, with the woman's head and blond hair bouncing off the green simulated marble floor. The sound of the gunfire boomed through the terminal. The blood splashed and began flowing instantly, but the three had no time to view it. They dashed outside to the waiting car, which sped away as soon as the door slammed closed. People in the terminal hardly noticed what had just happened.

The Zurich CIA office was located in Rüschlikon, with a beautiful view of the Zürichsee. It was a non-descript office building in a small office park off the Nidelbadstrass.

Luckily, it had its own infirmary because both Katanga and Kirby were in need of medical attention, Katanga for the leg and arm wounds he received during the Battle of Calloway Castle, as they had begun to call it, and Kirby for the shoulder wounds he received in the fight at the airport. But they were in high spirits now that they were back in friendly hands. But as they celebrated, the door opened and it was the Station Chief, along with his deputy, Sarah.

Both did not look happy.

The Station Chief squared off with Kirby, who was sitting on a stool, getting bandaged by an aide. He was seriously pissed. "You two have been stirring up a war in the CIA. Based on the burners that have been flying across my desk, either you deserve a medal, or you need to be arrested and sent to the CIA dungeon. Can either of you enlighten me as to the course I ought to take with you? Then, there's the matter of two wounded policemen and two dead CIA agents lying on the floor by Gates B/D in the Zürichflugen. What's with you two?"

Kirby related the research they had done and how it had exposed the human trafficking ring between the US, Caracas, Nigeria, and Switzerland. He did not name any of the people alleged to be involved. This information could only be divulged to law enforcement back in the US. Kirby still had no idea who he could trust, and there were two assassination attempts and a fresh bullet wound to prove it.

The Station Chief was not satisfied. "Why didn't you just surrender to the two agents today, instead of killing them, for Christ's sake."

"Sir, they approached us with guns drawn, no ID's, and not telling us who they were, and they shot first, at the cops and us. I'm sure there is plenty of camera footage to back us up. And one of your guys was waiting in the First Class Lounge to jump us, and wasn't asking questions, just pulling out his gun. What was that?"

"What? That wasn't one of my guys." The Chief took another slow look at them. "You guys seem to have more enemies than just us." Then he looked away, and said, "Well, anyway, I'm going to have to hold you here until we get this all cleared up. And I want you to hand over the information about this mess that you say proves your cockamamie story."

Claire clutched the shopping bag a little tighter.

Kirby reached for his coat lying on the table next to the surgical bed that Katanga was sitting on. He felt for the disk that he had carried in his right inside coat pocket. It was cracked having been nicked by the bullet that hit Kirby, and it probably slowed the bullet that hit his shoulder. He pulled it out and looked at it. The disk had a whole quarter-section broken out of it, and was covered in his blood.

The Station Chief grumbled, "Well, that's just great. Are there any other disks?"

Kirby replied slowly, "They were blown up along with my two analysts, Kent and Bob, when their plane exploded just after take-off. Then he looked at the Chief, and said, savagely, "Doesn't that sound like evidence of rogue action to you?"

The Station Chief grumbled again. "It still doesn't clear you of the charges I've seen out of Langley. I am going to hold you in confinement until we can organize a court of inquiry."

"Sarah, would you escort your friends to the confinement area. And put that woman in a hotel room somewhere. She's got to be a witness to all these crimes and shenanigans."

Sara stood up, and told them, "Follow me." As they walked down the hallway, Sarah looked around to make sure they were alone. "I'm sorry it turned out this way. While you were getting treated, I arranged some transport on a cruise ship that's leaving from Rotterdam going to New York in a couple of days. I hope you know how to cook. Of course, you are going to have to take the Thalys trainLine from here. It takes about eight hours and runs right into the Eurosport in Rotterdam where the "Holland Rotterdam" leaves from. I'll leave all the tickets with you in case this mess gets cleared up soon."

She took them all down into the basement where the confinement area was located. It was more like a hotel room than a cell. It had a desk, a bed, and an attached bathroom. More importantly, it had a phone. But it also had an armed guard at the door.

Sarah added, "Sorry we have to put both of you in here. We only have one unit. I'll send some food down later. Also, sorry for all the traffic noise. This level empties out into the street through that fire exit just down the hallway outside. I hope that's not an issue." Kirby and Katanga looked at each other. That information would prove very useful.

"By the way, don't try to use the phone. Everything you say will go right to the Chief. But, if you want to get a message out, write it down and I will send a secure email for you. But only one message."

Kirby asked, "Can we have visitors, like Claire? "

Sarah was leaving, but she turned and said, "Hmm...I don't see why not. You're not guilty of anything yet. So, sure. I'll tell the guard. His name is Curtis, and he's my nephew. Please don't hurt him," she added, wagging her finger at us.

"Oh, Sara. Where did they put Claire?"

"She has a room in a little hotel nearby here. I'll send her by to see you. Curtis likes pretty women."

Katanga found a piece of paper from a bathroom paper towel. Kirby found an old blue pen in the top drawer of the desk. Kirby took the paper and bent over to write behind Katanga to shield the note from the surveillance camera. He writes:

"Ethan & Morgan - we're being detained by the CIA but can't tell you where. But we have a plan to escape and we need you to try to get some help to keep the CIA from tracking us down and killing us when we get home. They've already tried twice. The information we have will blow this whole thing open. Maybe the FBI can help."

Then he scrawled Ethan's email address on the bottom of the note and gave it to Katanga.

Katanga folded up the message and gave to his friend Sarah. As she took it, he held her hand. "Thank you so much for this. It really is a matter of life or death. Ours. And make sure it doesn't fall into the hands of anybody here. Even the good field agents have been told to kill us on sight. Thanks again!"

CHAPTER 98

Kirby and Katanga both needed rest, so they laid down on the single bed together and fell fast asleep. Four hours later, Claire came in the back door, which for some reason was unlocked. She had rested, bathed, and put on a red cocktail dress that was cut dangerously low in the front. She had applied her most sultry makeup, and of course, her Baccarat Rouge 540 perfume, the one that Kirby really likes. The one for which he pays $850 a bottle for 200 ml. Armed as such, she encountered young Curtis in the hallway outside the detention facility.

She walked up dangerously close to him, close enough that he could smell her perfume. Her red lips looked like candy. He looked at her with a combination of lust and fright.

"Hello....You must be Curtis. You are much bigger than your aunt told me you were when she asked me to come by and visit with you. You must be an athlete, what sports do you play?"

He couldn't move, nor could he speak.

"Curtis, do you mind if I go in and visit with my friends? As you know, they have both been wounded in battle, and could use a woman next to them to cheer them up. Is that okay?"

Curtis nodded rapidly, and replied, "I'm sure that would be fine. I play rugby. It's a very tough sport."

Claire looked at him with her most enticing look. "Oh, you play rugby. That's fascinating!" She moved even closer to him so that the curves of her breasts were almost close enough for him to touch.

"Can you unlock the door now, please? And could you just leave it open so you can see me and make sure I don't do anything improper?" She looked at the young man and winked with those smoky eyes.

Curtis struggled to find the right key with her beautiful body right next to him, but then he did find it, and when he started to insert it, she laid her hand on top of his, and whispered, "You have to push hard to get it in." and then she pushed the key in and turned it. Curtis was aware of a sudden tightening of his pants around his groin as he drank in the erotic moment.

She pushed the door open, and went in to the sleeping men and commanded softly "Wake up. We're leaving."

The men struggled to wake up, so she returned to Curtis. She went to him, put her hand on his shoulder, then took his hand and put it around her waist, touching the curve below. She did this slowly, giving Curtis time to really appreciate what she was doing, and then she pulled him in close and kissed him hard, moaning, "I love ruggers!"

Curtis pulled himself away, taking one last look, then bolted out the door, headed for the men's room.

Kirby and Katanga jumped up, grabbed the tickets, their coats, the sandwiches, and go-bags and fled out the door, down the hallway and out the fire exit to the waiting minivan. Claire's bag, including the beach bag in a Nigerian pattern that carried the precious documents, was already locked in the van's trunk. They piled in, laughing and high-fiving as they sped toward the train station. Kirby hugged Claire and said, giggling, "I almost had to stop in the bathroom myself!"

CHAPTER 99

The summer had just gotten underway, and me and Morgan were already bored and were sitting in the living room throwing the couch pillows at each other. We knew our Dad was on his way home, but we didn't know how or exactly when.

There was a knock on the door and we tensed up, and carefully went to the door. It was Colin.

"Come on in, buddy. You want to join us throwing pillows at each other, or did you have something else in mind? Besides beer; we're fresh out."

Collins said, 'No Mate, I don't want to throw pillows with you two girls. You promised me that I could learn to shoot. With all the action around here lately, I thought now might be a good time." I looked at Morg, and I could see the eagerness in his face, and I was bored stiff. Plus, we might need his help. "Ok, Col. Let's go do it."

The fact that we had the guns was widely known, so I didn't feel that we needed to hide them anymore. Morgan went upstairs to get one of the 30 round mags and one of the M-16A2's and brought it down and set it on the living room table.

"Colin, this is a very dangerous rifle. It can either fire one shot at a time, or fire like a machine gun, controlled by this selector switch, here. In "AUTO" it will fire three rounds each time you pull the trigger. And here's how you load it up. Put the magazine in here and lock it. Then pull this handle back to load it. Locked and loaded. Get it?" Colin nodded his head solemnly, practiced locking an empty mag in place, charging it, and then selecting ""FIRE" or "AUTO". "Ok, I've got it!"

We got into the Maserati with Morg as shotgun and Colin in the back, and headed for a remote dune out past the airport to finally educate Colin on being an American man. On the way, Morgan told him about becoming a "Ranger" if he ever faced a life or death situation.

As we went through a green light at the intersection of Main and Fourth Street, out of the corner of my eye, I saw a large semi-truck cab entering the intersection at high speed, deliberately targeting us. I slammed on the brakes, making the truck miss the passenger compartment and hit the front of the car instead. It plowed into us with an enormous crash sound of impact and crushed metal. The semi- tore off the front of the car and the engine, overturning the car, sending it sliding violently across the intersection with sparks flying, and leaving the Maserati spinning slowly on its roof as we slid to a stop. The truck that hit us kept on going. Morgan, who took the brunt of the crash was knocked out and we were both locked in our seatbelts upside down. Colin wasn't wearing a seat belt and was thrown against the right side door, then found himself lying on the roof with the M-16 next to him when the car stopped spinning. Then a tall man in a long black coat came out of a shop on the corner. He had thin blonde hair, and was wearing strange, round dark sunglasses. He seemed perfectly calm, and walked slowly like he was just crossing the street. Then, out of his coat pocket, he pulled a silenced pistol. As he got closer, I struggled with my seatbelt but couldn't get it to release. I yelled to Colin, "Shoot him! Shoot him!" Colin picked up the rifle, very hesitantly. The gravity of the situation was slow to come to him, but "RANGERS" entered his mind. He locked the magazine in and pulled the charging handle, then selected "AUTO" as we had shown him. As the shooter raised his gun and pointed it at Morgan's head, Colin pulled the trigger, firing a three-round burst into the shooter. The rattle of the rifle in the overturned car was deafening. The tall man fired his pistol into the air, and fell backwards, crumpling to the ground.

People came flooding out of the shops, and cars stopped to try to help. Someone came over to my side of the car, knelt down, and cut my seat belt, and I fell awkwardly to the roof. Two girls came to Morgan's aid, and slowly released him and supported him, then pulled him carefully out through the broken window. Morgan woke up, looked around, then asked one of the girls, "Hi, what's your name?" Then, I knew he was going to be ok, especially after one of them brought bandages.

Colin and I crawled out and surveyed the scene. Colin had left the M16A2 in the overturned car. I reached in and pulled it out. When the inevitable investigation started, I wanted to shield Colin, a foreign national who wasn't supposed to even hold a rifle in the US or the state of MA. And there was the issue of it being an automatic rifle.

The shooter was still lying on his back in the street, and there were several people standing over his body. His pistol was lying in the street and looked to be a suppressed Beretta, not a Glock, so this was probably a new player. Once again, we were not seriously hurt, this time thanks to the conversion-under-fire of Colin.

The Maserati held up well during the crash, and its big brakes allowed me to slow enough so that the truck hit forward of the passenger door, probably saving Morgan. Its engine was gone, however, lodged into the grill of a fast-moving north-bound semi. That truck should be easy to find with a Maserati engine and wheel sticking out of the grill.

Officers Collins and Watson arrived with lights flashing and sirens screaming. They quickly recognized the car, and the three of us standing by the car with minor wounds. I saw Officer Collins look, and he shouted, "Oh no. Not you two, and that damn car again!"

He nevertheless walked over to the car and asked, "Are you alright? What happened here, and who is that guy lying in the street?"

Morgan was cradling his right arm and a girl was holding a bandage up to the right side of his head. He snarked, "You are the law enforcement here! That's your job to find out!"

Collins snarked back, "Well, you two are the local spies in town and I'm tired of cleaning up these messes where these kind of guys keep showing up," pointing to the guy whose body was being loaded into an ambulance.

"I've already talked to enough witnesses to know that this was a deliberate attack, so you guys can go, but leave your little rifle here. It's evidence now, along with the dead guy's pistol. I pulled all the stuff out of his pockets and I know for sure he wasn't from around her. He had a Swiss passport. Does that mean anything to you?"

Morg and I looked at each other. Was this a visit from the 'Big Guy'? The FBI was going to love this!

One of the on-lookers was Mr. Frank, our one and only cab driver in Pocasset. He beckoned to us, and pointed to his cab. I nodded yes for all of us, and then we waded through the astonished crowd to his cab. He opened the cab door and we all crawled in.

He came around and got in, then turned to look at us. I said, "Home, please, Mr. Frank", and Frank grunted and took us back to Fort Calloway, which at the moment looked much safer than driving around town. We got out, and he drove off without charging us for the ride. Colin had ridden along in silence. His first experience in firing a gun was to use a sub-machine gun to kill a hit man. Not a bad start for our Aussie friend, but he was going to need therapy.

This new assailant was a mystery to us. Morgan was able to get his personal information from Ofc. Ray Watson. He was from Zurich and looked like a professional Swiss hit man. Unless things turned out exactly as they did, with Colin with a loaded M16 laying on the upside down roof, we would all be dead, not here, discussing it on the couch. We knew that until our Dad got home and delivered his evidence, including the identity of a Swiss hit man, to the US Government, we would be continually at risk. I thought about calling Tory, but this time it needed to be directly from me. I was the acting man of the house. It was time to call the FBI again. We needed protection.

CHAPTER 100

The bright red Thalys bullet train was already at the Zurich HB Station. Claire had timed her arrival at the detention room to coincide with the departure time of the train, plus it gave all three of us time for some much needed rest. The trains left every two hours so it was easy to turn in our vouchers for tickets and leave right away. They bought tickets on the 15:06 departure, which would put them into Rotterdam at about ten o'clock at night. They would need to find a place to stay until departure on the "Holland Rotterdam" at 1700, the next afternoon.

Kirby told them, "I got this new personal credit card a few months ago for times like these. It's using my French passport name and address so it should be hard to trace, at least until we get home."

They got to their seats just before the train began to move, and after watching the stunning Swiss mountains go by, they fell asleep again.

Kirby woke up at about eight o'clock and let the others sleep. He knew the CIA, or some part of it, was still searching for them.

He hoped desperately that, in the interval of his travel, responsible people in management in the Federal Agencies would investigate what happened at Castle Calloway, and start asking questions about company activities that were clearly illegal. He was carrying the only copy of the truth that was left, and he was putting his life on the line to get it to the right people so he could again feel safe to get on with his life, possibly with Claire and the boys.

As the train slowed down coming into Rotterdam, Claire and

Katanga woke up and started looking out the windows at the darkened town. They were pulling into a station near the waterfront and there were lights on what looked like dozens of ships, some moving with their red and green lights, while others were docked with their huge foredeck lights shining down on the whole ship.

Our ship, the "Holland Rotterdam" wasn't due in until early the next morning, so we needed a place to stay and to get something to eat. We found a cab, and between my English, Claire's French, and Katanga's German, we were able to have him take us to a nearby two-story inn called the Kuiperduin which had late-night snacks, and free breakfast. Unfortunately, the bar closed at eleven. We got one room with two single beds, Claire and I took one bed and Katanga had the other one. I finally got edged out and slept on the couch.

We still had the company Glock19 and six bullets. We were using my French ID and credit card so we couldn't be traced. This place was a small, inconspicuous hotel off the main road. We felt that it would be safe enough not to have a watch-stander. We were right. The next morning dawned bright and clear, so we had breakfast and then hung out in a small garden behind the hotel.

Now, for the first time, we reviewed our escape plan. First thing that morning, I called Capt. Stillman, Wendy's Dad of the Hyannis Coast Guard and explained our predicament, that we needed to get off the "Rotterdam" near Cape Cod, rather than risk entering New York and getting arrested, or worse. He and I were almost classmates at the Naval Academy, just a year apart, and classmates from a service academy would literally do anything in their power to help a "brother in arms". Katanga and I were also brothers, having been through armed combat together.

We had devised a plan, but we needed the cooperation of the Captain of the "Rotterdam" for it to work. That's again where I needed Capt. Stillman to make a Merchant Marine connection with the Captain of the Rotterdam. Stillman would have to convince him that this mission was important enough to national security to slow down his ship from its normal cruise speed of 24 knots to less than 5 knots when he was 83.3 miles south of Hyannis, precisely at position 41.00 N, 70.00 W at around 0300 in the morning, five days from now. At that point, the ship would be 189.6 miles East of New York Harbor and on course to New York through the shopping lanes.

We boarded, well, rather we snuck aboard the "Holland Rotterdam" that afternoon. We were masquerading as kitchen help, thanks again to Sarah, and because the Rotterdam had a light load going to New York, there was room in the crew spaces for us to hide out in the tiny crew berths for the four days until the drop-off. Plus, we were close to the kitchens, so we ate well the whole time.

But, we were not safe. Late one night on the third day, I heard screaming coming from down the hall. I ran down the corridor, to Claire's room, lit by only one single bulb, to find a big, black man with his arm caught in the door to Claire's room, struggling to pull it out. I could hear Claire screaming on the other side. I threw my weight against him and his arm came out of the door, broken and bleeding. Suffering with the pain from my gunshot wound, I started fighting with him, but he was much bigger and stronger than me, even with just the strength of one arm. Then, he jerked back and pulled a gun, a Glock19, out of his waistband, aimed it at me and pulled the trigger. I ducked to avoid what I knew was coming, and it only grazed the top of my head but disoriented me. I heard two more shots, and I fell. Katanga stood over me with our own stolen Glock, the barrel still smoking. The man fell to the deck, shot through the heart, twice.

Katanga spoke first, "You alright, Kirby? There's a lot of blood coming from your head." I reached up and felt the blood matting in my hair, creating a crust already.

I noticed that Katanga was looking with sadness at the body in the floor. "Did you know him?"

"Yeah, we worked together in London a few years back. He was a trainer. He taught me knife-fighting," Katanga said, with a chill of irony.

"I'm sorry. That didn't need to happen. It makes me even madder at those bastards that set us up."

Claire came out into the corridor, wrapping her robe around herself. "I was cold so I was coming down to your room. As soon as I opened the door, he was there and he forced his arm in. He dropped his knife over in that corner of the room."

"Well, what are we going to do with him? The crew will catch on and have to report it."

"Well, one of us is getting a roommate."

Claire cringed, "Not me. He can have my room and I'll sleep with Kirby." She was shaking from the attack, and came over to me for comfort. "When is this going to be over, my love? All this unnecessary killing. I want it to be over."

"Soon, I hope. We only have one more night."

Claire then noticed the blood dripping down my back from the bullet graze that I had just gotten. "Kirby, we have got to clean you up. You're ruining that shirt." She got a couple of washcloths from the bathroom and told Kirby just to hold it there until the bleeding stopped. Then she retrieved the first aid kit from the kitchen and bandaged his head.

Katanga observed, "They won't stop trying, especially since we're getting closer to New York. They wanted the three of us to come up missing somewhere back in Europe, and the evidence lost forever. Then they can go back to their old, very profitable ways."

I explained, "That's why we have to get off. Ok, here's the plan. We'll put him in Claire's stateroom, lock it, and we'll all stay together in mine. It'll be cramped, but they won't be able to pick us off one at a time.

The rest of the night passed without incident. On the fifth night, just before midnight, we heard the sound of a door being kicked repeatedly, with loud curses being shouted. The smell of the dead man was beginning to permeate the corridor. Then there was the sound of loud hammering, and a door opening. There were more curses as they found the dead body that had begun to smell, which is what brought them to that door. Then we heard them shuffle off, carrying the dead man, but there were no more noises after that. The smell of death still flowed through the hallway.

Then, later at 0200, we moved carefully to the lower deck, with Katanga and his Glock with four bullets leading the way. From there, we took a narrow stairway deep into the bowels of the ship, and then went lower still until we reached the Lower Hull Access Room. There was a large hatch in the side of the ship near the stern just above the waterline that could be opened to bring large pieces of equipment into the boat, or take large sections of systems out for repair. The fact that it was on the waterline made it easy to bring small boats or barges up to the hatch. It also made it easy to launch the ships' Rigid Inflatable Boat, or RIB, out of the hatch to carry out clean-up, rescue, or line handling duties. This particular foggy night, the RIB was embarking on a different mission. The only question was would the ship slow to almost a stop so we could open the hatch and launch it.

CHAPTER 101

We had enlisted two young crew members to go with us and aid with launching the boat and returning it to the ship after the drop-off. They were eager to go on our night-time, high-seas spy mission without any clue why they were doing it or who we were. Ah, the foolishness of youth.

Suddenly, the door back into the ship opened, and there was the Captain of the ship, Captain Lars Johansson. He was a tall Viking-looking man, with gray hair and a short beard, and piercing blue eyes. He took a look around, then looked at us like he was having a hard time believing what he was seeing going on in his boat. We stood still, at attention, waiting for his pronouncement. He reached for his walkie and commanded the bridge, "All Stop". We could feel the great ship slowing to a stop. We now had to face the dangers outside the ship.

"Get this little stunt moving. I can't just sit here waiting on you!"

Captain Johansson seemed to be ignoring the fact that there was an unexplained dead man on his boat. We opened the hatch using four large handles that hydraulically unlocked the hatch, and when it unlocked it slid automatically into a recess in the ceiling.

The ship had slowed to a crawl and the seas were relatively calm. The Captain spoke into his radio to the bridge, "Confirm All Stop." We only had a small time window to get underway. The RIB was housed in a large fiberglass container which would become its hull. Katanga pulled a rope handle on its side which caused the RIB to inflate and push its container aside. The RIB was over 14 feet long, and it took up most of the space in the room. There was an 50 horsepower outboard motor hanging on the wall, and Katanga and I manhandled it down and installed it on the transom. There was also a large red gasoline tank on the floor that Kirby set inside the RIB and hooked its fuel lines to the engine. This was just common spy stuff that Katanga had practiced many times in training, so it went smoothly.

We all put on the provided life-jackets, then pushed and pulled the big RIB to the edge of the hatchway. The Captain said, "Wait. You will need these." He reached into a small cabinet and pulled out a set of small rod-shaped devices. "These are red flares. Ignite them when you get to your destination. It will make you much easier to see. And Capt Stillman sends his regards."

Kirby looked outside to judge the swells and the dark waves. There was a gentle swell out of the East, and Kirby looked at his watch. On the top of the swell, it was time to go. "PUSH!", he commanded.

CHAPTER 102

It was a typical very foggy night in the shipping lane from Amsterdam to New York in the early summer. The cruise ship "Holland Rotterdam", about 190 nautical miles from New York, had slowed considerably as the fog closed in on them.

Morgan and I were waiting by the phone in the Ops Center of the Coast Guard station in Hyannis. I had insisted that I go along on the flight to help identify my Dad, and Capt. Stillman had somewhat reluctantly agreed. There were drug smugglers and fishermen in these waters at night, and he did not want to drop down on the wrong boat by mistake. Then, Capt. Stillman came out of the ops center, and ordered, "We're a Go, boys. Boat's in the water. Let's load up." Falk then came out of the Ops Center and followed Capt. Stillman into the pilot's ready room. The Rescue Swimmer, Tim, a wiry little guy, came over and gave me my inflatable PFD and directed me to follow him out to the chopper. It was still very dark, and the flashing lights, the jet noise, the pounding of the helicopter blades, and the smell of aviation fuel filled the air, adding to my level of excitement. I climbed up the few steps to the cabin door and clambered into the cabin, only lit by red nighttime lighting. It was just light enough for me to find a seat and buckle in. Tim, the rescue swimmer went around the cabin, checking his equipment in the dark stern of the chopper, and then he came back and put a radio headset on my head. Then he sat opposite me, giving me a big grin and a thumbs up. He reported "Swimmer and cargo bay clear", which I heard on the headphones. I returned his thumbs up, and within seconds, the chopper lifted off and we turned to the South and headed out to sea. I could hear very minimal radio traffic; I guessed this was not a routine mission.

At this time of night there were only a few lights; some sword fishermen leaving the docks to head out to the Grand Banks, and a few big ships headed into New Bedford or Providence. The sea was dark, and once we left the lights on the shore, it was difficult to distinguish between sea and sky. We gained altitude and then settled at a few thousand feet for our roughly one-hour trip to the South where we hoped to find my Father, his love Claire, and some guy named Katanga. I couldn't imagine how we would ever spot them. Tim slid the door open and I could feel the rushing wind. He signaled that I could take off my seat belt and go over to the door. I crawled over to the open hatch, and then felt Tim putting a safety lanyard on me so I didn't fall out into the darkness. There was nothing to see, really nothing at all.

Out in the "New York Approach" shipping lanes, on the "Holland Rotterdam", a light appeared down on the starboard stern as a hatch opened and five people were seen launching a large inflatable boat. They boarded the boat and sped away to the North.

Around dawn, I felt us slowing down and then going into a hover. Capt. Stillman had sighted the inflatable which had stopped in the water at the designated coordinates. I looked out the door and saw what looked like the lights of fishing boats way off to the East. Capt. Stillman and presumably, very unofficial Flight Officer Falk had picked up the signal from its red signal flares on the infrared sensor and had seen it on the choppers' radar. We hovered directly overhead, and Tim, the rescue diver jumped out of the helicopter, hitting the water in a tight vertical cannonball, and swam over to the inflatable. With the unnecessary help of two of the men on the inflatable boat, Tim was hauled in. I could look straight down, and in the powerful spotlight from the chopper, I could see five people in the raft. I guess Capt. Stillman didn't need me to identify my Dad because they were already on the cable, and one at a time, the three people on the little boat were being raised up into the helicopter.

Claire was first to be pulled up. I recognized her immediately from the one photograph we had, but she was wet, tired, and her black hair was in her face. She recognized me right away, and she smiled and grabbed my hand as she buckled into a seat. It was way too noisy to talk. My Dad was next up the cable, and as soon as I was able to, I hugged him as hard as I could. But he then he turned to look over the side of the helicopter, awaiting the next guy to be lifted out of the little rubber boat below us. As the new arrival got up to and filled the door, I could tell that it was a very big black man; he had to be Katanga. The diver then jumped back into the water, raising his hand for rescue. The two men in the inflatable waved and turned off to the West and sped away to catch up with the ship, still waiting for their return. The lights of the "Holland Rotterdam" were visible a few miles away.

The Coast Guard helicopter picked up the diver from the sea, logging it as a diver night training mission, and headed for home to its operating base, back to at Hyannis, about 88 miles north, or less than one hour away.

We didn't try to talk much as we flew back north in the awakening dawn. Dad leaned over to me and shouted, "How far is it to home?" I shouted back, "It's only about an hour." He grinned broadly. Dad was sitting next to Claire, with Katanga on her other side. It occurred to me that this sitting arrangement had a real, deep meaning, especially over the past week of hiding and traveling.

Tim kept the door open; it seemed because he liked to sit in the door with his feet out and watch the sea under his feet. The Sun rose slowly, spectacularly out of the sea like it always had, but there was something really different for me, sitting with these people with their amazing story.

As the helicopter settled onto the landing pad, the pilot, Capt. Rick Stillman, looked toward the lights of the ops building to see if the welcoming crowd was waiting there. From the cockpit of the helicopter, he could see the silhouettes of a half-dozen very agitated people inside the glass. He could also see a number of FBI agents standing guard around the pad and inside the terminal.

When the blades stopped spinning and the engine turbines spun down, the door on the helicopter opened, and four people got out and ran in the dark towards the terminal, ducking under the blades which turned very slowly at least ten feet over their heads.

When they got into the lights of the terminal, there were four very happy people coming into the light; a tall, lanky man, a young man who looked very similar, a big black man, and between them, a woman with long black hair blowing in the wind, and struggling to keep up with the three men.

"Dad, Dad, over here!" Morgan was running out toward the helicopter, and plowed right into Dad. Dad hugged him, and tousled his long blond hair. Morg could see that Dad was holding hands with a very pretty woman, the one with the long black hair. "Boys, this is Claire!" She looked at us with a huge smile and grabbed around us in a big family hug. Even though I didn't really know her, I knew what she had been through with our Dad, and I loved her for that. Maybe we really could start over as a new family. We all walked together towards the terminal building.

I saw Wendy walking out to greet her Dad, in his helmet and flight suit, who was just climbing down from the cockpit of the huge machine. Falk followed him down, grinning from ear to ear. This had been his first flight sitting in the cockpit of a Coast Guard helicopter, and for the first time, he wasn't wearing jeans and a T-shirt. He was wearing a Coast Guard flight suit, and although he probably couldn't admit it, Capt. Stillman probably let him fly it out to the rendezvous point. I did see the real co-pilot get out too.

I saw Colin running out to join Falk, who was staring up and admiring the white and orange-trimmed beast. I grabbed Wendy as she passed us and pulled her over to our moving group hug. "Dad, this is Wendy! He looked at her smiling beautiful face and red hair with its white bow, and said, "It's so damn good to meet you! And boys, this big guy right here is your Uncle Katang...er Ken."

As a big family lump, we couldn't pass through the double

doors, so we broke it up, Dad and Claire, me and Wendy, and Morgan hanging on to Ken "Katanga" Broussard, looking up to him like his football hero.

Once we were inside, we had a chance to talk. Wendy's Dad came by, and my Dad leaned over and grabbed his hand and shook it. "Damn fine rescue, there Cap'n." Captain Stillman, laughed back and said, "Glad you had fun! We needed the practice In long-distance night rescues!" Wendy gave me her love look, squeezed my hand and then went off with her Dad.

Falk and Colin were still outside, staring at the helicopter. The FBI agents milled around, still concerned about a threat.

Even Uncle Mark was there, and he and Dad shook hands and hugged, but I could tell that our Dad didn't think much about his brother's lack of involvement in our situation.

Then Dad pulled us all aside, "We are all going out to be guests at the Stillman's farm, just north of here. It's too dangerous for us to go home."

"The FBI is guarding the house from the CIA if you can believe that." He shook his head in disbelief. And they will guard us out at the farm, too. We'll go home as soon as it's safe."

CHAPTER 103

That night, the five of us gathered in the living room of the Stillman's guest house. It was a collection of rooms set in a circle around a central living area. There were FBI agents outside guarding us, walking around the house and grounds. We had all showered, re-bandaged our wounds, and found some clean clothes or bathrobes. Still, we looked awful. Everyone was draped in white bandages. It was surreal and yet comforting to finally have this new family together again, despite the awful events we had all experienced in the past few months. There was a knock on the door, and an agent stuck his head in. "Is it ok if she comes in?" I could see Wendy standing behind him. "Of course" I yelled out, and she came in, smiling at everybody and sat next to me and on me in the big chair.

Once we were all settled in, Dad said, quietly and very emotionally, "I am so glad that we are all here together and safe. I know the past few months have been difficult for all of us." He looked up and around the room. Morgan chuckled first, and then we all joined in laughing at Dad's terrific understatement. We all laughed until we cried, releasing the enormous reserve of tension we all felt.

Kirby Calloway had tears in his eyes, but he continued, "Tomorrow will be the end of me keeping a promise I made, not only to my friend, Muhari Clarion, but also to the two brave CIA agents, Kent Simmons and Bob Hayes, who died trying to get this awful story out and into the right hands. Tomorrow, Uncle Ken and I will finally get this evidence into the right hands, in this." He held up a brightly covered Nigerian shopping bag, and patted it. "Now I think we should all get a good night's sleep. Tomorrow will be a big day."

Everyone got up, hugged around, and then headed back into their respective bedrooms. I stood up and took Wendy in my arms. I asked her, "Where are you going to spend the night?"

She looked up at me with an inviting smile, "With you."

The next day, Kirby and Katanga got up before it was light. They put on their best borrowed suits. Kirby leaned over to kiss Claire, and then got the Nigerian shopping bag that they had all fought so hard for. The sun was rising earlier and earlier as the summer got started. There was an FBI SUV waiting outside, followed by another one full of agents, and preceded by an escort of two Boston police motorcycles. The escorts would be replaced by escorts from each major city as they rode south to Washington, DC. The convoy rolled on through Providence, Philadelphia, New York City, Baltimore, and into Washington.

It rolled on with police lights flashing until it arrived in front of the Department of Justice Building at 450 5th Street, and stopped. The FBI guards piled out of the rear SUV and surrounded the front SUV. Two men got out of the back and walked directly up the stairs. One, the lanky one, carried a beat-up but brightly colored Nigerian shopping bag. His companion was a very large black man. The doors were opened and several men came out and shook hands with the two men, slapping them on the back and escorting them in. The truth had arrived in Washington.

CHAPTER 104

Finally, some adults in our government, in the DOJ, the FBI, and, yes, in the CIA, got together to find out what really happened at Castle Calloway in Abuja, Nigeria and at Fort Calloway, Pocasset, MA.

The effort was led by Senator Rick Allen, the head of the Foreign Intelligence and Immigration Committee, and the husband of Georgia Allen. They had all read through the evidence that those two brilliant men, Simmons and Hayes gave their lives for, and finally accepted it and began looking for the players behind it all. Subpoenas were flying everywhere.

The first one to go was Dad's ex-friend James Weldon, who had not only protected the real perpetrators in the Company who were involved in making huge personal profits from human trafficking and drugs, but he was working with Kwandanbo to unseat President Muhari. He tried to discredit Dad, and then ordered my Dad's killing, as well as being directly responsible for the killings of Simmons and Hayes. He and his henchmen were dragged out by their heels to the CIA Dungeon that my Dad had been threatened with. I hope he never climbs out of the slime in the deepest part of the swamp.

It took a while to get through all the shell companies and fake foundations to get to George Washington Hilton. But they did, and he said he would resign, but I don't think the AG is finished with him yet. I would love to see him in an orange jump suit, if they can find one to fit the fat bastard.

As far as Horatio Sorobet, he is so protected by international laws, his position, and his power to just buy people, it would take an extraordinary effort to take him down. However, the FBI is continuing to pursue him through Interpol, and given the evidence that "spies like us" collected, they may take him down as well.

There is one very unpredictable and very dangerous loose end; Ruiz. One of his smuggling boats landed in the middle of the night in Providence Harbor eight nights after the destruction of the "immigrant school" in Caracas. The bodies that were found in Caracas were not immigrants; they were victims of trafficking and the persons who ordered their execution must be brought to justice. It's too easy for Congress to order the military to strike to cover up their mistakes and misdeeds as they did in this case.

Aboard the smuggling vessel that arrived in Providence after the Caracas attack, there was no crew or "passengers" aboard, just the familiar stench of human sweat, bodily wastes, and evidence of blood, lots of it. The poor people being trafficked are now in the evil hands of their new owners. And there were four packages of Chinese Fentanyl left onboard, eight kilos in all. There had been more, but many were missing from the box where these were found. Now there are a lot of people looking for Ruiz "RZ", but what became of him remains a mystery. We can make some guesses, but that monster will no doubt find other people to terrorize for profit or hate. We remain on-guard.

CHAPTER 105

Congressman George W. Hilton needed badly to get out of Washington, and Massachusetts as well. The arrival of a ship likely carrying human cargo into Providence had shaken him to his core. The questionable destruction of a warehouse in a foreign country that resulted in twenty-five human casualties has been laid at his door. And Ruiz was unaccounted for.

Luckily, he had a cottage up in New Hampshire, across the border, like many rich folks, especially politicians who have acquired them with help from contributors. He had decided to take his wife, Ellen, and his grown daughter Martha up to his cottage to get away from all the press scrutiny and cameras in his face every time he showed up in public.

The pretty white cottage was set in the woods by a beautiful lake. Across the lake were tall trees, and a small cove used by a flock of quacking ducks. The back of the house was a large porch, leading to a twenty-foot pier. There was a separate boat house where Hilton kept his boat and fishing equipment. Hilton wanted desperately to go fishing, to get away from the world, and be alone on the lake with just the sound of fish jumping and the smell of the pine trees.

His wife and daughter chatted happily as they unloaded the car and moved food, blankets, and drinks into what had been the shuttered little home. They planned to make a big dinner with George's favorite dishes; lamb, mashed potatoes, fresh green beans, and ice cream for dessert.

George couldn't wait to get out on the lake. He changed into his fishing clothes, and went out to the boat shed. He opened the door, and looked inside. Everything looked normal, just as he had left it, except for some opened boxes and old blankets spread out, kind of like a bed. Hilton sniffed; there had been vagrants in there before.

His 18-foot Grady-White fishing boat was there, suspended on its cables safely out of the water. His fishing rods were there, hung on a rack on the ceiling. He selected one, and laid it into the boat. He looked for his tackle box, then he realized that he had left it in the trunk of his car. He left the boat shed, thinking to go inside the house and see how dinner was progressing, and see if he had time to go out on the lake for a few casts.

He walked over to the back porch and looked through the windows to the scene in the kitchen.

There he saw his wife and beloved daughter happily setting out what they would need to prepare the feast. He went through the house and out to his car. He had asked a few of his security team to follow him up to the lake, but he looked down his long drive and didn't see their car yet. He remembered that they had been separated in heavy traffic on I-95 North, but they should be just behind by a few minutes. He got his tackle box out of the trunk, and took a last look down the drive. No cars, and no security team.

But then he thought, no matter, it was time to get out and tangle with a lake trout or maybe even a Muskie.

He lowered the boat into the water, and got in with his rod and reel, and turned the key on his old Evinrude outboard motor. It turned over lazily, but wouldn't start. It had been sitting all winter and wasn't worth the effort to fight with. He could just row out a few hundred yards, besides the exercise would be good for his health.

As he rowed out, he caught a whiff of the lamb roasting in the kitchen and his mouth watered thinking about what was to come.

He continued slowly paddling out until he was over a spot that he remembered was the skeleton of an old boat that had sunk there many years back, and seemed to be a good place to find fish lurking about. He decided to use a XFisherman 3" bass lure to start, and cast it out about 25 yards, then he started reeling it in, putting a little jerk-and-pause action on it. His mind slowly relaxed as he thought of nothing but fishing.

Suddenly, he heard a series of screams coming from the house. He looked back at the house but could see nothing out of the ordinary. Then, he was shocked to see his daughter Martha running towards the boathouse, half-clothed, with a swarthy looking short man chasing her. In his hand, he held a large knife.

Hilton cursed the fact that he hadn't started the outboard motor, but he gave it a few pulls on the start cord, and as he feared, nothing happened. He grabbed the oars and started rowing as fast as he could. He looked back at the boat house. Martha was standing there at the door, apparently pleading for her life. He could hear her wailing. He cried out, "No, no, please!" at the top of his lungs. The man walked up to her and she fell to her knees, looking up to him and crying. He turned to look out at the boat on the lake, and then he turned back, flipped the knife around, and plunged the knife deep into her chest. There was a short scream, then nothing. She remained in a kneeling position, but her head fell backwards onto the boathouse door.

The man, pulled the knife out of her, and her body fell onto the grass.

Hilton stopped rowing, letting the boat coast to a stop. The man on the shore beckoned to Hilton, come here, come here.

Hilton frantically weighed his choices. He assumed that his wife, Ellen, was now dead, lying in the kitchen, and his daughter, Martha, was now dead laying on the grass. He wasn't a brave man, and it seemed to his cowardly mind, that his best course of action was just to sit out in his little boat on the lake until his security team showed up.

He had no doubt now who the vicious animal on the shore was. It was Ruiz, come to take revenge on him and his family. He had escaped the attempt to burn him out in Caracas, and now he was here, waiting on the shore for a chance at killing Hilton.

Hilton had made his choice, and he paddled out a little farther in the lake just in case Ruiz tried to swim out to him. The only weapon he had was a paddle.

Then, suddenly, a figure appeared out on the porch. It was his wife, Ellen, her arm was covered in a bloody towel and her head was bleeding all over her body.

But in her hand she held a .38 pistol, an old gun that had belonged to her father. She had hidden it ever since Hilton had banned having any guns at the cottage.

Hilton's spirits jumped. Perhaps his wife could save them both.

Ruiz had not seen her and she walked slowly towards him. Then, when he noticed her and turned, she fired, again and again. Ruiz ducked the first two shots, but the last bullet hit him in the chest. He doubled over, but then he stood back up and stumbled toward her, raising the knife once again. She fired once more, missing him, and then he grabbed the gun out of her hand, turning it on her and firing it, but it was empty. He hit her across the face with it, then threw the gun into the lake. He grabbed her by the back of her head, and pulled her to him. Her eyes grew wide, and she turned her head, but Ellen stood firm as the monster Ruiz plunged the knife into her, and then stabbed her again as she fell.

Ruiz kicked her body out of his way as he stumbled onto the porch, dripping blood.

Ruiz fell into one of the lawn chairs on the deck, holding his stomach, and again gestured to Hilton, out on the lake, come here, come here.

The back door of the cottage burst open and there, finally, were the security men. Ruiz turned to them and raised his knife a last time as they shot him over and over. He fell from the chair onto the deck, and lay there, his blood mixing with Ellen's and dripping into the flowers along the porch.

The security men looked around and were dismayed at what they saw. Ellen Hilton was dead, lying on the deck, not far from the body of the dead Ruiz. His daughter Martha was dead, lying out by the boat shed, covered in blood. And Hilton was in a little boat, out on the lake, apparently paddling in circles. This did not look good.

CHAPTER 106

"THIS IS CNN. We have a very disturbing report coming from our sister station in Manchester, New Hampshire, WMUR Channel 9. On the phone, we have our local correspondent, Cynthia James. Cynthia, what can you tell us?"

"There is a very disturbing situation here in the woods near Greensboro. This is the summer home of Congressmen George W. Hilton. From what we've been told, one of the gardeners employed here went on a rampage and killed the Congressman's wife and daughter while Congressman Hilton was fishing a few miles away. He was returning from his fishing trip by boat when his security team arrived at his cottage and shot and killed the gardener, who we understand is an undocumented immigrant from Venezuela. He has been tentatively identified as Juan Ruiz. That's all for now, this is Cynthia James from near Greensboro, New Hampshire."

The CNN commentator continued, "This is so unfortunate for a family that has been through so much. Congressman Hilton is now facing an investigation into the activities of his foundation, that was run by his now-deceased wife, Ellen. Our condolences are out for the congressman and his family, and we wish him well."

CHAPTER 107

We were not surprised when that report appeared on the nightly news. We knew that it was Ruiz well before the CNN reporter identified him, and he was no gardener. We were all immensely relieved that the animal Ruiz had come to a predictably violent end, though the spin that was applied to the story was amazing. It was like no one wanted to take credit for ending that particular human trafficking and drug ring. With government officials usually flocking to the microphone to take credit, the only thing we Calloway's could surmise, with our best spying spider sense, was that this thing was so deep, so pervasive, that no one wanted anything to do with it. We would have to depend on Congressman Rick Allen and his wife Georgia to root it out.

My family now lives at Calloway Court, Shore Road, Pocasset, Massachusetts, USA. We Calloway's are done with spying for the time being. This is just the time we are taking to re-create our family, and to enjoy each other, at least until we go our separate ways again. We are well and complete for now. We have added to our family, which used to be just Morg and me. We now have a new Mom, a new uncle to replace the dysfunctional one, and my Dad, who is a Shining Star that served our country under huge pressure and in battle, and remained true to his commitment to a President of what we hope will become a prosperous and democratic country. And I have a girl who says she will love me forever.

As for what is next for me, I got a letter from the Department of Defense offering me an appointment to either the Air Force or Naval Academy, or West Point. I got a nomination from Acting Congresswoman Carol Valentina, who is filling the position of some bum ex-politician named Hilton. I'm still trying to decide, but no matter which one I choose, I AM GOING TO FLY.

ACKNOWLEDGEMENTS

Writing a first novel is a goal for many people, as they try to tell part of their life story in an entertaining and potentially profitable way. But, many never either start or finish it. "Spies Like Us" would not have been completed without significant help and encouragement from a number of friends and family members. First, two of my sisters, Linda Beyt and Noreen Bienvenu, who dug in and gave me feedback and many, many corrections to the work. Then, my two Air Force Academy colleagues, both best-selling authors, Buck Stienke (Black Eagle) and Andrew Ceroni (Meridian), who provided great coaching about self-publishing. I want to thank Kristin from 99Designs in Australia for my book cover design. Finally, my wife Sandy, who is my biggest fan and Senior Editor and the love of my life. I look forward to seeing you all at one of my in-person book signings.

CPSIA information can be obtained
at www.ICGtesting.com
Printed in the USA
LVHW050138211020
669276LV00005B/678